The Grotto's Secret

Paula Wynne

Prado Press

London, United Kingdom

Also by Paula Wynne

Create a Successful Website
Pimp My Site

Writers' Resource Series
Pimp My Fiction
A~Z of Writers' Character Quirks
101 Writers' Scene Settings

Torcal Trilogy
The Grotto's Secret

Author Contact & Copyright

Copyright © 2016 by Paula Wynne.

Paula Wynne/Prado Press
United Kingdom
www.paulawynne.com

Ordering information: Special discounts are available on quantity purchases. For details contact the author via paula@paulawynne.comFirst Published 2015 by Prado Press

First published by Prado Press 2016
24 Caunter Road, Newbury, Berkshire, RG14 1QZ

ISBN: 978-0-9934921-7-4

Cover Art: Travis Miles

Editors: John Harten, Ken Sheridan and Kim Farnell

Book Layout: Slavisa Zivkovic

Dedicated to two fantastic women

Merle Hawkins: Thank you, Mommy, for encouraging me to believe that I can be anything I want to be. Ana-Mária's love for her Madre reflects my love for you.

Adeline Boyder: Talking to you all these years, Gran, has eased the emptiness you left behind. Enjoy dancing in the rain, sweet granny-darling.

For Ken, my husband and best friend

And our supportive sons, Ryan, Kent and Niall

And all the conquerors who will never give up their quest to be authors

Never, never, never give up

Winston Churchill

1

London, Present Day

The note met the usual conditions. A veiled message on the envelope. A torn piece of paper. Scrawled handwriting with a cryptic letter.

Kelby Wade often received puzzling letters from aspiring entrepreneurs. She'd found this one on her seat as she'd returned from refreshing her face on the early flight from Dublin.

Her heart skipped a beat at the familiar phrase scribbled across the envelope: *Never, never give up.*

Kelby sucked in her breath, snatched up the envelope and slipped into her seat. Although it didn't have her name on it, she knew those words were intended for her.

Since her parents' death, her goal had been to look after her brother Gary. His life was determined by the essence of perseverance. Hers by regret. Before he left, he'd given her a gift, telling her to grab the chance to face her future without remorse. What had happened to him tore her heart apart.

She put her glasses on and pulled the paper out of the envelope:

> *I've stumbled upon an ancient secret with incredible*
> *powers. Someone is killing those who know. I won't give*
> *up until I find the truth. Please help me save them.*

Kelby had a sudden eerie sensation that Gary was watching her. She spun around. A man stared at her from a few rows behind. She met his steady gaze. Energy radiated from his tanned face, but there was no message in his eyes to suggest he might have left the note.

No-one else seemed interested in Kelby. Most passengers leafed through a book or magazine or stared at a tablet. Some were shuffling their reading materials into their bags to prepare for landing.

Swivelling back, Kelby bit her lip and frowned at the note. It wasn't Gary's spider writing, but the unwavering tone suggested he'd written it.

Kelby glanced sideways, wondering who had left the message. The young-gun across the aisle sat rigid in a tight three-piece suit and snored into his starched shirt and tie. He was clearly bored by the used car magazine on his lap.

The middle-aged lady beside her stared out of the window. Sadness etched her face as she clutched a grubby tissue. Kelby wanted to share how talking to her deceased mother had eased the emptiness in her heart. But she said nothing because sorrow made people creep inside themselves fired by their desire for solitude. Her own grief was still hidden deep inside her.

Instead, she reached into her handbag and drew out a travel-pouch of pocket sized tissues. In a gentle gesture, she tucked the packet into the lady's palm. They exchanged a glance, and by squeezing the lady's hand, Kelby told her she understood her loss.

Respecting the lady's privacy, Kelby settled back in her seat. An abrupt cocktail of smells wafted down the aisle. The aroma of coffee, bacon sandwiches and sweet-sticky buns struggled against the reek of sickly air-freshener trying to disguise a dirty nappy.

Kelby re-read the note and flopped her head back.

What the hell is this?

She'd heard it before. Everyone had the answer to the next best thing and the next big money spinner. But this intriguing request had no pitch and no plea for investment.

She fought the temptation to peek again at the man behind to see if his expression gave anything away. But, at that moment, the plane touched down in Heathrow and taxied along the runway. Even though she hated leaving Annie behind when she flew off to Prince Al-Bara's film locations, she loved the way her stomach tumbled the moment a plane took off. It gave her a sense of adventure.

While she waited for the seat belt sign to turn off, Kelby switched her phone on. It immediately vibrated and spewed out another disgusting message.

Since *Devil's Grotto* had first aired on TV, internet stalkers had been trolling her. As a reality-show host she mentored early business start-ups. Of course there could be only one winner, so the lively banter had turned into outright abuse soon after the first screening.

Every bit a private person, Kelby hated being recognised from the first series. And now word had got around they were preparing to film the second, the tweets got worse every day.

Well, she couldn't ignore the messages forever, considering the show required being active on Twitter and Facebook. If it weren't for Annie, she would ignore her phone. It would be more of the same garbage anyway. This time it showed a tweet:

@kelbywade U will meet the devil 2nite

Blood pumped in Kelby's ears. Her heart fluttered in her chest, a hooked fish wriggling to break free. She glanced out of the window at the passing runway buildings and tried not to think about the warning. Insulting and threatening tweets were a *really* annoying part of her job, but the trolls didn't know when to stop.

Kelby's day had just started, but she sensed something lay in hiding, waiting to attack.

2

At last the plane shuddered to a halt outside the terminal. Most of the passengers jumped up, and a babble of chatter erupted as people fought to grab their bags from overhead. Rising out of her seat, Kelby swallowed hard and tried to forget the tweet.

The man from a few seats back bumped into her and mumbled an apology. Although his eyes beamed warmth, they also signalled amusement at the pushing and shoving behind him.

Kelby reached to grab her briefcase, but he got there first and retrieved it for her. As he did so, an unruly pewter lock flopped over his deep frown lines.

'Thank you.' She gave him a quick once over. He wasn't a head-turner, but definitely easy on the eyes. His face had the lived-in look of someone comfortable with himself and enjoying life. Yet his body showed none of life's pleasures; it could have been carved by Michelangelo himself. Toned and athletic. Not an ounce of fat on him. The man appeared to be the strong silent type, with a mystique that made her heart sing. His salt and pewter stubble plied him with a certain panache. Who needed a silver fox when pewter foxes were on the loose?

As they queued to exit the plane, the Pewter Fox's old-fashioned scent made Kelby remember how long it had been since she'd had a man in her life.

She took a step forward. The Pewter Fox did the same and walloped straight into her. He muttered, 'Ah, so sorry.' The arms of his jumper hung around his neck over his tight shirt.

From the corner of her eye Kelby watched him stand his ground as someone shuffled forward and shoved him from behind, sending him tumbling into her once more.

'Me again. I keep bumping into you.'

She smiled at his gallantry by taking the blame for the thrust in the queue. At that moment, a subtle spark connected them, as delicate as a single strand of gossamer thread.

Another bump and he muttered, 'I'm not a stalker. Scout's honour.'

The thread severed and Kelby grimaced.

'Whoops, sorry, shouldn't have said that.' He flushed. 'I'm not getting this right, am I?' He lifted his hand to stop her answering. 'Please … ignore me.'

Confused by his choice of words, Kelby turned and faced the front. Thankfully, most of the passengers were in a rush and the queue slowly dissipated.

She hugged her coat to her chest to keep out the March morning mist and trudged down the gangway into the terminal, glancing at her phone again.

A photo of a man with a child on his shoulders beamed at her. Gary glowed with health while Annie's huge expressive brown eyes tugged at Kelby's heart. She would go to the end of the earth to protect them.

Kelby tapped a number and waited for an answer, hoping there'd be good news about Annie. The number rang and rang.

Her other hand still clenched the crumpled note. Keeping it hidden from prying eyes, she scrutinised it again and wondered what secret could be so deadly.

Kelby screwed it up tightly, annoyed it had hooked her interest. Someone was playing her. She wasn't prepared to be reeled into a scam, so she stuffed it into her handbag.

What's the ancient secret?

She shivered, although not from the bite in the air.

The note's words still lingered in the back of her mind, a stalker lurking in the shadows.

Someone is killing those who know.

3

Once in the terminal Kelby didn't have to turn around to realise the Pewter Fox was close by. His magnetism zipped through the cold room like electric sparks. Any man who looked at him would surely plan a trip to the gym once they'd compared themselves with his physical perfection.

Kelby made her way to pick up her luggage and called her office manager, Jimmy O' Rourke.

She tapped her fingers impatiently while she waited for him to answer. When he did she could hear the smile in his voice.

'Morning, Kel. I'm still jealous you didn't take me to Dublin. I wanted to show you a few of my ol' haunts. Was it any use?'

'Same old thing. The new bunch pitched to the producers. At least I don't have to do the Prince's yacht trip to Valencia. Oh, hang on.'

Kelby darted around the conveyor belt, grabbed her suitcase and dumped it beside her. 'Gotta go. I'll be there in an hour. Please boot Zelda up the arse. I still haven't seen those marketing reports.'

'Oh, by the way, Kel, I've squeezed in a new entrepreneur who's been desperate to see you.'

Kelby groaned.

'Don't give me that,' Jimmy admonished her, 'they pay you good money, remember. Anyway, this one sounds interesting. They have some kinda secret potion.'

Her heart skipped a beat. 'A what?'

'Okay, okay. I'm pulling your leg. They have a healing herb. Big hush-hush.'

Ending the call, she lugged her baggage to the taxi rank. Kelby tapped into her phone and panted at Jimmy, 'One more thing. What's her name,' she snapped her fingers, 'from the Blue Garlic?'

'Emma.'

'Yes, tell her to send her press release and do follow up calls.'

'Right you are.'

Kelby slipped her phone into her coat pocket, dumped her luggage into the first black cab in the queue and jumped in beside it. A smell of wet socks and unwashed bodies lingered on the seats.

As they pulled off for the trip into London, she wondered what the note meant, but her mind soon returned to work.

When the cabbie pulled up at the first set of traffic lights on the way out of the airport, Kelby caught sight of the Pewter Fox in the cab beside her. From the corner of her eye she spied him tapping his phone.

Immediately, her phone beeped with yet another message:

@kelbywade Devil waiting 4 u @ office. U will open
wider 4 me 2nite

The hair on the nape of her neck lifted and a tingle radiated down her arms. Her heartbeat boomed in her ears. What did he mean, he'd open her up wider?

Another thought struck her, and she glanced at the cab pulling off. The Pewter Fox was still engrossed in his phone. Could he have sent the message? She shook off the thought. A stranger from the plane? This was getting silly.

After a long moment, Kelby realised her fingers were going numb from clutching her phone so tightly.

She would *not* let these messages wear her down. Kelby slipped out her iPad and scrolled through her to do list. Within seconds her mind wandered to the envelope and the new meeting.

Were they connected?

If so, she'd soon find out who'd left the note.

4

An hour later, Kelby stared at a blood-spattered magazine. The parcel had been delivered in a recycled cardboard box tied with blood-red twine. Another strand stuck out of the middle to ensure she went straight to the centre spread.

At first she thought the editor had sent her yet another copy of her recent *Devil's Grotto* photo shoot with the two women mentors. But that was out of the question. The editor wouldn't mutilate her own magazine with such horrific graffiti.

No, it had to be the Twitter bully.

Her breath caught in her throat as she examined the red slash drawn across each woman's face. Kelby stared at the image, not knowing what to do. After a long moment, she lifted her reading glasses and bedded her knuckles into her eye sockets. Once she could focus again, she stole another glance at the grotesque graphics. The editor had entitled the article 'Drop Dead Devils'. Kelby slithered her fingers over the smooth-as-ice magazine centre spread, touching both women's faces. As her fingertip snagged a glitch on the lustrous paper, her eyes narrowed. She squinted at it.

Oh my God. Real blood!

She studied the red slashes across the women's necks, the vibrancy of the blood marring their creamy skin. As Jimmy entered and kicked the door shut, Kelby slapped the magazine face down on the desk.

'What does yours say?'

'You got one, too?'

Jimmy reached to open her copy, but she slammed her fist on it. She couldn't bear to look again. He yanked his hand away and tutted, 'That bad, huh?' The magazine rustled as Jimmy lifted his hand, waved his copy and opened it across his chest.

Kelby flinched at the words smeared in black gunk across her face: *How can you work for this devil?*

'Oh, for God's sake.' Kelby swept her copy of the magazine into the waste paper basket. 'I'm sick of them.' She bit back some of her brother's army language that would have made her mother ashamed of her.

'He needs a good belt.'

'That's your answer to anyone who doesn't toe the line.' She jumped up and stomped to the window of her sky-high barely affordable London office. Only the thought of competing against Teresina Piccoli with Jon Thompson watching from the side lines kept her paying the extortionate rent.

Her voice became hollow. 'Will they ever stop feasting on me?'

'Not while you're on one of the most popular shows on TV.' He ambled between their offices, sorting out the morning's post.

Kelby glanced at the Thames, at the boats chugging around the wide bends with tourists strolling alongside the river. The distant hum of a bustling London morning rose to their floor.

She pressed her hands into her chest. A deep longing filled her. She'd give anything to be strolling along, clinging onto a little hand while heading nowhere in particular. Kelby flung the thought away and marched back to her desk, her squat heels clomping on the wooden floorboards. *No time for silliness.*

Jimmy dumped a pile of post in her letter tray as Kelby lifted her bag and pulled out a child's picture. 'Oh, I nearly forgot.' She handed it to Jimmy. Behind her, in one corner of her office, hung a gallery of children's framed drawings.

Taking the picture from her, Jimmy said, 'Ah, another masterpiece.'

Kelby smiled with pride. 'This one is of Annie's new friend's swimming pool.'

They looked at the pencil drawing of a waterfall cascading from the top right of the picture. Sprays of blue pencil plunged into a pool below. Around the pool, large rocks were covered in green pencilled moss.

'More friends?' Jimmy's eyes widened.

Kelby wagged her finger in the air to prevent mockery spilling from Jimmy's mouth. 'Imaginary friends are healthy for children. Annie relies on them as her buddies and superheroes.'

'I thought most kids outgrew their imaginary friends by her age. What is she now? Nine? Ten?'

Kelby straightened. 'Never deprive a child of hopeful friends, Jim, it may be all they have.'

Jimmy said, 'True. Maybe her head's still dealing with the stress.'

'Maybe.' Kelby swallowed a lump. Even after all these years the gaping hole of losing her own parents as a teenager had never left.

Jimmy ambled out of her office. For the hundredth time she glanced at her mobile phone, hoping to see a message about Annie. Kelby tapped it and propped her glasses on her head while her thumb stroked the mobile's smooth screen. Again she rang to see how Annie was doing. As before, the number rang and rang.

'Damn!' Kelby dropped her phone and scraped her teeth on her thumbnail.

The phone beeped again. If it hadn't been for Annie, she'd have thrown the bloody thing away. For a split second she squeezed her eyes tight, unwilling to see another threat.

The phone beeped again. She sagged over her office chair like Annie's rag doll.

Kelby dropped her glasses onto her nose. A shiver clawed its way up her spine and her stomach tied itself in knots.

God help me. Not him again.

5

Serramonacesca, Italy

Barker enjoyed this killing malarkey. Although he'd never done it before, he had a gift for it. Thankfully his task in the Abruzzi Mountains was almost over; he only needed to do a few tweaks to ensure the cogs fell into place.

Job done.

He pressed send on his phone and tucked the device into his pocket.

Yes, he enjoyed playing with the she-devils. And neither of them had the foggiest that he was their cyber stalker.

Planning Teresina's death had been easy. As one of the show's producers the craziest ideas were pitched at him. Using them for his own means, he loved.

Both she-devils knew everyone on the show was testing this new device from one of the entrepreneurs.

As he touched the sun-warmed metal hood of the gleaming French-navy Maserati, he ran through his plans one more time. Some things he hated about this job, including sticking his hands up the wheel shaft. On the other hand, touching this graceful racer he loved.

He stood back to enjoy the sun glinting on the bonnet. The Maserati thrilled every petrol-head as it tore through the Italian countryside. Now it rested in silence on the paved drive. Beside the gleaming bonnet, twinned sculptured cypress trees guarded the Palazzo's baroque entrance.

Today was special.

Today Teresina would die.

A voice bellowed from the window, disturbing the countryside's peace. 'Majella! Did you hear me?'

Her yell bounced around inside the Italian palazzo before emerging from the ornate-stone arched windows on the mountain's breeze.

Rude or moody most days, Teresina Piccoli, heiress of the Piccoli Palazzo and one of the *Devil's Grotto* game show mentors, had something extra gnawing away at her today. A package had arrived that morning, gift wrapped in blood-red twine. The she-devil had received his anonymous threat.

Barker chuckled. She had no idea she would soon be pushing up daisies. He knelt and peered inside the wheel chassis. Then he pulled a device out of his pocket, dropped it into his palm and pressed a yellow button. The screen lit up. Next, he pressed the red and yellow buttons simultaneously, held them for a few seconds and waited for the zero to stop blinking.

His fingers slid along the inside of the alloy rim, found the best spot and snapped on the gadget. Tighter. And tighter still. He wriggled it one last time. Tight enough to do the job. He grinned and tapped the device, whispering, 'Do your thing, buddy, and do it at the right moment.'

During tests the device had failed high speed cornering when the load was greatest on the tyre. Teresina loved speed. The countryside was renowned for its winding mountainous roads so the device would do the trick.

The engine oil's sharp odour stuck in the back of Barker's throat, making him gag. Stretching back up, he filled his lungs with fresh air.

The tyre tread monitor settled to a steady blue haze at 0.0.

Primed. Ready to explode.

6

Kelby didn't bother to read her latest phone message and ignored the insistent beep. There were too many idiots using social media nowadays.

Jimmy took her phone and read the message, then dumped it on her desk in disgust.

Without looking up she said, 'That bad?'

'It's not only you. Teresina has been taken to the cleaners. I've learnt a whole bevy of new words from this fella. Horse-teeth. Dentist-done smile. Devil's breath. Viper. But mostly Teresina's called a man-eater.'

She muttered, 'I'd give anything for her ironing board tummy!'

'Nah, yer grand, you don't wanna be that skinny.'

'I do!' She looked at Jimmy askance. She envied the way Teresina attracted people to her like butterflies to a new spring flower.

'Maybe it's because she runs through Hyde Park in the mornings and doesn't stick her nose into her laptop as soon as she wakes up.'

'You've made your point.'

'I keep trying, but it doesn't seem to be getting through. Go spend your money. Live your life.'

'And who'll run this place?'

'Me. I'm overdue for a promotion, anyways.'

She gave him a ha-ha look. Turning her back on Jimmy, Kelby scribbled reminders about the week's targets on the whiteboard. Her thumb sneaked into her mouth and she slid her nail back and forth across her bottom teeth. Not biting, filing, she often convinced herself. It helped her to think of the perfect solution to whatever problem plagued her.

'Wish she would stop mouthin' in the papers about your latest bust up.'

Kelby spun around to face him. 'Which one?'

'Where you called her "Mafia money".'

Kelby groaned. She wasn't proud of her temper. That one had been captured on air.

'If you keep on at the cow, it'll make it worse.'

'I don't care! I won't have Teresina stomping all over me.'

He continued his telling off. 'It sends you more tormentors.' He tapped the magazine. 'Like this graffiti fella.'

'Don't rub it in.' Kelby sunk into her chair. 'Please print off Jason's new business plan. I'm also waiting for the NDA from the Beach Hut. Their application for home working pods looks exciting, but I can't go any further without signatures.'

She rubbed a lens cloth over a smudge on her glasses. 'And diarise a day with the producers. They keep changing things on set. I'm going to put them straight.'

'I'm on it. By the way, Miss Gappy called.'

Jimmy loved to give her mentees nicknames. The group was labelled the 'hunting pack'. She frowned at him, trying to put the nickname to a face. 'Miss Gappy?'

'Joanne, the gap-tooth. The marketing campaign you suggested is going gang busters.'

'I'd hate to know what nickname you have for me behind my back.'

Jimmy shuffled to the door. 'I see you're on that again, so I'll get outta your face.'

As he opened it, a myriad of chattering voices in the main office flowed through the door. The sound of an intercom squawking in the reception frayed Kelby's nerves. She darted to the door, leaned out to face a bunch of people and bellowed, 'Will someone get that?' They turned to gawp at her.

At that moment an office assistant dressed in spotted leopard tights and high-heeled boots scrambled out of the kitchen and headed to the squawking intercom. 'I'll get it!'

'Thanks, Zelda,' Kelby called out, relieved the squawking had stopped. She closed her door.

Beside her, Jimmy whispered, 'Those red smeared lips remind me of a leopard licking its blood tainted mouth after gorging on a carcass.'

'Oh, she's harmless.' Kelby strode back to her desk and plonked herself down at her laptop.

'Maybe, but she's not the brightest button.'

'Give her a chance. I have a feeling she'll show her true colours and prove herself.'

He shrugged. 'Not sure how long we can wait. Besides, I know you felt sorry for her when her mother told you how she had struggled to get a job after she dropped out of uni.'

Despite Zelda's questionable dress sense, Kelby liked her. Within days, she had settled herself into the office, overtly attentive at all times.

'But then, that's you all over, Kelby. Hardened honeycomb on the outside and gooey caramel on the inside. A real softie.'

Ignoring his summary of her, Kelby muttered, 'Don't you go spreading such terrible rumours.'

'Hah! That secret's in the can.' Jimmy chuckled. 'Hey, I have an idea. Maybe you can ask one of the girls to talk to Zelda about her clothes.'

Suddenly Kelby slammed her hand on her desk making Jimmy jump. 'Hang on! I have a great idea. You know I told you I wanted to get rid of those designer frocks I've been given for the show?'

He nodded suspiciously.

'Well, Zelda is the perfect person to find them a new home.'

'If *you* think so.'

'Done deal. I'll tell her about it later.'

'Anything else?' Jimmy asked as if he had nothing to do all day.

She slid an envelope across the table.

Jimmy lifted it and opened it. His eyes widened as he pulled out an air ticket. 'What's this?'

She shrugged. "You've been piling on the hours so I thought you might want a long weekend to see your mum.'

'But I can't take time off now, it's so busy.'

'Now look who's talking! Listen, Jimmy, you deserve a break. It's only a long weekend.'

He slapped the ticket at his palm and said in a soft voice. 'Thanks Kelby.' He scampered across the room, chuckling, 'Jaysus, when I turn up on her doorstep, my ol' mam will die of a heart attack!' As he grabbed the door handle, he spun around. 'By the way…'

Kelby looked at him.

'Barker is coming to fit the tyre tread monitor to your car tomorrow.'

7

Right now, Barker needed to ensure the device clinging to the Maserati would send Teresina off in style. Such a pity that majestic beast would soon end up as a twisted metal carcass at the bottom of a hairpin bend.

He whistled a tune she'd loved; Gloria Gaynor's *I Will Survive.* Quite apt with today's events unfolding.

Teresina had a private family event this morning. She was *always* late, so she'd be in a spin and race around the mountain.

Talk of the devil… Madame Millions belted out more demands. 'Majella! Are you ready?'

Barker heard a muffled reply wafting through one of the Palazzo's upstairs bedrooms. He smiled, knowing the ten-year-old would be preening in front of her full size mirror in her girlie bedroom.

'*Merde! Carino*… did you hear me?'

This time Majella yelled as loudly as her mother, 'I said, *yes, Mamma.* I'm tying up my hair as *you* insisted.'

'*Bene!* I need to make a quick call and then we're off. Nonna is waiting.'

'And so is Rome.'

Barker chuckled at Majella's response. Imagine naming your daughter after the mountain under whose shadows you were born and raised. Although that wasn't as bad as some names he'd heard. Kids today were named after superheroes, towns and even fruit, for God's sake.

He'd name his kid with elegance and beauty, a name that would prove his breeding beat that of any Italian aristocrat. A name like Grace or Kelby's little Annie. He'd always liked that name. And Annie was a cute kid. Thank goodness his mother hadn't been so tacky. He would've ended up called 'Tango' or 'Rioja'.

All told, Majella was a pretty decent kid. Anyone would think she'd be a spoilt brat with that old Italian money floating around, and a mamma who doted on her kid when she wasn't prowling for prey. Kids, he liked. Spoilt brats, he hated.

A downstairs shutter flew open, almost thumping Barker on the side of his head. She hadn't noticed him as she spun around to her desk. Barker had to stay out of sight. Luckily for him, Teresina never gave anyone on the TV crew a second glance.

From the corner of his eye, Barker watched her punch a number into her landline and flop into a luxurious leather chair. Her black espadrilles matched her sombre black dress and her grave face. The she-devil swung her heels onto the edge of her desk.

One thing she had going for her was her innate ability to transform her father's family ruin into a chic and glamorous yet classical home. The entrance hall's chandelier pendant was over the top, but she had a good eye for design with her edgy, contemporary pieces.

As usual, Teresina's shoulder length, limp black hair had been tucked behind her goblin ears. It shone as if someone had sprayed a can of furniture lacquer over her head.

Her stark dresses were always black with an occasional spray of white as if she were at a permanent wake. And those hooped earrings made her look like a tart.

Barker craned his neck like a giraffe over the elaborate wrought iron window decoration to peer into her office. On her desk a magazine lay open. Both women in the centre spread photograph had a large question mark splashed over them, etched in blood and dripping over their faces.

Because he'd sent it, he knew it featured the women entrepreneurs who appeared on *Devil's Grotto*. In it, each woman recounted their successes in helping their mentees pursue and hunt down their own riches.

In the magazine photo, Kelby's eyes were azure plunge pools in an island of complication. Every woman wanted eyes that colour. And it was obvious from the impatience radiating from her iridescent eyes that she couldn't care less about the photo shoot. The frown lines criss-crossing her forehead warned any prospective admirers that she had passed her sell-by date. She wore a fringe to hide evidence of a workaholic face.

Teresina leaned forward in her seat, looking into the camera and Barker could imagine precisely what was on her mind while the photo was being taken.

He gave a start as he heard Teresina suddenly bark into the phone, 'Kelby Wade, please.'

8

A twinge of annoyance shot through Kelby as Jimmy ambled back into her office. He hadn't given her a moment's peace that morning. 'What now?' She dropped her gaze and continued typing into her laptop.

'The man-eater's on the line.'

Kelby's head shot up. 'What! Teresina never calls. What does *she* want?'

'She won't say.'

She slid her thumb nail across her teeth.

'And?' Jimmy waited for her direction.

'I'm thinking.'

'Hurry up. She'll be brewing up a head of steam on the other end.'

'I don't care. I won't have her horns ramming into me.'

'I can see you're not in the mood for another fight with Teresina. The more you stay out of each other's hair the better for both of you.' Jimmy whispered, before putting the phone on loudspeaker. He raised a finger in the air to indicate he was about to speak and pressed a button. 'Sorry, Miss Piccoli. Kelby is busy with her mentees.'

Teresina blasted down the line, 'I have something she needs to know. It can't wait.'

Kelby's jaw dropped.

'I can disturb her if it's urgent.'

Kelby shook her head, mouthing: *No!*

Teresina snorted. 'Oh, for pity's sake, drop the bullshit. Kelby *will* want to know about this. We had a spat on the show last week, so what.' She let out a grunt. 'God's truth, she cannot afford *not* to hear this.'

'Hold on, please.' Jimmy pressed the mute button again and raised his eyebrows at Kelby.

'She's in one of her moods. She'll wind me up and stuff up my day.'

Jimmy nodded, un-muted the phone and said, 'Oh, Miss Piccoli, my mistake, a client has joined the meeting. If you'd care to give me a detailed message, I can slip it under Kelby's nose and ring you as soon as I get a response.'

'No! I *cannot* leave a message, you thick Mick!' Teresina spat. 'And I will not be giving *you* the low-down. Get your boss to call me.' She emphasised her Italian accent, '*Veloce!* I'll be on my mobile in my car. Got that? *Bene!*'

Kelby flinched as Teresina slammed the receiver down. 'Sorry, Jimmy. That was out of order.'

He'd been with Kelby for five years and she hated to imagine a day without him. She made a mental note to speak to *the cow* about it. Teresina had everything Kelby wanted, including a life away from the cameras with a child. But she was rude and arrogant, and *that* Kelby certainly didn't envy.

'Jaysus, she's a piece of work!' Jimmy muttered before leaving her alone.

Kelby glanced at her desk. Cables snaked along the oak, disappearing into her laptop which took pride of place amongst the techno gadgets. Some glowed with cyber glitter as they routed her to the world's web, while others blinked to announce their connection to her office data storage network. Each device reminded her of their right to be there with an ethereal cat's eyes' constant glare and a quiet electrical hum. This was her world, her real home.

All the tools increased her productivity, but she couldn't live without her laptop. If marooned on a remote island, she'd have to be mean with her time on it to savour the battery while trying to find an electrical connection. She'd be lost without it.

Jimmy swept in carrying a bowl of sliced melon and a freshly brewed coffee. 'Here you go. Your cantaloupe, madame. Sounds like antelope, only less chewy and not as likely to run away.'

Kelby smiled, 'No Yakult today?'

'Why are you still taking that stuff?'

'It's good bacteria.'

'So, you'll be full of friendly feckin' maggots!'

Her eyes stole a glance at the window and what lay beyond. 'It's only your funny bone that keeps me from firing you.'

'No-one else would do what I do, yer know.' He darted out.

Goodness knows what could be so urgent to make the Italian heiress lower herself to call her arch rival. Between abuse from internet stalkers and Teresina's heckling she'd had enough of *Devil's Grotto*.

Once again, her phone beeped. Automatically reaching for it, she hoped it would give her news about Annie.

Instead it spewed out another poisonous threat.

9

Barker had almost completed this part of his mission. Now he could slink back into the shadows and wait it out.

Old palazzos had kitchens and working areas where the owners never ventured. Teresina had probably instructed the back kitchen patio to be shrouded in palms and greenery to hide her servants coming and going.

It was a perfect place to watch his plan unfold.

The she-devil stood in the doorway with her vicious paws clasped to her hips. 'Majella, I'm not calling you again!' bellowed Teresina, now in a restless rage.

Well, soon enough the brat would snuff it too, but that was her mother's fault, not hers.

Teresina's heels echoed on the marbled patio tiles as she paced. 'Inez! My bags are ready.'

Even from a distance, her ranting cat-calls rang in Barker's ears. From his position on the kitchen patio, he saw an old lady hobble out from the palazzo laden with Vuitton luggage.

'Book my hotel in Rome, the number's on the dresser in the hall. Majella and I will be home in a few days. In the meantime, get the pool cleaned and the driveway hedges clipped. The house could also do with a spring clean — and don't think I'm not watching you. *I am!* I have eyes in the back of my head.'

From experience, Barker knew Teresina's emerald eyes glowed like those of the panther she emulated.

Inez nodded.

'*Bene, okay!* Don't forget to book my hotel in Rome. We're going there straight after visiting Nonna.'

No you're not, she-devil, you're not going to Rome. The thought sent a powerful surge of warmth that radiated down one side of Barker as though someone had plucked at his central nerve. It made his Johnson bulge his trousers.

'Majella wants to buy some pretty dresses after my meetings, but I have an awful man to meet.' Her nose snarled as she said, 'Wait till the *Bastardo* hears what I have to say!'

She tossed her patent leather handbag in the car and let out a roar without turning around, 'Majella!'

'I'm right here, Mamma.' A soft voice came from her side.

Teresina patted Majella's fluffy head. 'No matter how much you brush, you can't keep this fuzz down... can you, *carino?* Like your papa.' She jumped in behind the wheel.

Once again, she tucked her hair behind her goblin ears, and turned in her seat to check Majella was fastened into place in the back. Then the she-devil sped down the drive.

For a moment Barker watched the Maserati disappear over the winding hill towards Serramonacesca. He gave a salute and muttered, 'Drop dead... devil,' before he sauntered inside with a sudden lightness in his chest, and let out a deep gratifying sigh.

One down. One to go.

10

Kelby stared at the latest message:

> *@kelbywade Get your pussy ready 4 a beating.*
> *U will be raped B4 2nite's over*

Her heartbeat pounded against her ribs. Hot breath caught in her throat. *This has gone too far!*

Kelby's instinct was to hurl the phone at the wall and watch it splinter and crack, removing all traces of the violence it held. Instead, she tossed the phone back onto her desk and snubbed its clatter of disapproval. She yelled to Jimmy in his adjoining office and his head appeared around the door.

Kelby slumped back in her chair. 'To do the show, I signed up to being hounded. I know I have to have rhino skin, but this...'

Jimmy loped over to her, picked up the phone and read the message. 'The bastard!'

'It's about time the cops stopped this abuse. Please get them in here asap.' She shook her head in disgust. 'Call Twitter. They must have policies about this kind of thing happening.'

Before either could speak, her phone beeped again:

> *@kelbywade I'm not going 2 go away. I WILL B in*
> *your face*

Kelby gasped. 'It's as if the bastard's right here in the office listening to us.' She stood and glared at her team of workers. Everyone had their head down and a phone to their ear.

'You think it's one of *them?*'

Kelby sunk back into her chair and tossed her phone to him. Jimmy grabbed it in mid-air with a well-practised catch. 'I'm sure some fellas from Dublin's north side would love to pay this tormentor a visit.'

'I don't play dirty.'

'Maybe it's time you did.'

11

An hour later Jimmy pranced into Kelby's office with a cat-that-got-the-cream expression on his face. 'The cops will be here any minute.'

Still deeply engrossed in a financial spreadsheet, Kelby looked up.

'And you wanted to see the leopard.' He waved at Zelda to enter.

While Jimmy hovered nervously, Kelby watched Zelda saunter into her office. Before the girl had a chance to spread her effervescence around the room, Kelby said, 'I have something special for you to do today.'

'Okay, Kelby.'

'Jimmy will give you an office credit card and I want you to go to Hamleys and buy the best toys for Down Syndrome kids.'

Jimmy and Zelda's jaws dropped.

'Act as though you're a kid again and find the most exciting ones, okay?'

'Sure, that sounds fun. How much do I spend?'

'A couple of hundred or so will be fine.' Kelby turned to Jimmy and held out her hand, 'Card please?'

Still puzzled, Jimmy dug in his wallet and handed her the company credit card and she passed it to Zelda.

'And another thing, I have a pile of designer dresses I want to get rid of.'

'Ooh, sounds fun!'

'Don't get too excited. The studio tends to dress me in frilly sleeves that get in the way and long skirts I keep tripping over.'

Zelda giggled.

'Anyway, can you find the best way for me to get rid of them without the studio getting offended?'

Zelda threw her arms in the air and exclaimed, 'Why not give them to a charity? They can sell them and make money. You'll get oodles of PR. And ...' she drew out her final comment, 'the studio will think you're a saint.'

It was Kelby's turn for her jaw to drop. She stared at Zelda and gave Jimmy a smug glance. 'What a brilliant idea!'

Zelda spun around in a pirouette. 'Ta-dah! Everyone happy.'

'Can you handle it, please?'

'Oh, Kelby, I'd kill if anyone else took on the job! I'll get right on it when I'm back from Hamleys. Any particular charity?'

'Actually, there is. Help For Heroes. And the National Eczema Society — split it between them.'

'Yuck, I know the one. The scaly red patches that make them look like lepers.'

Kelby flinched.

As Zelda clomped out of Kelby's office in her high-heels, Jimmy called after her, 'And buy everyone a round of sarnies.'

Zelda shot Kelby a questioning glance.

'Sure.' Kelby smiled and waved her off.

Within seconds, Zelda's head popped back around the door. 'Own up. Who did it?'

'What?' Jimmy started towards the door.

Zelda whispered, 'The pigs are here!'

12

Kelby watched as Jimmy led the two policemen into her office. She indicated the soft seating in the corner. 'Please take a seat.'

Young Police Constable Pike resembled a string-bean, thin and gaunt like a marathon runner. PC Gardenia, turkey-necked and cagey, allowed his less-seasoned colleague to take charge and stood silently while PC Pike said, 'Great show, it's very popular. I believe you're currently filming the next series.' His eyes betrayed the tension inside him and Kelby wondered if he was being supervised by Turkey-neck.

Sitting opposite them, Kelby explained how she had to maintain a social media presence, but some dimwit had started trolling her.

PC Pike scribbled notes, flipping back and forth between pages to check what he'd written. Beside him, PC Gardenia stared over his shoulder in silence.

She finished by handing PC Pike her phone. 'You can see the messages in there.'

The young officer took his time scrolling through the threats she had received earlier, nodding now and then.

Biting back impatience, Kelby pushed her glasses on top of her head and blinked to focus on PC Pike. 'What are you going to do about it?'

'What do you expect us to do, Miss Wade?' PC Gardenia appeared suddenly energised. 'This sort of thing is to be expected when you're in the spotlight.'

Kelby bristled. 'I'm sorry, but I don't accept that. People don't need to behave this way to anyone, even to someone *in the spotlight.*'

'Well, most people don't bother the police with such everyday matters.'

'Can't you hunt him down and stop him before he gets it in his stupid head to act on any of those threats.'

'They are only tweets at the moment —'

PC Pike interrupted his colleague, 'Twitter should sort this out for you by closing the offender's account.'

'But can't you get someone to watch my house in case this idiot tries to break in?'

The Turkey-neck's excess skin flapped about his throat as he shook his head. 'If he comes around, then call 999 and we'll come straight round. But for now, we are very understaffed due to the budget cuts and very busy with real threats.'

His monotone voice made it hard for Kelby to concentrate. There were too many things whistling through her head.

Opposite her, PC Pike fidgeted uncomfortably and added, 'Miss Wade, we can't put surveillance on you just like that, but we —'

PC Gardenia butted in, 'Listen, many celebrities face this kind of thing, and they get private security firms to guard them.'

The younger officer seemed bent on trying to help and said, 'We'll discuss it with our supervisory officer, but we have to manage your expectations.'

She slumped back in her seat and narrowed her eyes. 'You can't do *anything*?'

'As I said, we'll speak to our super —'

'Yes, yes, I know.' Kelby jumped to her feet, 'you have to manage my expectations.' She marched to the door. 'If that's all, officers, I'll take it from here.'

As PC Pike reached the door, he turned to her, took her hand and wished her well.

When they were gone Kelby spotted a cloud drifting past the window forming into a one-eyed gargoyle that scowled at her. Maybe Jimmy was right. Even if Twitter closed his account, he'd rise again with another account, a new obnoxious user name and the same abusive torch. How could she ever hope to win if she didn't play their game?

She spun around and marched to the door linking her and Jimmy's office. 'Jimmy, please get Jon Thompson on the line.'

'Sure, anything I need to prep before you speak to him?'

'No thanks. The cops won't help. As executive producer, Jon should handle this.' She sighed. He wasn't the show's only producer, but he was certainly the most difficult.

'Will do.' At the door, Jimmy stopped. 'Ah, I nearly forgot. Your herbs are sitting in the boardroom.'

For a moment Kelby didn't understand, then it dawned on her. As she readied to meet the new mentee, she recalled the cryptic note. Could it be linked to this sudden and urgent meeting?

Intrigue spiked into her, and she hurried towards the boardroom. She couldn't wait to find out the ancient secret. And what made it deadly.

13

Before she entered the boardroom something prickled at Kelby's neck. She jiggled her shoulders to stop the tingle taking control of her whole body.

Then, it dawned on her. He was close by again and now she was imagining he was in her office.

Oh, my God! He was!

The Pewter Fox sat right there in front of her, his finely carved fingers draped over a petite woman's arm. Her nerves went into overdrive. Firstly, at the sight of him, and secondly at seeing him so intimate with another woman.

Get a life, Kelby!

She moved to the boardroom table and as she took his outstretched hand, a sensual current sizzled through her.

The Pewter Fox said, 'Hello, Miss Wade. Thank you for seeing us at such short notice. I'm Doctor Roy Robson.' He shook his head, 'I know how that sounds. Rob Roy and all that.' He smiled. 'Mum loves history.' As his hand clutched hers, she tried to release herself from his grip. He suddenly let go as though he had been jolted by a spark. 'Sorry.'

Kelby smiled. She sank into a chair opposite him, thankful to be off her wobbly feet and stared at the attractive Spanish woman sitting in front of her.

'And this is my sister, Marina Peña.'

Marina's face appeared as though someone had painted it with its sultry stare, its arched, thick eyebrows and pouting lips.

Kelby's mind was spinning as she muttered, 'This morning ...' She couldn't think of how to ask if he'd been following her. That was stupid; he was simply another businessman on a flight. But she couldn't help blurting out, 'Were you follo—'

The doctor interrupted, 'We just happened to be on the same flight.'

Marina's eyes lit up. 'Roy was visiting medical colleagues in Dublin to help me find the right home for my discovery. That's why the big rush to see you today, Miss Wade.'

'Please call me Kelby; formalities give me a headache.'

Marina started to open a folder, thick with documents, but Kelby stopped her. 'Wait, I have very little time now. Give me the nuts and bolts. Sum up your pitch in one sentence.'

Marina opened her mouth to speak, but Doctor Robson jumped in first. 'We've stumbled on an ancient secret. Something incredible. But there's a problem ...' His voice dropped as he fixed his eyes on Kelby, 'It could be deadly if it falls into the wrong hands. We're hoping you'll help us stop that from happening.'

Kelby gasped.

14

Kelby stared at the doctor, 'So it *was* you who left the note.'

His mouth twisted into a sheepish grin.

'Good pitch.' She grinned. 'Tell me more.'

'Aside from being extremely rare, Marina's herb has extraordinary healing powers.' He turned to his sister. 'Will you tell Kelby how this started?'

Marina explained, 'My husband and I live in a rural part of Andalusia. Inland of Malaga. It's in the middle of nowhere. You wouldn't believe what we've found!'

'What?' Kelby tried to focus on Marina, but her brother butted in before she could continue.

'Marina's home has been in her father's family for generations. They own thousands of acres of land. There are some ruins Marina wanted to develop.'

'My husband, Pepe, he thinks it is good for me to keep busy.' An elaborate shrug showed her amusement. 'At first I thought of renovating the ruin as a yoga retreat, but I changed my mind.'

'Why?'

'¡Dios!

'I found a skeleton in the ruins.'

Kelby pulled a face.

'I found it in a cellar. Buried underground. I think they used to store preserved food in there. Once they heard about it, archaeologists got excited. They've started a dig to discover fourteenth century farm life. It appears the ruined *finca,* um, that's a small farm with lots of buildings. Now they're digging up spoonful's of soil at a time to see how medieval farms worked.'

'The thing is, Kelby,' Doctor Robson drew Kelby's attention back to him, 'is that this discovery wasn't just the ruins —'

Marina interrupted, 'I also found a book and a pile of old documents.'

'The important thing, Kelby, is that Marina has not revealed the true find to the archaeologists.'

Kelby loved the way he said her name. Once again, she felt the thread that had connected them briefly on the plane. She glanced from brother to sister. 'I'm not with you.'

'The *real* find is a journal.' Doctor Robson sounded impatient to get to the point. 'Marina *also* found a leather bound book hidden in a clay pot. It dates back to medieval times.'

Before she could stop herself, Kelby blurted out, 'Medieval? Most people come to me with modern gadgets or futuristic inventions.' She raised her eyebrows. 'First time I've had something medieval in here.'

Doctor Robson said, 'Here, Marina will show you.'

Marina's tiny hands slipped something out of her folder. With careful movements she unwrapped a layer of mottled mocha and buff leather. 'It's a medieval girdle book. I think it was handmade by this author.'

Kelby leaned closer to the leather clad book.

'Look,' Roy flipped back a long flap of leather with a knot on the end, 'the book is bound with two pieces of wood covered with leather.'

Kelby noticed the leather had been pasted to the boards with an extension of leather knotted at the end.

'*¡Mira!*' Marina held the knot up in the air so the book hung upside down. 'See, when you lift it up to read it, the book's the right way up.'

Kelby raised her eyebrows and nodded. 'Clever idea.'

'They would slip the knot under their belt to carry on their bodies.' In a gentle motion, Marina placed the book back onto the table between them. 'Here, take a look.'

The book had a symbol etched on the cover.

Kelby gasped and held a hand across her chest. 'I *know* this. I see it every day.'

'What?' Marina glanced from Kelby to Roy, her frown darkening her golden glow. 'You've seen this book before?'

'No. Never.' Slowly, Kelby reached into her blouse, keeping her eyes on Roy's face. His eyes widened.

Kelby pulled out a chain with a pendant hanging from it and said, 'My brother Gary gave me this before he died.'

In the middle of her palm lay a pendant with a large, curved X inside it. The symbol was an exact replica of the image on the book.

15

Kelby lifted the chain over her neck and placed the necklace on the table between Roy and Marina.

'How did he know the symbol?' Marina asked.

Kelby shrugged.

'Maybe he saw it on the internet? Apparently, it's one of a few ancient symbols no-one understands. A cipher that has never been cracked. I've been researching and —'

Roy touched Marina's arm to quieten her. 'Don't go into that. Kelby has very little time and it'll just side track us.'

But Kelby stayed on the subject and said, 'Gary did some cycling training in Spain before he died. Could he have seen it there?'

'Possibly. But where?'

'I think he was cycling around the Sierra del Torcal.'

Marina and Roy gaped at each other and Roy said, 'That's near Marina's find. It's too close to be a coincidence. Do you know any more about this?'

'Nothing. Except he came home and had this made for me.' She fondled the pendant and frowned, 'I remember him saying he was onto something, but he went quiet for a while and then—'

Kelby dropped the chain back over her neck.

Marina said, 'At first we thought the two CCs was something to do with the occult. When I was a child I heard whispers of a secret society in Torcal so I looked up symbols and I found out there is a secret society protecting medieval manu—"

'Not now, Marina, we must finish this before you discuss other issues.' Doctor Robson whispered to his sister. His gaze swept back to Kelby, as he said in a gentle tone, 'The pendant's precious to you.'

Kelby nodded, reached out and lifted the ancient book. Her fingers traced the grooves, along the sides and corners. The book sent a bolt of exhilaration to every nerve fibre in her body, electrifying her.

Even though most of the outer brushed leather had cracked and dried out, something about this book touched her deeply, as though the author's warmth still radiated through it. She had spent the past ten years touching every conceivable product entrepreneur's invented. None of them had ever caused her to react in this way. Her heart skipped a beat as though a mystery rippled through the centuries and struck a chord within her.

Kelby fondled the knot. It gave her an odd sensation, as though she had stepped into the shoes of the creator, and now, centuries later, took the same pleasure and satisfaction in their handiwork.

A slight bump near the top caught her attention, but she ignored it for the moment. As Kelby balanced it on her fingers, she muttered, 'It's so unusual.'

'*Si*, it's made to dangle the girdle from your belt.'

'Thankfully, otherwise it could bring their trousers down!' Doctor Robson grinned.

Marina slapped his arm in disgust, 'No!' She turned to Kelby and said, 'Anyone who carried girdle books in the Middle Ages wore dresses or habits, not trousers! My brother is full of, how you say, *diablura*.'

'Mischief.' Doctor Robson's eyes twinkled, 'That's my middle name.'

Kelby marvelled at how his face lifted as the corners of his eyes crinkled. A tender warmth filled her. Even as she watched this brother and sister's banter, it reminded her of Gary. Instead of filling her with the usual sadness she felt when remembering him, it gave her fond memories of how they used to tease in much the same way.

'Aside from my devilment,' he chuckled, 'one opens a girdle book pretty much in the way one opens any bound book. The only difference is there's the extra length of leather hanging from the book.'

Marina pulled Kelby back into the moment as she said, '*Es triste*, it's sad. Very few of these book carry-bags have survived.'

Kelby's index finger hovered over the book, resting like a butterfly on the stiff cover. 'It's beautiful. I've never seen anything like this before.'

Marina gleamed with pride. '*Mira aquí*, you see inside is an elaborate family crest and the word "Carbonela".'

Kelby pushed her glasses closer to her eyes and leaned in to examine the.

'Marina has done so much work on this. She found out there were a variety of ways in which medieval ink was made. In general, the recipes produced very long-lasting inks that typically don't fade.'

'Don't we need gloves to touch it?' Kelby kept her gaze on the book.

'But this is not papyrus, it's parchment!' Marina spoke as though everyone should know the difference between papyrus and parchment.

Doctor Robson blushed and explained, 'Parchment is a strong material. Remember, it's animal skin, and not like papyrus or paper in consistency. Pages made from early papers or papyrus are fragile, turning them can cause damage.'

Marina chipped in, 'And wearing gloves can make it worse.'

'Yes, true. But Kelby is right to ask because medieval books are not to be taken for granted.' Doctor Robson said to Marina.

Kelby squirmed in her seat.

'I checked with an old friend of mine from university who's now an expert on this. Tim studies medieval documents across the globe. He said institutions have different policies. He's never been asked to wear gloves in the British Library's manuscripts room. And he was only asked once to wear gloves when he was consulting a heavily illuminated manuscript in the Bodleian Library in Oxford.'

His eyes stayed on Kelby making her uncomfortable. 'Tim said the gloves make sure hands don't mark the parchment, but it could be beneficial for parchment to absorb the natural oils on fingers.' Doctor Robson chuckled, 'Either way, it's best to make sure our hands are clean.'

Kelby saw Marina's outstretched hand. A sharp lemon odour filled the room as she wiped her hands.

'Phew!' Kelby finished wiping her hands. 'I wouldn't want to ruin this lovely old book.'

'But of course, best practice is to handle it as little as possible.'

'Okay.' Kelby said.

Each page illustrated details of a different herb in a flowing handwritten script. Beside the inked words, an elaborate decorated first letter, naming each herb had been drawn with intricate designs. Despite its age, every page in the book had high-quality drawings of the plant and its seeds.

'It seems to be a practical book.' Marina's voice filled with pride. 'Look,' she pointed at the page Kelby was on, 'There's details about each herb's medicinal properties and even directions for compounding the medicines extracted from them. They're on every page. And these are symbols of the different planets, a sort of shorthand showing medicinal properties. Astrology was a big part of medicine in those days.'

'What does this say?' Kelby pointed at a large A.

Marina leaned over and squinted at the words. 'It says "anemone". Then it goes on to explain its juice is applied externally to clean ulcerations, infections and cure leprosy or inhaled to clear the nostrils.'

As Kelby listened to Marina, the tips of her fingers tingled. Kelby shook herself and pulled back. The girdle book magnetised her. Locked in, Kelby leaned forward again, one hand still resting on the leather knot.

Marina's voice dropped to a conspiratorial whisper, 'When I was researching herbals, I came across a woman author who'd written several stories in Barcelona in 1492!'

Doctor Robson reached into Marina's folder and showed Kelby a printed list.

'They're now held in manuscript archives in Madrid,' said Marina. 'Some of these old documents are preserved in private repositories, such as Abadía de Torcal. My uncle runs an exclusive retreat there.' She glanced at her brother.

'Not now, Marina,' he said.

Marina sighed, and continued, 'But this particular author's work is in public administration.'

Kelby nodded and made some notes.

'I wanted to be a hundred per cent sure, so I went to the Instituto de Enseñanza.'

'What did you find?' Once again, the book winched Kelby closer. A shadow lingered between the pages, leaking an aura of a medieval struggle.

Marina tossed her head and twanged in her thick accented English, 'The stories appear to be written by the first female Spanish author.'

'Wait,' Doctor Robson cut in, 'she may not be the first as such. Remember Egeria.'

'We don't know if Egeria was Spanish,' Marina retorted.

Kelby watched the sparks fly between them and held up her hand. 'Can someone fill me in here?'

Doctor Robson cleared his throat, 'Um, sorry, Kelby. Nothing like a little tiff to add excitement.' He gave her his sheepish grin and continued, 'Egeria was a fourth-century female pilgrim who wrote an account of her pilgrimage to Jerusalem in Latin.'

Kelby watched him stroke his sister's arm.

'When Marina was researching she came across Egeria. While we're not sure who was the first female author. We'd like to believe our journal author is the first, because of her numerous short stories and her detailed journal.'

Marina leaned forward, 'Si. There's so much written speculation about her, yet no-one can say what happened to her. Her disappearance is a mystery.'

Suddenly a thrumming vibrated through Kelby's veins.

'What was her name?'

'Ana-María de Carbonela.'

16

Ana-María de Carbonela stood on the rocky ledge beside the waterfall inside the cave. She loved how the sun glinted on the surface of the pool below. A fine spray from the plunging water drifted over her body, cooling her and drenching her skin.

Even though the cave smelt damp, and the acrid stench of mould clung to the back of her throat, María loved this secret place.

Her grotto thrummed with life.

The constant drip of water. Insects scuttling from one hiding place to another. Underground passages that breathed out odours of damp earth with crevices to explore. In her living *cueva*, with its strange setting, she considered herself a passing visitor.

From her perch high in the hollowed out cave, she could see the sea mist clawing its way into the *valle*. Around her the day sparkled with life. Yet in a few hours the mist would wrap itself around everything in its path making it impossible to see the pond below.

She loved being alone in the wild countryside. Ever since Madre had drawn a map to show her how to find the grotto, she had spent many days lying by the pond and dreaming. Whenever she came to collect the *estraño* herb from the rocks, she took her time exploring the cueva.

She had been unable to tell Madre that cleaning the house and cooking bored her. Or that she preferred to live in another world inside her head.

On the clearest days, the distant mountains called to her. One day she would journey to the sea. Maybe even hide on a boat and write a story about a girl who sailed to new lands.

Like *La Reina Isabel*, the queen María admired so much, she wanted to journey to new places. Unlike the queen, she didn't have the means to see new towns and learn about the people. And like the monarch, María had blue eyes and chestnut hair. But she kept her clothes simple. The looser the garment the easier it was to run through the fields and woods. When at home with only Madre around, she didn't worry about her appearance. Her mother sewed gowns with trailing sleeves that hooked onto branches when María collected wood. Or dipped into the water buckets at the well and became drenched in the washing tub. But even Madre had not given in to the scandalous fashions of tighter-fitting garments with lower necklines and lace to create a form-fitting shape that girdled at the waist or hips.

María usually preferred to wear a smock and hose, and refused to wear a girdle and a bonnet or hair caul, but she had no choice when they went to church. Otherwise the town people would frown on Madre's unruly daughter.

Delighted she could discard her woolen garments in place of a lighter linen for the coming warmer months, she had thrown her tunic beside the pond. One day she would write a story about a girl who fashioned easier garments for women to wear, much like those men wore. For a moment she imagined how Queen Isabella would look dressed as the king.

A shiver tickled María's spine. Her uncle had taught her about a French martyr, Jeanne d'Arc, who had been burnt at the stake because they couldn't understand why she dressed as a man, even though she helped the French defeat the English invaders.

María didn't want to reject the gender roles; she simply wanted to dress in a manner that gave her more freedom for country life. Girl's garments didn't suit that.

Annoyed, María shook herself to stop her thoughts running away with nonsense. Dressing in men's clothing carried a death sentence.She wasn't about to be caught for such a foolhardy *perversio*. Besides, she had to start gathering the sticky herbs for Madre.

She leapt to her feet. The only way to cross the grotto was to swim.

As she stepped to the edge, she focused on the blue iridescent gleam right in the middle where she dived in. A slimy surface covered the water's edge, where it escaped through the cave and over the grass verge into the pool below.

A distant sound startled her.

Her head snapped from side to side as she glanced around and listened. A strangled bleating cut through her secret world and sliced into her.

Without hesitation, María dived off the rocky ledge and plunged into the green underground lake. Her head shot out of the crystal clear pool. Gasping from the cold current, she swam a few strokes across the shimmering water and climbed out over a natural stone wall. She ran through the rocky tunnel and clambered down the cliff into the shallow pond below.

After wading across the stream, and clawing over the mossy rocks, María grabbed her linen tunic off a dangling branch and pulled it over her head. Holding up a hand to shelter her eyes from the sun, she listened for the direction of the animal's cry. As she leapt across the river cobbles and up the opposite riverbank, María spotted a baby mountain goat struggling to break free. He strained his rear hoof between two sunken boulders. Blood caked its front right leg.

María skidded to a halt and crept closer. The goat veered to the left, away from her. *¡Hola, guapo!* What a handsome little goat you are.'

It didn't know what to fear more: her or the rock trap that snared its leg. María cooed reassurance. 'Shh. Quiet now. María is here to take care of you.' She winced at the sight of the goat's mangled leg. Its head reared as it bellowed for its mother to help. María grabbed the goat's tiny horns and held its head in a vice-like grip. She reached to hold its leg still. The little goat had incredible strength as it bucked around in her arms and bleated.

Dropping to one knee, María leaned forward and lowered herself over the goat, forcing it to the ground. Whispering to keep it calm, she lay on top of it with her back raised in an uncomfortable arch. With both arms now free, she tugged on the rocks, pulling them apart. Her natural lithe build had blessed her with the strength of any young man.

Still tucked under her, the goat started trembling. Its eyes rolled back in its sockets, a sign of death. With one final wrench, the skin lacerated along her fingertips as she lifted the mangled hoof from between the rocks.

Using her teeth, María tore a strip off the bottom of her tunic. As she wrapped it around the wound, the goat's warm blood spurted over her hands and slithered down her arms like a nest of baby red snakes in flight.

Still whispering to keep the animal's spirit alive, María stood. The poor creature probably wouldn't survive. The wound was deep, and the leg dangled at an awkward angle. She had no-one to turn to. No-one except Madre.

Even though her mother went to church every week, the priest condemned her for healing the sick and helping peasants who couldn't afford to see a doctor. So Madre practised in secret; her herbal remedies had saved thousands of their local people from suffering.

Since Madre had started picking rizado off the rocks beside the pond, her fame had grown and now people travelled many days to consult the *medicina*. If anyone could help the goat, Madre could.

By using the grotto's secret.

17

María's stomach grumbled. The smell of onions braising in the pot with freshly picked herbs and a chunk of wild boar made her mouth water. Madre had been paid well for helping another baby into the world last night.

She watched Madre mash the rizado into a pulp. Next, she smeared the green, sticky pulp on the goat's wound.

'Ana-María, you must stop bringing these animals home.'

'We can milk this one.' She gave Madre a coy smile.

'We barely have money to feed our own mouths. Pray tell, how can we feed these?' Her arm flung wide. Outside, a menagerie of rescued animals clucked and sniffed at the door.

'One day I will be paid for my writing, then we will have plenty of money to feed them all.'

'That is another thing you must stop.' Madre washed her hands and without wiping them dry, clapped them on the layers of wide skirts hiding her hips. 'Ana —'

'Mama, call me María!'

Madre threw her hands in the air. 'I pray you! Why do you make life difficult for yourself?'

'I know what you are going to say. I do not want to get married and stop my writing.'

'If you refuse to marry you can take refuge in a convent where at least you could enjoy being a clever woman. The nuns at *Abadía de Torcal* would love you to write for them.'

As María crossed her arms, her stomach muscles tightened. 'Madre, being with child or being cloistered in a monastery are unacceptable to me!'

'It is a humiliation for our family. Padre would want to see you married.'

Padre's death had resulted in her remaining unmarried — much to her relief. Thinking of Padre made her blurt out, 'When Padre did some work at the abbey he told me strange things go on there. And strange creatures walk the night.'

'¡He! Alas, I shouldn't have allowed Tío to put that nonsense in your head.'

'Not nonsense, Madre. Learning.'

'Learning indeed! When he took you under his wing to give you an education, it was supposed to teach you to be a good wife to a wealthy husband.'

'Mama! I am a good maiden with upstanding virtues. I don't need a husband to make me any better.'

Long ago Tío had given her history lessons. Saint Catherine of Alexandria stuck in her mind the most, mainly because she'd refused to get married. María knew how she'd felt.

'You miss the point, mi querida, I was hoping because his family are money lenders, he could find you a husband amongst the wealthiest, most powerful families of Spain.'

'Madre, you of all people know I am not in need of a wealthy man to make me happy. It is absurd! If they gave girls books and taught us what Tío has shown me, women would be as knowledgeable and as happy as men.'

'Ana-María de Carbonela! You cannot talk like that. If someone hears you …' Madre shook her head. Her voice dropped to a whisper, 'I know you are writing about this. Do not give Tío any more of those manuscritos. Your writing will get us thrown into prison. The monarchy would not like to hear the things you write.'

María swung around. 'He betrayed me!' So Tío had told her mother about her last manuscrito. She had asked him to send it to people in Barcelona who would listen to a woman's voice.

'No, Ana-María. He would not betray you. He wants to protect you, but he is proud of you. He sent it wherever you asked without my blessing.'

María exhaled and stared at the fireplace where more of her work lay hidden. She wouldn't give it up. Not for anyone. Not even Madre.

'As you will.' Madre snorted and lifted the goat off the kitchen table. 'But take heed, your thirst for learning will bring problems on your head.' She dumped the goat into María's arms and inclined her head towards the back door.

Instead of taking the goat outside, María ambled to the fireplace. She placed the goat on an old rug in front of the fire, tugged the hairy little beard under the goat's chin and patted his head. She rose and turned to her mother. 'I will not give up my writing Madre, like you will not give up your medicine.'

For a long moment, mother and daughter glared at each other. Both defiant, both trying to force the other to consent. Finally, Madre huffed and wiped her hands on the apron covering her fleshy belly. 'If you must do this writing, confine it to religious matters. Or write a journal about my medicine so you can learn about things that will one day be useful to you.'

A spirited bleat echoed around the room. They spun around to see the goat trying to stand on his wounded hoof. María's jaw dropped as she watched the little goat already putting pressure on his hoof and limping a step or two. Could Madre's rizado work that fast?

'*Ya está!*' Again Madre's hands landed on her swaying hips. 'You see; he will walk soon.'

María's eyes lit up. 'Yes, Mama, he will walk soon.' She stepped forward and hugged her mother. '*Gracias.* Now too, I have seen what many of your patients tell me. You are a miracle worker.'

'No, Ana-María.' Madre wagged her finger. 'We do not want to offend the Church. I am not a miracle worker. I only use natural remedies to help people. That is all.'

'I will write a manuscript about your *medicina.*'

With a rough hand, Madre cupped María's cheek. 'You are a good girl, Ana-María. One day you will make a good wife and a good mother.'

'One day, maybe. But now I will start with this rizado plant.'

They glanced at the goat again.

María smiled.

He had been cured by the grotto's secret.

18

Barker's thoughts ran wild in anticipation. If only he was there to see the terror in Piccoli's eyes as the tyre burst and she couldn't control the beast. He wanted his face to be the last the bitch ever saw.

Making money had been exciting at first, but the gloss had soon worn off and for the past few years he'd had his nose to the ground, sniffing out something to rock his socks.

Slowly his plan had formed. Of course, he'd mulled over it with many cups of camomile tea on countless nights trying to figure out how he'd remain anonymous. It had turned out to be easy although setting up the show had tested his patience with Teresina constantly bitching at him. That's why she had to be the first. And for other reasons he preferred to forget.

A thought suddenly struck him and he grinned. He had the perfect solution to make her think of him before she died.

Barker called her mobile.

19

Teresina's head pounded. 'Majella, turn that music down!'

Majella fiddled with her phone and instead of the monotonous drone lowering, it filled the car with a deafening beat.

'Majella!'

'Sorry, Mamma. Wrong button.'

Within seconds Majella lowered the volume, but it still thumped in Teresina's ears. Her nerves prickled. She was late for Nonna and nobody, but nobody was ever late for Nonna.

She switched on the air-con and breathed in the instant blast of cool air. She hated the Italian heat; it exhausted her and made her listless. And she preferred to keep up her fiery and passionate reputation.

'Call Inez and tell her to make sure we have adjoining rooms.'

'Mamma, don't badger her. She will do that anyway.'

'Okay, *carino.*' Teresina glanced at Majella. 'Can you send a text for me?'

Before Majella lifted the phone, it started ringing through the speakers, filling the car with more chaos. Teresina glanced at the dashboard and grimaced at the caller's ID.

The Bastardo.

She barked into the phone, 'Don't tell me you're not coming.'

'Of course not, I'll be there. How's the car handling?'

'You think I can't handle this car? I've been driving this sexy beast for years!'

'Oh, you're capable. That car becomes you.'

'*Esatto*, exactly! I don't know why I've been asked to assess the show's stupid devices.'

'You know the drill. We check the products entrepreneurs' pitch to the show so we can see which are suitable for the next series.'

'*Bene*, okay! I'll see you in Rome. We're going there straight after visiting Nonna.'

'How's Majella?'

'Why the sudden interest?' Teresina prickled. He had no idea what would be handed to him in Rome.

'I thought I heard music in the background.'

'Yes, some stupid hip-hop.'

'Ahh, nothing like the good ol' tunes.' He broke into song with a piece of the chorus from Gloria Gaynor's *I Will Survive*.

'Listen, you may have nothing better to do with your time than sing to me, but I have things to do.'

Teresina gripped the steering. Annoyed at him for making her remember the past, she struggled to concentrate on the hairpin bends coming into Serramonacesca.

'I'll see you later.' She hit a button and cut the call.

20

Kelby frowned, confused by the information about herbs and ruins. Impatiently she asked Marina, 'What has this got to do with what you found on your farm?'

'It's the same woman.'

'But you said the documents weren't named.'

'I went to the Bibliotecas Públicas del Estado and other archives in Madrid. *Herbal de Carbonela* is still in print today. I took the herbal guide I'd found in the cellar and matched the two. They're identical. It's been rewritten and reproduced, and many new authors have taken the information and published their own herbals.'

Doctor Robson said, 'Strangely, we found lots of information about a sailor named Carbonela who was associated with Christopher Columbus, but not much about Ana-María. She disappeared late in 1492 after her herbal journal was published.'

'Have you tried to contact an expert?'

'*¡Dios!* It's more than that. I think the skeleton we found in the ruins is Ana-María de Carbonela's! If it is, she deserves to be honoured but I don't know how to go about it.'

Roy patted his sister's hand again, 'More important is finding out more about this plant. The herbal journal names a herb called "rizado".'

'Which,' Marina interjected, 'has never been found! I spent hours on the internet reading documents and days in libraries and museums.'

Doctor Robson nodded. 'Carbonela's herbal says rizado was mixed with other traditional remedies. It speeds the healing process. Carbonela's stories —'

'¡*Eh,*' Marina slapped his arm, 'call her Ana-María. Don't refer to her by her surname.'

Doctor Robson turned back to Kelby. 'Marina's right. Ana-María's chronicles reflect the healing process. Take one of her stories archived in Madrid. It's about a woman herbalist who concocts a potion with incredible healing powers. She does this inside some kind of secret grotto near an underground waterfall.'

Marina said, 'Maybe this herbalist was her mother.'

Doctor Robson cut in, saying 'The herbalist in her story was named Carmen. She may have been Ana-María's mother.'

'Why do you think that?'

Marina flipped the book closed and pointed at the symbol again. 'The two C's are back-to-back. They could stand for Carmen Carbonela.'

Kelby stared at it. 'Hmm, I see the two C's now. When Gary gave me the pendant I thought it was an elaborate X.'

Doctor Robson said, 'It could be either.'

Marina shrugged. 'If it's two C's I wonder if that was Ana-María's way of honouring her mother's knowledge.'

'Marina thinks Carmen named the herb. The first mention in the journal is listed as "rizado", which means "curly", so it must be a funny looking plant.'

Marina shuffled more research documents. 'I found an old book on the Spanish Inquisition. A woman from the Granada area called Carmen was condemned as a witch. It doesn't give her family name because they didn't know much about her.'

'But you said you lived near Malaga. Granada is miles away.'

'*Lo sé*, I know, but in those days the whole of our area fell under Castile de Granada. That was eventually divided into Andalusia, and later Malaga got its own province.'

'I see. So, this Carmen was a witch?'

Doctor Robson's steady gaze bored into Kelby. 'She may have been a herbalist, but the Inquisition would have considered her an heretic.'

Marina chipped in, 'Maybe they accused her of being a witch because she mixed herbs to make medicines.'

Doctor Robson, lowered his voice and leaned closer to Kelby, 'Heretic or witch or neither, Rizado needs to be protected.'

'Protected?'

Doctor Robson and Marina looked at each other.

His intense gaze penetrated Kelby's as he said, 'There's a lot of noise on the web about this herb and why it hasn't been heard of since the Middle Ages. The big pharmaceuticals have been trying to find it and replicate it.'

'Ancient secrets breed weirdos.' Marina added.

'Rizado could be extremely powerful in the right hands.' Doctor Robson threw his jumper back over his shoulders.

'And *mortal*, deadly, in the wrong hands!' Marina exclaimed.

Kelby frowned. 'I've lost track here. What are we talking about now?'

'Haven't you heard of rizado before? Not even from your brother?'

Kelby's jaw dropped. 'My br-brother?' She stammered, 'What's he got to do with this?'

Doctor Robson came around and knelt beside Kelby. His hand rested on her arm. 'Kelby, many of the people interested in rizado are extremely dangerous.'

Marina nodded in agreement. 'With the speculation out there, rizado will be attractive as a big money spinner to many *diablos*. Do you know what this could be worth to the pharma sector?'

Kelby's gaze swung across the table between brother and sister. 'I can imagine! But I'm confused. Why me? I don't know about the pharmaceutical sector.'

'The world is full of evil, *perverso*.'

'Wait! You said something about my brother. What's he got to do with this?' Kelby touched her phone and her screen-saver image of the man and child lit up. Gary and Annie. The two most precious people in her life.

They glanced at the phone, but Kelby clicked it off.

Doctor Robson's grip on her arm tightened. 'Kelby, we came to you because we think your brother was murdered.'

21

26 April 2010, Andalusia, Spain

Gary Wade puffed up the steep incline. Slivers of sweat trickled out of his cycling helmet, down his nose and through his panting lips, leaving him with a salty mouth.

His good leg cramped and strained to reach the top. Strange how his other leg spun around effortlessly, despite it only being half a leg.

He had set himself a fifty kilometre ride for the day. Nothing too severe, yet not too gentle either with a manageable gradient and a couple of climbs to get his heart monitor beeping. Strapped across his chest, it sent his distance, speed and heart rate, as well as the route's incline and decline, to his watch.

On the four-hour ride, he'd set a good pace, keeping in high gear as often as possible but still enjoying the countryside rolling past him.

Gary glanced over his shoulder. Around them green rolling hills meandered through the Guadalhorce Valley between Malaga and Marbella.

As usual Mark had shot ahead. His friend may be better up hills, but boy, oh, boy, Gary would punish him on the straights.

Now Gary had committed to do the charity cycle for *Help for Heroes*, his school friend was a good buddy to join his training programme. They'd always been fit, but this trip around Andalusia would make his legs stronger.

As he powered up the hill, he grabbed a few mouthfuls of water. A few sips were better than large gulps. He unzipped his cycling top to allow as much air as possible to cool his overheating body as he made the ascent. Gary concentrated hard on his breathing. Nearly at the top.

He glanced at the tall ladder of bizarre limestone formations towering over the landscape. Despite its steep rock faces, El Torcal plateaued on top into a vast labyrinth of rocky crevices. Sierra del Torcal was next on his fitness hit list. They were hiking it tomorrow before they returned home for the charity ride.

Mark had planned a perfect send-off in the mysterious monastery *Abadía de Torcal,* clinging to the cliff edge, which now served as an exclusive spa retreat. Their famous hot stones treatment apparently worked miracles. He couldn't wait to feel the effects on his gammy leg.

It had long been his dream to climb the 1,300 metre elevation to check out the spectacular pinnacles and spires in the geological curiosity. Another field-test to spur the new leg into catching up with his body and mind. El Torcal wouldn't beat him. No-one would. Never. Not even the Afghan who'd launched the rocket that blew off his leg.

His first prosthetic was a basic model from the UK's National Health Service, which allowed him to stand and walk, but was nothing special. The stump made him feel as if he was walking on stilts with his phantom foot constricting as if it had been glued into his shoe.

He'd consulted specialists and now his legs were designed to crack most sporting activities. This particular leg could pivot at the ankle and included a robust shock absorber that could endure heavy drops when walking down steep hillsides.

With his family by his side and a growing pile of new legs, he had so much to look forward to. He loved this. The freedom of riding in the country and exploring a new culture. Totally awesome.

In a burst of exhilaration, Gary started the incline, all plans driven from his head. Blowing hard, he concentrated his eyeline at a point four metres in front of the bike, keeping his pedal rhythm steady. Now and then, he flicked his eyes at his watch to check his heart rate was holding a steady one-fifty-sixty rate. With his cardiovascular coming under pressure, and his quads starting to burn, he preferred staying in the saddle rather than standing on the pedals, forcing himself to accept the pain. The more he increased his endurance capabilities now, the better he'd cope during his Lands' End charity ride. Even though he was gasping for air, a thrill flooded through him.

As he reached the brow of the hill, he glanced over the other side. Mark wasn't even a speck of dust in the valley. Gary frowned, hoping Mark hadn't taken a wrong turn and got lost. Sure, the place was out on a limb, but they'd gone over the Guadalhorce route a few times so he should be on track. Maybe he'd gone into the bush for a leak.

Gary bolted over the brow and the road fell away dramatically. Gathering speed, Gary's mountain bike hurtled down the hill at forty kilometres an hour. As he raced down the treacherous descent, he clung to the handlebars. While he tried to maintain balance, he corrected the bike's desire to drift towards a steep cliff on the side of the road.

Suddenly his front tyre hit rubble and veered to the left. He corrected the steering, but couldn't stop it gunning into a gully along the rocky verge. Gary's heart raced. Sweat saturated his armpits.

The wheel took on a life of its own.

The front tyre crashed into a crag and rammed between two huge boulders, wedging itself like an arrow into bark. Gary jettisoned forward, his arms and legs flailing, automatically preparing to cushion his landing. Instead, he somersaulted and his left shoulder smashed into the bedrock. His cycling shirt ripped on a jagged point, tearing his skin beneath. A sharp blast of pain bit into his arm.

As the back of his helmet struck the granite wall, Gary lost consciousness.

22

Gary's eyes fluttered open. It seemed as though a pneumatic drill hammered in his head, as if builders were digging up the dirt road right behind him. He tasted copper in his mouth and knew he'd bitten his tongue.

For a moment, his memory blurred. Within seconds, he became aware everything ached. It felt as though his hip was smashed. Thankfully, his left side had taken the brunt, but he wasn't sure how much his right could endure with a third of it missing. Slowly and carefully, he wriggled his toes. Then he flexed his joints, from his ankles to his neck. Nothing bust.

Instant relief swept through him. Abrasions, criss-crossing his palms and elbows, left blood smears across his clothes. Suddenly, a vision of his daughter stood in front of him, her thin cotton shirt billowing in the fresh mountain breeze.

'Annie? Is that you, pumpkin?' he croaked, blinking his eyes to focus on the silhouette blocking the sun. No, it couldn't be Annie, this angel was much older than his at home.

Gary smiled and raised himself onto his shoulder. '*Buenos días.*' As the movement sent another flash of pain through his upper body, he grunted and bit away the agony.

'*No se mueva!*' The girl repeated herself in stilted English, 'Don't … move.'

From the corner of his eye, he saw a long, bloody gash almost slicing his bicep in two. He shifted his flank and jabbed his other elbow under him. Leaning on his right side, he glanced at the girl. She knelt at his side.

Long tendrils of dark hair fought to escape her riding helmet while her bronzed skin glowed with a sheen. The sun was warmer than earlier, so he tried to shake the pain from his head, but it refused to budge.

The girl pointed. His eyes followed her finger. In the field to his right a horse grazed happily, its ebony coat gleaming. He snorted, his glossy mane shaking off the flies.

'Can I?'

Gary looked back at the girl kneeling beside him. Her slim, bronzed hand dipped into a leather pouch and came out a slimy green. Without asking again, she smeared the green slime down his torn bicep.

Amazed at the girl's self-assurance, Gary watched and tried to guess her age. Probably twelve or thirteen, but with her self-confidence she could easily pass as a young adult.

The cool, damp paste instantly relieved the needles of pain piercing his muscle. He frowned and peered at her fingers massaging the jelly-like seaweed into his wound. His nose wrinkled. It smelt like a dirty fish tank. The dark oozing blood faded from a ripe cherry-red to a military green. He gaped as his blood was absorbed into the slimy jelly and disappeared, taking with it the dull ache of his bruised shoulder.

'Gee, that looks and smells yuck, but it feels great.' He was going to say it was gold dust, but he'd learnt not to use slang with Spanish people, as most of it got lost in translation.

She laughed and said in perfect English, 'Yes, it's gross, but it works a treat.'

'Hey, you're English.'

'Bit of both.'

He watched in shock as the jagged flesh seemed to knit together. A shout tore his attention away from the wound. Down the track, Mark's legs gyrated, biting on traction to get to them fast. Again, Mark yelled out, 'You okay, buddy?'

Gary waved. 'I'm in good hands. This little angel saved the day.'

The girl grabbed Gary's water bottle lying near him with its lid open. She tilted it upside down and a drop leaked out. She emptied the rest of the slime from her pouch into the bottle. Only then did he notice the strange symbol branded into the leather. A curly X with equally strange motifs scrolling beneath it.

'What the hell is that?'

She shrugged and grinned. 'It works for Midnight.' She inclined her head to the elegant pony nuzzling dried grass in the field.

There was a skid as Mark's brakes crunched gravel and chewed up dirt. Mark called out, 'You loafing again, Wade?'

The girl stretched out her hand. 'Nice to meet you, Wade.'

'Wait. Don't go. I want you to meet my friend.' He didn't want to frighten her off by saying he wanted to find out more about the stuff and where she'd got it.

As Mark strode towards them, removing his helmet, the girl ran off, waving and calling out, 'One more should be all it needs to heal. *Hasta la vista.*'

He didn't even know the young angel's name. Gary stared at the symbol, fixing it in his mind. Maybe that would lead him to the source. Again, he stared in amazement at the pesto-like paste on his arm. He couldn't see underneath the slime, but the wound had stopped bleeding with a strange tightening sensation. He may have to tone down his story of what happened. Mark would certainly give him stick about stinking like a pond. If it could be successfully tested, it might give him a hike in salary. That would make Stacie happy. She refused any help from Kelby.

Thank goodness the girl had left him a sample. He didn't want to go back with stories about his arm being injured — with nothing to prove it.

Then he'd *really* be without a leg to stand on.

23

Gary stared at Gorden. Why on earth was he reacting that way? By now the slime paste reeked even more than it had a few weeks ago in Spain. The beer fridge in his man-cave shed at home stunk to high-heaven, but he wasn't going to give up his last sample without some kind of commitment from MG.

'The test results are confidential.'

'But *I* gave you the stuff. *Surely* you can give me an idea of how things are going.'

The sounds of cars revving and taxi horns vying for their space in the bustling London traffic outside didn't do much to steady his nerves. Mark had told him he didn't have the mettle to stand up to a global conglomerate such as MG. But he dug his heels in deeper. He wouldn't let Gorden get the better of him. No way.

'You expect us to believe some girl gave you this paste which healed the wound. You don't know what it's called or what it does, but it healed your arm super-fast — though you can't prove it.'

Gary nodded, agitation rising from his stomach. The thought of a potential pay rise had disappeared with the results of the wound on his bicep. This gunk was incredible. It had to be seen to be believed. All he wanted was the promise of doing the right thing, but the whole story had started to stink, more than the sample.

'What are you expecting? Miracles?' Gorden scoffed.

Gary stood his ground. He wasn't stupid; he'd done his homework. 'I checked with the scientists. They told me they'd found something amazing.'

Gorden's face froze. 'Oh, they did, did they?'

Suddenly Gary realised he'd put his foot in it. His only sodding foot. He didn't want to get the fellas in trouble.

'Let's make a deal. You tell me where you *really* found it and I'll show you the test results myself.'

'I told you, I didn't get her name.' They didn't buy his story about a young girl healing his arm and their questions had made his hackles rise. Without mentioning any of this to Stacie or Kelby, he had done some nosing around of his own. Getting cosy with the scientists had upped his ante. Even better, finding out about an ancient secret remedy had given his story strength. But listening to this crap wasn't cutting it with him. He estimated what this would be worth on the open market, but he had hoped the company would work with him. It might not help amputees grow back their limbs, but the potential to speed up other forms of healing sparked his interest.

'What if we flew you there to get more samples? Would that do it for you?'

'Gorden, I've already told you, I have no idea where the girl came from. But, sure, flying me over to scout around could help me find her and get more of the stuff.' He flexed his bad leg.

Gorden slumped back in his chair and locked his fingers around the back of his head. Gorden's gaze was meant to disarm his adversary, but Gary wasn't rattled. 'Before that I want your written assurance any more samples will be openly tested and findings will be shown to the UK and EU drug testing councils or whatever they're called.'

Gorden gave a discreet cough. Gary stiffened. Damn, he should have looked up the name of the drug testing place. Being armed with that kind of info would have given him more kudos with Gorden. *Damn, damn, damn!*

What did Kelby say? Forearmed is forewarned. She said those who know something is coming are better prepared to face it than those who don't know. He could kick himself, despite having only one foot. Paying attention to that kind of insider info would have allowed him to be one up on Gorden. More importantly, it would have allowed him to prepare for trouble.

'Listen, Wade, if you're buying time to get MG to offer a big payout, forget it.'

'What?'

'And don't even think about trying to sell it on the black market, either. You'll get yourself buried in shit.'

'Hey, I don't need this crap. I brought you something I stupidly thought would interest MG. It seems I was wrong.' He spun on his good heel and marched to the door. Under his prosthetic foot, the floor squeaked and released a faint smell of pine floor cleaner. For a strange moment it reminded him of the hospital where Annie was born.

'Wait! You're our only link. We'll send the scientists with you to Spain. They'll support you in any way possible.'

Gary swivelled his head and eyed Gorden. 'And you'll make that promise?'

'Yes, I will. You're a decent bloke, Wade. I can see that now. You're only interested in getting the benefit out to the world.'

'What did you think?'

'Sorry, I should've trusted you from the word go.' Gorden rose to his feet and held out his hand. 'Start over?'

Gary hesitated, but decided to trust Gorden. *Who else would believe his strange story?* He strode back to Gorden's desk and shook his hand.

'What would you like to do first?' Gorden asked softly.

'I have a tiny bit left at home in my shed. Why don't you get the guys in the basement to start processing it while we head to Spain to see if we can find the girl?'

'Not downstairs. We'll do further tests in 42A.'

'Where's that?'

'Under lock and key.'

'Why?'

'Some people will kill to get their hands on this.'

24

As she sat upright in the boardroom chair, Kelby's heart pounded against her ribs. Her body seemed to be suddenly filled with wriggling eels. The shame of Gary's assumed suicide had caused her years of pain and grief, and shame on her family name. More than that, his passing had caused a gaping hole no-one would ever fill. Although she often spoke to him, as she did her mother, his death still saddened her.

Now, these people were saying he'd been murdered!

'What are you talking about?' Her words barely came out as she struggled to breathe.

Still on his knee beside her, Doctor Robson said, 'When Marina was researching rizado, she found some unexplained deaths. Like Gary's.'

Marina added, 'They were linked to rizado but each one had,' she curled her fingers in quote marks, 'a *reason* for their death, so there was no further investigation.' Marina pulled out more notes from her folder and slid them across the table to Kelby. 'See this man? He's an experienced diver, but he died at the bottom of the ocean. They said he made fatal errors with his kit.'

Kelby looked at a printed website story about the diver. His sun-blond tousled hair and piercing green eyes held her gaze.

'This one,' Doctor Robson tapped his finger over another printed sheet, 'died on a long run through the Brecon Beacons. He supposedly had a heart attack, but he was perfectly fit and healthy.'

'Roy has five more case studies to show you, but they are depressing enough without knowing your brother is amongst them.'

'How is Gary connected?'

'All these people worked for Mata Gordo.'

'What?' Kelby gasped.

Still kneeling beside her, Doctor Robson pointed at the diver. 'This fella was a young scientist.' His finger moved to the other story showing an older man in the London Marathon. 'This chap trained him. They died within months of each other.'

'Gary worked for Mata Gordo!'

'He was their security analyst, wasn't he?'

'Yes. He'd been injured in Afghanistan and had to be discharged. For ages, he struggled to find something else. I wanted him to work for me, but he refused. Said he wouldn't let me do any more for him. He would rather work for a security agency than be seen as the "paid brother".'

Doctor Robson rose to his feet and returned to his seat opposite her.

Kelby continued, 'An associate of mine discovered Mata's security had been breached a number of times. Gary did a presentation on how bad their systems were. And what they needed to do to fix them, so they hired him.'

'Well, he must have been successful because the trail of deaths halted for a while.' Marina sighed.

Kelby slumped back into her seat, exhaling loudly, as though exorcising a demon. 'Why would he be killed? He didn't do anything wrong.'

Roy answered, 'I think he found out about the other deaths.'

Kelby stared at the doctor. Confusion hammered inside her head.

'Maybe he found out about them and wanted to report them so they had to quieten him too.'

Kelby gasped, her hand clutching her mouth. Gary murdered! 'I couldn't believe it at the time.'

'He was doing loads of stuff for *Help For Heroes* to show other soldiers being back in civvy street with a serious injury wasn't so bad after all. He had even been training to cycle from Land's End to John o' Groats.'

Roy explained to Marina, 'That's the whole length of Great Britain from south to north.'

'*¡Dios mío!* That's a long way.'

'Yes, he was going to cycle for about two weeks to raise money. Why would he commit to that and then … then …' Kelby choked up. She pulled herself together. 'Mata said he had consulted their in-house counsellor. They said he'd been terribly depressed about his injured leg and the issues with his prosthesis.'

Roy frowned. 'It doesn't sound as if he was suffering from depression.'

'He wasn't!'

'Did you see any signs?'

'No, and neither did his wife. In fact, we saw the opposite.' She jumped up and marched to a picture frame hanging on the wall. She unhooked it and stepped back to the table. 'Gary gave me this when my first business failed. I was gutted and thought I wasn't capable of managing a company.'

Inside the picture frame a quote by Winston Churchill read: *Never, never, never give up.*

Roy frowned at the message and stared up at Kelby, his eyes a mixture of emotion.

For a moment they looked at the frame. Then Kelby said in a soft voice, 'Is that the kind of man who would give up?'

Roy patted Kelby's arm. 'You were obviously very close.'

'We were orphaned in our early teens so I had to look after Gary.'

Marina said, 'I'm sorry to hear that.'

'It was a long time ago.'

'But it never leaves.' Roy's eyes held Kelby's for a moment.

Kelby nodded, knowing Roy understood the gaping hole that losing a parent left. Then an abrupt thought shot into her mind. 'The envelope! How did you know?' Kelby's gaze drilled into the doctor's, silently demanding an answer.

'I didn't.'

Marina said, 'Roy lives by that motto.'

'So did Gary.' Kelby whispered.

A warmth crept into Roy's cheeks. He cleared his throat, tapped the images laid out on the table and asked, 'Can you see the connections here, Kelby?'

The pictures of the dead men stared at her. She didn't answer, but looked into Roy's eyes.

'Marina realised the deadly value of her find, and when she showed me this, I wanted you to see it.'

Kelby swallowed the lump in her throat. She couldn't decide whether to be relieved Gary hadn't committed suicide or scared about the deadly implications. A sudden coldness clenched the core of her being. 'Do you know if Mata Gordo did it?'

'We have no idea.'

'So you don't know who is responsible for Gary's and these ... these deaths?'

Roy shook his head. 'No. But they're linked to rizado. Whoever is doing this is powerful and they'll do anything to keep their secrets hidden.'

'That sounds a bit paranoid.'

'I know, but we're in danger.'

His words hung in the air for a breath-taking moment, then he softened his tone, 'They'll stop at nothing to find rizado.'

25

A light knock on the door brought Kelby back into the moment. She waved her hand to her office assistant holding a tray of coffee. 'Come in, Zelda.'

In a flash, Marina had wrapped the book and hidden it inside her folder. Kelby's stomach dropped. She wanted to keep the book, but it was their find, not hers.

Zelda entered and flounced to the boardroom guests. She placed the coffee cups on the table.

Marina wove a strand of hair around her finger and, glancing nervously at Zelda, she said in a low voice, 'Ana-María wouldn't have known what gave rizado such incredible healing power.' Marina let the strand of hair go. It sprung up into a coil.

Doctor Robson also dropped his voice to a whisper. 'Rizado coming onto the market will devastate Big Pharma.'

Kelby waved Zelda away. 'Thank you.'

Behind Kelby's guests, Zelda busied herself clearing older coffee mugs beside the overhead projector.

The doctor said, 'Since the journal was found in Madrid's archives, it's been speculated that rizado –'

'Sorry Doctor Robson,' Kelby interrupted and turned to Zelda, 'Thank you, Zelda. *That* will be all.'

Doctor Robson kept his voice low, 'It appears rizado aids each component it's mixed with. Basically, it acts as a catalyst. It needs testing, of course, but it's possible it will enhance any drug's capabilities and speed up the healing process.'

Instead of leaving, Zelda cleared her throat and asked, 'Anyone want milk or sugar?'

Kelby answered, 'We'll sort it out, Zelda.'

Zelda lifted the tray with the old mugs and clomped back to the door. Roy jumped up to hold the door open for her — Kelby suspected it was to ensure she left. After closing the door, he slipped back into the seat opposite her as he poured the milk for Marina and Kelby.

'Sorry about that, Doctor Robson.' Her cheeks warmed with embarrassment over Zelda's eager efficiency.

Ambling around the table, Doctor Robson placed a coffee in front of her. 'That's fine.'

Back in his seat, the doctor left his coffee black. 'Call me Roy. Formalities give me a headache too.'

Kelby smiled. Then the reality of their pitch slammed into her. Gary murdered? Tears in the back of her throat threatened to swell up. She almost knocked her coffee over when her hand went to lift her cup. Despite trying to piece it together, her thoughts were in a jumble.

Could the book's secret *really* change the world?

26

Kelby started pacing the boardroom. Her heels tip-tapped across the floor, and she made a mental note to ask Jimmy to get her shoes re-heeled.

She spun around to face Doctor Robson and Marina and asked, 'I still don't know why you came to me. I told you earlier, I'm not into the pharmaceutical sector.' Kelby rubbed a sudden hive of goose flesh.

'For your brother's sake, help us locate rizado. If you want to carry it through we'd love to have you on board. If not, it would be great to give us a personal intro to Jon Thompson.'

For a moment Kelby was puzzled and then said, 'Of course, Jon's into that sector. I think he has shares in some kind of health clinic. So this may be right up his street.'

'He'll see that rizado could affect every drug in the market.' Roy forced her to lock eyes with him before he continued his summary, 'The implications this could have on the industry are untold. Globally. The business potential could be enormous. And that's what makes it so dangerous. The big problem is … can we trust him?'

'I think so. He's not my favourite producer, but I'm sure he'll keep this under wraps. What else do you need?'

'Finding rizado is only the start. There'll have to be studies on how it affects medical treatment, especially in the early stages.'

'One thing's for sure,' Kelby smiled, 'I don't have access to the sort of money that would be needed.'

'It might even help in preventative medicine. If you've ever known anyone chronically ill, you'll understand what a difference it will make.'

Kelby kept her eyes on the doctor, but thought of little Annie.

At that moment her phone beeped.

Kelby grabbed it, hoping against hope it wasn't the stalker. Instead, her phone had reminded her about her conference call with Jon. 'Talk of the devil,' she said and stood abruptly. 'I'm sorry Doctor Robson, Marina.' Tapping her watch, she walked around the boardroom table, 'I have a conference call.'

As Roy rose to his full height, he asked, 'Are you going to help us?'

'I'll consider what you've told me today.'

'When will you decide?' Marina lifted her precious leather book.

Kelby stared at it, reminded again of the mystery hiding between the pages. Her breath quickened. She wanted to suggest she kept the girdle book, but it wasn't her find.

Marina stepped closer and said with a desperate tone in her voice. '*Por favor,* please, help us to stop the deadly big business people chasing after rizado.'

Roy stretched beside Marina and again placed his hand on her arm. Each time he did it, the gesture calmed her.

Kelby's phone beeped another reminder about her call. 'Sorry, now I'm late.' She led them to the boardroom door and held it open for them.

Roy said, 'Let's find it and prove what it can do.'

Jimmy gave a polite cough behind her. 'Sorry to disturb you, Kelby, but Mr Thompson is on the line.'

'I'll be right there.' As Kelby stepped away, Roy touched her arm to detain her.

Kelby squirmed. She imagined being alone with him and her heart fluttered.

'If you do get involved there will be huge risks, so please don't say anything to Mr Thompson until we can work out more details.' He leaned closer. 'The note on the plane ... I had to tell you about Gary.' He paused for a moment, and added, 'And that *you* are in danger.'

27

A thread of suspicion coiled in Teresina's gut. The Bastardo hadn't sung to her for more than ten years. Even then, he only sang to her in his toneless voice when he had something on his mind and couldn't figure out how to spill the beans.

What was he trying to tell her?

They'd managed to keep up a veneer of friendliness — at least until the show.

Recently he had started to get too friendly again. Her showdown with him in Rome would put him back in his place.

'Was that your favourite song, Mamma?'

'Long ago. Not now.'

Majella's music crept up a few notches, distracting Teresina's eyes from the road. The Maserati veered to the right. Teresina eye-balled the steep cliff and yanked the steering.

'I heard that other man singing it.'

The car careered into another sharp turn.

'Please send a text for me.' She spun around the bend as the road ascended into the hillside town. Then she swivelled her head to Majella. 'What man?' A coil of suspicion unfurled deep inside her.

Majella lifted her phone to send the text. 'The one who came from the show.'

Teresina frowned. 'I told you not to go near strangers, so how do you know he was singing that?'

'I heard it through my window, Mamma.'

First the magazine and now that old song. Without a doubt, he was up to something.

'If you heard it how come you know it was a strange man singing?'

'Because Mamma,' Majella sighed with exasperation, 'I peeked at the man from the studio.'

Teresina shook her head. She hadn't bothered meeting anyone else from the crew. There were so many who came and went, mostly setting up the new products they had to test.

'He had this tiny thing in his hand. Kinda like an iPod. He stuck it onto the car.'

She hit the brakes and skidded into a sharp right twist in the road. 'What did he look like?'

'Like a man, Mama.'

'Give me more details than that.'

'I couldn't see him properly.'

'Majella!'

Majella huffed. 'Tall and skinny. *And* red hair.'

'Oh my God! The Bastardo!' Teresina grabbed Majella's hand and shook it. 'Quick. Find Kelby Wade in my phone. Send her a text. Tell her to call me urgently.'

'Mamma, you can ask me nicely, you know.'

Teresina ignored her. She thought of the voice singing to her. He had never resorted to violence; it wasn't his style. But she wouldn't put it past him to threaten her. She'd seen a different side to him that night and she didn't want to see it again. The magazine had been a clear threat. The blood spattered across her and Kelby's faces showed he had become unhinged.

Teresina raised her voice over Majella's music. 'Wait! Send the text later. First, look in my phone for Gabrielle and call her.'

Within seconds, Majella had connected the call into the dashboard and Teresina panted at Gabrielle, 'Listen, if something happens to me, send the same letter to Kelby Wade.'

A voice boomed through the car speakers, 'Nothing is going to happen to you. You're being paranoid.'

'I'm not! He's up to something.'

'Well, you'll soon find out when you hand the letter over. Are you on your way to Rome now?'

'No, first we're visiting Nonna and then we're heading out.' Teresina clung to the steering as her beloved Maserati curved into another sharp bend. She didn't care it took the corner at high speed; she had other things on her mind.

'Listen, chill, okay? Everything is ready for your meeting. You'll be fine.'

'Thanks, see you later.'

Even though her lawyer thought she was being paranoid, Teresina couldn't stop thinking about the voice singing to her. It had been a long, long time since he'd done anything that showed he remembered their affair ten years ago.

Maybe he'd got tired of the blackmailing. Maybe making him pay for Majella's tenth birthday party had pushed him over the edge. For ages she had wondered what would be the final straw. But he kept yielding to her demands, so she kept pushing him. They'd always been that way together. Now she wondered if he'd reached his snapping point.

His voice filled her head, blotting out logic. Her gut churned with dread. She had better warn Kelby. Their lives were in danger. 'Majella, call Kelby Wade. Do it quickly. Tell her I've already left a message. But she must call urgently.'

Majella tapped into her mother's phone once again.

But then the tyre exploded.

28

Zelda shoved the loo door shut with her high-heels. Using her longest nail she plonked the loo seat lid down and squatted onto it.

She rummaged in her handbag and fished out her mobile phone. Pressing a number listed in her favourites, she waited. When someone on the other end answered, she whispered, 'More news.'

'Go ahead.'

She twirled a finger around her red, tong-straightened hair and pouted. 'I want double. This is big-time info.'

'Go ahead.'

She gawped at the phone and asked, 'Are you *really* gonna give me double?'

'If the info is worth double, Zelda, it's yours.'

She tugged on her leopard spotted tights., 'Okay, this couple came in today. Just after madam landed from Dublin. She was in some kind of temper, by the way. She gave me a grilling cos I didn't answer the doorbell on first buzz. I'm not the feckin' receptionist, you know. Why should everyone have to answer the door cos they're passing? What was eating her buns? I don't know.'

'Get on with it, Zelda. Someone might hear you.'

'How do you know where I am?'

'I have eyes everywhere.'

'Bullshit. *I* am your eyes!'

'Who came into the office, Zelda?' The man's tone was clipped.

Even though she was trying his patience, she didn't care. She was entitled to her opinion when madam got up her nose. Which was most of the time.

She stuck with the job because the pay was good. Besides, it was fun spying on people, and bonuses paid for more nips and tucks. Her boobs used to be like lemons but now they were well-stacked. It paid off — now she was noticed by every man on the street. But her bum still sagged and her saddlebags needed attention.

'Zelda?'

She leapt out of her cosmetic to-do list and mumbled, 'Some missie came in to pitch her business idea. Creamy skin I'd die for.'

There were a lot of things she'd die for.

29

Teresina coughed and struggled to breathe as the smell of burning tyre and melting tarmac caught in her throat. Another loud bang blasted into the car.

Beside her, Majella shunted forward, her body immediately thrashing back again as her safety belt kept her from hitting the dashboard. She screamed as her head bounced against the head rest and slammed into the window.

With one eye on the road and the other on her precious daughter, Teresina saw blood running into Majella's eyes from a gash across her forehead. She battled to hold the steering wheel with one hand. 'Majella! Are you okay? Majella! Answer me. Wake up.' Teresina stamped on the brake and tried to steer the car to the edge of the road.

Instead of slowing, the Maserati spun out of control, zigzagging across the road. The metal rims scraping the tarmac shrieked around them, echoing across the valley. As the car hit a gully on the verge, its rims crunched on gravel.

Glancing again at her daughter's head lolling on her neck with her chin rolling across her chest, Teresina clung to the steering wheel. Her beloved Maserati flew through the air, over another hairpin bend and crashed down a steep cliff on the other side.

Then, it slammed into a tree half way down. All sounds blackened out.

The last thing Teresina heard was the voice singing to her from earlier.

A familiar voice singing *I Will Survive.*

30

As Zelda revealed her news, she smeared her lips with Dior's latest red lipstick. When it came to make-up, nothing rivalled the power of red lips. A crimson pout could elevate any of her fake designer brands. More importantly, it upped her sexiness and made a statement in one red swipe.

'Anyway, she was going on about some big farmer. Apparently, this fat slob is somehow going to change the world. They said it would cause a tsunami. Now, that's what I call *big* news!'

The voice became alert and attentive, 'Could it be Big Pharma?'

'That's what I said.'

'Be careful, Zelda. Tell me exactly what she said.'

'I always do!'

'Not always.' The voice sighed. 'But this time I *am* sure you're going to be precise with your information.'

Zelda wanted to spite him by insisting she wouldn't tell him anything if he used that tone again. But she remembered the last time she had done that. It cost her a big bonus. And besides, a tummy tuck was more important than some cretin giving her the third degree.

'The man who came with Miss Penn-ya said this stuff —'

'Who was the man?'

'I don't know, but I heard Jimmy say he was a doctor.'

'Go on, Zelda.'

'He rattled on about some diary found in Madrid's archives.'

'Is that it?'

'Well, if you'd wait a bit, and stop interrupting me you'd find out the real bomb, wouldn't you?'

Silence on the other end of the phone.

'Are you *really* gonna double me up?'

'I keep my promises, Zelda.'

She flicked open a hand mirror and rubbed her lips together to ensure the red went from corner to corner.

'Well…'

'Oh, yes. They said their risotto would —'

'Risotto?'

'Yes, that's what I said, didn't I?' Zelda started getting annoyed with him. Being his mole was one thing, but putting up with him doubting her ability was another.

'Risotto is an Italian rice dish, Zelda. How can a rice dish do these things you're talking about?'

'Okay, maybe it wasn't risotto. Maybe it was rizz-otter. Or riz-aydo. You know, rizz. Like rizla ciggies?'

'You've earned the bonus Zelda, but I need the name of this product and these people.'

'Okay, well, they said when you mix this potion with speed, it can heal anyone!'

Silence on the other end of the phone.

She loved the impact she had made and regretted not asking for a triple bonus. 'How about that?'

Zelda heard the ladies' room door open and she fell into her warning voice, 'Listen, Mum, I'll tell you more when I get home. See you later.'

Zelda cut the call and flushed the loo. She left the cubicle and washed the lipstick smears off her hands, giving her lips another once over. They looked great. Anyone would think she was a catwalk model.

As she left the ladies room she smiled to herself in the mirror and perked up her new boobs. One more bonus coming up. But first, she had to get the stupid product name. Jimmy couldn't be bought; she knew that. The red pout didn't do the trick either. That wouldn't stop her from sneaking into his office and taking the information she needed. A tummy tuck was worth breaking and entering.

Besides, Barker had plenty of money to burn.

31

Back in her office, Kelby thought about the cryptic note on the plane, and how she had sensed the doctor had left it for her. She had known their paths had collided for a reason, and her body still tingled where he'd touched her.

Jimmy marched into her office and asked, 'Should I put Mr Thompson through?'

Kelby nodded.

In her chair, she swung around, faced the river and filled her chest with a deep gulp of air. She needed it when she spoke to Jon Thompson. She knew his file off by heart.

Name: Jon Thompson.
Status: Millionaire Entrepreneur
Devil's Grotto: Executive Producer

Something made Kelby mistrust Jon. There was a weird little red flag that flew at half-mast when he was around. What was it about him that made the hairs on her neck stand up? Anyway, right now she needed him. She pressed the green button on the handset and said in her breeziest voice, 'Jon. Good morning. I need your help.'

Kelby spent the next five minutes telling Jon about the Twitter troll and how his threats were escalating. She finished by saying, 'I had the cops over, but they're too short on resources for surveillance. I don't want any weirdo pulling anything funny on me.'

'Don't worry. We'll get a security system plugged in.'

Kelby swung around in her chair. 'When I bought the house it had a security unit installed but I've never used it.'

'We can set that up for immediate protection.'

'Will you get the show's network security people to send someone to guard my house?'

'Better than that, Kel. I have the perfect chap in mind.'

'That's a huge relief.'

'Hawk recently left the army to start his own business. He's a smaller outfit than the big boys. He may not have all the latest gadgets, but I trust him with my life. So I'd trust him with yours.'

'Thank you Jon. I appreciate your help.'

'No probs.' He was silent for a moment, then he asked, 'Any new pitches since the Dub Fest?'

It was things like that, that tossed the red flag back into the wind. 'No new pitches, Jon. It's only the usual old stuff.'

'You sure? I know you can't resist squeezing in as many as you can.'

Kelby's gaze shot up and roved over the office. Lately, she'd had the feeling Jon knew everything that happened in her business. Surely none of her team would betray her? She scribbled a Post-It to Jimmy:

Suss out if there's a rat snitching on the hunting pack.

Jon launched into his weekly update about the producer's expectations. Unable to sit still while he droned on, Kelby opened a gold embossed envelope. An invitation to board Prince Al'Abbas Al-Bara's yacht for a sea fest dropped onto her desk.

Kelby frowned. As executive producer alongside Jon, the Prince had lavished the show with extravagances. During filming there were pitches for the next series in exotic places, such as an ancient castle steeped in Irish history and inhabited by ghosts. She had agreed to do the Irish Fest because Jon promised Teresina would go on the yacht.

'Jon?'

He stopped in mid-sentence. 'Yes.'

'I've told you once, and I'll tell you again. I am *not* going on this stupid cruise!'

'Ah, so you got the invite.'

'This is the third time you've sent it and the third time I'm declining.'

'What's up, Kel? Scared of a little water under your feet?'

Kelby's jaw dropped. She'd never told Jon bloody Thompson or anyone else about her fear of water.

'Face it, Kelby, you know what the Prince is like. Come hell or high water, he'll get you there, he'll find a way to ensure you board that boat.'

'Over my dead body!'

32

Zelda peered at her computer screen. Luckily, she had been given the naff end of the office, so no-one could see her screen.

She often chatted on Facebook when she got bored, but with this new titbit from her mole-hole in the corner, she had more to toy with. She fired up Chrome and googled: riz-otto. As Barker thought, Italian recipes. So she tried searching for variations of 'big farmer'. As Google spat out thousands of results, she squinted at her screen.

Shit! 'Big Pharma' *was* used by the pharmaceutical blokes. She read a few pages, but soon got bored with reading about how a New York pharma company had sales of over forty billion dollars. Or the Pharmaceutical Executive Magazine's annual ranking of the top fifty pharma companies.

She gave up and tried typing in 'big pharma and risotto'. To her amazement, Google spat out thousands of search results. For 'rizado'.

Another typo. She had to get her spelling under control. She sighed and started browsing through each link. After an hour of intense reading, her eyes throbbed.

Scanning through pages and pages about herbs, she spotted something about a Spanish witch who was burnt at the stake because she had written a book about herbal potions.

Zelda shuddered.

The thought of flames licking at her boots and burning her feet chilled her to the bone. Her old lady had four cats at home and the neighbour once said he'd burn them if they peed on his front door mat. Yikes, she didn't want to snuff it in such a sick way. She blew at a strand of hair from the corner of her mouth. For now, she had what she needed.

If that gorgeous hunk pitching to Kelby had found the secret, it could be worth more than Barker's piddly bonuses. Zelda rubbed the tip of her finger along her lips and pouted. Huh, now Barker would think she was an airhead after her remark about speed. This rizado looked cool.

As long as Barker didn't cock up, this could be big. Huge! If she got her paws on Kelby's contacts, she'd be able to bypass Barker and tell her spy stuff to the pharma blokes. Who and where that would be, she had no idea. One step at a time. First, the hunk's contact details. Then she'd figure out if it was worth squeezing Barker for more money or if she should go over his head.

Zelda slumped back in her seat.

Bloody hell! This rizado must be one of the longest ongoing searches since the birth of the internet. That meant real money.

33

Barker languished on the pool steps, each big enough to hold a sun lounger. He sipped a cup of camomile tea and sent a message to Teresina. That would prove his alibi.

He stepped out of the pool, dried himself and ambled inside. A few minutes later, with another camomile tea and a magazine in his hands, he slipped into a wicker chair under a large parasol near the pool. At last, coercing Zelda in Kelby's office had paid off.

A quick google had led him directly to the rizado. Pages and pages of speculation. One of the biggest players in the market was Mata Gordo International. His investment with them gave him a yearly globe-trotting income. One journalist had even tried to blow the whistle on the pharma giant for hiding their research. Strangely, the same idiot had managed to get himself crushed in a skiing accident.

Barker's heart raced as he thought about one of his first investments. Homerton Grange had started as a clinic for alternative medicine, but over the years it had become a centre for testing new drugs. Maybe it would come in handy when he got his hands on rizado and it needed testing.

But first he had to find it. And he knew just where to start looking.

Barker lifted the magazine into his lap. Teresina's big pull out quote said: *Facing my secrets in my forties has been a liberating experience.*

'What secrets are these, Teresina? Your secret was my fear. Remember our pledge? Some secrets are meant to die with us.' Flames of resentment shot through his veins.

Kelby's pull out quote countered her co-host's: *Life's too short to harbour secrets.*

'Never a truer word said, Kelby. If only you knew what's coming your way.' Barker's hand locked into a fist.

No matter what, he had to find the rizado. And who better to spar with than Kelby? While new ideas gallivanted around his head like roving vagabonds, he finished his camomile tea. 'Mmm… so far you've been a delight to toy with Kelby, but now the hunt begins.'

Barker released his locked fist and closed it over his groin's impatient throb. That's what he loved about Johnson, he always joined in the excitement. Any minute now he'd cream the pool.

This would have to be a fast one. He knew what would send his Johnson off the deep end. Barker closed the magazine and fanned the pages. He raised his finger and held it up for a moment and in one swift motion slid it along the edge of the glossy paper.

Ouch! He hated paper cuts. But painting faces with the blood, he loved.

In slow motion he drew a bloodied X over Kelby's face.

34

Kelby marched into Jimmy's office as he pointed his finger at Zelda. She frowned and asked, 'What's going on?'

They both stiffened as Kelby waited for an answer.

Jimmy relented. 'I caught her having a good ol' snoop.'

Zelda piped up in quick defence, 'I was only trying to find the name of that gorgeous man who came to visit you this morning.'

'Why do you want his name?' Jimmy fired at her.

'I wanted to ask him on a date? Is that so wrong?'

With a strange bolt of jealousy, Kelby wanted to slap the pout off the girl's fish-lips. Instead, she said as calmly as possible, 'Zelda, how did you get on with the toys?'

'Ooh, what fun it was. There's a few shopping bags in your office.'

'Thanks, I'll drop them off tonight.'

'I've been on the internet and found something interesting.'

Intrigued, Kelby waited for her to finish.

'Your dresses will fetch those charities big money. They're thrilled, by the way.'

'Jimmy has a spreadsheet–'

'Sorry to interrupt, Kelby, Jimmy gave me the spreadsheet with the details. I've sent it to the charities. Was that the right thing to do?'

'Of course, good work.'

'It's been an exciting project to work on. Have you got any more I can help with? I love this sorta stuff,' she dropped her voice, 'Or even secretive tasks.'

'Nothing at the moment, but I'm sure I'll find something.'

Zelda lifted and dropped her shoulders and strutted to the door.

'By the way, Zelda…'

Zelda spun back to face Kelby, her eyebrows arched in expectation.

'If you want to know anything, ask me or Jimmy. We'll see if we can help. Best you don't wander around our offices or it could be seen as snooping.'

'Fair one.' Zelda's eyebrows dropped as she mumbled, 'Sorry.'

As Zelda slunk away, Jimmy muttered, 'I don't trust her.'

Kelby handed the gold yacht invitation to Jimmy. 'Please send that back to Mr Thompson. If I've told him once, I've told him a hundred times. I am *not* going.'

Jimmy glanced at the invite and shrugged. 'Sounds fun to me. You're grand to be on the Al-Bara yacht. It'll be like a week in a spa. Says here,' Jimmy flicked at the edge of the invite as if it was a fly, 'you'll relax in a jacuzzi or sauna, enjoy body massages and soak up the Mediterranean sun.'

'Hah! No way. Not me. Wouldn't dream of it.'

She marched out of his office and back into her own with Jimmy close on her heels, saying, 'I heard you telling the Devil about—'

'It's not your job to listen to my calls.'

'It is. In case you forget something. *Remember.* Your own instructions!'

Kelby dropped her head closer to her laptop screen to hide the flush. She had asked him to remind her of things because she sometimes forgot under pressure. Kelby placed her glasses on her laptop keyboard and wiped her grainy eyes.

'You gotta make time for dating. Not with him. But ever since you ditched your man —.'

'He left! Not me.' The mention of her ex-husband raised prickles of irritation on her skin.

'Cos you work too much. You gotta stop and smell the roses.'

'You smell them for me. I haven't got time.'

'By the way, why did you decline the Devil's date? He has everything a woman wants. Looks. Millions. Power. Fame.'

'Everything I don't want.'

'He'd be a right good catch.'

'Well, I'm not fishing at the moment.' She waved him away with her eyes indicating the door.

As Jimmy left, muttering he was going to set up a few dates for her, Kelby's phone beeped again. Her breakfast turned in her stomach. Kelby's finger twitched as it hovered over the message.

Oh God. What now?

35

In her cottage kitchen, María lit a candle and carried it to the table. On top of the dry clothing she hadn't packed away, sheets of parchment balanced precariously. Beside the clothes sat a small, squat, glass ink bottle. She placed the candle on the table, wincing as a drop of hot wax splashed onto her finger.

María loved this room. It reminded her of her father. As the village stonemason he had built his family home with his bare hands. She used to sit at his feet and listen to his reports about the houses he had built. From one-room cottages with a loft for the family to sleep in, to castles with grand kitchens and magnificent rooms for the family to entertain their friends. Those tales had fired her imagination, filling her with a desire to tell stories of her own.

True to his word, her father had given his wife a huge cooking area. Build from stone, it featured alcoves down the side and wooden racks to store her mother's clay pots. Metal and copper pans hung inside the hearth and long handled ladles were fastened to iron hooks in the ceiling. The cottage floor was cobbled with stone from their own land.

A few quills lay drying beside the fire. María hated plucking the geese to steal their feathers, but she needed the quills to write. Tío had taught her to harden the quill by thrusting it into hot ash in the hearth, stirring it until it softened. She then flattened it under a heavy pot and finished it off by rounding it in her fingers. For the past year Tío had taken her stories to his family in Barcelona, and always returned with more parchment.

María had learnt to make her own ink by breaking up oak galls and mixing them with soot, wine, water and gum arabic.

It hadn't taken long to complete the herbal manuscript. Ever since her little goat had healed, she had worked late into the night burning candle after candle to write about Madre's *medicina*. To make it easy to read, she had taken four sheets of parchment, folded each in half, and tucked one inside the other. She did this until the *Herbal de Carbonela* looked like the books Tío had used in his lessons.

Before María had written a single word, Madre had insisted she swore on Padre's name to keep it secret and hidden.

Her mother had drawn pictures of herbs and beside each one María had written their medicinal uses. Most remedies used a small portion of rizado.

Madre had tried growing the *estraño* herb in the croft, but for some reason, which was beyond Madre's knowledge of plants, it appeared to need the grotto's water to feed it.

María had never defied Madre. But when the herbal was complete, it was too *magnífico* to keep hidden or secret. Only this one time would she go against Madre's wishes so she could prove her worth as a scrivener. She was proud of Madre's skill and wanted to show off the herbal manuscript.

After she had witnessed how effective the herb was, she regretted writing that first made-up tale. It had told of a woman healer who had created a secret potion that cured any ailment. She had based her story on Madre, but had imagined the woman healer journeying around the country to treat the sick. It had ended with her summoned to heal the queen. The queen then gave her a majestic castle from which to practise her *medicina*.

At the time she had been innocent and not aware of the wonders of rizado. Now she knew that kind of healing power was best kept secret.

For many nights she had agonised about her decision to go against Madre's wishes and send the herbal manuscript to Barcelona. At the last minute she had removed the detailed notes about the strange herb and left the manuscript intact. With a tremor in her stomach she had presented it to Tío when Madre was nursing a dying woman. He too agreed the details and drawings were *magnífico*. And as such it should be shown off. By assuring Tío a published copy of her manuscript would be a gift of pride for her mother, she had convinced him to keep it a secret from Madre.

María tensed. Never again would she lie or be deceitful. Or keep secrets from Madre. Already it ate at her day and night.

From now on she would busy herself with stories about the people she met each day — such as the locals who visited Madre to have their babies delivered.

Tonight, a new story would flow from her quill. María lifted a sheet of parchment and wrote the first thing that came into her mind: *The Grotto's Secret.*

36

Kelby flinched at the sight of a text from an unknown caller. What the hell? How had the Troll got her number? She read the message:

The news. Watch now! BBC 1.

The image of the magazine with bloody slashes around their necks flew into her mind. Kelby sprinted into the board room, grabbed the TV remote with clammy hands, and flicked the TV to the first news programme she found. A red breaking news ticker-tape ran across the bottom of the screen:

Italian heiress, Teresina Piccoli dies in Italy a few
miles from her home.

Kelby gasped and slumped into a seat, eyes glued to the scenes playing out in front of her. Police cars lined the valley clinging to the hairpin bend. Their blue lights flashed warnings to local villagers taking a morning drive. Three ambulances, almost jack-knifed beside each other, had their back doors ajar, while paramedics rushed up and down the steep slope. Two of them carried a stretcher. A white sheet concealed a slight hump.

Kelby let out a groan and covered her mouth with a clammy hand.

Time seemed to tick in a thick muddle.

Teresina can't be dead, she just called. Only an hour or so ago.

As she watched the news, Kelby's teeth sawed against her thumb nail in time to the beat of her pounding heart.

Debris was scattered across the cliff, including what looked like a bumper split in two. A small suitcase with clothes flapping in the breeze lay further down the hill.

Far below a car had slammed against an electricity pylon. Its nose crumpled into the windscreen as though the vehicle had been concertinaed like a biscuit tin crushed against a wall. Watching in horror, as the scenes of devastation marred the beautiful sunny valleys of the Abruzzo Mountain, Kelby heard the journalist repeat the story.

'As I said, Miss Piccoli was on her way to meet her ageing mother for her birthday.' The journalist looked over his shoulder. 'It's a terribly sad day for Abruzzo and the Majella Mountain people. Teresina made them proud when she hit the *Sunday Times* Rich List. And then she appeared alongside some of the UK's most successful venture capitalists in the popular, yet extremely competitive entrepreneurial game show, *Devil's Grotto.* A sad day indeed.'

Once again the camera panned over the wreck of the car. The reporter continued his mournful tone, 'Miss Piccoli's ten-year-old daughter, Majella, is thought to be one of the bodies recovered.' The journalist was silent for a long moment as the image repeated the scene of the medical team carrying a small sheet-covered body to one of the ambulances. 'Majella was named after these spectacular mountains.' He swung his arm to show the backdrop.

The news presenter asked, 'What do we know of the vehicle?'

'Maserati has commented that her car was new and not the cause of her careering over the hairpin bend. They will do a thorough examination of the wreck.'

'Do we know what happened?'

'Not officially. It's rumoured by some of the locals who witnessed the accident that her tyre burst as she sped along these precarious roads, but I've been told by the Italian *polizia* we'll hear when they're ready to inform us.'

'Thank you.'

As the presenter moved on to the next story, Kelby sat still, chills coursing through her as if someone was strumming her nerves like a guitar. Guilt competed with the horror of the magazine graffiti, and together they caused havoc in her mind.

She hadn't been in the mood for Teresina's lashing tongue, but she wondered what had been so urgent to make Teresina call from Italy.

What had she wanted to tell her? She had said it was urgent and now she was dead.

Pinning her arms around her stomach to stop nausea creeping up, Kelby stood to pull herself together. Her hands trembled with regret.

What had she wanted? Why had she called? Did Teresina know something was going to happen to her?

But how could she know about her own death?

37

Still numb from shock, Kelby gaped at the man filling her doorway. At least six foot six and ugly as hell, he held out his hand. 'Miss Wade? I'm Charlie Hawk. Please call me Hawk.'

He looked more like a thug than a security advisor, but she offered him a seat. Clearly uncomfortable in his jacket, he took it off and slung it over the arm of the sofa. 'Firstly, I need to understand the nature of the threat. How did this start and how long has it been going on?'

'Jimmy will show you the messages.'

'I'll need to assess how much of your information is publicly available. And I'd like full details of which social media this person is targeting.'

'There's no time. I need protection.'

'Miss Wade —'

'Please call me Kelby.'

'Okay, Kelby, it's my job to put your safety first. I'll put you under surveillance and keep you under tight rein, but the other information will help me create a profile of the stalker and build an evidence package to give to the police.'

She nodded. 'Yes, yes, of course.'

'I strongly recommend you move away from your home address. We can set you up in a hote —'

'No way! I'm not going to live in a hotel. My schedule won't allow it.'

'But I strongly suggest —'

'I won't be bullied into hiding in the shadows. I'm staying right here. And at home. Find another way to protect me.'

'Do you have any security at the moment?'

'No, apart from an alarm in my house, but I've never used it.'

'Okay, that's a step in the right direction. We need to know when someone is on your property though, not just inside your house. I'll get my colleague to do a security audit. We need to validate that your system is fit for purpose and we'll make recommendations to improve your security.'

Kelby nodded, feeling overwhelmed.

'Once your home's secure, we'll sort things out here. I noticed anyone can get in here.'

'That's because it's a standard office.'

'Okay, I get that. But we'll need to prevent access to your floor. We'll have to hand out badges to anyone coming here so we can vet and validate your visitors.'

Kelby groaned inwardly, but nodded her head, trying to figure out how she would fit this fuss into her hectic schedule.

Hawk reached into his oversized jacket, drew out his wallet and fingered the pouches. As he pulled out a card and handed it to Kelby, something else fluttered to the floor. Kelby lifted it. Two faces beamed at her. Hawk dressed in military uniform with his wife in a lacy wedding dress. She was so petite, she was tucked under his arms.

'Apologies, Miss Wade, er, Kelby. I didn't mean to throw that at you.'

'That's okay. Beautiful wife.' Kelby handed him the frayed picture. 'I see you were in the forces.'

He nodded. 'Yes. Royal Engineers. We built bridges and roads in Afghanistan a few years back, but when Sandy wanted to start a family.' He shrugged, looking sad and forlorn.

'I know how it is.' For the third time that day, Kelby relived the pain of losing Gary.

'Anyway, I can make more money working for myself.' He chuckled. 'It will help pay for the kids.'

'How many do you have?'

'First one on the way,' Hawk pulled out another picture and showed it to Kelby.

She stared at an ultrasound image, and didn't tell him she had wished hundreds of times that she could show off hers.

'Sandy wants a football team of them.' His voice filled with pride, 'I built the nursery. I can't wait to see my kid.'

Kelby smiled and handed him back the image.

He stretched and rose to his feet. 'I'd better get on with things. Can we have your keys?'

'Of course.' She strode to her desk, fiddled in her handbag and gave him her house key.

'Is anyone going to be following me ... you know ... in case he tries something?'

'You don't have to worry about a thing, Miss, um, Kelby. I am your PPO.' At her frown, he explained, 'Your personal protection officer.'

'Thank you. That's a huge relief.'

'Don't worry. You're safe now. I'll bet my life on it!'

38

Kelby had been so engrossed in tapping on her laptop she hadn't noticed the day had long ago slipped into night without any fanfare.

Car horns tooted and taxi cabs blasted in return as far below London took on a new persona. Without looking Kelby knew the vibrant night-life would be aglow with light spilling out of the many pubs, restaurants and ground floor offices lining the Thames.

From far below, animated chatter and rowdy laughter drifted up. The tinkling sounds of people living a happy life sent a pang through her. A longing for her own little family nest.

Since Teresina's accident her phone hadn't stopped ringing. Every Tom, Dick and Harry reporter wanted to know what she thought about Teresina's death.

Questions came at her from every direction. When last had she spoken to Teresina? What was she like to work with? Had she known little Majella? What would happen to the show now? On and on and on it went.

Jon's plea for privacy on the evening news hadn't made any difference, although surely people realised the crew was grieving?

Engrossed in her own Google search on the rizado, Kelby didn't hear Jimmy enter her office. He slammed her laptop lid shut, almost snaring her hands. 'You have to get out of here. Go see Annie.'

Kelby leapt out of her chair. 'What the hell?'

Jimmy stood his ground with his arms folded across his chest. 'Go. She needs you.' He aimed his pointy chin at her, 'You know I'm right. Get out of here, boss.'

She grumbled, irritated more with herself than him, 'I'll do these reports later.'

'Don't you dare work over Annie's sick body!'

As she packed her red leather briefcase, Jimmy followed Kelby's pointed gaze at Zelda, who was leaving with some other staff. 'What do you want to do with Zelda's shopping?'

'I'll take it with me.'

'I spoke to Karen and she's going to take Zelda under her wing on the clothing issue. And I called Twitter. As we suspected the account had false details and they've closed it.'

Feeling a rush of relief, Kelby exhaled hard. The threat had hung over her all day. She hadn't wanted to leave the sanctuary of her office in case some twit followed her and tried to carry out his threat.

'And Big Boy is waiting for you in the lobby.'

She chuckled, 'It didn't take you long to find Hawk a nickname.' With renewed determination, she grabbed her briefcase and shot out of the door.

Jimmy grabbed the shopping bags and followed her. In the reception, he helped her into her coat, 'Here. It's fierce windy out there.'

The lift button bleeped. The shaft came to life and swooshed up to collect her. She stepped inside and murmured, 'Thank you Jimmy.'

He shrugged. 'Yer grand.'

A smile tugged at her mouth and lit her eyes. She nodded at him with a lump in her throat.

As the lift descended she thought for the hundredth time about the earlier tweet: *You better watch your back, you'll be raped before the night is over.*

The night wasn't over, but at least with Big Boy nearby there wouldn't be any more rape threats.

39

It was bad enough María had exposed Madre by writing of a woman healer although with a different name in a different town. Even worse that she had broken her promise to keep the herbal manuscript a secret.

As before, Tío had sent it to his family who *rápidamente* sent word that it was good enough to be made *publicus*.

They'd never been so rapid in their messages to Tío and they complimented the author on the manuscripts vast amount of in-depth knowledge.

Every week in church she prayed the woman healer story had been lost on its way to Barcelona. Now she prayed for the herbal manuscript to go missing.

In the candlelight, María peered at the title of her new story: *The Grotto's Secret*. A shame no-one would get to read it, but she couldn't risk people coming to the grotto. Thankfully the doomed manuscript never once mentioned the grotto or its location.

No, she had to change her idea. *The Grotto's Secret* would have to remain in her imagination. Leaving the rest of the page empty, she slid the story title into the notes about rizado. With parchment so scarce, she hated leaving an empty page. Maybe she'd return to it with a different story to tell.

María ached for another opportunity to treat a wounded animal. Each time she used rizado she had learnt more about how it worked.

Over the last few weeks, she'd thought of little else but healing, hoping she'd been blessed with the same gift as her mother. The only skill she possessed was seeing people in her head, doing things they shouldn't be doing. Alas, some would verily say that was a sign of being insane. *Loco*. But María waited for the day when her stories would be admired.

With Madre in bed, María took the opportunity to carry out a task her mother wouldn't *permitir*. She listened for a moment and heard Madre's faint snoring from her bed.

With the stealth of a viper, María unwrapped a long piece of soft leather that bound the secret copy of *Herbal de Carbonela*. Instead of giving it one layer of leather for the original binding, she had covered the book with two layers of leather, one on top of the other.

Now, using a yard of twisted thread, María stitched a small square just below the knot. Once she had bound the two strips together into an invisible pouch, she hid Madre's map of the grotto inside. She stepped back to check her work. The only way the secret pouch would be known, was by the slight raised mark of her stitches on the leather skin.

Pleased with herself, María hid the book in amongst the *lavandarium*. Madre never checked the clothing to be washed because it was María's task. Later, the *Herbal de Carbonela* would once again be hidden in a clay pot in the cellar, but before she did that, she had one more *tasca*.

Through soundless movements, María unwrapped another long piece of soft leather she had found in Padre's workshop and held it close to the candlelight.

In the same way she had made a binding for Madre's herbal book, she would make another book, but this one would only need one layer of leather binding.

She wanted to carry her writing with her to the grotto, hidden on her body, so she could make up stories while staring across the valley towards the sea. Maybe she'd write that story about a girl like her having a sea adventure.

With Madre's herbal journal still *fresco* in her mind as her *modus*, one more time she copied the making of the book. From Padre's workshop she had taken two pieces of wood to make a cover for the front and back of the block formed by the parchment pages.

She turned the ends of the leather over on the inside of the front and back boards and then pasted them down. At the bottom of the book, she extended the leather, from covering the boards, into a long flap and knotted the end. She stroked the leather strip for a moment, loving the softness tickling her fingertips.

Glancing over her shoulder to check Madre was still asleep, María felt her heart beating faster. With trembling fingers, she slipped the knot under Padre's belt. With the leather extension at the bottom of the book, her book hung upside down. When she lifted it, as if to read it, the book was the right way up. Although Tío had shown her many similar books, they were scribed and ready for reading, but her book was empty and waiting to be written at the grotto.

With her book complete, María paced in front of the hearth watching the dying embers. Practicing how to wear it, María let it dangle from Padre's girdle that she now wore under her garments. Although she hated a girdle over her tunic, this one would allow her to hide her book. It felt odd to have the leather book slap at her thighs.

Suddenly a loud bang made María jump.

40

The lift from the car park basement rose into St Adelaide's Hospital. Its doors pinged open and Kelby stepped into the private hospital's reception. Thankfully, Hawk hadn't insisted on coming with her. She had been looking forward to this moment.

Her special time with Annie.

With her phone glued to her ear while she lugged shopping bags and listened to messages, Kelby ran head first into an older couple.

'Whoa!' The old gent raised his hands, leaning them back in a theatrical pose.

'Oh,' Kelby muttered, 'I'm so sorry.'

His wife gave a loud tut and shook her head. Kelby backed away, apologising again. Embarrassed by the thought that people milling around the private Surrey hospital might recognise her, she dropped her eyes to the floor and rushed down the crowded passage, weaving between people.

In her haste she didn't spot a doctor ahead of her backing out of a room with an armful of papers. Kelby banged head first into him. Her shopping bags of toys slipped out of her hands and thumped to the floor.

His arms flew into the air, his fingers attempting to grapple the neat pile of documents. Splat. The papers hit the floor and scattered, fluttering away as if they had been looking for an opportunity to escape his clutches.

The man rose to his full height.

Kelby groaned.

Doctor Robson peered at her. 'Hey, calm down. What's the rush?'

Even though his lopsided boyish grin sent waves of excitement to her nerve endings, she couldn't let on what effect he had on her. Without meaning to, she snapped at him, 'You should look where you're going.'

'No, *you* crashed into me.'

She shook her head, '*You* backed out of a room in reverse without even a glance at who was coming by.'

'Kelby, this is a hospital. People generally don't fly down these corridors at a hundred miles an hour.'

'Hah!'

'You shouldn't be here if you're in that kind of rush. There are some good race tracks near here. Try Silverstone or Brands Hatch.' Although his tone sounded brusque, his eyes beamed amusement, 'Both will suit your needs.'

Her jaw dropped. 'What? You're the clumsy one. You started it this morning on the plane!' Kelby's hands found her hips, and without realising she adopted one of Teresina's poses.

'Am I supposed to be intimidated?' He dropped onto his knees to retrieve his flapping papers.

She mirrored his action; a hot flush prickling her skin. 'I'm sorry, I didn't mean that. I'm rushing upstairs to see someone.' Bent over, Kelby started to help him collate the papers, but sudden embarrassment at her silliness overcame her. 'Sorry.'

Without another word she straightened, grabbed the Hamley's bags and rushed off. As she reached the top of the stairs, her phone beeped to announce another text had arrived.

When U R finished @ the hospital, bitch, I'll B @ yours

41

Kelby's glare lifted from the stalker's text and moved down the stairwell. No-one was there. No-one knew where she was. Except the doctor. And Jimmy. And maybe a few late-leaving staff members who had seen Jimmy chasing her out of the office.

She jabbed the last number dialled on her phone and panted into it, 'You there, Hawk?'

'Everything okay, Miss Wade?'

She exhaled and said, 'I just got another message.'

'I thought Twitter had closed the guy's account. I'll get right onto them.'

'No, this time it was a text message.'

'You want me to come up?'

'No, I'll be fine. I'll see you later.'

As Kelby deleted the message, she butted into someone else and groaned. *Dear God, how many more times in one night!*

'Ah-hah! The famous sister-in-law arrives.'

'Hello Stacie. I thought you'd be gone by now. Aren't you on nights this week?'

Stacie raised one pierced eyebrow in her annoying know-it-all way. '*That's* why you're so late. Trying to avoid me.'

'In case you've forgotten, I have three businesses to run, another five to chair as a non-exec and ten mentees to babysit. Oh, and a reality show to film.'

'Poor Kelby! Too busy to live.' Stacie brushed past her.

Kelby smelt cigarettes on her clothes and gawped at Stacie. 'I don't believe it. You come here stinking of smoke in front of Annie!'

'Ooh, look who's on the prowl again today.'

Any snide remark from her sister-in-law was enough to goad Kelby into retaliation. They took up their usual stance on opposing sides and faced each other en garde, ready to lunge with verbal swords.

'You're not fit to be her mother.' Kelby instantly regretted her words, but couldn't bring herself to apologise.

'What about you?' She grabbed Kelby's coat sleeve. 'You come here full of cat's hair. Look. It's all over you.'

Kelby looked at her coat.

'It's zebra-like with that horrid cat's hair.' Stacie leaned forward and sneered as she sniffed. 'You even smell like cat's pee.' She glanced at the shopping bags and scoffed, 'I'm surprised the shops allowed you in.'

Behind Stacie, Kelby spied a group of nurses watching with interest. One of them had the cheek to sneak in closer to listen, intrigued by yet another round of fireworks.

'Your fag-butt stink will bring on another asthma attack.'

'So will that cat's hair!' Stacie backed out of Kelby's smell zone. 'So don't you dare,' she wagged a finger in Kelby's face, 'accuse me of being a bad mother. You'll never be a mother — good or bad!'

Stacie marched off leaving Kelby seething. She glanced around and found all the hospital eyes on her. She ducked her head, half in shame and half with pride. As she darted towards Annie's room, she spoke to Gary in her head, as she often did. *Sorry Gaa, I did it again. I know I promised last time, but I can't help it. Your wife riles me.*

A nurse came out of Annie's room and bumped into her. 'Ahh, Miss Wade, lovely to see you.'

'Hi, Rosalind, how's my girl today?'

'Why not see for yourself?' Nurse Rosalind Potter stepped aside to let Kelby pass.

As she did Kelby shoved the shopping bags at her. 'You told me you're fundraising for a Down syndrome charity. Will this help?'

Rosalind glanced into the bags and gaped at Kelby. Before she could refuse, Kelby said, 'It's just a pile of freebies I get sent. You know, people think I want their latest products.'

'Are you sure? It looks so expensive.'

'Course. They're cluttering up my office so I hope you can do something with them.'

'Of course! Yippee, we can do lots of raffles. Thank you, Miss Wade!'

'It's nothing.' As Kelby slipped into Annie's room and closed the door, she spotted the other busybody nurses circling around Rosalind's toys from Hamleys. Thank goodness she had insisted on a private room.

No eyeballs in here to ogle at her.

42

Kelby settled into a seat beside Annie and looked at her frail body. As she slept Annie looked peaceful and calm. As well as regular acute asthma attacks that led to hospitalisation, Annie had eczema which had flared up soon after Gary passed away.

Overnight, Annie's pearly skin had become itchy red patches with thick scales. She'd been a happy little girl, full of jumping beans and always wanting to be outside playing with her menagerie of insects. Now she was self-conscious about being smothered in creams and not able to participate in school sports because her skin was always itchy and sore.

When her asthma flared up and had her choking for breath, she had to be admitted to hospital. Each time the attacks were worse and led to different treatments that hadn't worked. It annoyed Kelby when the doctors didn't take it seriously enough.

After insisting on paying for private care for Annie, Kelby had expected to see more visible signs of her health improving, but her hopes had dropped. She'd have to speak to the doctors again and boot their asses to get that new treatment from the States. Stacie wouldn't have any experimental drugs used on her daughter, but Kelby took it upon herself to get the doctors to convince her sister-in-law to try anything new.

Annie stirred, her eyelids fluttered open and she turned to face her. Kelby gave her a little wave. Annie beamed, despite the horrid plastic tube stuck up her nose and taped across her translucent cheeks. Her thin hand reached out and her voice croaked, 'Aunt Kel! I've been waiting all day for you to come.'

Kelby refused to let her voice crack. 'And I've been waiting for you to wake up to chat to me.' As her heart pumped, Kelby savoured a rush of happiness radiating through her. But the rush soon faded and guilt took over. Jimmy was right; she worked too hard. She should have come earlier; Annie needed her more than the hunting pack.

Annie lifted a sheet of paper off her bedside table and handed Kelby a drawing. With a pink, scaly finger, she pointed at a pool of water with two figures splashing about. 'That's where May-ree swims.' She picked at a patch of red and tender skin on her arm. 'And that's me with her.'

Kelby reached out and stopped her scratching. 'Is this May-ree who told you about her waterfall?'

Annie whispered, 'Her waterfall is a special place no-one has ever seen. It's inside a cave. Her secret treasure is hidden in the cave. She found a bull painted on the rocks. He's called Toro.' Her nose screwed up. 'She hid her secrets near his horns.'

Kelby leaned in, pretending to be intrigued.

'She has another secret too.'

'Ooh, and what's that.'

Annie's voice dropped to barely a whisper, 'She drew a map and hid it inside her book bag, like my school bag, only hers is old-fashioned.'

Kelby nodded.

Annie's energy bounced around as she changed the subject, asking 'Aunt Kel, tell me about the time Daddy's friend jumped on you.'

'You mean in the pool?'

'Yes.'

'When your daddy and I were small —' her voice cracked, 'we were on holiday and one of his friends jumped onto my back when I was swimming across the deep end. He hung on my back like a monkey, but he was so heavy I nearly drowned.'

'Could Daddy swim?'

'Yes, when he joined the army, he swam across the English Channel. He was training to cycle across England.'

'You mean with his new leg.'

Kelby nodded, struggling to hold back the tears.

'I wish he would come back from heaven to teach me, but May-ree's going to teach me to swim.'

'Daddy wanted you to be a fish like him.' Kelby made a mental note to get Jimmy to find a private swimming tutor when Annie was discharged.

'Can you swim, Aunt Kel?'

Kelby swallowed hard. 'No, I can't.'

'But you're grown up. Grown-ups know how to swim.'

'Not all. Thousands are too scared.'

'Are you scared?'

Kelby nodded.

'Why? Because of the boy who jumped on you?' Annie patted Kelby's hand. 'Don't worry Aunt Kel, we'll learn together. I'll do it if you will. And I won't jump on your back, neither.'

Kelby leaned over and hugged Annie. 'Okay, deal. But you better get out of here quick!' She couldn't tell Annie she had no intention of keeping her promise.

'My new friend can swim.'

'May-ree?'

'No, Corinna.'

Kelby tried to recall if this was another pretend friend or a real one. 'Is she that little girl next door?'

Annie shifted her jaw side to side and nibbled on her lips with a mischievous glint in her eyes.

Kelby nodded. 'Ah, *that* friend.' Annie had a school-yard of invisible friends.

'I told Daddy about her. And he's been talking to her too.'

Kelby nodded and let out a silent *phew*. To help Annie come to terms with Gary's death, Kelby had encouraged Annie to talk to him.

'How old is Corinna?'

'She's ten. I can't wait to be ten.'

Kelby fluffed Annie's head. 'You're nearly there.'

'Who's your best friend, Aunt Kel?'

'You.'

'Mum says you're Becky-no-mates.'

'Sometimes being Becky-no-mates is best.' A seven year-old couldn't be expected to understand being friendless helped avoid hurt and disappointment.

Annie glanced over Kelby's shoulder and dropped her voice to a whisper. The look on her face was of a child spy about to reveal a global conspiracy.

'Aunt Kel, can you keep a secret?'

43

Once again Padre's hand-carved door rattled under the weight of a man's fist. Still testing out her book, María gulped and bit her lip. A deep sense of foreboding clutched at her stomach.

With her stomach churning, she jabbed the quill lying on the table into an old cotton chemise. She rolled up *The Grotto's Secret* and ran across the cobbled floor. Leaning into one of the stone alcoves, she tucked her writing materials at the back of a blackened pot.

Madre appeared in the kitchen, rubbing her eyes.

María had always been proud to watch Madre deliver a baby onto its mother's breast. Over the past few weeks of learning the *medicina* secrets, her love for her mother had swelled.

The door shook under the persistent fist.

'Ana-María, the door!'

María scrambled to open it and a shaft of moonlight crept in. A man shoved past her into the kitchen and demanded, 'Where is your mother?'

Madre stepped into the candlelight and asked, 'Fernando, your wife is ready so early?'

'She is in much pain; I could not bring her to you. You must come quickly.'

Without hesitation, Madre pulled a gown over her chemise, grabbed a shawl, threw it around her shoulders, and said, 'Ana-María fetch me some mugwort from my baking room.' She turned to Fernando and explained, 'It induces labour. It will assist the birth and afterbirth. And it will help to ease your wife's labour pains.'

When María returned a few minutes later with a pile of dried mugwort, Madre kissed the top of her head. 'Throw that jasmine you crushed into my basket, Ana-María, it will help to calm the new mother.'

With haste, María did as she was told.

Madre picked up her basket, which she kept prepared for an emergency. 'Feed the animals and follow me in the morning. I will need you to help clean up.'

'Of course, Mama.'

At the door she gave María a pointed look. María didn't follow her mother's gaze but just nodded curtly to assure her the journal had been hidden.

When the noise outside had subsided, and the night had calmed back into silence, María poured water from the bucket into a pot and set it over the fire to boil. She prepared a vegetable and chicken stew for Madre and fed the animals. It would be a long night and day. Delivering babies had long ago bored her. She preferred to spend her time writing, or with the animals in the fields, but Madre needed her.

By the time she left their Finca, and started walking through the night to help Madre, a deep sensation that something terrible was about to happen chilled her.

A cool breeze had whipped up the valley from the direction of the sea. María pulled her shawl closer to her neck, enjoying the roughly woven warmth of the wool. Clumps of clay from the recent rain stuck to her boots.

And then something rustled in the trees ahead.

44

Barker dumped his overnight bag and briefcase on the kitchen island and flicked the kettle on. His flight had arrived late and he'd had to tackle heavy traffic on the M25 to get to his London home.

Living in London, he loved. Fighting its impossible traffic, he hated.

He sifted through a row of teabag tins and chose camomile to calm his mind. He dropped the teabag into his teacup, lifted his briefcase and ambled down the hall.

Passing his sitting room, he glanced at the leather lounge suite, as white as virginal daisies. The curtains draping elegantly to the sides were as white and looked pearlescent with the uplighter shining on them. He'd decorated it to prove his clean sexual tastes. Only to himself, of course. Teresina hadn't put a foot in this new home.

In his study, he placed his briefcase on the desk, opened it and switched on a lamp. In the corner, he lifted a gift box and spun back to face his desk. He knelt down to a safe hidden under his desk and removed a wad of money. Next, he swathed the pound notes into tissue paper and tucked it into the box.

Inside the lid of the briefcase, a letter opener gleamed. Its decorative handle showed off an angel with expanded wings. Barker grabbed a roll of red twine and sliced through a long strand.

He carefully wrapped the money bundle into the box, closed the lid, and tied a bow with the red twine. Zelda's find had become an important cog in the mechanical process. It hadn't taken him long to notice that after his last payout, Zelda had been away from work for a week, returning with a brand new set of ripe, fleshy breasts. She must have paid handsomely for them.

Barker placed the parcel into his briefcase ready for posting and ambled back to the kitchen. The kettle whistled. He poured boiling water onto the teabag and hummed. As the brew steeped, he carried the china tea cup across the marbled floor and set it down before settling into a leather sofa.

Barker reached for his phone, dialled a number and asked to speak to Matt Gorden. When the chairman of Mata Gorda International hollered down the line, Barker cut to the chase. 'Gorden, have you heard of something called rizado?'

A long silence on the other end.

'Gorden? You there?'

'I'm here.'

'So you know about the *Herbal de Carbonela* being dug up in the Madrid archives and opened to the public.'

'Of course, we've known for years. We received a sample of it ages ago and we've been trying to replicate rizado ever since. Why are you asking?'

Without giving his game away, Barker filled Gorden in and ended by saying, 'I'll get my hands on it soon. What did the results show?'

'It was only a small sample so we couldn't do much. But it's amazing. Rizado heals burns and cuts in hours. Our scientists added it to some antibiotics and it made them ten times more effective. If you can get your hands on more, we'll do more tests. Why don't you come in and discuss it?'

After arranging a meeting for the following day, Barker cut the call. He lifted a magazine from his coffee table and it fell open to the centre spread. He rubbed a finger along the page. As before, it slit his finger. Staring at the blood made him smile and swelled his Johnson.

He smeared the blood across the two she-devils. Each incited a different fire into his belly: Teresina made him pulsate with revenge and churned up anger, and Kelby, with her secret potion, gave him an exciting new project.

'You will give up your new secret, Kelby. I have lots of ways to make you spit it out.'

Barker released Johnson, straining inside his trouser zipper. Above the magazine faces, Barker's engorged penis turned purple.

Like his next victim would soon be.

45

Kelby leaned close so Annie could reveal her secret.

'Promise you won't tell Mum.'

'Tell her what?'

'Promise properly.'

Kelby dropped her voice to match Annie's scheming tone, 'I do solemnly swear, Miss Annie Wade, I will not tell Mum your secret.'

'You're not allowed to swear. You'll get me into big trouble.'

'I solemnly swear I will not swear.'

Annie giggled and tapped the tip of her finger on Kelby's nose as if it were a magical wand granting special powers. 'Okay, you pass the test.'

'Soooo? What's the big secret?'

Annie equalled Kelby's lean-in and came nose to nose with her. 'I lied to Mum.'

Kelby's eyebrows shot up, and she tried to stop her jaw from dropping. 'Annie!'

'But it was a small little lie, not a big bad porky pie.'

'Fess up, girl, or I'll have to start swearing again.'

Annie's face creased into a delightful mixture of conspiracy and mischief. 'Everyone is allowed to bring their pets to school for show and tell, but I'm not allowed hairy pets.'

'Pumpkin, you know that's because you'll have a bad attack from a puppy or kitten.'

Annie nodded, clearly resigned to her fate. 'I told Mum I had to have a pet.'

'But what about the goldfish I bought you?'

'They don't count.' She consoled Kelby by patting her hand. 'I couldn't take a goldfish bowl filled with water to school the way Mum drives!'

'Ah, I see your point.'

'And imagine Mrs Greenwood's face when Marcus tips up the bowl and Emily starts crying and won't stop. *So*, I told Mum I needed to start an ant farm for a school project.' Annie gripped Kelby's index finger and yanked on it, 'Remember your promise.'

'Brownie's honour.' Kelby saluted Annie.

'No!' Annie's eyes grew large in horror. 'It's like this, Aunt Kel.'

Kelby smiled as Annie tapped three fingers of her right hand up. Her thumb and little finger bent and touching as her hand rose to an imaginary cap. Inside her palms, white scaly flakes stood out on the pink tender skin.

'All my friends have got normal pets, but no-one's got an ant farm. When I show and tell they think I'm cool.' Annie's face lit up. 'Marcus stopped calling me "sniffer". And Kathy won't stop hanging around me. She wants to know about my ants, even though she normally flicks my nose and calls me Rudolf. And guess what …'

'What?' Kelby waited in anticipation.

'Sam has stopped calling me a leper!'

Kelby flinched. She hated how cruel the kids were to Annie. In particular, her hands had caused a fuss at school. None of the other kids wanted to touch her. It took constant reassurance from the teachers Annie's skin wouldn't harm them, but that still didn't help. Even simple actions such as washing her hands, picking up her school bag or pulling on her jumper to go into the playground distressed Annie.

'Everyone wants to be my friend and even Emily thinks I'm an ant hero.'

'You know something, Annie? You're starting to sound like an entrepreneur.'

'What's that?'

'A crafty, little so and so who thinks up clever plans that will give them what they want. And they take big risks to go for it. Like you. Many of them will lie too.'

Annie chuckled behind her hand clamped over her mouth. 'I only lied cos Mum said she hates ants. Says they give her the creepy crawlies.'

'I'm with Mum on that one.'

'I think she'll starve them while I'm in here. You know Mum doesn't bother much about food.'

'Then you better get your bum out of bed pretty fast.'

'I'm better. *Please* tell the doctor to let me go home.'

'I'll do that.'

'Can you keep another secret?'

'Are you the chief of the secret service?'

Annie giggled behind her hand.

Kelby loved the way her eyes twinkled with mischief.

'Spit it out.'

'Corinna told me she saw a man killing her mummy.'

Kelby gasped. 'Annie!'

'It's not me, Aunt Kel, it's Corinna. And she's not lying neither.'

'Annie, where do you hear these things?' Kelby glanced at the TV on the wall. She'd have to tell the nursing staff to curb Annie's viewing. She must be watching things Stacie would never allow her to watch at home. The child had an active imagination, but this was getting out of hand.

'Annie, you must be —'

Annie rolled her head over on the pillow. 'I won't tell you any more if you won't believe me.'

Kelby stood and marched around to the other side of the bed and pulled a face at Annie. 'Okay, secret service, how does Corinna know these things?'

'She said before they went shopping she heard someone singing outside so she peeked out. She saw a strange man with something that looked like a tiny iPod in his hand. He stuck it onto their car.'

Kelby almost dared not ask, but did anyway. 'And then what happened?'

'She said the car went bang.'

46

A branch cracked underfoot. María froze. Her eyes darted left to right. The moon had disappeared behind a cloud, and for a moment she held her breath. Then, someone stepped out of the shadows and lowered his hood.

'Don Behor!' María blurted out in surprise.

Although Behor de Catalon wasn't her uncle, she considered him to be, and called him *Tío* — uncle — to show her affection.

'*Shalom aleikhem*. Peace be upon you.' Tío folded her into his arms and with a big hug drew her into his flowing green robe. He finished the embrace with a kiss on the top of her head as Madre did.

'But what are you doing out at this hour of the night, *mi querida?*' Whenever he called her *my dear* his tone softened with affection.

Tío dressed elegantly in fine silk and linen. Today his tappert's large sleeves revealed a jubba underneath to stop the cool spring night breeze from piercing him.

María explained what had happened and asked, 'And why are *you* out so late, Tío? Is there a *problema* with my stories?'

Tío placed a hand on her arm and said, 'Not that kind of trouble, *querida*. But I was on my way to tell Carmen some terrible news.'

María's heart pounded.

He lifted the wide-brimmed woollen hat he wore and rubbed the top of his head. He only removed his hat when he was worried. 'I've received news from my family in the Basque region.'

'Come Tío, let us turn back and talk in the cottage.'

They walked in silence for a few minutes. María's heart lifted when the animals gathered around her legs as they neared the cottage.

Inside, she threw another log and a handful of twigs on the glowing embers. Kneeling, she blew on the embers. A spark licked at the twigs and flames leapt around the log. María straightened and watched Tío pull out a tiny hardened leather costrel and threw back a gulp of *vino*. María had heard Tío tell Madre he drank his vino for medicinal reasons.

'*Con salud, querida,* with good health. A drink will calm my nerves.'

'What has happened, Tío?'

'It is God's will. You must get this news to your mother as soon as you are able.'

María nodded and waited while he took another smaller sip of his calming wine.

'It is happening, *querida*, for many years there has been rumblings that *los djudyos* — the Jews — will be banished from Al-Andalus.' He sipped again and breathed deeply.

María stoked the fire.

'The Alahambra Decree is an Expulsion Edict because of the Catholic *reconquista* of Spain.'

María swallowed hard.

'Isabella and Ferdinand — that *azno.* He is a jackass.'

María suppressed a cry of shock. Tío was clearly distraught. She had never before heard him speak ill of anyone, especially the monarchy, but he trusted her.

'They've ordered Jews to convert to Catholicism. If they don't, they'll be executed.'

María's jaw dropped.

'We have to leave or die.'

47

Kelby slowly awoke. At first she didn't know where she was and opened one eye to look around. The chemical tang of newly washed floors reminded her she had fallen asleep beside Annie.

Her laptop had gone to sleep on Annie's hospital bedside cabinet. Kelby tapped her phone: 01:44.

Annie's peaceful face lay within arm's reach, although Kelby resisted the urge to stroke her cheeks in case she woke her. The poor little thing had such a wild imagination, no only having invisible friends, but now believing they were real people with real dramas.

Outside the room, someone whispered, 'She has no personality.' The busybody nurse clearly intended to be heard. 'Yep, she doesn't say a word to us, just types away.'

'Shh, she'll hear you.' That sounded like Rosalind.

'No way, I've got the heating units on full blast; you wouldn't hear a devil roar behind her.'

'That's a terrible thing to say,' Rosalind chastised. 'She's kind to me and she's often here visiting Annie, even though someone like her probably gets invited to all kinds of fancy events. But no, she doesn't bother with that, she'd rather sit with Annie.'

'Hey!'

The flooring squeaked as the gossiping nurses spun around to face the male voice invasion.

'Give her a break. She's been here for hours.'

The voice came closer. Kelby dropped her head, pretending to be asleep. *Oh, no. Not him again.*

From the corner of her eye, she spotted the hairy caterpillars peering through the blinds.

Outside, Doctor Robson whispered, 'Look, she's fallen asleep in there.'

'Yeah, laptop still on and all.'

'Did anyone offer her a cuppa?'

Silence.

'Shame on you. All of you!'

His footsteps squeaked along the chemically clean floor. Kelby tiptoed to the door. The nurses had ambled off down the web of corridors. Stuffing her laptop into her briefcase, she blew a kiss to Annie. Kelby crept along the corridor and out of the hospital, extra careful not to bump into anybody.

Surrounded by conifers that reached for the moon, the car park scattered long shadows. They followed her every step as though they wanted to pounce on her ankles and tackle her to the ground. Her breath jammed in her throat, shafting up in desperate gasps.

Where was Hawk?

Hidden amongst the branches, an owl fluttered its wings and hooted, spooking her.

Kelby spotted Hawk inching his car towards her. Phew! Yesterday was only just over, but she wasn't taking any chances at this spooky hour.

The stalker's last words still haunted her: *See you at yours tonight.*

48

The sombre house greeted Kelby with silence. She hated the dark. Always had. A blast of wind blew her inside and growled as she stood beside Hawk.

Kelby slipped off her shoes in the hallway, her nerves still jumpy. In the tomb-like silence, she could hear the rooms resting and emitting stray sighs like a dormant monster deep in slumber.

She placed her keys on the wall keyring holder and their jangle echoed around the kitchen. Suddenly, they heard arguing as a man and woman's voice came from the lounge.

Hawk followed the echoes.

Kelby's breath caged in her throat as she tiptoed down the hall after him. Her muscles cramped with dread.

At the point where a blue haze oozed out of the living room, Hawk stopped dead. He pushed the door open with one finger. Sounds reverberated around the room, bouncing off the furniture and whirring straight at Kelby like a ghost being exorcised. The door nudged open enough to reveal the culprit.

One of Fat Cat's soaps.

'It's only the telly,' Hawk chuckled.

Kelby slumped against the wall in relief as he pushed the door wide open to see Fat Cat fast asleep on top of the old square TV. Below him, one of the BBC's soaps blared as some haggard old female had it out with a younger man.

'Hah, soap re-runs at this hour of the morning!' Hawk grinned. 'You forgot to switch it off.'

'No, not exactly.' Kelby blushed. 'I leave the TV on for the cat in case he gets lonely.'

'Oh. Okay.'

'It started after my ex left.'

The stupid bastard had left her for a young tart he'd got pregnant, but Kelby had no intention of sharing those details with Hawk. She recalled the endless photos of her ex on Twitter and Facebook that showed him loading his Porsche with leaving-home-luggage. And the people gloating at what had happened. In the end, she'd sold her Chelsea home to get away from them. Now she hid out in the sedate yet prestigious, tree-lined celebrity drive near St George's College in Surrey. The agent had boasted that Elton John and Cliff Richard were neighbours; not that she cared. She had bought privacy.

Kelby sighed and said in a low voice, 'Leaving the TV on was more to do with my fear of being alone in the dark.'

'Don't worry. The dark scares a lot of people.'

'Mine comes from the night when my parents left me and my brother with the babysitter for an odd night out.' She swallowed hard at the haunting memory.

'How old were you?'

'Just a teenager.'

'What happened?' Hawk's gentle voice prodded her to get rid of her demon.

'At midnight the babysitter left. I waited alone in the dark all night with Gary. In the morning one of my aunts arrived with the police and told me about my parents' accident.'

Hawk's huge arms wrapped around her.

'I know it sounds daft,' her voice muffled against his chest, 'There were no mobiles in those days and no way for me to get in touch with my folks, so I hid Gary in a wardrobe and climbed in with him.'

'It's okay.' Hawk patted her shoulders.

'I'm brave in public, but a coward on my own.'

She pulled out of Hawk's arms, lifted Fat Cat and gave him a quick cuddle.

Back in the hallway, she watched Hawk check the house and then he showed her how to use the alarm. Thanking him, she watched him slide back into his car right outside her door. 'I won't be far. I'll keep checking around the house. I'm here if you need me. Just call.'

Darting upstairs to her bedroom, Kelby slipped off her bra and pulled on a pair of Calvin Klein boxers. She often bought the soft t-shirt ones without the Y-front in Harrods, pretending they were for a man friend. She hopped into bed, careful not to disturb Fat Cat who was curled in a fluffy ball on the bottom corner.

With no hope of a decent night's sleep, Kelby slipped between the cold sheets. For the first time since her divorce, she regretted being alone.

After reading two pages of *The Economist's* world news, Kelby realised she hadn't registered a word. Every sound outside magnified in her mind. The wind swept through a garden pergola, creaking around the grapevine arbour. It played havoc with the roof tiles, lifting them one by one, as if to tease her with frightening sounds. Somewhere downstairs a tap dripped. Although it drove her nuts, she wouldn't get out of bed to find it and stop the irritating drip.

Dumping *The Economist* on her bedside table, she opted for her latest Dean Koontz novel. She soon gave that up too. Fine thing to be reading with someone prowling around her garden. At least with Hawk there, no-one would get inside.

Kelby hit the light switch and snuggled under the duvet, curling into a foetal position. Her king size bed was a cold, vacant void without a man's warmth. She tried to empty her mind and get some sleep.

Fat chance.

49

Kelby crept around the house, trying to get away from a dark figure, but the more she tried the slower she went.

He yanked her from behind. Throwing one of her shirts over her head, he tugged it tighter and tighter. A large hand closed over her mouth. She coughed and spluttered, struggling to breathe.

She came around with her hands and feet bound to a chair in the kitchen. The dark figure made himself at home, munching on left over quiche and sipping on an open bottle of Rioja. For hours, her attacker taunted her. 'You deserve to be raped,' he hissed, 'A she-devil like you needs to be exterminated.' A loud bang on the door stopped his ramblings.

With a jolt, Kelby woke from her nightmare.

Too afraid to move, she lay under the warm duvet. For a long moment, she listened for someone at the door. Silence. Nobody there. It was only a nightmare about being tied up. Yet, it had been so real, she had felt the rope chafe her wrists. What a relief. The threat was over. She had escaped.

But how come her bedroom stank of stale tobacco?

The banging in her head refused to abate; she had to take a headache pill. Forcing herself up, Kelby rose in slow motion, her eyes taking in every square inch of her bedroom.

No sign of an intruder.

Kelby crept across the darkened room, fearing her attacker would appear from nowhere. Her ears were on red alert.

Calm down! She shook her head.

After a quick shower, she opened a drawer tangled with panties and bras. Distracted, and multi-tasking with her hands going in different directions, she lifted out a pair of knickers and her finger slid across the smoothness of paper.

Kelby frowned as she pulled out a magazine.

The same blood-smeared magazine centre spread stared back at her. This time, Teresina had been blacked out. Her glossy smile was scarred by the horrific graffiti while Kelby's face had been smeared with a large bloody X.

She inhaled sharply. Glancing over her shoulder, her eyes checked every nook in her bedroom, and focused on the entrance, half expecting the attacker to be silhouetted in the doorway.

Kelby's thumb instinctively popped into her mouth and her bottom row of teeth shaved along the nail.

Then, her spine recoiled with a new realisation. The internet stalker must have had something to do with Teresina's death. His message was clear; she was next on his list.

Kelby bolted down the stairs, flung the door open, yelling to Hawk.

But his car was gone.

50

'*El Dio que mos guadre*. May God preserve us.' Tío's usually smiling face contorted.

María stared at Tío. Still dazed, she muttered, 'Oh, no, poor Moshe and Ribka will be terrified.' She couldn't face the thought of her village friends being sent away and asked, 'Why are they doing this?'

Tío's voice dropped to a whisper, 'They have lots of different reasons. The king's more powerful if everyone is Catholic.'

'But why? We have so many different religions in Granada.'

'Yes, *querida*, but the king and queen want to increase their political authority and weaken opposition.'

A deep frown creased her brow.

'Remember when we talked about Granada being the last bastion of Moslem rule?'

María nodded.

'It was only a few months ago, in January, that Granada was conquered from the Moors, and the reconquest was completed. We have a few months to convert to Catholicism or we must leave Spain.' He lifted his hat and rubbed the sweat off the top of his head. 'They want to rule the world.'

María jumped up and poured herself some water.

'My family have decided to fund a sea captain who is looking for sailors to help him find new worlds.'

'Cristóbal Colón?'

Tío jolted upright in his seat, his face aghast. 'How do you know this, *querida*?'

'You taught me when we did our lesson on the new world. The Italians call him Cristoforo Colombo, don't they?'

He slumped back in his chair, muttering, 'Yes, yes, of course. This news is driving me *loco!*' He tapped the side of his head.

María touched his hand. 'You are not a crazy person, Tío.'

'Bah! Now they want Colón to find a new route to India.'

'But you told me Isabella had turned his request down because it cost too much money.'

'*Si el emprestimo era bueno, emprestava el rey a su mujer.* If making loans were good, the king would lend his wife.' Tío shook himself as though the thought of the king distressed him. After a moment, he scratched his head and said, 'Yes, yes, too much money, even though the rewards will be great.' He stretched his body as though the conversation gave him backache. 'The treasury has estimated that the expenditure for three ships and crew will be about the same as it costs the young royals to entertain a visiting noble for one week.'

'How do you know so much about Colón's quest for money?'

For a moment Tío stared at her, then he dropped his voice as though someone might overhear them, 'You can never say this aloud, *querida.*'

Holding her breath, María hung onto every word he uttered.

'My family are related to him.' He waited for his words to sink in and continued, 'Not many know of his Jewish origins. He is from a Converso family. *Djidio bovo no ay.* There are no stupid Jews.'

Taking a deep breath, María asked, 'Does the King know of this?'

'As I said, not many know Colón is a Converso.'

'But if they support Colón, they can take control of the world and all its people!' María's heart beat so loudly she hoped Tío couldn't hear it.

'Yes, *querida.*'

'Will your family convert? They have been so helpful to me.'

He remained silent for a long moment.

Tío sighed deeply and dropped his voice so low she could hardly hear him, 'We have little choice.' Tío said in a trembling voice, 'In their search for would-be heretics, they're torturing confessions out of those who have converted.'

'Are they allowed to do that?'

'They can do whatever they want. They are even seizing the properties of convicted heretics.'

'You are not a heretic, Tío.'

'Bless you, *mi querida*. But in their eyes I am.'

'What will you do?'

'Up till now my family in the north were blessed. They had the money to buy their way out of trouble if it came their way.' He sighed. 'Money is the solution to many problems, *querida*. Now they are going into hiding and I will go with them.'

'Until when?'

Beside her the fire leapt over the logs, eating at any crack in the wood. As it spat and crackled, its heat warmed her cheeks.

'Until this persecution is finished, we will leave our homes as they are until we can return to them. But listen, *querida* ...'

María squirmed in her chair. A tremor in her spine tickled the base of her neck.

'There is more.'

51

Barker tossed a fifty quid note at the driver and stepped out of the black cab into the early morning drizzle. A wave of foul-smelling heat, pumping out the smell of petrol fumes, rose from under the vehicle.

He hated travelling in cabs. They stank, and who knew what slob had sat on the seat minutes before him. But it was the only way to travel in the congestion zone. Although he was on a stealth mission, most people came to Harley Street's prestigious medical mecca for private consultations about everything, from depressing terminal illness to conceited cosmetic body reordering.

Earlier, he'd had Kelby's car fitted with the same device that killed Teresina. Every time he thought of how he could get away with his plan, adrenalin surged through him, setting his whole being on fire. He couldn't believe he hadn't discovered this rush before. A meticulous killing strategy thrilled him more than any business plan.

Rain splattered on Mata Gordo's Victorian arched windows. Its facade begged passers-by to peer into the windows. Barker pressed the buzzer on a highly polished, black door. He wondered if Mata Gordo purposefully added a thick veil of mystery to their entrance. They certainly kept secrets like stones kept silent.

The door buzzed and clicked open. He stepped upon the shiny wooden pine floors of Mata Gordo Pharmaceutical. The smell of the place, pristine and lemon-like, caught him high in the nostrils. Medical smells, he hated. Lemon freshness, he loved.

Apart from the receptionist's muted phone conversation in the next room, the imposing gabled lobby was silent. Only the occasional pigeon, flapping against the high octagonal tower's skylight, disturbed the peace. For a split second he imagined himself to be inside an elaborate doll's house.

The click-clack of his heels on the pine floor brought the receptionist scuttling into the hallway. She extended her hand, half bowing her head, as the ultimate show of respect.

Without doubt, she would have signed agreements to keep her trap shut about the goings on in here with the high profile clientele, political and medical.

The receptionist ushered Barker into Mata Gorda's inner sanctuary. The plush décor eased Barker's beating heart. It hadn't stopped tapping against his ribs since Zelda had given him the ultimate coup de grâce for destroying another she-devil.

Rizado consumed his thoughts — almost taking over his game plan. Once his research had revealed its immense potential, everything would slot into place.

He needed to find Kelby's secret plant.

52

Within seconds of slamming her front door Kelby heard footsteps crunch on her driveway. She peeped through the keyhole and saw Hawk passing the window.

She darted outside. 'Where've you been?'

Hawk smiled. 'Morning. I've just finished patrolling the grounds.'

The fire in her veins immediately melted and she softened her tone, 'I thought you'd gone.'

'Why? I told you I'd be here all night.'

'Your car ...' Kelby stretched her neck and saw it parked at the bottom of the garden behind the shed. She suddenly felt terribly stupid.

After she'd explained to Hawk, he said, 'When we did the audit I did a sweep of the house for bugs, but I didn't do an extreme sweep. This may have been there before I set things up.'

She nodded.

'Or it could be a threat from within. I wonder if this person knows you.'

'But who?'

This time Hawk shook his head.

Kelby made coffee to settle her nerves while Hawk made a few calls. Hawk's colleague Roger, came over and drove Kelby to work while Hawk scoured her house and grounds to see how someone could have infiltrated the security system.

An hour and a half later Kelby swept through the glass double door of her office and spotted Zelda glued to her PC in the far corner. She hung her coat in reception along with a row of other wet, bedraggled and sad-looking garments.

She didn't want to face another day of tedious mentee meetings. After the initial thrill of being on Devil's Grotto, the gloss and glamour had quickly worn off leaving her with the dull ache of being in the public eye. She rued the day she had let Jon Thompson twist her arm to be on the show. At the time, it had sounded fun with lots of opportunities to meet new people. But now, with the trolling, it was too much hassle.

Kelby dumped her briefcase on her desk and delved inside to rescue her laptop. It whirred into operation, ready to power her day.

Greeting the early birds as she marched through the office, she spotted Jimmy. He waved at her and she nodded in return, knowing a hot cup of coffee would be in her hands in a few minutes. What would she do without him?

After an update on her security, she said to Jimmy, 'Please call Stacie, I've been trying her mobile and her home number, but she's not answering.'

'What's the message if I get hold of her?'

'Put her through, I have to talk to her.'

'Another bust up?'

Kelby dropped her gaze. Jimmy was too damn intuitive for his own good. 'Get onto Stacie. ASAP!'

'I'm on it.' Striding to the door, Jimmy asked, 'How's Annie?'

'Much better, thanks, but not out of the woods yet. The poor little thing looks so pale with those tubes stuck in her face.'

'Did you get any sleep? Or did you spend the night working on those reports?'

Ignoring his question, she asked, 'Have you heard any more about Teresina's accident?'

Jimmy shook his head.

'Get me everything you can find on it. Call Jon or the producers, they'll know the latest.'

He saluted and disappeared.

Kelby slumped into her seat and stared at the dark thunder clouds crowding in around her window. She'd have to quit the show; she couldn't tolerate this troll infestation.

A flurry of unfamiliar voices filtered into her office, and Kelby glanced through the internal window facing her staff.

PC Pike and Turkey-neck stood in reception staring directly at her.

53

Barker stared at the lard arse in a three-piece suit. Being CEO of one of Europe's most affluent pharmaceutical companies gave Matt Gorden an inflated ego and plenty of excuses to overindulge. If he wasn't suited up, he'd look like the Michelin Man.

Before Barker had time to say a word, the lard arse propelled him into another extravagant room and ushered him to a chair in front of a plush oak desk.

Gorden slumped into his leather seat, which squeaked as he went down. 'Did you find it?'

'Almost there.' Barker tried to control his irritation. 'What can we do in the meantime?'

'Nothing happens without the goddamn plant.'

'Agreed, but we need to hit the ground running as soon as we find it.'

Gorden bristled; his tone barbed, 'Listen, Barker, you've been around these woods long enough to know that new medicines go through rigorous tests.'

'Of course, but if rizado is such a life-saver, we should get the process ready for when it comes in.'

'Not that easy.' Gorden shook his head. 'Let me explain.'

Barker ignored him and tried not to scowl. 'If rizado stacks up, it will revolutionise the drug market.'

Gorden said, 'But first we have to file a new drug application to allow rizado to be tested on humans in clinical trials. That's the biggest hurdle.'

'The trials will show it's not hype. From what I can see, this stuff will benefit the industry.'

'Uh, huh, but some would say rizado is too risky.'

Barker had the feeling Gorden wasn't keen to bring rizado to the market.

'Anyway, we'll use Inter Mezzo as our sounding board on this one.'

'They're a bunch of criminals in white coats.'

'Good God, man, why do you say that?'

Barker cleared his throat. 'MG's annual reports show they've prevented at least three of your new medical innovations.'

'That may be your view, but hundreds of medical organisations belong to the Mezzo. They check every stage of a clinical trial before deciding if a new medicine is safe.'

'What are you saying? I get the distinct feeling rizado doesn't excite you as much as it does me.'

Barker hated being strung along by idiots.

Idiots like Gorden.

54

With eyes burning from lack of sleep, Kelby glared at the two policemen. Ever since Gary's death, she'd hated the police because she believed they hadn't investigated it properly.

Kelby bit her lip, intending to make a big song and dance about it, but not yet. She couldn't risk telling anyone about the rizado findings.

Parking his skeletal body on her sofa, PC Pike asked, 'We'd like to talk to you about Teresina Piccoli.'

Kelby nodded her head.

PC Gardenia gave her a smug grin. 'We wanted to find out about your relationship with her. We know you've exchanged insults.'

Kelby reeled inwardly, but kept a controlled exterior and said as calmly as she could, 'That's personal.' She crossed her legs, wiping her clammy palms along her thigh.

'Not when it's on national telly.'

'It's a reality show, what do you expect?'

'Did you have to have a slanging match when she won the first mentoring round?' The Turkey-neck absentmindedly swung the loose skin under his chin back and forth. 'Seemed a bit odd to me.'

Kelby cringed, hoping the idiot police constable couldn't hear her heart pounding. She couldn't think of a sharp retort and rubbed her hands along her leg again.

'You okay, Miss Wade? You look a little nervous.'

'I'm pushed for time. My diary is stacked and I have lots of calls to still make before my meetings start.'

PC Pike took over the conversation. 'We understand, but we have lots of interviews to do to help the Italian police.'

PC Gardenia jabbed his elbow into his young colleague's ribs. Raising his eyebrows, he indicated something in the notepad.

PC Pike flipped the notepad closed and asked, 'Is it true Miss Piccoli said that,' he dropped his head in embarrassment, 'Sorry to repeat this, but she said you're way too ugly to be on the *Sunday Times* Rich List.'

'She did.'

'And what did you do about it.'

'What could I do? Have her dropped in the ocean with an anchor tied to her ankles?' Kelby immediately regretted her words. *Good God, what's wrong with me!* Of all the moments to display a flash of temper.

As before, PC Pike scribbled his notes while PC Gardenia rubbed Kelby up the wrong way. 'Did you retaliate by calling her ...' he tapped his colleagues notepad and emphasised his words, '*Mafia money.*'

'I apologised for that remark. I admit she did rile me. We'd been under tremendous pressure with a hectic few weeks of twelve-hour days on location. The pressure erupted and we had a tiff on the show.'

'Is that how it was?' PC Gardenia's eyes penetrated hers.

Kelby squirmed; he was bent on driving her into a corner of suspicion. She tried to remain patient. 'PC ...' Her mouth opened and closed, but his name wouldn't come out. *Damn, not good. They expect people with a smidgeon of respect to remember their names.*

'PC Gardenia.'

'Thank you. What you didn't see is Teresina riling me and provoking me off camera. She had an incredible knack of winding people up.'

'No-one is forcing you to take the bait. Or is that part of the show?'

'I suppose you could say that. It's not something I want to do,' Kelby said, her eyes glued to him, 'but the pressure the producers place on the team is ridiculous.'

He held her stare, but blinked repeatedly as if he didn't believe her.

She continued, 'It's a reality show. That's what we have to do. We also have to put the contestants under pressure. Make them sweat and get jumpy so they stumble and forget their pitch. That's how we find the strong ones, the ones worth fighting for.'

'Thank you for explaining, Miss Wade.' PC Pike scribbled notes in his book.

'Any more questions, officers? I'm sorry, but I'm pushed for time today otherwise I'd offer you a coffee.'

'Your man secretary already did.'

Kelby winched. Jimmy would go ape if he heard them call him that.

'We declined. The coffee, that is.'

She rose to show them to the door.

'One more thing, Miss Wade.'

Kelby groaned.

PC Gardenia pushed out his chest as though his body stance should intimidate her. 'Miss Wade, your man secretary told us Miss Piccoli called about something urgent.' He pointed at Jimmy outside her interlinking window. 'Why did Miss Piccoli call you?'

'I have no idea. I wish I knew.'

'Then why did you refuse her call?'

Kelby prickled. 'I didn't refuse her call. I'm sure Jimmy explained, I was in a meeting when Teresina called. I was due to call her straight back after my meeting ended ...' Her voice faded as guilt consumed her.

God, how she wished she had taken that bloody call.

She avoided the police officer's eyes and wrapped her arms across her chest while her mind raced.

Both men stared at her. She could see the older one didn't believe her, while the younger seemed too nervous to voice his opinion.

Eventually Turkey-neck nudged PC Pike. The string bean cleared his throat and said, 'Miss Wade, are you aware Miss Piccoli's call to you was her last call before she died?'

Kelby gawped at him. 'No. I'm so sorry to hear that. Do you have any more details about her accident?'

'Such as?'

She blushed. 'I'm not sure … how did it happen? More importantly how *could it* happen? She was an excellent driver. She even had another Maserati imported to use over here.'

'The Italian police are keeping us informed of new developments.' PC Pike's voice sounded far too official.

PC Gardenia added, 'What my colleague is *trying* to say, is that the Italians are still investigating the incident. At this stage, they're taking anything into consideration, even foul play.'

'You say that as though …' her voice trailed off, her earlier morning thoughts suddenly became real. Should she tell them about the magazine found amongst her knickers? They didn't have time to check that out. Besides, Hawk would handle it.

PC Pike frowned. 'As though what, Miss Wade?'

'As though this wasn't an accident.'

PC Gardenia's smug glow returned as he said, 'No, Miss Wade, we didn't indicate that at all. *You* did.'

'Maybe the stalker I told you about was also after her.'

'Unlikely, but we can check into it.' PC Pike shook the notepad as though trying to squeeze answers out of it.

Turkey-neck stepped to the door, saying, 'Miss Wade, if we have more questions for you, we'll be in touch. Everyone is a suspect until this matter is cleared up. Even you, Miss Wade, even you.'

Kelby flinched. She couldn't believe they were treating her as they would a suspect. Then reality hit Kelby.

Oh, my God. Teresina must have been murdered!

55

Time slowed as María waited for Tío to explain what other bad news he had brought. Yet her pulse quickened.

'There is *una problema* for healers.'

'Is that because the Holy Office is against women healers?'

'Yes, yes, that is correct,' he croaked, 'the Tribunal del Santo Oficio de la Inquisición.'

María swallowed hard, dreading what would come next. Tío had taught her about the Inquisición Española and how the king and queen had intended to maintain Catholic rule in their kingdoms.

Tío took the last sip of his vino medicinal and shook the leather pouch close to his ear. 'Please, *querida. Una gotika,* a little drop. I must keep drinking. This news has my heart skipping a beat in my chest.'

María wished her mother kept mead in the cottage. Instead she reached for a jug and poured him a cupful of wine, hoping he didn't notice it had been watered down.

Tío said, 'I warned your mother about the men who have been trained as doctors. They believe knowledge is harmful to women. I also told your mother how the nobility have been cultivating their own university courses to be trained as doctors.' Tío leaned over and patted María's hand. 'Have faith. One day, *querida,* your little stories will be big.' He tapped his head. '*La pacencia es media cencia.* Patience is halfway to wisdom. You have a good head on your shoulders.'

He'd often told her how smart she was and she'd beamed with pride. Now, she sat in glum silence.

'Like your mother,' he patted her hand again, 'you too will make a fine *balabaya,* a good homemaker.'

María tried to smile at his faith, but it turned into a sardonic smirk. 'Tell me of *el problema* for Madre.'

Tío drank deeply from the cup and accidentally slammed it on the table. His eyebrows asked for more and María topped up his drink.

'Your mother is useful to our village. Most of us would be in ill health without her remedies.'

'And as a *komadre*. Most of the children around here would not have been born without her.' María added with pride.

'Yes, you're right. This village would wither away without your mother.'

María cursed under her breath and covered her mouth in shame.

'It is okay, *querida*, we know your mother is a good woman. *Quien bien faze, bien topa.* He who does good, finds good.'

'Yes, it is terrible so few women are educated.'

'That is why your mother asked me to teach you privately. The life of most women is to sweep, wash and raise children.'

Tío drained the drink as if just speaking of these heinous crimes parched him. María refilled it, not wanting their *conversatio* to end.

'*El Dio que nos guardre de medico y de endevino.* May the Lord protect us from doctors and fortune tellers.' Tío scratched his head again. 'The church has legitimised doctors. So wise women like your mother are now viewed as heretics. If any of the villagers fall sick or die unexpectedly, your mother could be accused of being *una bruxa*, a witch.'

María bolted up in her chair. 'Mama, a witch? Because she is skilled at midwifery and her *medicina*?'

'Si, *querida*. If a woman dare to cure without studying, she is a witch and must die.'

María felt the hair rising on her back and rocked forward in her chair.

'Priests can command anyone knowing a wise woman to reveal her name, so the church can report her as a heretic.'

María wished she could stand up for Madre and show the church what good her mother did for the local villagers.

'Sadly, if anyone accused your mother of being a wise woman, she would be bold enough to show the children she has delivered, and the people she had healed. And that would be all they need to condemn her.'

María leapt to her feet. Behind her, the rickety wooden chair crashed to the floor. She ignored it and started pacing in front of the hearth.

'We still have faith there will be peace. We must be *confiensa*.'

María couldn't understand how Tío could be confident; her armpits felt clammy and her insides were boiling.

'*Un buen siman*, querida, a good sign.'

Madre wasn't a heretic or a witch.

But what if *La Reina Isabel* believed such nonsense?

56

Barker watched Gorden through slitted eyes. Most of the time the runt was hard to read.

Like now.

Gorden squeezed his chin. 'Developing a new medicine takes at least ten years and costs a couple of billion.'

'I'm not worried about that. Rizado will be worth more.'

'Maybe. But less than twelve per cent of new medicines on clinical trials are approved.' Gorden peered far too intensely at him as though part of him enjoyed having superior knowledge.

Barker stared back, refusing to be humiliated by this trumped up prick. 'We don't have to make it so long-winded.'

'The rizado must go through the right process before it even gets to human subjects. And there are regulations for testing on people. There'll be control groups monitoring the whole process.'

'Okay … And?' Barker's tried to keep the barb out of his voice.

Gorden swivelled in his squeaky leather seat and placed his foot on an open drawer at the side of his desk. 'And we can't have Herman Schmidt sticking his nose in. He had the nerve to accuse us of exploiting people in the Indian and African trials.'

'Who?'

'You know, the scientist who founded WMW.' Gorden pointed his stumpy finger at a cork board with hundreds of press clippings stabbed with colourful pins. They reminded Barker of Stacie Wade's ear studs. And they gave him a great idea to shake up Kelby.

'The World Medical Watchdog.' Gorden rattled on.

Barker shook himself, forcing his focus on the runt.

'They investigate pharmaceutical activities in poorer countries. He has the cheek to insist test patients receive medicines after the study is over.'

'Most of those monkeys live in extreme poverty. They don't get medical care. They'll jump at the chance of free medicine. And they won't realise or even care if it's tests,' Barker said dismissively.

'Too risky. Schmidt will tear us to pieces.' Gorden gave him another intense stare. 'After hearing that, I hope you're not disappointed.'

'What do you mean?'

'You're still in the pro camp?'

'Why not?' Taken aback, Barker asked, 'Is there any other camp?'

'Think of the cost to the industry if suddenly there's a way to speed healing.'

'I'm not with you.'

'Pharma could lose billions in lost revenue from medications that slowly heal or don't even heal, but people buy them anyway.'

'So, you're saying it's better to stop rizado hitting the market? Just because it will rival traditional meds?'

'Good God, man, not me, but some in Inter Mezzo may believe the impact will be terrible for the economy.'

They were silent for a moment. Staring each other down.

'Sounds as if you're in their camp.'

'I'm neutral.'

Barker didn't believe it; he could hear the tension in Gorden's words. They radiated between the lines, ballooning the invisible implication into a whole new significance.

Without moving a muscle, Barker tried to absorb the concept for a moment, but the thought of the billions he could make still gave him an instant hard on.

'Don't bother about them and their opinion. The board will take a vote and decide.'

Barker had heard enough.

Gorden and Inter Mezzo thought rizado would kill the pharmaceutical industry.

57

Kelby accompanied the policemen to the lift. PC Gardenia asked to use the bathroom and Kelby waited for him in awkward silence with PC Pike.

After a moment, the police officer glanced over his shoulder and stepped closer to Kelby. 'Listen, Miss Wade, I don't believe Miss Piccoli's accident is connected to you. I'm just doing my job.'

'Like you did with Gary's death?' Kelby regretted the words as they spilled out of her mouth.

His voice dropped, 'I know you're still peeved about that. Between you and me, his death wasn't properly investigated.'

Unsure if she should bellow at him or be thankful someone had believed her, she asked, 'Can you do anything?'

'What?'

'Re-open the case. Dig deeper. Find out what happened.'

'I'm not sure. I'll have to ask my boss, see what the process is for such a thing to happen.'

'But —'

They heard a mini jet roar of air from the loo hand blower. Pressing the lift button, PC Pike said in a low voice, 'I'll do what I can. If I find out anything, I'll give you a call.' He handed her his card. 'In case you need to get hold of me.'

'Thank you.' A wave of guilt shot through Kelby for thinking the officer was conspiring against her.

PC Gardenia slapped Pike on the back, 'Come on, lad, we're done here.' He stepped into the waiting lift without saying goodbye.

As PC Pike joined his colleague, he nodded his greeting but his eyes told Kelby he understood her anguish.

As Kelby entered her office her head felt lighter with the knowledge someone might be able to help her. With sudden inspiration, an idea bolted into her head. What if Gary had kept any notes about rizado at home? Maybe that would help Roy and Miranda. And possibly give more evidence against the person who killed Gary.

As soon as the doors closed, she yelled at Jimmy, 'Did you get hold of Stacie?'

'No answer.'

'Try again.'

'But —'

'*Now*, please!' She had to make things right with Stacie. And find Gary's personal papers without Stacie getting suspicious.

Within minutes, Jimmy popped his head around the door, looking as though he was afraid it would be bitten off. 'Can't locate her.'

Kelby threw her head back on her mesh chair in exasperation. Keeping her feet still, she swung her knees from side to side. She had to do something.

'Jimmy, cancel my meetings. I'm going out.'

'What's going on? Something's eating at you today.'

Kelby shoved her laptop into her briefcase. 'I have to see Stacie. Keep trying her. If you get hold of her, tell her I'm on my way over.'

'Shall I get Hawk to come around to pick you up? He called to say he's still busy at your place sussing out how someone could have broken in.'

She stopped dead in her tracks. Seeing Stacie was a personal matter. It wouldn't be pleasant. Not something she wanted witnessed. 'Don't worry him, he's busy finding out what happened at home. I'll let him know where I am.' She flew out of the office and darted to the lift with Jimmy on her tail.

'Wait, I've gotta tell you about that stupid device on your car.'

'Tell me later. I'm taking a cab.' She pressed and held her finger on the elevator button.

Jimmy shook his head and mumbled, 'How am I supposed to explain this?'

At last the lift hissed open and Kelby jumped inside. As it closed she shouted a reply, 'You'll think of something.'

On the quick descent Kelby's temples throbbed. So much happening so fast. Too much to take in and no time to work out the tangled mess.

After the lift deposited her on the ground floor, she strode to the edge of the street and hailed a cab. As soon as he skidded up to her, she yanked open the door, hopped in and dumped her briefcase on her lap. She gave the cabbie an address in Kensington.

When the cab pulled up at her destination, Kelby paid the driver and rushed to Stacie's office.

She knocked and waited.

Silence.

She hammered on the old-fashioned brass door knocker to announce her arrival.

The stench of cigar smoke wafted from around the side of the building. Poking her head around the corner, she spotted two workmen in paint-stained overalls. One puffed while the other belched over his Pepsi can.

Kelby called to them, 'Hi there, is Stacie Wade in?'

'No, darling, we're renovating the office. The boss said she could work at home.'

Kelby bit her lip and thanked them. Damn, she'd have to fetch her car. It was still in the office car park from yesterday.

For a moment she thought of calling Hawk. But going to Stacie's would only be a short trip.

She'd be back in no time at all.

58

Barker jumped to his feet and started pacing the room in front of Gorden's desk. 'I came here for results, not a lecture on how long-winded the process would be!'

Gorden held up his hands, 'Listen, there's good news. You bring it in. You'll be more than handsomely rewarded.'

Barker had a choice to make.

He could go along with their ruling, and risk losing a personal fortune, as well as lose control. Or he could stay in the driving seat to take possession of the world's providence.

Not only would he be in command of a large infinite revenue, he would be a global icon. Bill Gates had revolutionised the computing world, and Tim Berners-Lee the online world. Barker would revolutionise pharma.

Imagine, he'd be more than a hero. He'd be a god.

For a long time, he had been bored with making money. Of course, he'd rather be rich than poor, but he needed more. Something compelling only he could achieve. That's why his plans for killing Teresina and Kelby had set him on fire again. Having anyone and anything at his disposal excited him. He could get rid of who he wanted when he wanted. Nothing would stop him. He'd never thought about being a world leader, but now it tempted him.

Barker was prepared to go to any lengths to get results. He had the money, but was running out of time. If Inter Mezzo wasn't interested in bringing rizado to market, he'd do it himself.

In front of him, Gorden shrugged. 'There's nothing stopping you from being the next Eli Lilly or Glaxo Smith Kline.' He gave Barker a caustic smile.

Barker returned it with a stony glare. 'Let's face it, it's speculation so far. An old witch became famous for a journal about herbs.'

Gorden must have realised Barker's fury because he prattled on. 'Listen, this is confidential. We have done solid research.'

This time Barker reeled in shock. 'With the rizado?'

'I can't divulge any more. We tested the rizado secretly, but we need more samples.'

'Where did you get it?'

Gorden clamped up again. He shook his head. 'I can't tell you. But the person who brought it to us showed signs of a remarkable recovery.'

'So rizado does work!' Barker stopped pacing and flung his head back onto his neck. 'Jesus. After all this time, the secret's revealed. Rizado may be a life-saver!'

'Calm down,' Gorden rose to his feet. 'Don't shout, I don't want anyone to hear about this.'

'Why? You scared the news will leak?'

Gorden opened his mouth to speak, but Barker threw his hands in the air between them. 'There're people who would kill to get their hands on the stuff.'

Nodding his head slowly, Gorden whispered, 'You're right. I'm sure they would.'

59

By the time María reached Fernando's house, dawn teased the horizon with a streaking silver aurora. She found Fernando and Madre outside kneeling beside a small mound of freshly turned over earth.

María glanced from Madre to Fernando.

He sobbed and banged his fists in the clods of soil while Madre patted his back to comfort him. María took a step forward, but a hand shot out behind her mother's back commanding her to keep away.

María stood still and waited until her mother stood and shuffled over to her. She grabbed María by her elbow and led her away. María opened her mouth to speak, but her mother's warning glance silenced her.

They were nearly home when Madre finally asked, 'Did you feed the animals?'

'Of course, Mama.'

'Then why are you here so early?'

'Because I have terrible news.'

'My news is worse. The poor woman fought all night. She had been in childbirth for hours before Fernando came home and wasn't able to get help.'

'What happened, Mama?'

'I tried to turn the *bebé* inside her, but she is a Portuguese woman with small hips. She is not one for raising children, too *frágil*. The *bebé* died before he was born.'

'Oh, Mama, I am so sorry.'

'Me too, Ana-María. Rarely do children die in my care.'

In the breaking dawn María saw her mother scrutinising her hands, turning them this way and that, as if to try to understand what they did wrong.

'What is it, Ana-María?'

María dropped her gaze, feeling guilty for spying on her mother. 'Nothing, Mama.'

'You came so early to tell me nothing?'

'Oh, no, I too have terrible news.' María's flustered words tangled themselves around her tongue. Her legs wanted to collapse beneath her as she stuttered, 'Let me give you some hot stew. And then I will explain.'

The story of the still-born child chilled her to the bone. This could bear bad *problemas* for Madre. She wanted to get her mother inside and warm her up before she told her of Tío's visit.

Things were getting worse.

60

After Barker left, with no fixed agreement between them, Gorden listened to his secretary's heels clicking across the oak floors. He had asked her to call Inter Mezzo in Copenhagen, the Europa agency that evaluated new medicinal products.

As he waited to be connected, he stood at the window with his hands clasped behind his back.

Working within the opulence of one of the most famous streets in London had its advantages. Compared to ever-bustling Oxford Circus a moment away, Harley Street was pleasantly peaceful.

The earlier downpour had abated, leaving a steady drizzle, but that wouldn't stop the tourists herding into the nearby fashion stores.

To his right, the balustrade balcony boasted an intricate pattern. It reminded him of one of Carbonela's drawings of rizado's frizzy leaves. What a mystery this plant had been. Years of speculation and failed attempts to find it, grow it and replicate it. The whole Wade saga had been a mess. Great that Gary had brought home the strange slime from Spain, but they didn't buy his story about a young girl healing his arm. But he got suspicious about their questions and started nosing around. Finding the 42A lab had been the straw that broke the crippled athlete's back.

Gorden's phone buzzer echoed around the office. He stepped over and lifted the receiver.

A voice on the other end barked, 'There's more rumours about rizado. What's going on over there?'

'Barker's close to finding it.'

'Speak up.' Lars Jurgen shouted.

'But there's a problem —.'

Jurgen interrupted, 'Put Olaf on the case, he'll find it before Barker does.'

Just hearing the name made a shiver spiral down Gorden's spine. As a bouncer turned professional liquidator, Olaf the Dutchman specialised in blotting out snitches. He had already left a trail of rizado bodies. Thankfully, the cops had never smelt a rat.

'Be careful, Jurgen, we can't afford to lose another lead.' Gorden fumed. Years ago Jurgen had decided Wade was trying to sell rizado on the black market. Before Gorden knew it, his new security analyst had topped it. He'd been pretty pissed off. 'Wade was our only link. I'm not losing the trail again!'

'Calm down Gordie!'

Gorden bit back his next remark. After they'd checked Wade's training schedule in Spain, he'd sent his scientists to several possible sources, but they'd come back empty-handed.

'You still on those blood pressure tablets?'

Gorden ignored Jurgen, and saw Barker emerge from their building. He watched him for a moment. Barker ran along the wet pavement trying to hail a cab. In amusement, Gorden saw him step into a puddle.

'You there?' Jurgen's voice bellowed down the line.

Shaking off his irritation, Gorden said in a softer tone, 'The results of the rizado tests have kept us waiting and hoping something would surface. Now Barker has a connection to it, we have to work with him to find it.'

Jurgen scoffed. 'No doubt his source is Wade's wife or sister. More likely the sister because of her connections on that stupid TV show.'

Gorden didn't want to agree with Jurgen so he kept quiet.

The German's harsh voice broke the silence, 'Find the rizado. I'll work out what to do with them.'

61

Almost two hours later, fuelled with caffeine, Kelby stepped on her beamer's accelerator. She headed down the country lanes, heading towards St Adelaide's Hospital. There was a chance Stacie was at the hospital with Annie.

A mist hung overhead, making the road barely visible. Kelby sipped her Costa coffee while her other hand rested on the top of the steering wheel. She hated that the new-car smell had long gone. It had been replaced with the scent of stale coffee, and Fat Cat's pee from his last vet trip. Both odours still clung to the back seat fabric. She made a mental note to get Jimmy to book a car valet.

Her thoughts zipped to the magazine blackening out Teresina's face. Then just as quickly, they fizzed to the police questioning. Her mind tried to connect the dots.

Someone must have killed Teresina and was after her.

Kelby veered up to the stop sign, but didn't stop. Instead, she slowed down, her glance darting in both directions. No cars so she accelerated.

Keeping one eye on the road ahead, she tapped her phone and listened to the endless ringing in her bluetooth headset.

'For God's sake, Stacie, pick up!'

She tried again. No answer.

A faint squeak that sounded like something rubbing under the bonnet filtered into her thoughts. Twitching her nose, she caught a burning odour coming from the passenger side. It smelt as though a plastic grocery bag was stuck to her exhaust.

Kelby peered into her left wing mirror.

Nothing different.

The road had tight curves and high banks up the side. If she pulled over, there was a risk someone would ram her from behind.

As she slowed to look for a lay-by, a silver rusting sports car hurtled up behind her. She signalled him to help her. When she caught sight of the boy racer, with his Lonsdale cap sitting side-saddle on his head, and a fag hanging precariously from the side of his mouth, she knew he wasn't the knight she needed. He revved his engine and gestured at her to move over.

Kelby gagged on the reek of burning rubber filling the car.

The boy racer pulled out in front of her. He held up his middle finger. His rusting bullet shot forward and disappeared around the corner.

'Bloody idiot!' she yelled at him.

At that moment the beamer hit an obstacle on the slick road.

62

Gorden coughed politely. Jurgen had remained silent for so long he' thought the German had hung up.

As chairman of one of the most respected European pharma associations, Jurgen got off on pressing people's buttons. Fair play to the man; he'd found huge success in a complicated industry.

Jurgen had set up his company with funding from the European Union and the pharmaceutical industry, as well as indirect subsidies from member states, to work with new European medicines coming onto the market. The IM's main responsibility was the protection and promotion of public health, through the evaluation and supervision of medicines.

Although the German had publicly stated his directive to secure the free movement of herbal medicinal products within the European Union, the bastard had no time for natural medicine.

Jurgen's voice broke into Gorden's thoughts, 'Where does MG stand on this? You've had scientists on this for years.'

'Trying to replicate it in secret hasn't been easy. The sample was too small. We used it up quickly.'

'There's cockroaches crawling all over this.'

'Good God, don't I know it. Some heretic die-hards think they've solved the mystery.'

'But you'll get there first,' Jurgen's tone turned menacing, 'won't you, Gordie?'

'Of course!'

'You still want it hitting the market?' Jurgen asked.

Gorden imagined himself wringing the German's neck. It was the only way he could deal with him. 'I've said this for a number of years now. I wanted to replicate it to analyse it. But I believe it should not reach the market.'

'Good! We have to stop them believing rizado will advance other treatments. If the public gets wind of this, there'll be uproar. They'll expect miracles. We have to cull this *schwein kraut* now before it takes down the industry.'

'What's the plan?'

'Get Olaf on Barker's tail. If he moves, we move.'

'Right away.'

'Olaf will sort it out. The bastard won't leave a footprint. Keep me updated.' Jurgen barked one last time and cut the call.

Slumping into his leather seat, Gorden dropped his phone into the cradle. He kicked the bottom drawer shut and spun his seat around to face the window.

The responsibility for rizado had fallen into his lap. His company wanted it found. Jurgen did too.

But for entirely different reasons.

63

After disabling the alarm by punching in the code, Barker entered Kelby's house. He stopped, listening to the sound of voices.

Strange. Kelby wasn't home. Annie was still in hospital, and Kelby had no other close family. And Hawk had finally left the house after searching it all morning and was now on his way to watch Kelby at her office. She didn't employ a housekeeper so he couldn't imagine who was talking.

He peered along the hallway. A blue haze emanated from a room at the end. He stalked towards it, treading lighter than a cat.

Fat people with heavy footsteps, he hated. Slim people who walked with grace, he loved.

At the door where the blue haze spilled onto the hallway rug, he stopped to listen. He slipped his nose through a crack in the door. One eye peered around the room, taking in everything.

Kelby must have forgotten to switch the damn thing off when she left home that morning.

Barker prodded the door open with his toe.

Meow!

He jumped back, expecting a cat at his heels. Peering into the darkened room, he could just make out the stupid fur-ball slumped on the top of the TV. He sidled towards the cat and stroked it. 'Here, pussy. Here, pussy.'

Being friends with the cat helped his next move.

First, he had to find the rizado. Though she'd been promised a bonus big enough to pay for nips and tucks across every part of her, Zelda hadn't managed to find contact details for the mysterious couple.

For the next hour Barker went through Kelby's home. Starting on the top floor, he searched through her bathroom cabinets and wardrobes. He slipped open her drawer of bras and smiled to himself. She had found his magazine message.

Next, he combed her office, rummaging through her desk drawers and filing systems.

Nothing.

Not finding what he was hunting for, he hated.

The cat. An idea struck him. One that would cause lots of pain and anguish.

To both Kelby and her sick niece.

64

For the tenth time since Barker had left him, Gorden stood at his office window. His hands, behind his back, played the snaking game, squirming around each other, releasing and coiling again.

He usually didn't let such things bother him. There'd been enough practice over the years. So many stinkers had stuck their sharp noses into Mata's business and he had to have them exterminated. If only he could do the same to Herman Schmidt. He had to find a way to blot him out, but right now he had other fish to fry.

Gorden spun around and dug in his top drawer. His hands shied away from the mobile phone as though a viper was about to strike him. He hated the thing. So intrusive. So demanding. So impersonal. Yet the stupid device created privacy for certain phone calls.

Finding Olaf's number made his lips curl. He wanted nothing to do with that man, but he didn't trust Barker any more than he trusted Jurgen.

Olaf answered on first dial. '*Ja*, Gordie.'

Gorden winced. Olaf had picked up the dratted nickname from the Jurgen bastard. Trying to ignore the rush of blood prickling the surface of his skin, he said in a calm voice. 'Tag three.'

The exterminator didn't need it spelt out. He knew the priorities.

Tag three. Observe.

Tag two. Threaten.

Tag one. Exterminate.

Gorden gave him details of where Barker would be and cut the call. He tossed the mobile back into the drawer, slammed it shut and ambled to the window.

Soon he'd know who Barker's informant was. And he intended going directly to the source.

65

Back in Kelby's kitchen, Barker glanced around. The pungent smell of burnt milk competed with the aromatic tang of coffee beans. He shook his head at the sink overflowing with coffee mugs and stained with sticky lumps of coffee granules.

He'd filled his own kitchen with mod-cons with easy-clean surfaces and microwave meals for the odd days he ate at home. None of this airy-fairy warmth and homely malarkey. His step-mother had been childless until he came along, so she'd never cottoned on to baking fresh bread or pies.

Barker scribbled something on the Post-It note lying on the counter and stepped back, smiling at his handiwork.

What a lovely soft pussy you have.

Maybe the cat's disappearance would get her to reveal her secrets. She might even spill the beans on rizado. And where he could get more.

But now he had other urgent tasks on the boil.

Kelby's car would pack up soon like Teresina's had done. He'd better hurry into the studio for his producers meeting so his alibi was solid.

Oh, lordy, lordy, lordy, these games he played with Kelby were intoxicating. Even Johnson stirred.

An idea struck Barker. Perhaps a quick workout for Johnson. He glanced around. Where could he leave his mark? Spurt on her office desk? How about on her kitchen counter where she'd prepare her next meal? Or in her bed and pull back the covers without her knowing? Maybe even leave them open.

Barker opened his fly and released Johnson.

So many enticing options.

66

Kelby glanced at her rear-view mirror. The mist had thickened so she couldn't see what she'd hit. Her hands trembled as the car shuddered through the steering wheel. It wobbled for a moment and suddenly the steering became heavy and difficult to control.

A perforation sound, similar to that of Annie's bicycle tyre puncturing, reverberated through her head.

Thankfully, the road was empty. Any earlier or later and she'd have been caught up in the school run or mummy-coffee-morning traffic.

Kelby hung onto the steering wheel as the car slewed to the left. Gripping tightly with both hands, she used all her strength and energy to keep the vehicle facing forward. It refused, pulling to one side, and drifting into the opposite lane. Kelby yanked the wheel to correct the steering. Her handbag flew off the passenger seat, spilling its contents, and her gym bag dropped into the foot-well. Kelby ignored them as she battled with the steering.

A loud bang startled her.

The noise was unlike anything she had ever heard. Kelby thought the car was exploding beneath her.

Then came a whoosh. Flap. Flap. Flap. Flap.

Black hailstones of rubber flew in every direction. Kelby's scream rose above the metal rim grinding and scraping along the slippery tarmac. Without thinking, Kelby lifted her foot off the accelerator. Instead of slowing down, the car plummeted forward.

She slammed on the brakes.

For a split second, the car swung in imbalance. Kelby watched in horror as it swerved and fishtailed out of control. She screamed again as the car dived into a 360-degree spin.

The BMW shot up the muddy left bank.

Kelby held her breath in terror. The car nose-dived back onto the road. It shot across both carriageways and plummeted down the embankment. Its bonnet crashed through a farmer's fence and its wing mirror shattered.

The car slammed into a tree. Its impact shunted Kelby forward. The air bag hissed as it exploded out of the dashboard with a loud crunch of breaking plastic and snap of buckling dashboard.

The huge stiff balloon struck Kelby's head, slamming her mouth against her teeth. The sting felt as though someone had slapped her face with a large rubber band.

With the putrid smell of fuel in her nostrils, Kelby blacked out.

67

As the full moon lit her path through the woods, María glided through the night. In her mind she created stories of a young girl being a goddess to wild animals.

Like her new *femella*, her own ears were ripe for the sound of someone in need.

Before the Inquisition had taken full force, Tío and his *mishpacha* had slipped away in the dead of night. She missed him and his wise acceptance of a woman's importance to the village. One day he would get word to her. Of that she was sure; he kept his promises.

When Tío had left and panic spread to their village, María had insisted on gathering the rizado at night to prevent strangers seeing her carrying bunches of smelly herbs. She wasn't afraid of the dark; she was more afraid of what would happen if the Inquisition found out about Madre.

Or her.

María lived with a secret fear. The story about a woman healer who had created a secret potion that cured any ailment worried her. Every day María rose early to pray the journal had never made it to Barcelona. To compensate for her stupid *errare* she did her chores far quicker than she had ever done. Madre often gave her a suspicious frown and laughed it off as her daughter being overly protective.

Before going to collect more rizado she had stewed another chicken. She learnt as a child to rub sage and rosemary into the meat to bring out its flavour.

Ambling along the meadow towards her *finca*, María gazed around the moonlit farm with pride. Outbuildings sprawled around the cottage. Long shadows from the animal sheds reached out and moulded their distorted fingers onto the farm's most revered outhouse — Padre's workshop.

After Padre had been trapped in a building collapse, Madre had refused to clear out his tools. She often sat amongst his things and talked to his spirit. Her mother even said that when she spoke to Padre, a turtle dove appeared nearby. Madre told her these birds only had one mate. Sometimes Madre said strange things.

Candlelight inside the cottage twinkled at María through the shutters, welcoming her to a broad thatched home with smoke wafting through the louvre. Yet the overhanging thatch suddenly seemed to lean to one side and frown at her.

The front door stood ajar.

María's pulse quickened. Madre always insisted on the door being shut to keep the fire's heat inside. Then raucous laughter spilled from the cottage. María stopped dead in her tracks.

Men.

Only horrible men laughed that way. Loud and vulgar. The harsh tones disturbed the peace.

These were not the sounds of *amigos*.

Panic gripped her.

Where was Mama?

68

Kelby came round to the sounds of voices. Disoriented for a few seconds, with a loud ringing in her ears, she struggled to breathe.

An acrid smell hung in the air, suspended amidst dust that had blasted out of the air-bag. Kelby coughed and spluttered. The air-bag had deflated almost as fast as it had inflated and it now hung limp between her legs.

Through slitted eyes, she glanced at the destruction. Her beamer's bonnet was embedded in a tree, hissing and fizzing in the afternoon drizzle.

A man and woman peered in at her. The woman asked, 'Can you hear me?'

Kelby nodded.

'Do you remember what happened?'

She nodded again, still groggy and trying to recall the details.

'I'm Janet. I'm a first aider. Me and Brian are going to get you out of the car.'

Kelby whispered, 'Thank you.'

'Can you feel any pain?'

'My head hurts.'

Janet said, 'Yes, hun, you've got a nasty bump on your forehead. Anything else?'

Kelby shook her head, smelling fuel. 'Petrol ...'

Brian opened her door and released her seat belt. "The crash may have jammed some metal into the fuel tank so we've got to get away from the car, just in case.'

Janet said to Brian, 'The smell does seem to be getting stronger.'

He glanced at the bonnet. 'The fuel line may be sheared.'

'Will it explode?'

'Not sure, but if a cut fuel line sprays fuel around on hot metal, it could be enough to start a fire.' He lifted Kelby out of her seat. 'Come on, let's go.'

Kelby started trembling; even her teeth chattered uncontrollably.

Janet clutched Kelby's hands. 'It's okay, dear, you're in shock. The ambulance will be here any minute.'

'Here,' Brian steadied her, 'let me put my arm under yours.'

Kelby's legs buckled under her so Brian sat her back into her car seat.

'Let me check your legs.' Janet prodded her legs and lifted her arms. 'No bleeding.' She peered at her front and back clothing, asking, 'Can I take a quick look?'

Kelby nodded, closing her eyes as Janet lifted her shirt to examine her stomach and back. 'A few bruises, but thankfully, no bleeding. When the paramedics get here, they'll do a full check of those bruises to be sure there's no internal bleeding.'

Brian exhaled hard, 'Phew. Let's get you away from the car.'

While Brian guided her, Kelby stepped gingerly away from the carcass of her car. Around her lay shattered glass. A shredded tyre. The bonnet concertinaed into the tree. The fence had scraped the doors and battered her wing mirrors into a pulp.

Instinctively, Janet grabbed Kelby's bags out of the passenger foot-well.

Brian held his arm around her shoulders as she struggled to walk. 'You sure there's no pain?'

'No. I just feel wobbly.' Kelby stumbled away from her crashed car in a daze.

Suddenly the air was sucked into a deep, hollow voomp. They spun around.

Clouds of black smoke hovered over the car. A cacophony of sounds came from under the bonnet. Clanging and popping where nuts and bolts in the engine burst. Whistles of hot air searing pipes. Bangs and booms from hot metal expanding as a few rogue flames licked at the bonnet. Glass shattered and clattered to the ground.

Brian shoved them forward, 'Come on! Quick!'

As they scrambled away, flames shot out, engulfing the vehicle in a mist of thick black smoke and bright orange flames.

Kelby glanced over her shoulder. The text threats flashed through her mind. The magazine graffiti. The news of Teresina's accident. At first, the stalker seemed to be toying with her, as Fat Cat would slap around a wounded rat in her garden. Yet, like a slow burn, he had ramped up the heat.

Now he intended to kill her.

69

Olaf flexed his biceps and studied his tattoos. The red dragon was by far the best. It brightened his bulging muscle, bringing attention to it everywhere he went.

He glanced at Barker's mansion. No movement for the past hour.

He had only been watching Barker for a day, but already interesting cockroaches had come out of the woodwork. Barker, the cat and a devil. Interesting.

Settling down for the night in his new Lexus, Olaf thought about his former life. Being a bouncer had its benefits. Busty tramps in tight mini-skirts desperate to get into an exclusive club would do just about anything. A quickie around the corner in the dark alley would buy their night's entrance. A joust up the *aars* bought them a month's free ride. But he'd left that life.

Being a pharma rat exterminator paid higher bonuses. This job paid twice. First, Gorden gave him a pile of cash, then, when he took the same information to Jurgen, the old bastard paid as well. Luckily, he had sussed neither trusted the other.

Now he didn't have to take any old clubbing slut up the back.

Picky. He loved that English word. He'd become picky. Money could get anything. If he wanted to admire a red dragon while he bent over some slut, he ordered it. The escort agency had a long list of tarts with dragons tattooed on their backs.

But being an exterminator had its downsides. No gambling with the other bouncers to see which slut wanted a month's club entry. No quickie around the corner to spike up his night.

Glancing at his Rolex, Olaf sighed. It was going to be a boring night.

Yet his *animaal* instincts were calling.

70

Kelby's eyes fluttered open. The constant flurry of activity had woken her. Machines beeped. A medicine trolley rattled past. Patients coughed, their families offering them soft whispers of reassurance. Somewhere along the corridor a baby cried. As a machine alarm went off, a nurse's feet shuffled with her shoes squeaking on the floor.

From the bed alongside hers, a persistent rush of air tunnelled into someone's chest every few seconds. It was followed by a subtle sucking sound and a long gurgle. Kelby grimaced, imagining blood and pus being sucked out. She wanted to roll onto her side, away from the sounds, but her body ached too much to move.

Everything was a blur. A nightmare where she couldn't escape. She began to recall the accident, the two people helping her get away from her car, being brought to the Surrey County hospital by ambulance.

A reek of vomit mingled with detergent and body odour wafted around her. The air hissed as a nurse sprayed sanitiser to remove the smell of misery and sickness and despair.

Kelby closed her eyes again; it was easier to keep them closed.

'What are the baseline obs please, Karen?'

'Pulse 80 and regular, BP 120 over 70, O2 sats 98% on air, resp rate 14 and GCS 15.'

Kelby's eyes shot open to find Doctor Robson leaning over her.

'You again!'

'I get around.'

She smiled at his wriggling eyebrows. 'You've left St Adelaide's?'

'No. I consult privately there. My NHS practice is here.' He glanced at his watch, 'In fact, I was leaving when I saw you lying here. Thought you might be relieved to see a familiar face.'

'Thank you.'

Karen glanced between the two of them, fiddled with the knobs on a machine beside her bed and showed him some notes.

After he had finished taking her pulse and scrutinising the bump on her forehead, he asked, 'Can we call your husband to help you home?'

'Why do I need a husband?'

'Okay. So, no husband. Anyone else?' His eyebrows moved up and down his forehead.

Those eyebrows again! She wanted to reach out and hold them still. 'I don't need anyone to chaperone me. I'm perfectly capable —'

'If you stop chattering, and listen for a moment, I will explain.' He waited, watching her face.

Feeling like a naughty child who'd been scolded, she nodded.

'You're pretty shaken and you shouldn't be alone. I could keep you in here for the night to check on you.'

She threw her hand in the air, her fingers quoting a headline. 'Prisoner Wade held hostage. Her crime: being a lonely old hag. Her punishment: locked in hospital for the night.'

His chest expanded as he straightened.

They stared at each other.

Finally, she gave in and whispered, 'I'll call Hawk.'

'Your …' he shook his head hoping she'd finish the sentence, but she couldn't think of how to describe Hawk. Maybe she should fess up and tell the doctor about the threats and Teresina's murder.

'Good night, Kelby. We'll give you a sheet on post-head injury advice and precautions to heed at home.'

As he turned, he pulled the curtain back around her cubicle bed and said softly so only she could hear, 'We wouldn't want anyone recognising you, now, would we?'

Kelby's cheeks flared. With a dull drumbeat thumping inside her head, she muttered, 'I have to get out of here.'

No way was she staying the night in hospital. Even if she wasn't safe at home. She should call Hawk, but she needed someone close to be with right now.

Only one person outside her family fitted the bill.

71

Kelby watched Jimmy packing her things and mumbled, 'Thank you for collecting me. I couldn't face asking Stacie.'

'Sure, but you've gotta listen to your man in the white coat. He knows what's best. Everything he said back there could happen. You could be alone and get a dizzy spell and no-one would know.'

'You're normally not a drama queen, Jimmy. Don't listen to him.'

It took ages to be discharged and collect her belongings. When at last the nursing staff handed over her briefcase and gym bag, Kelby dived in and checked her laptop.

'Phew. I had visions of it being cracked.'

'That's all you're worried about?' Jimmy grabbed it from her and shoved it back into the briefcase.

'Can you get me a hire for a few days until we sort out my car?'

'Kelby, I drove past your beamer on the way here. *That* will not be fixed any time soon. Consider it a write-off! Besides, you have Big Boy.' He stopped packing her things and swivelled his head to frown at her. 'Why didn't you call him? He should've taken you to find Stacie.'

Her teeth went into action and scrubbed along her thumb nail while she considered her options. 'You know what Stacie's reaction would have been.'

Jimmy rolled his eyes with suspicion. 'Come on, let's get you home. The Big Boy will be worried sick about you.'

'Later. We're going to see Annie first.'

'You heard what your man said. Home, bed, rest. I'll cancel your meetings for the next few days.'

'Thanks Jimmy. But I have to see Annie first.'

'Okay, a quick visit. But then you'd better keep out of trouble.'

72

Kelby hobbled out of the lift. She normally took the stairs to Annie's ward, but her whole body still ached. She shuffled close to the wall so she didn't topple over.

Jimmy was right; she needed to rest, but Annie always came first. Jimmy had stayed in the car to call off her meetings.

When Kelby limped into her niece's room, she found Roy examining the charts while Annie slept peacefully.

A sensation of pleasure belted through Kelby.

'Hello again.' Roy whispered, 'I thought as much. Can't put you to bed, can we?'

'What's wrong with visiting my niece before going home to rest?' She smiled and stroked Annie's thin leg over the hospital blanket. 'What are *you* doing here?'

He tapped on Annie's charts. 'Annie's doctors have treated her asthma symptoms with inhaled corticosteroids.'

Kelby glanced at the notes, not understanding any of them.

'Mm,' Roy mumbled, 'although they're the preferred treatment for young children, they can possibly slow —' He stopped in mid-sentence and cleared his throat. 'You know I shouldn't be discussing Annie's treatment with you.'

She stared at him, her eyes pleading for help.

He lowered his voice, 'Have you worked out her triggers?'

'Yes.' She whispered, 'Sadly for poor Annie, it's pets, and she so desperately wants a kitten or a puppy. Even a rabbit.'

'And pollen from grass and flowers?'

'Not as bad as pets, but yes, they're there too. And smoke.' Kelby glanced over her shoulder, then whispered, 'I keep telling her mother to stop smoking. She has a fag as she gets here and hugs Annie reeking of smoke.'

'That may be an irritant. She may not actually be allergic to it —'

'I know! But it does bother her. Like her skin,' Kelby pointed at Annie's hands, 'Sometimes the red, scaly skin gets thick patches of white scales. She gets so upset about it.'

'There's no way of predicting the next flare-up. And worrying about it will get Annie to pick up on the anxiety. A laid-back approach is best.'

Kelby touched his hand, forcing him to look directly into her eyes. 'What can I do? I can't stand seeing her in this state.' Her voice was barely a whisper, 'Ever since her father —'

Roy put his hand on her arm. 'I know. It's a terrible worry.'

'The doctor said the stress of Gary's death caused the eczema.' She cleared her throat, 'Annie didn't know the ins and outs. She just knew her daddy wasn't coming home anymore.'

Kelby watched as he moved effortlessly around Annie. Without waking her, he checked her drip and the tubes going into her nose.

'Anaphylaxis is the worst. With Annie's weak heart, a severe allergic reaction can cause respiratory arrest.'

'At least it's not likely to kill her.'

His look showed her how wrong she was.

73

Still searching around their home for her mother, María's breath jumped in rapid gulps. She crept across the cobbled toft on which Padre had built their home. Madre would have tried to escape if soldiers came to their house.

Her mother's soft melodious tone would single itself out from the crude voices. Although some of the shutters were rotting, María strained to peek through them into the narrow windows. As she tiptoed backwards, around the rear of the house she bumped into something.

¡Bah!

María sighed in relief. The water barrel, almost empty after a poor winter's rainfall, stood in her way. She ducked behind it and headed towards the front door.

Suddenly someone booted the door wide open. María slipped back into the shadows and sneaked behind Padre's workshop. Her dry mouth felt as if she'd eaten a sheet of her writing paper. Standing in the dim light from the front door, the soldier, wearing a leather jerkin, fiddled at his groin.

¡Uf!

María slapped her hands against her cheeks and watched in shock as he relieved himself right on their doorstep. Within plain sight of the privy!

After a few vile body noises, the leather jerkin soldier went inside.

María wondered if Madre was hiding in the underground cellar. Padre had built it to store the wild boar and buck he smoked or salted after being paid in livestock by local villagers for building more rooms onto their homes. As if he were creating a treasure trove, he had buried it inside the back of the stable. As a child María had loved to hide in there. Now it shrouded the second copy of the herbal journal. And the rizado papers she had removed from the copy Tío sent to Barcelona.

But it would have taken Madre too long to lift the heavy wooden door, scramble down the stone steps and secure it quietly behind her.

With the stealth of a snake, María slunk between the donkey's stable, the goat's shelter, the pig stye, and the hen and goose houses. The animals recognised her light tread and didn't cry in alarm. In the day the animals grazed in the lower croft, but María penned them in at night, especially the hens and geese, to keep them safe from wild animals.

Careful not to bump into the pile of firewood or step on any of the sprouting vegetables and sprawling herbs in Madre's garden, María searched the bake house in the middle of the croft. A heavy feeling in her stomach made her nauseous. Her mother was nowhere to be found.

¡Por dios! By God, what will I do now?

Trembling, María took sanctuary behind Padre's workshop and picked at the splintered wood. She watched the cottage for a long time and listened for her mother's voice.

Finally, it came.

In a piercing scream.

74

Kelby swallowed the lump in her throat. She couldn't stand the thought of any more harm coming to her family.

Roy cleared his throat. 'I'm not trying to frighten you.'

She dropped her chin and peered at him over the rim of her glasses. 'Or to get me to try your herbs?'

He chuckled. 'When we find rizado, it would be great to try it on Annie's skin.'

Kelby tried to get a word in, but he protested again.

'Seriously, Kelby, she's on the wrong treatment.' He tapped the charts again. 'I won't interfere. Get her mum to talk to the doctor. It's not good seeing her vitality crushed by what they're pumping into her. Try natural alternatives.'

'I've been saying this for ages, but I can't get Stacie to agree.'

'I'm not an expert on sister-in-law relationships so I can't help there.'

A smile tugged at Kelby's lips. He had obviously heard the rumours of bust ups with Stacie. 'What else can I do?'

Roy said, 'I can authorise new tests if that's okay with you.'

Kelby nodded, 'Yes, please.'

'And make sure there are no triggers at home. Get her outside as much as possible to adjust to what's around her. She must learn to live normally, without being cocooned inside.'

Kelby's face lit up as though seeing the light for the first time.

'Being vigilant with Annie's skin protection is vital. But there's so many other benefits, such as natural vitamin D found in sunlight.'

'We could all do with a dose of that.'

'She has a lovely little personality.' Roy came closer.

That first spark that connected them on the plane twined around them one more time.

'You're so good with kids.'

The thread became taut and Kelby wanted to sit and talk to him without any interruptions.

'Probably from growing up with two kid sisters. Annie needs to get out there and take life by the horns.'

'Funnily enough, she has been talking about a bull. She has this imaginary friend who lives near a waterfall and is going to teach her to swim. She said May-ree has hidden secret treasure beside her bull in a cave ...'

Roy frowned at her. 'May-ree?'

Kelby read his expression and chuckled. 'Not the same one, obviously.'

'But a strange coincidence.'

75

A shiver crept along Kelby's back as though a droplet of water was meandering down the rocky path between her spine nodules.

'Has Annie had visions in the past?'

Kelby thought for a moment and said, 'She has lots of friends, they come and go. I've always encouraged her to speak to her dad. It helped me as a kid to get over the loss of my parents.'

'Yes, talking to their loved ones can be healing for people. It's good for her to know he's there.'

The thread between them tightened again.

She smiled at him. 'So you believe in that?'

'I haven't had any experience myself, but lots of my patients have told me similar stories.' He puffed out his chest. "Besides, I've grown up between two cultures. My Spanish family are religious; the other side are the opposite.'

'I'm neutral. I feel Gary around me a lot of the time, especially when I'm stressed. But it hasn't made me run off to a séance or anything weird. I prefer to keep my beliefs and feelings private.'

'That's the best way.'

Kelby suddenly recalled Annie's big secret chat. Goosebumps rose on her skin. 'Come to think of it, she did tell me something weird ...' Her voice faded as she tried to recall Annie's words. 'At the time, I didn't make a connection, but —' Kelby looked into his eyes. Her jaw dropped.

'What?'

'She told me her friend's waterfall is a secret place no-one has ever seen.' Kelby's fingers pressed against her forehead as she strained to remember Annie's exact words.

'That gives me an eerie feeling of déjà vu.'

Kelby stared at him through her fingers. 'Um. What did Annie say?' Silence hung in the room for a long moment. Then, Annie's words floated into Kelby's mind, slowly like the first drops of snow. 'Annie said her friend's waterfall is inside a cave. She gave me a picture of it. Jimmy is getting it framed for me.'

'A waterfall inside a cave.' Roy looked thoughtful for a moment. 'I wonder if …' He reached out and laid a hand on Kelby's arm. 'Could it be?'

'I don't know. But Annie said her friend drew a map and hid it inside her book bag. She said her friend's book bag was old-fashioned, but similar to her own school bag.'

Still reeling from shock, Kelby's head swayed from side to side in slow motion. 'I wonder if the rizado map is hidden inside the book!'

Roy took her arm, 'Come on, there's only one way to find out.'

Once in the car park, Roy marched her to Jimmy's car. 'Jimmy, I'm taking this bruised and battered patient home. She needs rest.'

Jimmy looked up in surprise. 'What about Hawk?'

'I'll call him.' Kelby opened the back door and retrieved her briefcase and gym bag. At least she could take off her suit and change into something comfier. She came around to Jimmy's window, his eyes wide. 'I'll be at home if you need me.'

'Grand. Just what the doctor ordered.'

Roy waved at Jimmy as he drove off. He turned to Kelby. 'Hawk? I thought you didn't have a hubby.'

'He's my security guard.'

'What?'

'I should've told you. I was having Twitter threats. At first I thought it was a bozo thinking he was clever to frighten me, but after you told me about rizado, his threats got worse.'

'My God! Kelby, I'm so sorry.'

'What for? It's not your fault.'

'By telling you, this has somehow escalated. Do you trust Jimmy?'

'With my life.'

'So, if it's not him, who?'

'That's why Hawk is watching my house.'

'You'll be safe with me.' He stopped her strolling beside him with a hand on her arm. 'Are you sure you still want to find out if Annie is right about Ana-María's map? You've got a lot going on, and now you've seen the risks.'

Kelby exhaled. 'I'm prepared to take those risks. I need to find out who killed Gary. And why.'

76

Sitting beside Roy in Costa, Kelby listened to the clattering of the pouring rain against the windows. It splattered over the street lantern, making it look like an illuminated shower cubicle on the pavement. Gushing water swept along the streets and cascaded into the gutters.

The ambient sound of pouring rain with water dripping from the roof reminded Kelby of her mother. Adelaide Wade had loved the rain and used to dance in it with Kelby and Gary. It was her mother's way of teaching her children to accept the miserable weather.

Inside, the day's bustle had slowed down with only late commuters shrugging off the weather for a coffee or sandwich on their way home.

When checking the chalk boards with brightly coloured coffee and chocolate options, Kelby had been sorely tempted to divert from her regular course of coffee. But in haste she had ordered her favourite Colombian. Now she absentmindedly ran her finger around a coffee stain ring on the wooden table. As her eyes fixed on the leather pouch tucked inside Roy's open briefcase, she thought Roy's café macchiato looked too small.

Huddling over the book, they stared at it. After a long moment, Roy lifted the leather pouch but left his briefcase lid open so any nearby coffee drinkers wouldn't see the contents. 'Give it a go.'

She looked at him in surprise. 'But it's your book.'

'I know, but you remembered Annie's secret. Go on, have the honours.'

Kelby's hand rested on the mottled leather book. After a moment, she held it by the large knot. She lifted the book from inside and gently placed it inside Roy's briefcase. Next, she lay the girdle bag between them and looked into Roy's eyes.

He smiled at her, showing his encouragement. They leaned over the bedraggled looking leather skin. Kelby opened it and stretched it from corner to corner. The base, which held the inner book, had been sewn into a watertight wrapper. As before, the book electrified her.

When she'd first touched it, she had felt a slight bump somewhere. The soft inner skin felt creamy under her fingertips. Near the top where the strip of calf pelt joined into the knot, the leather bunched up. Stroking each section with long separate lines, Kelby studied the leather binding. Then her heart skipped a beat.

Her finger caught a tiny ripple. She leaned right over and whispered, 'Here, take a look.'

Roy's fingers joined hers, caressing the soft leather. She clutched his hand, guiding it to the small nodule near the handle's knot. 'Feel that?'

He nodded, excitement lighting his face.

Kelby tugged the mottled skin closer, tucking it between them. In the dim light, she squinted at the leather, examining it carefully. Suddenly, she gasped and exclaimed, 'There! Look, there's some kind of seam sewn into the handle.'

Roy grabbed his phone and pressed a button. In an instant, light shone onto the leather. Kelby held the knot under the beam. Together, they stared at a tiny pouch sewn almost invisibly into the leather flap.

The author's secret radiated under her fingertips.

77

'Roy,' Kelby whispered, 'this means Annie … Annie …' Kelby couldn't find the words.

'I know.' His gaze locked with hers.

For a long moment, they stared at each other.

'How can we unpick it? We can't risk damaging what's inside.'

'Here.' Roy held up the knife he had used to butter his toasted bun.

'But that will rip it.'

He ran his thumb along the blade. 'It's not nearly sharp enough.'

Kelby delved into her briefcase and rummaged around. After a minute, she exclaimed, 'Yes!' Lifting a keyring, she smiled triumphantly at Roy.

His brows puckered as he asked, 'Keys?'

'No, silly.' She held it in the air and pointed at a Swiss army knife dangling on the keyring. 'This was my dad's. When he passed away Gary treasured it. Strangely enough, just before he went cycling in Spain, he gave it to me, telling me one day it would come in handy.'

'Too right he was.'

Kelby dumped the keys beside Roy and ran her fingers along the line of thread. She wriggled it until it loosened enough to see a tiny loop in the stitch. Then, she splayed out her palm to Roy and said, 'Scalpel.'

'Pardon?'

'Scalpel. You know, the army knife.'

'Ahh, sorry, doctor. I'm new to this.' His smile lit his face as he fumbled with the army knife, and finally de-tangled it from the keyring. Then, he slapped it into her still outstretched palm. 'Scalpel.'

Kelby grinned. Using the tip of the knife, she slid it under the loop of thread and severed it. Searching for the next stitch with her fingertips, she repeated the process until there were more loops visible.

'Phew.' Kelby exhaled the tension in her chest. 'This is mind-numbing. I'm so scared I'll damage what's inside.'

'You're doing a great job. You should've been a surgeon.'

After each tiny stitch was loosened, she slit them with the army knife. Eventually, a thin line of broken thread revealed a hidden pocket. 'Now what?' She looked at him, his nose close to hers.

'Go in, Doctor Wade.' His warm breath brushed her cheeks.

Her fingers ghosted over the soft leather, tracing the line of broken thread. Sticking her index finger into the hole, she poked around inside, careful not to sever any other stitching.

The tip of her finger touched something soft inside, sending an electric shock through her. 'Roy!' she cried out. 'Something's inside.'

78

With Madre's scream ringing in her ears, María bolted out of her hiding place, raced to the cottage door and peered inside. Three soldiers sat beside the kitchen table eating the stew she had made earlier.

They had tight hose tucked in calf-high Moorish boots of red Moroccan leather, but one had removed his boots to dry his toes. Despite the warmth from the fire, a cloaked soldier had a blue wrap draped over his shoulders. At his feet, her mother lay crumbled in a heap, naked.

For a split second María's breathing suspended. Then, she burst inside, shrieking, '¡*Dios santo!* God, what have you done to Mama!'

The leather jerkin soldier roared, 'Who the hell are you?'

María fell at her mother's feet. A terrible acrid smell, similar to charcoal-burnt bread, caught in her nose.

Her mother's eyes flashed with determination as she whispered, 'Keep your promise to me, María. And don't tell them who you are.'

Streaks of dirt smeared her mother's face where a cross had been cut into her flesh in the middle of her forehead. Her wimple had gone and in its place her chemise had been wrapped around her head like a turban.

'Is this your son?' The leather jerkin soldier jabbed the toe of his boot between Madre's legs. He swung around and kicked María in the stomach with his heavy boot.

María clutched her sides, her breath knocked out of her. Muscle spasms rocked through her, making her swoon. She squeezed her eyes shut tightly against the ache in her stomach and struggled to catch her breath. After a few minutes she gasped, 'Why are you doing this?'

'She is a witch and must be punished.'

'No! Mama delivers babies. She does nothing else. My father was a respected stonemason in Granada. His skills were requested at Cerro de las Torres, and the Alora Castle on the hill.'

'*Silencio!*'

'But you must listen, his skilful trade was also procured for building the Alcazaba in Antequera. And the Alhambra Palace. He was a person of authority. Such a man would not have a witch for a wife.'

'There are signs of witchcraft here.' He pointed to her mother's basket. 'I see potions and *medicina*. And there are chickens and pigs outside and even a goat to sacrifice.'

As María wiped the back of her hand across her sweating forehead, Padre's cap fell off and revealed her long bronzed locks.

'Ah, hah! A young woman dressed as a man.' The unbooted soldier sucked the stew's juices off his fingers and said, 'So you must be the heretic Ana-María de Carbonela.'

María stared at him. How did they know her name?

Leather jerkin kicked her shins when she didn't answer. 'You're not fit to dress as a man. Only men have the balls to fill breeches. Dressing as a man will see you burned!'

79

With a precise, yet slow tug, Kelby drew out another piece of calf skin leather, tucked inside like a crumpled, dog-eared business card. She stared at it and then at Roy.

'Open it!'

Kelby obeyed, lifting the top corners first. The skin had been folded over a few times. Picking at each layer, she opened the leather wad into a square, half the size of a paperback book.

Kelby and Roy stared at it for a moment, then Kelby said, 'It's true.' She shone his torch onto the ancient leather strip covered with inked markings.

Roy threw his arms around her, squeezing her close. Then he took her head in his hands and placed his lips on her forehead, giving her a warm, squashy kiss. 'You did it, Kelby, you found Ana-María's map. Now we can find rizado!'

Kelby didn't move. She wanted to stay awash with the glow of this special moment. Time stood still. The gossamer link wove a web around them, once again uniting them in the book's enigma.

Suddenly a thrumming vibrated through Kelby's veins. Feeling overwhelmed by the lure of Roy's magnetic energy, and the tug of the map's mystery, Kelby shook herself and pulled back.

She couldn't explain the curious hold the book had on her. Ana-María's shadow lingered over the map, pulling Kelby's attention back to the inked markings.

The tip of her index finger traced across the top of the map and stopped on an arrow beside the word: Antequera. 'Those look like mountains. And these are probably trees.' She pointed to little upside down V marks. Shapes of trees were dotted around a central point where a river gushed out and down through the bottom of the map. Above the river, a large dark hole took prime position in the middle of the map.

Suddenly, Roy gripped Kelby's arm. His steady gaze pierced into her. 'Kelby, let's go and find the grotto.'

She stared back, aghast. 'You have patients to see.'

'I can work miracles.'

'Maybe you can, but I have a business to run.'

He smiled mischievously. 'Okay, okay, I fess up. I'm off for the next two weeks. Marina wanted to see what's happening with the dig. And I wanted to study the herbal journal. Now's the perfect chance. We're flying back in the early hours.'

'Tomorrow?' Kelby frowned.

'I can't believe the time.' He tapped his wrist watch. 'Costa will be closing soon.'

She peered around. The dimly lit coffee shop had emptied and the staff were cleaning up.

'We've been here for hours. Let me buy you a quick bite at the pub over the road, they'll be open for another hour.'

The more time she spent with him, the less clumsy he became. And the less his eyebrows wiggled.

'You coming?'

Kelby's heart fluttered. The thought of being far away from London with this man gave her the jitters.

'Besides, you're supposed to be in bed tomorrow. You can pull a sickie, I'm sure the boss won't mind.'

Her eyes twinkled. 'I don't have a flight.'

'Let me see what I can do. Maybe Marina will sacrifice her seat. She wants you to help her with this.'

'What about my hubby?'

'Your hubby?' His faced dropped.

'Hawk.' She tried to hold a straight face, but couldn't hold back a smile. 'I'll tell him I did judo at school. That'll impress him.'

She chuckled, still not sure if Hawk would buy that, after someone had broken into her house right under his nose.

Roy still stared at her, his eyes questioning.

For a dizzy moment, she had the urge to let off a scream. Instead, with a racing pulse and a half-smile, Kelby said, 'Okay, Rob Roy. Let's go and find the grotto.'

80

With map in hand, Kelby and Roy headed out of Malaga airport. He had managed to wangle changing Marina's ticket to accommodate Kelby. They only had time to rush home for her to collect her passport.

It had taken a lot of persuading to get Hawk to accept her plan. Roy by her side, and her being anonymous in Spain helped, but Hawk argued the stalker would know her movements no matter where she was. Eventually, Roy had convinced him, for the time being, she was safe with him. Now, with the sun slanting in at her, she peeled off her tracksuit top and flapped her t-shirt. 'I love this weather. The worst thing about back home is never seeing blue skies.'

She cracked open the can of Fanta Limón and passed it to Roy. For herself, she twisted open a bottle of cappuccino and took a long swig.

Heading up the Cordoba motorway, Roy pointed out landmarks along the way. 'I must take you to Antequera sometime.'

Surrounded by mountains on both sides of the road, Kelby slouched in the hired car, listening to his soothing voice.

'It's known as the heart of Andalusia, because it's so central to Málaga, Granada, Córdoba, and Seville.'

Kelby couldn't stop caressing the calf skin map. It made the trouble worthwhile.

'The town's partly Roman and partly Moorish.' He glanced at her and back to the road. 'If you love this medieval stuff, you'll love Antequera's two Bronze Age burial mounds.'

She opened the map and studied it. 'Do you know where we're going?'

'No, but we have clues.' He indicated to turn off the motorway at Casabermeja and drove under it, heading into the countryside. Roy pointed at the unusual graveyard. 'They're famous for burying their dead standing up.'

White headstones stood upright, facing in one direction, as if the occupants were gazing down the valley towards Colmenar, keeping their eyes off the northern mountain peaks. Behind the cemetery, a large sixteenth century church tower dominated the town. The mountains that had cocooned her only minutes ago suddenly disappeared, and Kelby studied the contrast where hills, trees and fields merged. 'It's so green here. I imagined it to be dusty and dry.'

'This part of Andalucia is exceptionally beautiful. Look.' He pointed at the huge rocky outcrop in the distance. 'There's Sierra del Torcal.'

'No wonder Ana-María drew it like that on the map. It looks like a solid chunk of rock.' The mountain made Kelby think of a long table and she muttered, 'It's like a king's banquet table.'

Roy chuckled. 'More like a rock climber's dream. Marina's uncle runs a fancy spa retreat up there. I'll get you the most fantastic hot stones treatment you've ever had!'

They wound between meandering hills. Farmhouses, sprinkled here and there, had white plastered walls with red tiled roofs. Many surrounded a central courtyard and shaded patios. Several grander rustic homes featured turrets and towers with romantic balconies and wrought iron detailing.

A bronzed man in overalls chaperoned a herd of goats. Roy slowed to let them pass. As Kelby leaned out, an earthy stink hit the back of her throat, rendering a sensation of eating goat's cheese.

A few kids bucked and horned each other. Some of the milking females struggled by with swollen teats dangling between their legs. Before she could stop herself, Kelby muttered, 'God, I thought mine were bad!'

Roy flushed a deep tomato shade. Letting him blush in peace, Kelby sipped on the dregs of her coffee and placed the empty container in her bag. She loved Roy's sweet nature and old-fashioned manners.

The thought of going back home and not being with him all the time saddened her. More than that, the gravity of finding the truth about Gary's death weighed heavily on Kelby. She tried not to think about the rizado murders Roy and Marina had shown her. She couldn't let them get in the way of their mission.

After finding the grotto, she had to go back, with or without Roy. She had to find out who'd killed Gary.

And why.

81

After fifteen minutes, Roy and Kelby passed a couple of white-washed Spanish villages and were right in the heart of the valley. Another turn into the country took them along a bumpy track for half an hour. The wild countryside and undeveloped views down the meandering valleys to the sea beyond the mountains gave Kelby a strange sensation of knowing this place.

Apart from a steep hillside village in the far distance, the valley was lush with green wheat fields and rolling hills, shadowed by layer after layer of rocky mountains to the west. Kelby had never been here before, but she felt an incredible peace descend on her.

Only the occasional farmhouse dotted the landscape. Aside from that, everything was field after field of green wheat.

When Roy headed over a hill and snaked through an olive plantation, Kelby pulled a sceptical face. 'With the tourist industry as it is today, how come no-one has found the grotto?'

Roy pointed at what seemed to be a never ending boundary. 'It must be on Marina's family land. See that fence? They have hundreds of acres.'

Her gaze followed his finger.

'They've farmed this land for centuries. It's enclosed with large gates at the farm exits. That's to keep out travellers who camp wherever they like. Did you see the house back there?'

She twisted her neck to look back. 'Yes.'

A long tree-lined drive led to a sprawling homestead with umpteen outbuildings, barns, and a stable block. The outbuildings and stables had red tiled roofs showing an affluent land owner.

'Marina's father and my mother live there. His brother lives over the ridge. He runs the hot stones retreat. The whole area is mostly their family, with a few holiday homes in between.'

'Wow, lots of land.'

'Yes, it dates back a few centuries. There's a ton of money left in a trust to ensure the land stays in the family. It's been handed down from generation to generation to keep it as private land.'

'Will we see your mum?'

A smile crept across his face. 'Of course, *luego,* later.'

Roy steered the car up a dirt track and stopped in front of high gates. 'Open Sesame!' he bellowed out of the window. As if by magic, they started opening. She looked at him, frowning, only to see him waving a remote control. 'Modern technology can be so handy.' After driving through the gates, he pointed the remote backwards. In the side mirror Kelby watched the gates close behind them.

'Have you seen a skeleton before?' Roy asked.

82

Kelby gaped at Roy as he drove along the rutted track. 'Do you mean the one Marina found?'

He nodded and pulled up on a verge. Leaning over Kelby, he pointed out of her open window. 'See down there, that's Marina's ruins.'

A few cars were parked to one side with a handful of people on their knees. A man in a straw hat scurried between them.

'That guy's the archaeologist. He has volunteers and other specialists on the dig. They want to find the foundations of the original houses and outbuildings. I'll show you later. I'm sure you want to see the cellar where the skeleton was found.'

Kelby grimaced. 'I hope it's been removed.'

'Oh yeah, it's gone for bone analysis so they can determine exactly how old it was.'

'You mean how old the person was. Remember Marina told you if it's Ana-Mariá, she has to be honoured.'

'I know, but we also can't draw much attention to this place in case it brings anyone else trying to find rizado. There's so much undercurrent noise about it on the web, I wouldn't be surprised if a weirdo came asking. Quite frankly, after the body count Marina uncovered, I'd prefer to keep my family out of it.'

'Yes, of course!'

'But when Marina gets a bee in her bonnet, there's no stopping her. When we see the folks, don't mention any of the rizado stuff. Marina is keeping that part between us because her dad hasn't been well.'

Roy started the car and they rumbled onto the track for another five minutes. 'Ana-Mariá doesn't show a homestead on here so we have to follow the map's symbols. Remember, she would have walked to the grotto.'

'She may have had a horse.'

'Possibly, but let's assume not.' He drove around a hill and pulled the car under a shaded copse of trees. 'If she needed to walk to get the rizado, it could have taken her a few hours.'

He tapped the map in her lap. 'I think we're somewhere here. Come on.' He jumped out of the car.

Kelby followed him and placed the map on the bonnet. Together they leaned over it.

'That's Torcal behind us.' He turned the map so Ana-Mariá's mountain range was behind them. He suddenly leapt onto the bonnet and climbed onto the roof. 'As a kid, I wanted to be the king of the castle.' He grinned at Kelby.

'You're *still* a kid. Get down.'

'No, I have a bird's-eye view from here.' He bent over and grabbed the map from her hand. 'Right, I think we're looking for this forest.'

'You know,' Kelby stopped to think, 'I don't recall seeing any woodland along the way.'

'Yeah, Spain has deforestation issues.'

Beside her head, Roy's feet shuffled as he turned his body direction. 'Nothing that way.' His feet inched around again. 'Nothing over there. Wait...'

Kelby's head shot up. 'What?'

'Hmm, not sure. There's a small rocky outcrop over there, but I don't see a huge forest as the map indicates, only a bunch of trees.'

'Maybe Marina's ancestors chopped it down for firewood.'

'Yeah, possibly. As most were.' He leapt off the roof and landed on both feet like a gymnast.

Kelby stared at him, waiting for his verdict. 'So?'

Roy flicked his thumb. 'We're hiking that way. It's the only bit that looks like on the map.' He tapped the grotto in the middle of the map. 'More importantly, I see something that looks like a heart-shaped hill.'

Kelby glanced at the map, her eyes widening. 'Of course. I hadn't noticed it before.'

'Nor me. But it's clearly visible on the ridge. Come on, let's go find the grotto.'

83

After striking west and climbing a hillock, Kelby followed Roy along a rugged trail, enjoying time outdoors and being away from work. Even more important was being in the sun with this adorable man. Despite being in a place she'd never been before, in a country she didn't know, she felt much safer than at home.

They strode through a thick copse. The green canopy reached high, hiding the blue sky and sunny day. Suddenly, the wood broke and they stepped up to a shallow pond. Kelby looked at the map and back to the pond. 'This must be it. The map shows a pool surrounded by bushes.'

Trees grew around the pond, some even spreading their roots into the clear shallow pool. They stepped across a path of rocks to the other side of the pond. From here, the entrance within the trees, was concealed.

A calming peace settled over Kelby. Soft background sounds soothed her. Water gurgled around the rocks. A sudden breeze rushed through the branches. Now and then, the occasional tweet of birds in the woods stabbed at the silence. A pair of pigeons cooed in the towering treetops.

'Is that it?'

Kelby noted the disappointment in Roy's voice. She watched him shade his eyes and glance around in each direction.

Staring at the rocky wall above the pool, Kelby said, 'There's got to be more to it than this.' She loved the sun warming her back. Tempted to lie back on the small stretch of grass beside the pond, she yawned. 'Annie said the waterfall was inside the cave, but I can't hear anything.'

'It has to be here somewhere.' Roy took a few steps back and held out his hand to guide her. Kelby clung to his fingers as she balanced her way across the water. On the other edge of the pond, he stopped. 'Listen. What's that sound?'

'Can't hear anything.' Kelby slumped on the prickly grass with an overwhelming feeling of wanting to dip her toes in the water. 'Hang on, there *is* a distant sound. Like rushing water. It's a bit hollow.'

'Maybe it's behind this rock wall.' Roy shoved his sunglasses to the top of his head and used his hand to shade his face while he examined the area.

A lazy glance took Kelby's attention to the rock face behind the pond. On the far edge, she spotted something and pointed. 'That looks like a little waterfall, but not the one I imagined from Annie's friend.'

Long grass grew along the edge of the rock face. About two metres above the ground, sheets of water cascaded into the pool, looking as though they came out of a mirror.

Roy ambled towards it, muttering, 'Maybe the vegetation is hiding something.'

The solid chunk of rock behind the pool loomed over them with a menacing glare. Half way up the rock wall, a cavity appeared. To Kelby it looked like an eyelid. As she stepped closer, the hole gaped, as though the craggy rock monster had flicked one eye open to peer at its intruders. 'Roy! There's a cave in the rock.'

His head swung back and nodded. 'Yeah, you're right. Maybe it's our grotto. Let's take a look.'

They headed around the pond towards the rock wall. Looking up, Kelby had no idea how they were going to scale the rock face.

As they neared the slab of limestone, a shadow beckoned. María's grotto had woven its spell on her just like the girdle book had

Kelby's pulse quickened. If only Gary had left notes. If they found rizado she wanted to prove someone had killed her brother.

Roy suddenly darted forward, yelling, 'Look!'

For a moment Kelby watched him scrambling over boulders surrounding the mirror waterfall. Then, she darted to him, breathless with excitement.

Roy bent down and fondled a mossy creeper. It was spread over the rocks around where the water cascaded into the pool. 'See this?'

Kelby bent down alongside him, trying to balance on the slippery rock. Beside her, Roy ran his fingers along the frizzy leaves and down the stem. Kneeling on the bank, he fiddled around the base of the stone. For a moment, he tugged at something, and started chuckling.

Kelby watched in fascination. 'What *are* you doing?'

With a triumphant yell, Roy yanked the plant out of the ground. He leapt up and threw his free arm around Kelby, hollering at the sky, 'I think we've found the rizado!'

84

Although Zelda had tipped him off that Kelby was home recuperating from her car accident, Barker hadn't been able to find her.

The cat incident had forced her underground. He had searched her house again with no sign of her or her security guard. Then he'd called Zelda, demanding more information. Despite her snooping on Jimmy's calls, she hadn't found anything. Kelby had disappeared.

A loud buzz brought Barker out of his thoughts. He grimaced at his phone. 'Yes, Gorden, what can I do for you?'

'The tables have turned.'

'What?'

'I know you're after rizado, but Jurgen has Olaf on the case too.'

'Why?'

'He doesn't think you'll find it.'

Barker put his phone on loudspeaker so he could sip his camomile tea.

'He knows your source.'

For a moment, sparks fused Barker's anger. He had seen this coming. When he'd told Gorden about rizado, he realised Jurgen would stick his kraut nose into his plans. But he had expected to find it before that happened. He took another sip of camomile and said in his calmest tone, 'What's Olaf going to do that I can't?'

'Think this through. Olaf has resources that belong to the devil.'

'What tag is he implementing?'

'Two.'

At that level of priority, Jurgen had taken over. 'Why did you let him get involved? You know what happened to Wade.'

'Wade was another story. He knew about the lab's body count.'

Barker stared at his phone.

'Besides, he threatened to take MG's secrets to the press. We couldn't let him stop our research.'

'You shouldn't have snuffed him.' Barker wondered whether he shouldn't have got Gary the job at MG. 'Well.' he continued, 'I couldn't tell you this before, but Wade was the source of the sample.'

'What?!'

'He had an accident on that training thing he did in Spain. He came back with a small scar on his arm and said it had slit open and someone had given him this stuff which healed the wound. It sounded like puffery to me, but we got our scientists onto the sample he brought back.'

'Did you find out where he got it?'

'No, as much as Olaf tried, he couldn't find a thing. We had people there doing the same route Gary did, but nothing.'

'Did he go with anyone? Maybe they know.'

'Tried that too. We offered his cycling mate the world to let us in on the secret, but he played dumb.'

Barker sighed; he had liked Kelby's brother. The guy had been young and energetic and ready for anything.

'You there?'

Barker heard the panic in Gorden's voice. 'Why are you telling me this?' He didn't trust the runt. He wouldn't be surprised if Gorden was playing Jurgen. And vice versa. Cheats, he hated. Playing them at their own game, he loved.

'I think Jurgen will order Olaf to go straight to a three, so I wanted to see what you could get first.'

'Let me get this straight. You want me to find rizado before Olaf does.'

'That's what I said.'

'Why, Gorden? Don't you trust Jurgen to share it with you?'

Silence. Ah, ha. As he suspected.

'If you want me to beat Olaf and Jurgen, you need to come clean.'

'About what?'

'Where are your scientists doing the rizado tests?'

Silence again.

'Gorden, think about this. You work with Jurgen because you have to. Your new drugs have to pass through his agency. Whether you want to get rizado onto the market or stop it doesn't matter to me. I will find it anyway and do what I want with it.'

'Your point?'

'Jurgen is a powerful man. Possibly more powerful than you. You said a few minutes ago that Olaf has the devil's resources. Those resources don't come easily, even to paid thugs. They come from Jurgen, buying in whatever is needed to get the job done.'

Barker waited for his words to sink in.

Losing sight of Kelby, he hated. Keeping people at his fingertips, he loved.

'If you give me everything you have on rizado, I will find it quicker. And you can tell Jurgen to go fuck himself.'

Barker enjoyed hearing Gorden clearing his throat. The fat runt was squirming. He had him where he wanted him.

Another ace in his game plan.

If he found out their rizado secrets, he could decide where to take the stuff when Kelby found it. If they were genuinely interested in keeping it on the market, he could name his price. If they weren't, he'd suck them dry of information and find a buyer. Even if it meant taking it to the black market.

Gorden hesitated and said, 'Okay.'

Barker smiled inwardly. It was about time Gorden revealed his part in the closely guarded conspiracy.

85

Kelby's hand clutched her mouth to stop herself inhaling the pond's fishy smell. 'This is rizado?'

'Maybe.'

'But I thought rizado was a herb. Isn't this moss?'

'No. Moss grows best in damp places. But it's a simple plant with no root.' He dangled the weedy thing in the air, his usually spotless fingers caked in mud. 'See, this has a root. It's a herb, smell it.'

Kelby leaned over and inhaled deeply. The herb's pungent scent filled her head with crazy thoughts of staying right here in this secret grotto with him.

'Remember rizado's full name in the journal?'

'Yes, Marina said rizado meant curly.'

'Uh, huh. It also means frizzy, see the leaves.' Roy spread the tiny fronds apart and rubbed each one between his fingers. 'Feel it.'

Kelby followed his example and groaned, 'Eeuw. It's sticky as hell.' She bent down and wiped her fingertips on the grassy bank.

'The rest of its name is *pícaro*. That's Spanish for "rogue".'

'You don't expect herbs to grow on rocks.'

'Exactly! Marina searched to see if there was anything like rizado growing anywhere else in the world. And there isn't.'

Kelby dipped her hands in the pond to get rid of the awful stickiness. She glanced at her hand in the cool water and cried out, 'Yuck!' Yanking them out, she pointed to a slick of slime clinging to the rocks. 'Look!'

Frowning, Roy leaned over and ran his hands through the water. Each time he lifted a wad of the algae, most of it slipped through his fingers, leaving a frothy slime in his palms.

With both hands leaning on the pond's stony bank, Kelby angled closer to get a better look. Shoulder to shoulder with him, she asked, 'What's that?'

'I'm sure it's plankton.'

'I thought plankton only lived in the sea.'

'No, they can thrive in any surface water.' He held her gaze. 'Some rare varieties make the water green because of the chlorophyll in their cells.'

Kelby flicked a piece of slime off his palm.

'They get their energy through photosynthesis and need a well-lit surface layer. The organic pigments give it colour.'

'So?'

'The pigmentation nutrients are the medicines! It's the colour in the plankton that has the most potent medicine.'

Kelby nodded thoughtfully, 'Okay, what's this got to do with rizado?'

'Maybe the rizado has fed off the plankton for centuries. And phytoplankton is such an important source of oxygen,' his voice rose with excitement, '¡Por dios! By God, of course! It could also protect human life!'

'What do you mean?' Kelby coughed to force the huskiness out of her throat. She wasn't sure if he could sense the air prickle as much as she did. Being up against him and discovering a secret that could change the world, turned her insides to mush.

'Phytoplankton bypasses the body's essential energy currencies, so you feel a lift almost immediately on ingesting it. This is probably rizado's secret.'

Kelby's eyes were glued to him. The combination of his presence, the herb's heady scent and their incredible discovery was impairing her attentiveness. 'I don't get it.'

Still fondling the slimy plant, Roy explained, 'The plankton releases key nutrients into the water, so maybe the rizado can only live in this one pool.'

'What if it was planted into another plankton source?'

'Not sure if it needs these conditions to thrive. Scientists say that phytoplankton is one of the world's most important plants. They're even saying it's the future for pharma.'

'Why?'

'Because it provides the earth with over ninety per cent of our oxygen.' He shifted on his knees. 'And it's got every mineral needed by us mortals. It's a power house of healing.'

Kelby sat up straighter with a sharp intake of breath.

Roy said, 'It could even cure cancer!'

86

Kelby stared at Roy. 'Cancer? This slimy green stuff could fight cancer?'

'It's got to be tested first, Kelby,' Roy said, 'But plankton contains hundreds of potent phytochemicals that work in synergy to protect the body's tissues. So it's possible.'

The corner of Kelby's mouth tugged into a smile as she watched him use slimy green fingers to count the benefits.

'It cleans the blood and removes toxins.' He tapped another finger. 'It also enhances oxygenation and circulation.' Another slimy finger flicked up. 'It reverses abnormal cell division that can lead to cancer.' Roy stopped talking and waited for his words to sink in.

'How do you know this?'

He slipped off his shoes, rolled up his trousers and waded into the middle of the pond. 'I did my thesis on the use of traditional herbs in modern medicines.'

Kelby raised her eyebrows. No wonder he raved about herbs. None of the doctors she had encountered before, had approved of natural treatments.

Kelby focused on the undiscovered plant resting in his palm. This could help sick people. Those who spent so much time living in and out of hospital. They needed to find a way to make sure it reached the right people. Not just those who wanted to make money from it. It could mean a breakthrough in medicine.

Roy stood and ambled around the pond, calling over his shoulder, 'It's like a whole food medicine.'

'Food medicine?' Kelby tried to absorb the medical facts. This kind of techno jargon wasn't her bag.

'Yeah, because it contains hundreds of vital nutrients. They work together to alkalise the system, nourish the cells and strengthen the immune system.'

After a few paces, he dropped to his knees again and dangled his hand into more green sludge. Kelby followed and used a broken twig to poke at the algae.

'I've read that if we took one teaspoon of phytoplankton a day it would save us from degenerative diseases. And yes, it could be the cure for cancer!' He threw his hands in the air and shouted with joy, '*¡Cáspita!* Imagine what rizado could do!'

Kelby enjoyed watching how his body became animated, like a boy with a new toy.

'This is amazing, Kelby.' He yanked more rizado out from under another rock. Kelby watched as he smeared the frizzy leaves across the top of the rock turning it into a sticky paste. He turned to her and smeared the paste between his hands and opened them to her.

'Kelby, this could help Annie. Phytoplankton helps with asthma and skin disorders.'

Her eyes widened. 'Really?'

'But I mustn't get too excited. It hasn't been tested.' His gaze fixed on Kelby. 'I want to take some rizado home to test it. I also need water samples to check the plankton.' He suddenly stopped wading and cursed, 'Damn!'

'What?' She thought he had stubbed his toe.

'I didn't bring a test tube.'

'Oh, wait.' Kelby scrambled around and dug in her handbag for the coffee shake bottle. She dipped it into the pond at a spot where the algae wasn't spreading across the top and rinsed out the dregs of the coffee a few times. Then, she held it high. 'Ta-dah. A water sample.'

Roy guffawed. 'You're a great companion. You found the map, and now you've come up with ways to prove rizado's properties.'

Kelby glowed. 'It's not sterile, but it should get you started.' Her voice dropped, 'I'm not sure how or why, but I feel as though this is another link in the chain at discovering what happened to Gary.'

'Yes, I keep hoping we'll see something that looks like the symbol he gave you.'

Kelby gazed around the secluded pond. 'Me too. This place is amazing. I can see why it's never been discovered.'

Roy followed her eyes. 'It's hidden behind the woodlands on land that's been privately owned for hundreds of years. Can't go wrong there.'

'And it looks like a pile of rocks. Nothing interesting from the outside.'

'And even if it was found, who would know that this,' he curled his fingers into quote marks in the air, '"moss" could heal the world?' Roy waded back to the grassy bank and stepped up beside her.

Kelby whispered, 'That's why Ana-María's grotto has kept its secret for centuries.'

'We found her secret. You and me. It's taken centuries, but *we* did it. What a team we are.'

They stared at each other in silence. The thread thickened as though an invisible silkworm wove it around them, encapsulating them into their own cocoon.

Kelby pulsated with excitement. 'The possibility of Annie and other people with long-term illnesses being healed is overwhelming. If Gary knew his death might give us a way to save his daughter —' She choked up.

Roy dropped the rizado and stepped closer, so close that her eyes struggled to focus on his face at such close range. His breath caressed the fine hairs on Kelby's cheek. Without thinking, she stepped even nearer to him. They stood for a moment staring into each other's eyes. Gradually, with a shy awkwardness, Roy pulled her towards him and brushed his lips against hers. A moment later, as though suddenly realising he shouldn't be doing that, he pulled back.

But Kelby tilted forward and nuzzled the tip of her nose along each of his eyebrows in turn. Before she had finished, his mouth met hers, this time without hesitation. They stood beside the rizado pond locked in an embrace.

And the world around them paused.

Suddenly Kelby's phone vibrated in her pocket. She jumped and grabbed it, flinching as she read:

The rich bitch even allows a cat into hospital.

Her finger flicked open the attached image. Kelby gasped as a spasm of pain bolted through her. In the photo, Annie, still wired up through her nose, smiled at Fat Cat curled up on her hospital bed.

87

Grunting in agony, María refused to grab at the tingles shooting through her feet where the leather jerkin had kicked her. Instead, she focused her eyes on the naked body beside her. Her mother's turbaned head lay on the cold floor slabs. She crawled closer and stroked the turban. It flopped to one side and fell off.

María jerked back; her jaw dropped. She blinked in disbelief. Her mother's head had been shaven. Clumps of long dark locks lay scattered in front of the fire.

'Mama! Your hair!'

As she lifted the shaven locks the burnt bread smell became noxious. María flinched, trying to suppress the bile rising in her throat. They had burnt Madre's hair.

From the corner of her eye, María spotted a dagger on the table matted with blood and hair. The sharp blade was about the length of her foot. Her eyes checked the other soldiers, but she couldn't see if they had the same lethal weapons.

The leather jerkin turned to the others and said, 'Should we shave this one too?'

He lifted the dagger and twirled in around and around. Its tapered point carved a tiny hole in the wooden table.

'*La bruja* didn't have any markings of the devil in her hair, but this young one might.'

La bruja. The witch.

88

Kelby's heart hammered against her ribs. *Oh my God!* Hairs lifted on her arms. What would this bully do next?

'I have … to,' She stuttered, 'to … get back to …'

'Kelby, what's up?'

'Nothing!' Her voice trembled, 'Please. Take me to the airport. I need to get back.'

'Why? I thought you'd want to stay and see this through.'

Her fingers tightened around her phone. Beads of sweat pinpricked her forehead. 'I do, but I don't want to get you involved or they'll come after you too.'

'Who?' He grabbed her phone and held it up. 'Another threat?'

'No. Yes. I mean, please don't get involved. They don't know about you and —'

'Kelby. I'm involved. I got you into this. Stop worrying about me! What's happened?'

She showed him the image of Annie.

'The bastards! Come on.' He rolled down his trousers and slipped on his shoes. 'We'll get a last minute flight. I'll call the cops on the way.'

Roy spun around and leapt across the pond. Instead of picking her way carefully across the water cobbles, Kelby stumbled across, soaking her shoes. She gulped down her panic as her stomach turned to stone and her chest heaved with painful spasms. All she could see in front of her was flashing images of Annie wheezing and spluttering. Doctor Willow had warned that an asthma attack could be fatal. And Roy had explained the connection to heart disease.

The bastard had gone too far. Her mind buzzed with planning options. 'Maybe Hawk can help.'

'Okay, you call him when I get the cops.'

'I'll have to tell Stacie something about what's going on so she understands the threats.'

'Remember, Kelby, you're a valuable asset now.'

'Why?'

'If they're after you, it's because they think you have information they need. They may even think Gary passed something on to you before he died.'

She turned to stare at him and almost tripped when he uttered his next sentence.

'But that information may help to keep you alive.'

89

After hours of hanging around Malaga airport, there was a cancellation so Kelby and Roy managed to catch the last flight home. Despite making several calls to Stacie's unanswered phone, Kelby hadn't been able to get any news about Annie.

Back in England, the dreary evening weighed on Kelby as she sat impatiently beside Roy in a cab that weaved its way to St Adelaide's. The events of the past day hardly seemed real. Finding a hidden map and tracing it to an ancient secret. Discovering a plant with alleged healing powers. Warming herself in the sun by a tree-lined pond in Spain. With her own Indiana Jones.

Hearing Gary may have been murdered and the poor other souls struck down by conspirators, Teresina's death and the implications of her own car crash, seemed in the distant past.

It also bothered her that the Troll had suddenly gone off line. His Twitter account had been closed, but he'd somehow found her number. For the hundredth time, she wondered if someone in her office was spying.

When the cab finally pulled up at the hospital's front entrance, Roy tossed a few notes at the cabbie and leapt out.

As they entered Annie's room, Stacie blocked Kelby's path. Over her sister-in-law's shoulder she saw Annie looking like her favourite rag doll, slumped back against the pillows. Roy marched past her and started examining Annie. Over Stacie's shoulder, Kelby couldn't mistake Annie's lifeless shape from her earlier asthma attack.

No Fat Cat on her lap.

'Where's Fat Cat?'

Stacie gasped. 'So it *was* you! Is that all you're worried about? Your stinking cat?'

'No! God, no!'

Kelby tried to step past Stacie, but her sister-in-law grabbed her arms and shoved her away. 'Don't be so stupid.'

'I think you kept it secret in that gross briefcase of yours. I wondered why you carried it. You hide your life in there!'

'For God's sake, keep your voice down.' Kelby's muscles started jumping under her skin, as though they were competing in the hurdle race at Annie's school's sports day.

Rosalind shuffled them out of the room. Kelby glanced at Annie, sick to her stomach at the little weak body wheezing and spluttering, choking on thin air that wouldn't give her body any release.

Outside the room, Stacie pointed at Annie. 'You see what you've done!'

'Why on earth would I bring the cat here?'

'Annie told me! Because of the secret!'

90

Out of the blue, it dawned on Kelby. Stacie thought the secret was bringing Fat Cat to visit. 'Wait!'

'No! I cannot believe you'd stoop so low. You knew this would happen!'

'Of all people, you know I'm worried about Annie. That's why I'm spending so much on this hospital.'

'Fuck you, Kelby Wade.' Stacie stuck her middle finger right in Kelby's face. 'You're trying to control my family again, like you did Gary. If you hadn't insisted he got that job, he'd still be here.'

'Look,' Kelby pulled out her phone, 'Someone set this up.'

'Don't give me that bullshit!'

Stacie slapped the phone out of Kelby's hand. It clattered to the floor and slid along the corridor as though it also wanted to get away from the argument. Stacie marched off. 'I don't want you near my daughter again.' Stacie yelled to Rosalind and pointed at Kelby, 'I want her banned from visiting.'

Rosalind gasped. 'But Miss Wade comes every night.'

'I don't care. She made this happen. She brought on Anne's attack. I don't want her near my daughter.'

The nurse looked from Stacie to Kelby and stuttered, 'But what about Annie?'

'Anne. Her name is Anne, not Annie as Miss Wade calls her.'

'But Annie … Anne loves it when Miss Wade gets here.'

Stacie threw her hands in the air. 'Are you listening to me? I am Anne's mother and I have the right to deny visitors. I am telling you now to get your boss here and ban this woman from this hospital.'

Rosalind stared in silence. Her eyes darted between Stacie and Kelby. Stacie leaned in and stuck her diamanté studded-nose into the nurse's face. 'Do you hear me? Get her thrown out. Now!'

Kelby ran back to the room, but Stacie was on her heels and dived ahead before she reached the door. 'Leave my daughter alone!'

Rosalind waved away Kelby and Stacie, making it clear she didn't want either of them near Annie.

From outside the room, Kelby heard Roy ask the nurse, 'Update please.'

'We checked peak flow and did a chest x-ray. Also checked oxygen saturation whilst on 100% oxygen.'

He nodded and listened to Annie's chest. 'It looks like the attack was severe.'

'Her respiratory rate is so high I can't hear her breathing clearly.'

'Her airways are restricted. Nurse, please make sure the blood gases are checked immediately.'

'Yes, doctor.'

He glanced at Stacie and said, 'It will show how much oxygen and CO_2 are in Annie's blood.' He turned back to Rosalind. 'And give her a nebuliser with salbutamol and ipratropium to open her airways, IV steroids and IV aminophylline.'

'Who are you?' Stacie rounded on Roy. Her wide set shoulders still blocked the doorway.

Behind her, Annie's sad eyes filled with tears.

'I'm Doctor Robson.'

'Where's Doctor Willow?'

Rosalind answered, 'He's off today.'

While Stacie swayed between Roy and Rosalind, Kelby made a snap decision. Annie was suffering because of her. The cyber bully had hurt Annie to spite her. She had to stay away until she could find the swine — and stop him. She stepped back from Stacie and held up her hands in defeat. 'Okay, okay, I'm going.' She looked at Roy. 'I'll see you downstairs, Roy.'

'There! You see!' Stacie bellowed at the nurse, 'Guilty as hell.'

Ignoring Stacie's comment, Kelby blew Annie a kiss off the palm of her hand and slunk away. Limping down the stairs, her heart ached more than her bruised body. She loved Annie more than anyone.

Now she had to find out who was threatening her.

91

The silent house disturbed Kelby. No blue haze from the TV slipped out of the living room to greet her. No arguing from the cat's soaps or sirens from the latest evening news. Instead of the comforting hum, the house screamed silence.

Although Roy and Hawk entered the house with her, it still gave her the creeps. Hawk hadn't left her property since her break-in and she felt sorry for his pregnant wife at home.

Exhausted from lack of sleep, and distressed at seeing Annie in that condition, Kelby shuffled into the kitchen to brew a pot of coffee while they decided their next move. Every muscle in her body ached. She held both hands against her temples to try to stop her head pounding. She didn't want to involve Hawk any more than they already had. Knowledge of the rizado murders would put him in danger. Even though he'd been recruited to protect her, Roy had suggested they keep Hawk on a need-to-know basis.

Something kept steering her towards searching to see if Gary had left any MG notes. Unlike most men, her brother had been organised and made to-do lists. Despite having the house redecorated, so it didn't give her painful reminders of him, Stacie had left his man-cave exactly as it had been. If they were anywhere, they'd be hidden there. One thing she could say about Stacie, she had loved Gaa. It was the only thing they had in common.

Hawk and Roy ambled into the kitchen, still deep in discussion. Behind Kelby, Hawk was explaining to Roy how the stalker must have hacked into their security system to get the cat.

As she opened the jar of coffee beans, the fresh aroma wakened her exhausted mind. She turned the canister over and poured the beans into the coffee grinder.

Out flopped Fat Cat's severed paw.

92

María shivered. So it had happened as Tío said it would. They were calling her and Madre witches. They had even searched Madre's head for devil marking and now they wanted to do the same to her.

The unbooted soldier stood, stretched and yawned. 'Let's make her watch the spider.'

The thought of a spider crawling over her mother gave María the chills. She wasn't afraid of any animals, but creeping insects filled her with dread. Seeking comfort for the bubble of guilt billowing in her gut, María stroked her mother's spiky head.

The leather jerkin stopped playing with the dagger. He dropped it back onto the table and marched outside.

Another loud belch filled the room. The unbooted soldier stood and relieved himself against Madre's head.

¡Puf!

María yanked the turban to stop the full flow splashing on her mother. She hated how Madre lay there, unable to fight back.

¡Dios santo!

The stench of his urine mingled with the acrid burnt hair. Again, María swallowed the sour bile that shot into her throat.

From the table the cloaked soldier laughed and grunted, 'I'll do that on her bleeding breasts when the spider is finished with her.'

María balled her fists. The spider must be a lethal creature. She had to do something to save her mother. Using the edge of her tunic she wiped the urine off Madre's coarsely shaven head. The foul stench caught in the back of her throat, but she refused to cough and choke as her stomach heaved. She would not give these soldiers the pleasure of seeing her discomfort.

Madre's hand reached out and gripped María's arm and yanked her closer. Her eyes were ravaged with pain and discomfort. 'Promise me again, María.'

María noticed Madre had used her preferred name for the first time. She stared into her mother's eyes and read her sorrow and heartache.

93

Kelby screamed and flung the coffee canister in the air. As she stumbled backwards, her leg caught the end of the breakfast barstool. She crashed over it and landed in a heap on the marble floor.

Blood pumped in her ears.

Roy and Hawk rushed to her side. Roy knelt to help her up while Hawk cleaned up the coffee beans and Fat Cat's limb.

Kelby stared at the paw. 'I hate seeing dead things. In my school science class, I used to faint when it came to dissecting rats and studying anatomy. I spent those lessons in the sick room.'

'It's okay. You don't have to explain, Kelby, dead things aren't pleasant for anyone.' Hawk recovered the paw, wrapped it in a layer of paper towel and left the room, his head crowning the door frame on exit.

'Here, Kel, sit down'. Roy led her to the breakfast nook.

She slumped into a seat and sighed. 'We have to do something. This is getting out of control.'

'Listen, I didn't want to say this before, but everyone knows Willow is washed up. His private clinic at Homerton is the only place he should be practising. And even that's a stretch. What they get up to there is anyone's guess. I'm going to see him and find out if he knows anything.'

'I'll go with you.'

'No, stay with Hawk, you're safer that way. I'll be back in a couple of hours.'

When Hawk returned to the kitchen, Roy said, 'Hawk, I know you haven't been told the background details so I'll give you an idea of what we're playing with here.'

'Okay. Fire away.'

'Sit. It's a long story, but I'll cut it short.'

94

With a hot coffee to comfort her, Kelby sat listening to Roy brief Hawk. When Roy had finished, Hawk frowned. 'Sounds like a conspiracy.'

'Yes, exactly,' Roy paced along the kitchen tiles. 'A number of other people have had *accidents* covered up. My biggest worry is that Kelby is a critical link. She's in terrible danger. They'll stop at nothing to get what they want.'

Kelby sipped her coffee and muttered, 'They have resources and ambitions you can't even imagine.'

Roy had left out key facts about rizado and the historical trail. Hawk was better off not knowing those details. He just needed to know the threat's potential so he could make plans to protect them.

Beside her, Hawk asked, 'Who are these guys?'

'We don't know. Not for certain. But we suspect it's a large pharmaceutical company. As far as we can see, they are the only link to the deaths.'

'How did they get inside if the house was alarmed?' Kelby shook her head in disgust.

'We had the pins changed on the initial audit, so there must be an insider who knows the code. I'll report this to the police.' Hawk straightened and towered over Kelby and Roy. He cleared his throat and said, 'Um, Kelby, I have to tell you something.'

Kelby stared at him. A flutter in her stomach.

'I have to admit I'm a bit out of my depth here. I appreciate Mr Thompson giving me this opportunity, but I don't think I can give you the kind of protection you need.'

'What?'

'This is a bigger threat than I imagined. We need full operational support.' Hawk counted on his fingers as he went through his list, 'We need video surveillance. We need a response company who can take counter measures. We need someone to evacuate you and your family when the threat gets severe.'

Kelby watched him as he waited for his words to sink in. She couldn't believe he thought this had become too much for him. Or that she needed this other kind of security.

'A bigger company can manage access control points at your gates and in your office. They can have more people patrolling the perimeter. They will monitor the entire house to check for any blind spots. They can even create a reinforced room inside with pre-rehearsed procedures. They'd design a whole system around you.'

'That sounds perfect.' Roy glanced at Kelby to see if she agreed.

'Basically, they will have the resources to create a secure bubble around you. Unfortunately, I don't.'

Roy turned to Kelby, 'Listen, we have to do what Hawk says until we find out who *really* is behind this. We may suspect MG, but we need evidence to stop them.' His voice dropped, 'They won't stop at Annie. They'll go on until they get what they want.'

'Okay, what's next?' Kelby scrutinised Hawk.

'I'll make some calls. I know a brilliant guy, Frank. His company can handle this easily.'

'Hawk, in the meantime, please stick to Kelby. I have to go and see another doctor we think is mixed up in this, but I don't want you to leave Kelby's side. Is that okay?'

'Of course.' He fixed his eyes on Kelby. 'I won't leave you.'

Roy stood to leave and Kelby jumped up. 'Wait! I have to go and see Stacie. I can't leave things as they are.'

'Not now, Kel. Give her a day or so to simmer down.'

'She shook her head, 'I can't. There's too much at stake. I know she won't listen, but I have to warn her. And I want to ask if she remembers anything before Gary died.'

Roy hesitated.

But she hurried on, 'I'm not giving up on this. Not when we're so close to finding the truth. I know ...' her voice dipped so she cleared her throat and repeated, 'I *just* know Gary is guiding me. I'm not sure how, but I *know* he wants me to find something.'

Roy opened his mouth to speak, but Kelby held up her hand. 'I *have* to do this. For Gary.'

Roy's eyes darted to Hawk.

'I'll be careful.' She touched Roy's hand. 'Besides, Hawk won't let anything happen to me.'

Roy glanced at Hawk, and Kelby saw something pass between the two men. *They've exchanged a silent agreement to keep me safe. No matter what.*

As she watched Roy leave, Kelby experienced a strange tearing sensation. In such a short time he'd become such an important part of her life, and she wanted to get to know him better. Kelby hoped the bond between them wasn't about to be severed.

95

Olaf crept through the bushes lining the high wall along Kelby's driveway.

Hiding his prized tattoos didn't appeal to him, but on this rare occasion it needed to be done. A dark green sweater covered his bulging muscles. It opened enough to expose the dark mass of hair curling into the hollow in his neck. As he crept closer to Kelby's mansion, Olaf wondered what she'd think of the surprise tucked into his pocket. He was still thinking of a way to drop this one on the devil.

After watching Barker for a day or so, it hadn't taken long to work out how he'd tormented Kelby with the cat in the hospital. It came in handy having someone on the inside able to get the alarm code to bypass security.

Olaf enjoyed watching Barker's game plan. A rich guy playing killing games impressed him. He could be as picky as he pleased. He churned the word around in his mouth: pi-ck-ee.

Ja, a great word for someone like Barker. And now someone like him.

Finding a spot where he could see directly into Kelby's living room, Olaf disguised himself amongst the shrubs. For a long while he stood still watching the giant security bastard with the devil. And another strange man. Maybe her lover. No bother to him, he'd soon find out more about the stranger.

After instructing him to step up to a Tag Two, Jurgen wouldn't dream of telling how to do it. He simply paid handsomely when the job was done. Olaf knew this would escalate to a Tag One. It smelt of dead rat.

As long as it looked like an accident, Jurgen would be happy. But not him. That part had started boring him. He wanted Tag Four where he could make the body disappear. The dividends would be taking control of what happened to the body. He could even get pick-ee about dirty deaths.

More than anything, he yearned to use his *animaal* instincts on this job.

Suddenly the stranger stood and the devil threw her arms around him.

Ah, huh. The lover. That complicated things. Because he might know things he shouldn't.

This would earn him a big bonus from Jurgen.

Suddenly the door flung open. Within minutes, the lover crunched on the gravel drive and climbed into his dust-covered Land Rover.

For a split second, Olaf hesitated. So they were splitting up. No problem for him. Even better to get the devil first and sort out the lover later. Should he follow? No, the devil was more important. The lover would have his turn soon enough.

Olaf twisted his Rolex. He had plenty of time.

There was no rush; no rush at all.

96

Sitting beside Hawk as he parked along the road in front of the terraced houses, Kelby said, 'Sorry, Hawk, I have to go in on my own.'

'But we agreed —'

'I know, I know. Please. This is a private matter between me and Stacie.' Even though Hawk was a gentleman, she didn't want him in on this conversation. Nor did she want him or anyone to be rifling through Gary's private space.

'I'll give you five minutes then I'm coming in.'

'Give me ten, no fifteen. Please.'

Hawk's jaw set, making his large head look like that of a grotesque statue.

Kelby swallowed hard as she left the car. *Hawk must think I'm dithery.* She had given him instructions to have this other security bubbling around her, and she insisted on being alone. Only for a few minutes. As soon as she found Stacie, she'd hurry back. She'd even get Stacie under Hawk's protection — if she could convince her stubborn sister-in-law.

With painstaking stealth Kelby opened Stacie's garden gate and trod silently along the pathway. Wild flowers, wispy and lanky, coloured Stacie's small patch of garden, like a child's finger painting. It contrasted with the solid green patch of freshly mowed grass next door.

In front of the blood-red door, Kelby hesitated. Stacie had said that in feng shui, her red door was symbolic of an opening of 'chi energy'. Shaking herself to ward off her own silly insecurities, Kelby rammed her knuckles against the painted door.

No answer.

Behind her, the wind toyed with one of Stacie's metal chimes creating a melodious tune.

To be fair, Stacie was a doting mother. She made it a hobby to make wind chimes with Annie. They collected shells and hung them from a piece of driftwood. A school ruler had different coloured pencils dangling from it. Stacie's creative side led her to use natural rods, bells, metal, wood and any other objects to construct suspended tubes to be played by the wind.

Somewhere in the garden hung a kitchen colander with an array of cooking utensils clattering against each other in the breeze. Kelby hoped it didn't annoy the neighbours. Ignoring the chimes, Kelby called out several times. She jumped off the front steps, and squinted into the living room window, using her hands to cup around her face and peer into the house.

She did the same at the kitchen window. Dishes were piled high above the sink and alongside it. Although she often rushed off and didn't wash her stream of coffee cups, she always loaded the dishwasher to stop the kitchen looking cluttered. She could imagine the air ripe with mould spores from stale food sticking to the plates. Something Annie didn't need.

Kelby tapped on the window and called to Stacie.

There was no movement.

At every window she did the same, yet no sign of Stacie. She tried Stacie's mobile again to see if she could hear it ringing in the house. Maybe she'd left it at home. Or worse, maybe she was at home and hurt with no way of getting help.

The number rang and rang.

Kelby slipped the phone back into her trousers and stepped into the shadows.

Thankfully, Kelby thought, old habits die hard. Gary's shed-turned-man-cave key lay hidden in the exact spot where he'd hidden it. In a stencilled military-type font the solid wooden door warned visitors: Command Bunker.

Kelby eased the key into the lock, stopping halfway to listen for any sounds. She took a deep breath and held it tightly in her chest. The key turned easily without fuss or scraping sounds. She turned the knob slowly so it didn't squeak.

Behind her the door groaned shut and clanked into its lock. As she slipped inside the shed, she almost knocked her head on a bunch of Gary's brightly coloured beer caps suspended from a wooden beam. For a moment they clattered against each other before calming down. Kelby frowned. Strange wind chime.

One wall had a full-length movie screen. A parachute had been strung across the ceiling and military helmets hung on hooks. Her heart ached to be amongst his things again. They say only the good die young, but it was so unfair.

As she stroked his military mementoes, she spoke to Gary, 'Talk to me Gaa, tell me what you did with your notes.'

Kelby glanced at the wall. Photos showed a hectic life of activity. Pride during his passing out parade. Various images of military friends. Parachuting. Diving in the Med. Cycling through the Spanish mountains. Solo yacht sailing. Jumping off high cliffs. Skimming across waves on a rubber dinghy.

Something caught her eye and Kelby leaned closer to one frame. She frowned and stroked the cold glass. Gary stood amongst a group of high school friends at their leavers' ball. Beside him Gary's friend, who had jumped into the pool and clung to her back when they were kids, grinned into the camera. Abruptly, Kelby recalled Annie asking her about the incident. How did she know about it?

Shivers ran through her. She lifted the frame off its hook to peer closely at the boy. She clasped the photo to her chest, absentmindedly stroking it. How did Annie know about that? Could it be ... ?

Kelby shook her head. No way, now she *was* losing her marbles. Gary couldn't have told his daughter about that incident from beyond the grave. As she pondered on her crazy thoughts, Kelby's finger caught a snag behind the frame. She flipped it over. A thick strip of parcel tape ran across the bottom near the frame's edge with a slightly raised surface.

Kelby's pulse quickened. The glow of finding the map radiated into her once again. She dug her bitten nail against the tape, wishing it was longer to catch the edge. After a minute of scratching at the corner of the tape, she finally hooked a tiny piece. In seconds she had ripped off the tape and found a concealed piece of paper. With trembling fingers, she opened the note in Gary's handwriting:

Homerton Grange Clinic.

Under a scrawled address, his note read: *Staff entrance, down the dirt track. The Lab. 42A.*

Kelby read it three times. Were his notes there? Maybe something in this place had got him killed.

Wham!

Kelby jumped at the sudden noise outside.

97

María wanted to turn her eyes away so Madre wouldn't read her guilt, but her mother's eyes held hers.

'Say nothing of the journal or they will do these terrible to you too.'

María's voice cracked, 'Never. Your secret is safe, Mama.'

'Try to run. Don't fight back, you have no chance.'

María nodded; she couldn't tell her mother she had no intention of giving in. She'd rather die than be violated or imprisoned or whatever else they had planned for her and her mother. Instead, she told Madre in silence: *I will never give up.*

The unbooted and cloaked soldiers spoke at the top of their voices, eating the stew with loud burps and grunts.

Again, Madre took the opportunity to whisper to her, 'I don't think it could be one of my patients. But maybe —'

'Tell me, Mama, I will find them and kill them.'

'Fernando's wife thought her bebé would live. She couldn't understand it was inside too long in the wrong position.' Her words were consumed with agony.

María wished she could take her mother's place.

'She didn't see Fernando and I. We pulled it out with the cord tangled around its neck.'

'I will find her Mama and —'

Despite her struggling to speak, Madre hissed, 'She is not to blame, María. You will do her no harm.' She lay her sheared head back on the stone floor, looking too exhausted to say any more.

Madre was right. This had not come to them from a woman's baby dying. Taking a deep, guilty breath, María closed her eyes, overcome with the desire to confess her sin of sending the story and journal to Barcelona.

The leather jerkin kicked the door open with his boot and barged back into the kitchen. María stared as he inserted a metal claw into the fire. As the flames heated the surface, she could see two sharp U-shaped points on each end that looked as though they pinched together.

Blood pounded in her ears.

Dios santo!

This was their spider.

98

The maze of terraced houses enabled Olaf to sneak past the security giant waiting in the car. The security guard surely couldn't see much with his head buried in the car ceiling. It must be a pain to be so tall. Literally a pain in the neck if you had to keep bending low.

He'd have to be crafty when it came to the giant's turn. Taking him down wouldn't be a problem. He had strength in the hard muscular dragon. It was the guard's height that would make killing him interesting.

But first the devil.

He crept to the shed and peered in the window to see what the devil was doing.

Years ago, this place covered in military memorabilia had been his first hit. Jurgen had insisted Wade had copied information and hidden it somewhere at home. Without making it look like a robbery, Olaf had done a thorough search of the house and garage. As he strained one eye to the side of the dusty glass pane, he knocked over a broom.

Olaf cursed under his breath. *Bliksem!*

He flattened himself along the wall and waited a few minutes, knowing the devil would be peering out.

Still in his green camouflage sweatshirt, he gave her a few minutes to calm down and wormed his way backwards behind the shed. She would exit any minute now. If only his heavy legs hadn't got in the way, she might have found what he himself had searched for a couple of years ago.

But he must have spooked her. Never mind, the spooking would soon be taken a step further.

That's when the fun would start.

99

Kelby's nerves were instantly on guard. She peeped out of the window at the back of the den. A garden broom had fallen over. She glanced around, expecting to see someone stalking her.

Now she berated herself for telling Hawk to wait in the car. As she had told him before, coward on her own!

With her heart hammering in her chest, she held her breath.

Kelby listened. Silence.

Only a light peaceful, musical tinkle of another wind chime hanging on the corner of the wooden roof.

Folding the note up, she took another look around Gary's man-cave, knowing she'd have to come back and search it more thoroughly. The note had alerted her. He had other information hidden in here somewhere.

Right now, Homerton Clinic called. She had to go there. She was too far down the line to stop now.

A crunch of gravel outside.

Kelby froze. Someone was there. She wanted to call out to see if it was Hawk, but realised with the maze of alleyways on the housing estate, he probably hadn't seen which house she'd entered.

She pushed her back against the wall. Moving only her head, she peered out of the window.

No-one in sight.

With her eye so close to the wall, Kelby could see something further along the wall under an army helmet hanging on a nail. She ducked under the window and swung the helmet to one side.

Gary's right army boot, from his amputated leg, hung by its lace on the wall. Kelby picked the boot off the nail and hugged it to her chest. Closing her eyes, she leaned in to smell the leather and polish still clinging to the boot. Gary had kept his boot even though it had never felt the warmth of his foot again. Tears threatened so she opened her eyes and gazed at a pattern on the boot.

Kelby gasped.

A replica of her pendant had been scratched on the boot. Except the replica had other symbols joining it, creating a full diagram.

What does this mean?

The drawing looked like a code. She stared at it and traced her finger along the curved X and then along the lines joining it.

Along the sole of the boot she could see tiny writing and squinted at it. Gary had etched his favourite words into the rubber: Never, never give up.

No time now to work out what the code meant. She peered out of the window again. Hawk wasn't far; she needed to get out of the garden and run down the row of houses.

For a long moment Kelby stood still before deciding it was safe.

Somewhere in the trees outside a dove cooed. Kelby glanced as the pair flapped down and settled on the nearby fence. They watched her with their beady eyes.

A strange sensation crept into her, as though Gary was up there, somewhere, watching over her.

She snuck out and locked Gary's man-cave, then she slid her back along the wall, stepping sideways, crab walking along the back of the shed.

At that moment, her head caught in a tangle from a chime that boasted an assortment of Stacie's earrings. She batted the strings of earrings away and suddenly, the hair on the nape of her neck lifted.

A human ear, studded with multiple earrings, dangled in the breeze.

100

Kelby gagged and dropped Gary's boot. Without a shadow of a doubt the ear belonged to Stacie. She swallowed the bile that hung in the back of her throat and stunk in her nostrils. She wanted to scream, but kept it bottled inside her. Instead, she blinked rapidly.

The piece of flesh was blistered and charred. Some parts were mustard yellow and leathered while others had burnt black bits hanging off. Scorched flakes of blackened skin had peeled away, yet the ear still flapped about in the breeze on Stacie's wind chime alongside her other earrings.

Kelby grabbed her phone and called Stacie. It rang and rang. No answer. Kelby gagged. She bent over and clung onto her heaving stomach.

When the nausea finally subsided, Kelby straightened. As she stood, a piece of paper fluttered alongside Stacie's ear. Shivering with the horror of it all, she read the note:

Find rizado. We want it. If you blab to anyone,
Annie is next. Don't look for her.
She's under lock and key.

Every instinct wanted to scream. She wanted to tell them, whoever they were, where to find rizado.

First, she had to find Annie. Kelby had no idea where, yet she had to start by searching the address Gary had hidden.

They had forced her to play their deadly game.

101

Olaf chuckled. The ear hanging on one of those stupid wind chimes had scared the shit out of the devil. He could have given her a showdown with the dragon there and then, but first he had to find out what she had found in the shed.

Still amused, he watched as the devil scurried down the garden path with what looked like an army boot under her arm and ran out into the road.

Women! Always needing something sentimental to hang onto.

Her erratic zigzag made him think of a frantic sprinter who'd missed the starting gun. His eyes followed her as she suddenly spotted the giant's car, sped up to it and hopped in. While she held up the boot to show the security guard, Olaf charged to his car hidden behind a delivery truck down the road. He decided to come back later for another poke around. He would easily tell if the devil had found anything. But now he had to follow her to see her next move.

A shot of adrenaline flashed through him. This Tag Two had become interesting. Even though he waited for the call for Tag One, he enjoyed following the rat's trail.

First the brother, then the wife and now the sister.

Feeling the heat of an impending battle warming his body, he pulled off his sweat shirt. Even with the day's chill biting at his flesh, he preferred to see his tattoos. The designs on his skin gave him different urges.

With one hand on the steering wheel, he flexed his fingers, crushing them into his palms.

Once again, his *animaal* instincts called.

102

As the cabbie sped along the long drive through the dense woodlands near the North Hampshire village of Homerton Grange, Barker spotted the rambling manor house that had been turned into Homerton Clinic.

A surge of excitement sent tingles coursing through him. He still couldn't believe a replica rizado had been tested right here under his nose.

Homerton Clinic of Alternative Medicine had been one of his first investments. He recalled Willow putting him in touch with Gorden about further investments in Mata Gordo, but he'd not linked the two. Now he realised Gorden owned the clinic.

Instead of entering through the buttercup-yellow front door, he strode down the side of the mansion. Landscaped gardens and park benches overlooking water features were part of the façade, hiding the obscure ailments and cures taking place inside.

Willow waited in reception. 'Gorden told me to expect you.' He took Barker's arm and led him along the corridor and down a flight of steps. 'And he told me what to expect from you.'

'Where the hell are we going?'

'To my office.' Barker nodded. 'You show me the money, and I show you my lab. Fair exchange.'

At the bottom of the flight of stairs, Barker felt as if he was sinking into the bowels of the building. The extravagant décor and fresh smells of potpourri disappeared, leaving this part of the clinic with stark white walls and the claustrophobic smell of disinfectant. Willow ushered him into a windowless room. His gaze indicated Barker in.

Barker placed his briefcase on Willow's desk and opened it. Inside, lined in the lid a letter opener's decorative handle showed off an angel with expanded wings. Using a matching magnifying glass with a steel shaft Barker scribbled out a cheque. 'I don't carry this sort of cash.'

'I know there'll be no trouble cashing it.' Willow said.

'And don't tell a soul I wear reading glasses.'

Willow's bony fingers stretched for the cheque, his mouth drooling. Barker yanked the cheque back. 'As patron of Homerton Clinic, I expect to see a return on my investment.'

Willow sighed. 'Your investment? Or the rizado information?'

True to his name Willow looked flimsy with a flaky core. Something about the moron gave Barker the creeps. Not many people had that effect on him. Maybe it was those skeletal hands flexing out of his oversized suit in an agitated dither.

'Both.'

Willow raised an eyebrow. 'As I expected.'

Barker scowled and his eyes levelled at Willow. 'You want the money?' He waved the cheque in front of the doctor's eyes. 'You'll notice it's double.'

Willow's eyes grew large, drunk with greed. Then, they narrowed at Barker. 'What's the price?'

'This should take care of the brat's private care and meds. Keep her doped-up for now.'

Willow's eyes fastened onto the cheque's zeroes, yet his fingers fiddled, leafing the paper corners and nodding like a rabid dog with a wagging tongue, desperate and eager to please.

The cheque had been signed.

Jon Barker Thompson.

103

Barker shook his head in disgust at the doctor who secretly tested new drugs on his patients. Washed-up and spineless, like driftwood on a beach, that was Willow.

Having morons at his mercy, he loved. But the morons themselves, he hated.

Willow said, 'Come this way. I'll show you what we've got so far.'

Barker nodded and followed Willow's lanky frame. In the reception a nurse called out, 'Doctor Willow, sorry to disturb you, but there's been an emergency in the MT.'

Barker saw Willow hesitate. The flaky doctor couldn't decide if his patient was more important than his investor. And MT was their code name for medical trials. He watched Willow for a moment and then helped him with his indecision. 'Go. I'll wait here.'

As Willow took a step to leave, another nurse stuck her head around the door, 'Doctor Willow, there's someone here to see you.'

'Not now. I have an emergency in MT.' Willow flapped his hands like dead branches in a winter wind.

Barker didn't know what patient awaited Willow or what bizarre treatment the man would execute. Nor did he care.

The nurse persisted, 'I know, doctor, but I thought you'd want to know about this too. A Doctor Robson said to give you this note. He said you'd fire me if I didn't give it to you immediately.'

Willow grabbed the note she gave him and opened it so he and Barker could see.

The Carbonela symbol stared back at them.

104

Barker followed Willow back into his gloomy windowless office.

'This is getting too much for me.'

Only now Barker noticed a sour tang of stale alcohol coming from Willow.

'Take it easy. I said I'd handle things from here.'

'I'm not happy about another doctor delving into this.'

'Don't panic. It's Kelby's stupid doctor friend sticking his nose into Annie's condition.'

'He's not a stupid doctor. Doctor Robson's a private consultant.'

'No big deal.' Barker didn't get intimidated by people's titles or status.

'I'm sorry Barker, but this is a big deal. The last time I saw Doctor Robson he was asking lots of questions about Annie Wade.' He flapped the note in the air. 'And if he connects me to the rizado tests, he can get me struck off the register.'

'Stop, Willow. You're hyperventilating.' Barker's upper lip curled.

'And what about my research downstairs?' If the Medical Council find —'

'They won't.'

Barker got the creeps talking to this man. For some reason, every agitated flex of Willow's skeletal fingers made Barker think of a hand reaching out of a grave. He tried to disguise the shiver that screamed down his spine. Ambling to the other side of the dingy room, he said, 'There'll be no evidence.'

'But there is. My lab is full of, um, test results.' Willow's hands fiddled with the buttons on his suit, opening and closing them. Through the gloom, the doctor's eyes gleamed like cat's eyes at midnight.

'Easy to remove.'

Willow stopped fiddling with the buttons. 'I don't want to be accused of unethical conduct or malpractice, or have my medical licence revoked.' Willow started panting. 'It'll ruin me.'

'Calm down! Robson knows none of this.'

'I don't want him snooping around here.'

Barker patted Willow on the back to reassure him. 'He won't be. Leave Robson to me.' His immediate goal was to separate Kelby and Robson. Together they were too powerful. He had to get her alone again.

'Will it be Olaf?'

Barker nodded. 'You lead the doctor to him. Olaf will take over from there.'

Willow's bony index finger lifted in a ghost-like manner as he pointed down a dark tunnel leading into the depths of the mansion. 'I'll take him to our dungeon.'

105

Kelby sat tensed and upright as Hawk sped along the drive through the dense woodlands near the North Hampshire village of Homerton Grange.

They had argued all the way. In a strange way it was just as well because it took her mind off the gross image of Stacie's ear dangling in the breeze. The shock numbed her senses.

Hawk kept insisting he take her somewhere safe, but she dug her heels in. 'I have to do this. Please, I know you have your job to do, but stick with me on this one last thing. Please."

'I'm not happy about it, Kelby. Do me a favour; call Roy and see what he thinks.'

To pacify him, she called Roy, but the call failed. She tried again. Immediately, Roy answered. 'Kelby! Good God, I have been desperate to get hold of you.' His voice sounded so clear and so close by.

'I tried to get you, but no signal.'

'Are you o—' His voice disappeared.

'Roy? Roy? Can you hear me?'

'Kelby, I'm . . .' the connection ended.

Kelby tried again. But it went straight to a dead signal. She squinted at the signal bars on her phone and huffed, 'No bars. Not even one.'

She waited a minute and tried again. This time Roy's phone went straight to voicemail. Kelby pocketed her phone and clung to the army boot. Her gaze kept wandering back to the symbol scratched into the leather. She glanced around. 'Look!' Kelby pointed to a rambling manor house which now appeared to be a clinic for alternative medicine.

Hawk tried again to argue with her. 'Kelby, I'm not happy with this. Let me take you somewhere safe and we'll get someone else to handle this.'

'Stop it, Hawk. You'll soon find out that when I make up my mind to do something, nothing can change it.' From the corner of her eye she saw his jaw tighten and lock.

With Gary's scrawl imprinted on her mind, she said, 'We have to follow Gary's instructions and go around the back.'

As Hawk continued along the dirt track, they noticed numerous signs saying *Do not enter* and *Private Grounds*. Another sign rattled Kelby. The blood-red triangle with bold black letters stating: *Warning Keep Out!*

Nowhere did Kelby see a signpost saying *42A*.

106

As Olaf kept a steady pace behind the giant's car, his phone vibrated on the dashboard. Without taking his eyes off the road, he answered in a gruff voice, 'Ja?'

'Where are you?'

'On the road to the clinic.'

'I thought you were tailing Wade?'

'I am.'

'Ah, so she is sniffing out the trail.'

Olaf kept silent.

'Perfect. Before you deal with her, pull in here. We have a man causing trouble.'

'Tall. Fair. Bushy hair. Tanned.'

'Yes.'

'It's the boyfriend. I saw him with her earlier. He left and I followed her to her brother's place.'

'What happened?'

'Nothing. She came out with an army boot. And now they're headed here.'

'She must have found something there to bring her to the clinic.'

'I will find out soon.'

'Okay, but first get over here and deal with him. I'll meet you downstairs. Willow said to tell you we're heading into the tunnel.'

Olaf cut the call. Strange how things had turned around, from tagging Barker to now working with him. No bother, he liked his style. One thing about rich men like Barker, they didn't like getting their hands dirty.

Pick-ee.

107

Beyond the clinic, Hawk and Kelby passed a walled garden and drove through more woods. Near the thicket, Kelby spotted a graveyard. Even though most manor houses had their own burial grounds, the sight still sent a shiver through her.

Dread swelled into her chest as Kelby edged closer to Hawk while he steered past a clump of dead, twisted trees that looked like gnarled claws. She imagined they wanted to reach out of the ground to grab her.

Then, a foreboding monster loomed ahead of them.

The abandoned mansion looked more like a small castle than a manor home. The winged flanks of the building spread towards trees on either side where a thickly wooded copse separated the two properties. Although someone had painstakingly restored the main clinic, this part of the property looked like it had crawled out of a horror movie.

Hawk parked and they stared at the once beautiful decaying mansion. Its peeling paintwork and overgrown courtyards told the story of a dramatic decline of a country house estate. Deteriorating buildings were connected by a web of overgrown patios. Some parts looked in danger of collapse.

'You stay here. I'll check it out.' Hawk opened the door.

'No way! I'm not staying here alone with that horrible building glaring at me. Besides, I want to see what 42A is about.'

Hawk grabbed her hand on the door handle to stop her opening it. 'First, let me have a quick recce. I don't like the look of this. I'll check it out to make sure it's safe and we'll go in together.'

'But —'

'In the meantime, why don't you try Doctor Robson again?'

Kelby hesitated, then sighed and nodded.

Talking to Roy would be better than sitting here alone.

108

After several minutes of chatting and laughing amongst themselves the leather jerkin reached into the fire with a thickly gloved hand. María's jaw dropped in horror as he lifted the red-hot claws of their metal spider and clasped them at the sides of her mother's exposed breasts.

Madre screamed in pain.

María's lunged at him. '*No!*'

The cloaked soldier jumped forward and kicked her in the stomach. María doubled over. Her stomach groaned in agony, and her eyes glazed as she watched the unbooted soldier lean over and lift her mother's sagging body.

Earlier, she hadn't understood why her mother wasn't fighting back, but now María saw why. Madre's naked body was covered in dark bruises and bloody scratch marks. It looked like a wild cat had torn off her clothes and shredded her belly. Her thighs, once a golden honey colour, now glowed with ominous purple welts.

The *bastardos* had beaten Mama!

After pinning her mother down with his boot in the crook of her neck, the cloaked soldier glared at María. His eyes defied her to try anything.

The gloved leather jerkin inserted the spikes into each side of her mother's breasts, penetrating them with a powerful grasp.

Again, her mother screamed in pain.

And fainted.

109

Watching Hawk's lofty torso striding to the old derelict building, Kelby's hand dug into the sling bag crossing her body. Taking her eyes off Hawk for a moment, she tapped Roy's number into her phone.

He answered on the first ring, 'Kelby! At last.'

Kelby exhaled with relief.

'Did you —' His voice faded.

'Roy? Can you hear me?'

'Listen Kelby …' the connection dropped again, but suddenly she could hear him, '… my messages.'

'Sorry, I didn't hear that.'

'Annie —' His voice dipped. Then, a moment later, it came back. 'Where ar—'

The line cut out.

Kelby's pulse raced. What was he saying about Annie? Did he know where she was?

Another five minutes and Kelby started to panic. Hawk had been away too long. Maybe he'd gone inside the mansion on his own, but he said he would come back for her. It must be safe if he'd done that. He probably thought he could find something without involving her.

A few more minutes passed.

Kelby couldn't stand it any longer. Her hand white-knuckled Gary's note. She turned it over in her hand for the third time to check if she could glean any more about what to do.

Forcing herself to open the door, Kelby stepped out of the car and peered around. Her heartbeat pounded in her ears. A breeze gusted up to her and lifted her fringe. A long drawn out squeak came from behind her.

Kelby spun around. A sign, swinging from a rusting lamp post, squealed its protest to the breeze. She looked closer and read the sign.

Homerton Hall Laboratory.

110

Olaf watched the giant and the devil taking the split in the road that led to Homerton Lab. Not many people knew about the place, so the devil must have found something.

Accelerating around the back of the clinic, he parked and entered the newly painted building through the side staff entrance. Knowing his way around the corridors came in handy.

He heard voices echoing through the maze of tunnels running beneath the house. For a moment, his imagination ran wild. He thought of the days when servants would have marched along here, to-ing and fro-ing between the two wealthy homes above. Before the old string of lights was installed, they probably used candles.

His breath caught in his throat. Lots of dragons would have roamed in the tunnels in those days.

The thought made him forget why he had come here. For a moment, he lost himself in *animaal* urges.

Then, just as suddenly, voices pierced the wild images raging through his head. Still lost, he thought it was that voice. The voice he had never forgotten.

But it wasn't.

It was Willow. His chest deflated as he exhaled hard. It disappointed him. The dragon had started firing up for revenge.

Willow, still talking to someone, drew closer.

'What's down here?' a strange voice asked.

'You said you wanted to know my connection to rizado. First, I'll show you toxicology research I have been doing.'

'What's that got to do with MG and the rizado?'

'Startling results.'

The voices were almost upon Olaf. He peered down the tunnel, making out Willow's skeletal figure with another tall one beside him.

The lover.

111

Although his body was raging with a fire wheel of burning memories, Olaf remained still. He had learnt to contain his smouldering urges.

He preferred to harness them. Keep them dangling in the air, just out of his reach. And when he needed them the most, he could reach out and snatch it. And use the strength it gave him to execute a Tag One.

At that moment, Willow looked up and caught Olaf's eye.

'I'll show you how my toxicology connects to rizado,' Willow stepped aside and indicated for the lover to move in front of him. 'Go ahead.'

Olaf pulled back into the shadows and into a junction in the tunnel. A tarnished light bulb near his head nearly gave the game away. His hand shot out and grabbed the bulb. He unscrewed it, despite the burning pain biting into his palm.

The pain was *niks*. The dragon had fired up.

As the footsteps were upon him, the lover said, 'I don't see what your toxicology research —'

Olaf swung his fist. It crashed into the lover's jaw, knocking him unconscious before he could finish his sentence.

'Thank God!' Willow whined, 'I was starting to think you weren't down here.'

Olaf knelt and took a closer look. 'What do you want me to do with pretty boy?'

'Whatever you like. I don't care. Let him rot in one of the downstairs rooms forever.' Willow fled.

Olaf dragged the leaden body along the tunnel. He better be quick. He had to finish off the giant and devil.

And the lover.

So much was happening so quickly. The excited pace set his pulse racing again.

The damp smell of the musty tunnel hit him high in the nostrils. Taking him instantly back to the dragon's forest.

And setting his *animaal* alight.

112

The unbooted soldier lifted the bucket of water beside the fire and threw it over Madre's feeble body. María heard her mother's flesh sizzle and burn as the warm water absorbed the heat from the red-hot tongs. Closing her eyes, María tried to stop believing the scene in their little family home.

All the memories of Madre delivering babies on their kitchen table, and healing sick people came flooding into her mind.

The laughter and merriment after the babies bellowed for the first time filled her ears. The smell of Madre's baking and the taste of a fresh pie filling her hungry belly. The sounds of Padre's booming voice as he came home laden with gifts of livestock, cloth and strips of leather.

María opened her eyes. Through slits, she surveyed the room, taking note of anything she could use as a weapon against these soldiers. A flush of adrenaline tingled through her body.

Madre moaned as another bucket of water was tossed at her. She opened her eyes and looked directly into María's. The cloaked soldier lifted his boot off Madre's neck and shoved her into a sitting position.

María's expression boiled in anger. Her mother's mouth moved silently. She leaned closer in time to hear her croak, 'María. The promise.'

María's nostrils flared. 'I will never fail you, Mama. Never!'

Suddenly, with the agility of a leopard, María sprang up.

113

Taking a deep and ragged breath, Kelby left the safety of the car. The imposing Victorian hall had clearly been built for spectacular living and entertainment. However, the building now seemed to sag in the agony of abandonment.

A pile of logs rotted nearby, giving sanctuary to night creatures. Debris of branches and dead leaves covered the paved slabs leading to the door.

Three floors with ornate window frames rose into turrets and chimneys. A large bay window surrounded the main door. At the ends of each winged flank were pillar-covered doorways. Many of the windows were cracked. Brambles climbed up, fighting to get inside the broken glass.

Kelby took a deep breath, lifted the huge door knocker and rapped on the door. It echoed inside the building, reverberating along the long hallway and disappearing out the other end. She waited. No answer. So she knocked again.

Still no answer.

After waiting for about five minutes, she tried the door knob, but it was jammed.

Blowing out her pent up tension, she sneaked along the house, peering into each window she came across. An eerie stillness hovered over the house. It seemed to loom over her like a demonic ghost waiting to strike.

Swivelling her neck, she glanced over her shoulder at the car. Hawk wasn't anywhere to be seen.

Damn. I should wait for him.

Kelby shivered and wondered what on earth she was doing with no clue as to what she would look for or find. But a strong instinct drove her on.

Suddenly the image of Gary giving her the framed sign with Winston Churchill's words came into her mind.

Never, never, never give up.

Taking a deep breath, an image sprang into her mind. The photo where Gary threw Annie up into his arms, caught her and cuddled her just as Kelby snapped the precious memory into her phone. With that image of her two most precious people, a new feeling crept into her. For too long she had lived with regret: first the loss of her parents, then her first business going belly up leading to her failure to conceive, Gary's leg tragedy and finally his passing.

He'd never let remorse get him down, saying loss of hope is temporary. When her business collapsed, he urged her to pick herself up and move forward. And she had. Now the sensation stiffening her spine was a new awareness. She had to accept her past without sorrow. Without her parents or her brother, she could face her future without fear.

Renewed perseverance zipped into Kelby.

At the end of the right wing, she stepped up to the covered door and tried the ornate doorknob.

The door creaked open.

Sweat dampened her armpits as she peered inside.

'Hawk. You there?' Even though only a whisper, her voice raced down the hallway and found an exit at the far end. It blasted out of a broken window and disappeared.

This time, she bellowed, 'Hawk, where are you?'

Again, her voice floated down the hallway and bounced around between the walls. With her heart thudding against her ribs, she stepped inside and peered around. It took her eyes a few moments to adjust to the dim interior.

Silence stretched along the corridor.

Thankfully, light spilled into the hall from the many windows, showing the decay and ruin. Once she was inside, the cold, desolate building clawed at her, as though relieved to finally receive a visitor.

As she stepped gingerly along the hallway, an earthy odour rose from the damp floorboards. Broken ceiling beams scattered her path. A painting lay on the floor as though the person hanging it had suddenly forgotten it. Unable to resist, she reached and touched the chipped and flaking walls. Saddened such a beautiful building had been left this way, Kelby imagined how it had once been, alive with the sounds of children playing, racing down the hallways and families chattering as they went about their daily routine.

That's how it should be now.

She could see lots of doors leading off the flaking hallway. Peering into each room as she passed, Kelby realised they were abandoned consulting rooms, filled with discarded books and papers. A few had windows swinging open on their hooks. One had birds nesting in what looked like a dentist's chair.

Feeling overwhelmed, Kelby tiptoed into the next chamber and gasped.

From the far side of the room, two white ghostly apparitions watched her.

114

Olaf ran through the underground maze. Sweat poured off his head. It rolled down over the dragon and soaked his t-shirt. This tainted tunnel ... it reminded him of another dark place. He had to get out.

Scuttling along the damp passage, Olaf placed his hand on the wall to keep himself steady. The smell of this place overwhelmed him, and once again he was in the forest where he had been abused.

That terrible wilderness still sired nightmares.

Fleeing. Over the forest floor littered with logging debris. At each turn the brush reached out to grab him, their woody talons thick with spikes and impaling thorns.

Stumbling. On overgrown roots and wind-toppled deadfall. Slashed by the oak thicket.

Tumbling. To the mossy undergrowth. Crashing to his knees. Unsure if the roots tripped him up or the dragon chasing him.

Plunging. Into a cavity surrounded by eroded roots. And debris. A rabbit carcass strewn about by its predator.

Explosions bursting in his head. That voice puncturing the heavy, oppressive air.

Sweltering. Heat consuming him. Sweat drenching him.

The dragon shooting bolts of flames into him.

For a long moment, Olaf lay curled up on the tunnel floor. Hugging his knees. Trying to rid himself of the pain. The shame. The fear.

Slowly, the same fear turned sour in his mouth. He spat it out, coughing up a lump of phlegm.

Flexing his bicep helped to remind him he had beaten the dragon. He glanced sideways at it bulging. Hard and high. He arched his arm a few more times and rose to his feet.

He had a job to do.

Grit and dirt crunched under his feet as he left the tunnel and exited the clinic, and the bright glare from the overcast day pierced his eyes. He had fired up the lover. Now the giant and the devil waited for their turn.

It only took a spark to flare up a fire storm.

115

Unable to run, Kelby stared at the two ghosts. Terror prickled her neck. Every hair on her body stood on end and her pulse accelerated into a frenzy.

The ghosts didn't move. Neither were they floating. They seemed too chalky with definite shapes.

Weren't ghosts invisible with only an aura of white?

Her breathing calmed. Taking the plunge to discover more, she stepped closer. They still didn't move. Another step closer.

Kelby blew out her relief. They were only garden statues with ivory dust sheets thrown over them. This was getting out of hand. If only she could find what Gary meant by '42A'. And if only Hawk would come back from where ever he'd gone. At least he was here somewhere and she'd find him any minute.

The next room she entered had once been a reading room. It still maintained a small semblance of dignity, with books lining carved shelves on either side of the room. Journals, covered in thick dust, lay scattered across the floor, while a coffee table waited to once again carry an afternoon tea. Outside, a row of barren trees shuffled their branches, looming in to see what the intruder was doing.

Across the corridor another room contradicted the decaying tranquillity of the reading room. Three wrought iron hospital beds on either side of the room shrunk back into the walls as though afraid of receiving new patients. This room had the stench of death.

Kelby's imagination ran wild with images of patients suffering unknown agonies. She bolted back into the hallway.

An amber glow lured her into a room a few doors further on. The mansion's kitchen looked as sad and forlorn as the rest of the house. Shafts of light shone through smashed holes in the glass windows and pooled onto the dust-covered floor.

As Kelby stepped carefully over smashed jam jars, she imagined the baker had thrown cinnamon in the air and it had filtered down to cover the entire kitchen. With each step the stench of mould and damp earth rose up to assault her nostrils.

A rusted ladle still perched in a roasting tin sat on the stove as though the chef had rushed out the door and hadn't come back. Ageing pan lids and burnt copper pots adorned the cooker set back into the wall, now crumbling around it. In the corner, cupboard doors swung off their rusting hinges spreading their shadows across the table, already littered with kitchen debris.

As she stood beside the rotting oak table, memories of her mother rammed into Kelby's mind. With unexpected clarity the smell of an apple pie steaming out of the oven took over the mildew stench. Kelby recalled apple pies with golden crusts sitting on a powdered counter where her mother rolled pastry.

As fast as it had arrived, the memory faded. She stood for a moment, struggling to retrieve it, desperate to remember those little details about her mother.

When she turned and glanced at the kitchen once more, it took on the bruised hue of decomposing flesh. Kelby swung around and tiptoed between the glass fragments. Out in the hall, she leaned against the wall. It was sad such a terrible place had reminded her of her mother, but she was heartened that some precious memories still remained inside her.

Still unable to find what she'd come for, Kelby suspected Gary's note indicated a room number. But none of these rooms bore signs. She fled, too afraid to look into any more rooms.

At the end of the long passage, a large arched landing area proudly showed off a carved flight of steps. For a moment, Kelby admired the stained glass skylight which sent shards of splintered colour down the dark stairs.

With a knot of dread unravelling in her stomach, Kelby peered down the curling staircase to the lower floor wondering if Hawk had ventured that far.

'Hawk?' she whispered.

Now convinced Gary's number indicated a room, she had to see if she could find it below. Picking her way between rotting floorboards, she crept into the basement of the derelict building. Each stair proved to be perilous as it squeaked and croaked under her feet.

Some had rotted away, others had holes where wood worms had eaten through the once solid oak. At the bottom of the creaking stairway, the musty odour became stronger, clinging to her nose.

Half way down another long corridor she passed a broken and rusting wheelchair, minus one wheel and the seat eaten by rats. The sharp stench of urine and musk grew stronger. She was heading deeper and deeper into the bowels of the mansion.

When Kelby thought she could take no more of this stinking place, a faded sign on the wall indicated an arrow.

And a number. 42A.

116

Leaping into the air, María kicked the uncloaked soldier leaning over her mother. He fell back, more overcome with surprise than hurt.

The unbooted soldier dropped the bucket and reached to grab her. María darted under his arms and spun back. She grabbed the bucket, dumping it over his head. Using the point of her carved wooden-soled clog, she stomped with all her strength on his toes.

'¡Ai-yee!' her war cry echoed around the room.

Then, with both hands, she barrelled towards the unbooted soldier, uttering another war cry. Her lithe body smacked into his. The force shoved him into the fire. His frightened yelp echoed inside the bucket. She spun around, grabbed the hair-matted dagger and hurled it into the flames.

The uncloaked soldier dropped her mother and scrambled to his feet, cursing.

María dived to her knees and grabbed two of the quills still drying on the edge of the hearth. With the instinct of a killer, she spun back to face him.

And plunged the quills into his eyes.

The man's screech filled the room. He gripped the quills, trying to pull them out, but tottered around like a drunk in a dark cobbled alley. He stumbled into the unbooted soldier who had wrangled the bucket from over his head, then he banged into the wall and passed out.

Beside the pile of clothing still to be packed away, María spotted her ink stained chemise.

The unbooted soldier came at her from behind.

Without thinking, she ducked, grabbed the ink stained chemise and tossed it high over her shoulders. His head caught in the loop of muslin that descended over the two of them. She yanked on it, jerking him into her back as the chemise suffocated him. Even though she had no chance against all three, she had to maim at least one. When the others came at her, she'd fight to the death.

The leather jerkin, still holding the tongs into her mother, let them go and jumped up. With her lips pulled back, María bared her teeth at him. He lunged at her with his huge leather glove.

María instinctively took a deep breath a second before the glove clamped over her mouth. She struggled against him for a long moment. She had to save Madre.

Nothing else mattered.

Without air to fuel her, María's strength ebbed away. The grip she had on the chemise behind her slackened, and the unbooted soldier's head came free. He grabbed her hands and twisted the chemise around them. In front of her, the leather jerkin held the glove over her mouth with his other hand on her throat.

María took one last glimpse of her mother's bloodied breasts and looked into her eyes.

Then her beloved kitchen went black.

117

Outside Homerton Laboratory Olaf slinked around the giant's beamer. Despite its age he loved the colour. Metallic shades reminded him of guns. Even though he hated guns and refused to use one, he still admired their fire power.

Nee, he preferred using his own body strength and turning his Tag into an *animaal* act. It was an art to use items around a killing scene. And this weird place certainly had enough creativity for him to use.

Most people would never guess by the look of him that he loved reading books, even soppy ones. The best ones took him away from his life and into another world where the seedy forest of his teens didn't exist.

The forest that had turned a boy into an *animaal.*

Others took him straight back to that day. Those stories taught him things school couldn't and steeled his resolve to stop the place haunting him.

Olaf clenched his fists and watched how his biceps jumped into sinew. He had no idea how the devil had found the lab but something in her brother's den must have led her here. That meant he hadn't scoured it properly after he'd silenced Wade.

A fault on his part. One he wasn't going to let Jurgen find out. The German would go totally berserk.

Olaf decided to sort this out first and head back to trash Wade's shed. He'd make it look like a robbery. Rather that, than not finding Wade's notes. Thankfully, MG trusted him enough to believe there were no notes.

All had changed with the devil sister's discovery of the rizado lab.

Olaf heard the ground crunching as a twig broke amongst dried leaves. He stopped and listened for other sounds. Apart from an occasional breeze rustling the dead leaves littering the drive, silence settled upon Homerton Lab.

He'd give the devil a few minutes to get stuck in the maze of corridors and hallways, then he'd corner her.

But first he had to go after the giant.

Rather than killing two birds with one stone, having them separated would give him two spoils.

More excitement for the dragon.

118

An eerie glow oozed out of number 42A. With a shaking hand, Kelby nudged the door open wider. It hung ajar. The painted number had almost completely flaked off.

A pungent stench pierced her nose. Death and chemicals formed a noxious concoction.

Her mind flashed back to her school days, and how once the science teacher had to call Gary to take her home. He had been only a little fella, but he had bravely taken his nauseous older sister by the hand, and walked her home. Now, she wondered why he had led her to such a disgusting place.

Inside 42A, Kelby immediately saw it was Homerton's hidden laboratory. As she sneaked inside, her shoes squelched on a sticky residue stuck to the floor. Something dangled in front of her face. Kelby jumped back, afraid a creepy creature had tossed its web to stop her entering.

Phew, only a long corded light switch.

She tugged on it and peered around. Opposite her, a fridge sagged into the corner. Cold air rattled through its pipes and echoed around the lab. The eerie sound reminded Kelby of films about people living under New York who communicated by tapping on pipes.

Next to the fridge a solid oak door looked as if it hadn't been opened in years. Above it, a wall clock ticked. A freezer hummed eerily in the opposite corner. Whilst it emitted only a quiet pulse, a variety of other sounds filled the room, including chiming beeps and blips from strange looking apparatus. Machinery boiled and bubbled with vats of unknown substances. Kelby shivered, refusing to imagine what they contained.

Despite the mansion's decay, this laboratory was equipped with the sophisticated tools of modern science: neatly stacked test tubes, beakers, flasks of coloured liquids and bunsen burners. Even an operating table.

An impressive sculpture with funny-shaped coils of glass glinted in the fluorescence. A large blackboard on the wall was covered in scribbles of unreadable notes and equations.

Kelby gagged at the stench. It made her eyes water. There were rows of containers of dead animals preserved in formaldehyde, some recognisable and other simply grotesque organs. She spotted brains sealed in a glass jar. In the bright light, a rabbit's two front teeth jutted out. Beside it a cat's wet furry head, soaked in chemicals, peered at her, its eyes transfixed in death. Its tongue hung out beside its fangs.

Nausea gripped Kelby. Why on earth had Gary led her to this sordid lab?

119

María came round and gagged on the ink stained chemise rammed into her mouth. Tied to one of the kitchen chairs, she opened her eyes to see her mother still on the floor in front of her.

In her fury, she hadn't thought about her own life. Everything she did was focused on saving Madre.

'She's awake.' A voice close to her ear smelt sour and rancid.

'Let's get on with it.'

A red-hot stick from the fire glowed in front of María.

'Close your eyes and you'll get the same treatment you gave our friend over there.'

María's gaze slid to the left to see the cloaked and quilled man slumped against the wall with her mother's apron wrapped around his head.

Keeping the glowing poker in front of her face, the unbooted soldier forced her to look at her mother. Once again the leather jerkin lifted the searing clawed metal spider out of the flames and clamped it to her mother's breasts.

Her mother let out another shriek and fainted.

María screeched into the gag. She struggled against the ropes, ignoring the sting of the rope rubbing her arms raw. In her attempt to get closer to her mother, she shunted the chair aside. One of its legs rocked on the uneven stone floor, and the chair crashed over. María's head slammed against the stone slabs, sending a jolt of pain through her.

The leather jerkin's glove ripped the metal spider out of her mother's breasts. The claws ripped and shredded Madre's soft skin.

Tied to the chair on its side, María lay still, her head pounding. The soldiers left Madre bleeding while they finished their stew and discussed what to do with her.

The leather jerkin prodded María with his boot. 'Where is the rizado?'

María's eyes widened and her mouth went dry.

He asked again, 'Someone told Queen Isabella about your stories. She demanded to see them and your heretic journal.'

María stiffened. Although shocked anyone other than Tío's family knew about her stories, María knew they would not betray her.

'If you do not give us this rizado to take to the queen, you will face the same beating as your mother.'

A sudden giddiness filled María's head. *Who told the queen?*

120

As Olaf slipped behind the derelict mansion, he glanced around. Spotting a long piece of weathered twine holding a vine, he jerked at it. It snapped.

He held it at arm's length and tugged it between his hands, but it tore into two threads. He shook his head in disgust and tossed it away. As he did so, he noticed more of the twine tucked closer to a rotting window. He yanked it and immediately felt it rub between his finger and his palm, giving him a rope burn.

'*Goed!*' He followed the twine with his fingertips and found the end. Unravelling it from the vine, he tucked it into his pocket. It helped to have a backup weapon. As he rose to his feet, he stumbled over a rusty old pipe, hanging off the wall.

Olaf's gaze followed the conduit and saw the water irrigation pipework would give way in numerous places. 'Even better,' he muttered, and wrenched the tube. Clumps of rust peeled off like crumbs falling from a fresh crusty loaf.

At the end of the corroded cylinder an oxidised tap leaked out a greenish-brown fungus. Although the fetid slime reeked of a foul-smelling pond, the tap tempted his imagination. He turned it and realised its inner parts had rusted up, but he ripped it off the wall bracket. Something extra to add to his weaponry.

He stopped and listened. Hearing the giant's footsteps around the back of the mansion, he started following with slow deliberate movements. His heart raced and sweat prickled in his armpits.

He wasn't afraid of the giant. Not at all. Thinking of how the dragon would slay the giant, excitement gripped him.

When his *animaal* called, he obeyed

121

Kelby wondered if the animal stuffed in the bottle was Fat Cat. She couldn't tell because the chemicals had bloated its face. Thankfully its eyes faced the wall.

Lots of the formaldehyde bottles had either evaporated or leaked out. The smell was dire, making breathing nearly impossible. As she reeled from the stench and shock of seeing so many dead things in one place, her hand clutched her nose. She glanced over her shoulder to the door, half expecting a mad scientist to jump out and stab a needle of some concoction into her neck to experiment on her.

The sudden venting of an air conditioning unit sounded like the release on the old steam train ride she'd enjoyed with Annie.

Inside an open cabinet, corked bottles of dusty medicines had illegible handwritten stained labels. Many of them had broken open with fumes leaking out causing the most putrid smell. Kelby switched on the desk's lamp. Beside it, a set of jars with medical labels showed a series of scientific equations.

One read: $Na+C=N$

Lots of squiggles with letters surrounded hexagonal diagrams showed letters: CI and HO.

Another read: $N > P = O$

For a moment, she examined a journal that lay beside the powder-filled jars. She turned the pages, but none of it made any sense. It appeared to be similar to Ana-María's herbal guide, except the images had dried leaves, dried seeds and petals crudely plastered into the pages with lines pointing to different formulas.

Then, something leapt from the page: *Natural Toxicology.*

122

Shouting that he needed to take the rizado to the queen, the leather jerkin's slammed his boot into María's body.

'Where is it?' he cried out, bringing another kick closer to her face.

María jerked her head back knowing it would only take one hard kick to shatter her jaw.

Most men didn't expect a woman to be as strong as her rage had made María. As soon as she broke free, she'd fight to the death like a mother lion defending her young.

'Answer me, or you will get the same beating.'

'She will get more than a beating.' The unbooted soldier leered at her, 'I want her first.'

'No, I will be first,' the quilled soldier muttered from his position against the wall, 'and I will take my time to punish *la puta* where it hurts the most. She will be begging for mercy.'

'And,' the unbooted soldier guffawed 'she will tell you everything to report to the queen. What is this rizado, anyway?'

The leather jerkin shrugged. 'I don't know and I don't care. I am the senior officer, so I will have her first.'

They banged their fists on the table as they started squabbling.

María took no notice. She tried to focus her mind on other things, but questions tumbled around: Who had told the queen about rizado? Had the herbal journal been published and shown to the monarch?

Behind her, María's arms twitched against the bounds of the ropes. How could she escape? And how could she get Madre to a safe place?

A loud bang on the door jolted her out of her reverie. A fourth soldier booted it open and bellowed, 'Who is next on watch?'

The leather jerkin bellowed at the young soldier, 'You are. Get back to your post.'

'I saw two inquisitors; they are going to burn their first witch.'

'You mean beat her.'

'No. Burn her.'

123

Inside Homerton Laboratory, Olaf listened to the hollow echo of footsteps. He followed them. Slow and deliberate. And silent. Stealth led to a surprise attack on his victim.

The devil had to be careful. The place had been abandoned a century ago, like the clinic next door. A lot of this building had been declared dangerous. No-one had even bothered putting up 'No Entry' signs.

When Gordo had spent millions renovating the clinic, he'd said he would do the same for this dilapidated side of the property, but he hadn't got around to it.

Using it for secret testing of drugs was a clever tactic. No-one finding the building by accident would attempt to go inside. It looked too creepy. And no-one would guess the two buildings were connected via stinking underground tunnels. They were ideal for transporting drugged test patients from one to the other.

When Olaf saw the place, Gordo had let slip it used to be an asylum for mental patients before the turn of the century. But whenever he came here, it reminded Olaf of the houses in the horror stories he read. The ones where humans turned into werewolves or other animals at dusk. Humans were basically *animaals*. They played the roles of humans, but everyone had the ability to turn, as he had discovered.

What tests they did here, he didn't know or care. His job entailed exterminating the human rats. At the beginning of his deal with Gordo, he'd been given a tour of the place. At the time he hadn't asked questions.

Why bother? He didn't want to know the answers. He needed to know what resources he had at his disposal. And he'd been given free rein to use anything right there in front of his eyes. From the demented lab to the bone disposal fire pit. Besides, the horrors inside the labs fuelled his imagination with ideas for his own *animaal* pleasures.

Who would have thought the sister would go the same way as her brother?

124

Still in 42A, Kelby opened the toxicology journal and glanced at the page. She leaned over to squint at the small writing. Half way, she spotted a paragraph that read: *Abrin is 75 per cent stronger than ricin — 3 micrograms can kill an adult human.*

Another entry read: *Strychnine tree. Strychnine and Brucine have a potent heart toxin called cerberin, similar in structure to digoxin, found in the foxglove. 30 mg gives a painful death from violent convulsions.*

Feeling perspiration prickling her skin, Kelby saw: *Digoxin kills by blocking calcium ion channels in heart muscles which disrupts the heartbeat.*

Intrigue and horror propelled her to continue reading:

White baneberries contain a carcinogenic toxin which has an almost immediate, sedative effect on human cardiac muscles and can easily cause a quick death.

Beside the journal, a tray of bottled jars sparkled under the lamp light. One bottle's label read: *Ricinus communis*. It contained dried seeds in a black and brown pattern. They looked like a bunch of thick blood-engorged ticks.

Another bottle had *White baneberry* written on it. Inside, clusters of small white balls with a black dot in the middle stared back at her. They reminded Kelby of Annie's doll's eyes.

Kelby shivered at a pile of seed pods that looked like red crab's eyes, sticking out of a dried husk. Near the jars lay a set of test tubes, wrapped together in an elastic band. Feeling a coil of dread snaking around her gut, Kelby straightened. Her gaze landed on a bloodstained lab coat hung on a hook beside the murky jars of mutant monstrosities.

Bile rose into Kelby's throat, choking her. She imagined a crazy scientist practising with dead and abnormal animals, trying to discover the components of rizado's healing elixir.

Maybe Gary led her here as proof that Mata Gordo were trying to replicate rizado. If she could find a way to prove what they had done to him, and the others, she could take the evidence to PC Pike.

Kelby had seen enough. Time to get out. A sudden thought struck her. Maybe Roy would understand the journal of numbers and poisons. She grabbed her phone and tapped his number. As before, it went straight to voice mail.

Before she could take another step, a door slammed upstairs, immediately followed by a loud creak on the stairway.

125

María gasped at the young soldier's declaration of a witch about to be burnt nearby. Like her, the unbooted soldier seemed to be in a stupor about the news.

'*¡Diablo!*' The unbooted soldier frowned. 'Heretics are supposed to be punished in their parish.'

The leather jerkin guffawed. 'Hah! Some of us get bored with parish punishment.'

'*¡Vaya!*' the unbooted soldier wiped his mouth with the back of his hand and spoke with his mouth full, 'Come on. Let's go and watch.'

Still slumped, the quilled soldier protested, 'We can't leave. We are on duty for our queen. Besides, I can't see anything.' The quilled soldier groaned. The other soldiers had patched his eye with Madre's torn chemise.

The young soldier at the door hesitated, looking from the quilled soldier to the others at the table. 'They said it is only a few hours' ride from here.'

The gloved leather jerkin rose to his feet and strode to the door while the unbooted soldier yanked on his boots and glanced at María. 'What about them?'

Shutting her eyes with her chin lolling on her chest, María pretended to be asleep.

'Leave them as they are. We'll come back to give the young one a spider.'

'She's a wild cat, she'll break free.' The now booted soldier grabbed his own cloak from the back of the room.

'How? She's tied up and gagged. She has nowhere to go.' The new soldier frowned.

'Hah! She's deadly. I don't trust her.' The now booted soldier pointed at the quilled soldier slumped over the table, 'We know what she's capable of. I don't want to see her anger again.'

The new soldier gasped, 'She did that?'

Although the now booted soldier was keen to leave, he hesitated. 'We'd better hurry back. If we do not find what Queen Isabella wants, she will have our heads.'

The new soldier lifted the quilled soldier to his feet and helped him limp to the door. 'We can find someone to look at your eye.'

María listened, hoping and praying the temptation to watch a woman die at the stake would take them away. Being imprisoned in this way would kill her spirit. Worse, her mother lay at her feet.

Dying.

126

Kelby listened. There it was again. Crreee. Craaww. Crreee. Craaww. The exact sounds when she descended the stairs earlier.

Someone was behind her. Following her.

Kelby dropped the journal, darted to the door and peered into the corridor. It must be Hawk coming back.

The staircase stopped creaking. Kelby backtracked her path to the base of the ageing stairs and looked up. Nobody there. But she had definitely heard the sounds. Picking her way up the rotten flight of stairs, she kept glancing at her feet to check her steps, and then upwards hoping to see a familiar face.

'Hawk?' she whispered.

The hall directly above had no door. A shadow stared back at her. Another skipped beat. She held her breath. No sounds. Then, Kelby realised it was a trick of her mind sending shards of panic into her. The shadow was an old tattered curtain blowing in the breeze from the broken window. Kelby exhaled hard. She had to go back for the journal and get out of here fast. Then a crunching sound came from one of the rooms off the hallway. Kelby's heart skipped another beat. Her breath caught in her throat. A sound came from above: heavy breathing. 'Hawk? Is that you?'

Her foot suddenly tipped forward into a hole. In panic, she yanked her foot back, realising she had to run and hide. If it wasn't Hawk, she had no way of fighting back.

The shadow materialised into a thickset man.

Not Hawk.

127

Unable to move, Kelby stared at the brawny man with his cropped head and a sinister glint in his eyes. Stocky and about her height, his thickset arms and legs looked like an inflated punch-bag. The air inside her jammed in her chest. His brightly coloured tattoos, showed a dragon spitting fire covered his arms.

Kelby snapped out of the terrifying sight's spell and asked, 'Where's Hawk?'

He lifted a finger in the air. 'Wait.' He spun on his heel. His heavy footsteps retreated down the hall.

Was he one of Hawk's security colleagues? He must have gone to call Hawk.

Taking another hesitant step up, Kelby heard the booming strides returning. A flash of relief shot through her.

Hawk was back. At last.

At that moment she leapt backwards as a large object crashed through the air past her and landed at the bottom of the stairway with a loud whumpfh.

Kelby grimaced in horror at Hawk's sightless eyes staring up at her.

A rusted pipe stuck through the hollow in his neck. An equally oxidised tap stuck out of his mouth. With blood dripping from different parts of him, Hawk's body looked like a giant garden statue fermenting into a corroding water feature.

The man placed one of his heavy boots onto the top step. 'Where did your brother hide the rizado?'

Although her instincts screamed at her to run, for a strange surreal moment she felt as though she floated above herself, watching the man advancing towards her in slow motion.

'I tracked Wade for months before I had to kill him.'

His words exploded into Kelby, rupturing the slow motion. After all this time, she had come face-to-face with her brother's killer.

Kelby spun on her heel and bolted down the decaying stairs.

128

As the sound of hooves clattered off into the distance, María shifted her weight back and forth, rocking the chair closer to the fire. Dawn peeped into the cottage window giving her new hope.

Thankfully, the soldiers' brutal lust for bloodshed had given her time to figure out how to escape. Up against the hearth, she felt the rough stone's edge against her wrists. María rubbed her arms, sawing at the ropes, her mind now focused on survival.

'Mama? Mama, can you hear me?'

Her mother lay still.

¡Por dios! Is Mama still alive?

María couldn't move far with the chair stuck to her back so she sawed vigorously against the stone ledge.

¡Bah!

It would take ages to saw through a few layers of rope. Her eyes searched the room. Even if she could find something to sever the ropes, she may not be able to right the chair back onto its feet, and hobble across the room.

'Madre, can you hear me?'

A faint wail came from Madre as she half opened her eyes and glanced around.

'We are safe, Mama, they have gone. They are coming back so I must get these ropes off.'

'María,' her mother's voice dropped to a hoarse whisper, 'when will they be back?'

'A day. Maybe two.'

'Get the journal, María, hide it in the grotto. They will ransack our home and find our secrets. We must keep them safe. Then, you must escape.'

'I will take you to the grotto, Mama. We will hide there until we can find someone to help us.'

Her mother lay still and silent.

'Mama? Mama, can you hear me?' María's breath caught in her throat. *Has Mama died?*

She glanced around the room one more time. Suddenly a noise outside startled her.

In shock María watched the young soldier step through the kitchen door. They were back. Although the thought of someone being burned horrified her, she had hoped they would leave. Maybe the others had left the youngest one to guard her and Madre.

Now they would never escape.

129

Kelby raced down the hall. As she swivelled her head to glance over her shoulder, she stumbled into the rusting wheelchair.

She wobbled, tried to right herself and tumbled sideways, crashing to the floor and thumping her head against the rusting wheel's frame.

Dust rose around her. Coughing and spluttering, Kelby jumped to her feet. Her mouth became engulfed with a bitter coppery taste, and Kelby realised she must have bitten her tongue.

Footsteps echoed along the empty corridor towards her. She glanced back. Punch-bag stepped off the bottom step. He looked in no hurry. That only meant one thing: the tunnel had no way out.

Kelby jumped forward over the wheelchair, now lying on its side. One wheel spun around in the air. Her gaze took in her only options: the lab door or straight ahead into the maze of tunnels.

She darted into 42A and slammed the door behind her. Punch-bag had killed Gary and Hawk. Maybe even Stacie. And he'd do the same to her.

Her heartbeat thumped in her ear drums, almost deafening her. Glancing around frantically, Kelby gulped on panicked air, looking for something to wedge under the doorknob.

Spotting a hefty oak chair at the desk, Kelby raced to it, dragged it across the room and butted it under the lab's door handle. Trying to quieten her breathing, she strained her ears for any sounds.

Silence outside.

Then … footsteps. Slow. Deliberate. Heavy.

Everything slowed as if she were in a dream from which she couldn't escape. It took only a few seconds for her to shove a pile of books under the chair's legs to wedge it tighter beneath the door handle, but it felt like hours.

She grabbed the light switch and yanked it, dousing the room into obscurity. Although she hated dark, closed up places, it would be easier to hide in the gloom.

A key rattled into a lock. Metal scraped metal as it turned. Listening hard, she leaned against the door, waiting to push back with all her strength. But the sound echoed from the other side of the room.

Kelby gawked.

She had forgotten the entrance beside the fridge. The door hinge creaked as it opened a fraction. In the darkening room, Kelby watched a sliver of light knifing in. Behind it a face became visible.

130

Slumped in her chair, María watched the young soldier digging into the pans on the table. He muttered and went to the pot beside the fire.

'They ate it all!' He bellowed, scraping out the last chunk of meat. Near the fireplace lay a few scraps of bread. He ducked and stuffed a crust into his mouth. Then another. When the bread was finished, he ransacked the rest of the kitchen in a desperate search to quell his hunger. The young soldier dipped in and out of clay pots and tossed ladles aside.

With a mighty roar he shoved the remnants of the soldier's meal off the table. The dishes clattered to the floor.

Madre opened her eyes. 'María? Are you ready to go?'

'Madre, be quiet.' María whispered, knowing her mother hadn't seen the soldier.

Madre glanced at the soldier and then fixed her eyes on María.

María's heart ached at the look in Madre's eyes. Sadness creased her mother's face as she too accepted their fate. They would die in their home.

Unable to find any food or water, the young soldier paced the room. Within minutes, he started coughing. María guessed a crumb of the dried bread had got caught in his throat.

He stopped in front of María, leaned over and plucked a handful of her hair. 'Where is your water?'

'In the well. We have none left here. They drank it all.'

'Where is the well?'

'Let me loose and I will take you there.'

He threw his head back and bellowed with laughter. 'Do you think me a fool? If I let you go, you will try to escape. I saw what you did to Paco's eye.'

María stared at him, her mind racing. This was her last chance to escape. 'It is far down the track; you will never find it.'

His hand shot out and slapped her across the cheek. María reeled. The sharp sting biting her cheek brought tears to her eyes.

'Tell me!' The young soldier coughed, spitting wet crumbs of bread in her face.

'Go down the track. At the bottom, turn towards the woods. You will see the well hidden amongst the trees.'

'You better not be lying, *bruja*!'

Without another word, the young soldier slammed out of the door.

María's heart beat faster. She had sent him the wrong way. *And* had not declared the water barrel behind the house.

Would he come back and beat her to death?

She had only minutes to get the ropes off and get Madre away from here. Her chin trembled as her gut filled with despair. She would have to burn the ropes off her wrists. Even as the thought entered her head, María knew the fire's heat would scar and cripple her hands. She would not write again. But she had to think on that another time. Now, she had to save Madre from these soldiers and get her to safety. Her sacrifice to her mother would be her hands.

María used her last remaining strength to lumber the chair closer to the fire. Its heat warmed her back. A flame touched her skin.

The ropes had to burn off fast so she stretched her arms backwards, further into the fireplace. White hot flames licked her hands.

María screamed in pain.

131

Kelby shuddered at the sight of Punch-bag's face. The look of rapture in his eyes when he'd told her he had killed Gary had hardened into a carnivorous daze.

Using both hands, he shoved the old wooden door. It banged open, swinging wildly on its hinges. The handle clanked against the steel operating table.

By Punch-bag's sides, his hands clenched and stretched continuously, as though flexing for a fight. No weapon. Only his huge hands and hulking body. He stepped closer to her with slow, steady movements.

Kelby stumbled sideways into the cabinet. The glass jars tinkled against each other.

'Where's Stacie?'

'What do you care?'

The roaring of her heartbeat deafened her. Her eyes focused on the red dragon blazing down his arm. 'Everyone knows you hate each other.'

She gasped again, remembering Stacie's severed ear swinging in the breeze. 'Is she still alive?'

With the heavy shuffle of a solidly built man, he stepped towards her. 'What do *you* think?'

In one swift movement, he reached and grabbed her around the back of her head. He stuck his thumb into the hollow of her neck and pressed her into the mad scientist's desk chair. He leaned over her, his face rammed into hers. 'You shouldn't have stuck your nose in. Haven't you heard the saying *Let sleeping dogs lie?*'

She squirmed in her seat. Punch-bag yanked her hands and held them over the desk. 'You have to stop mothering him. Even with him dead, you're still doing it.'

Spikes of adrenaline raced through her mind, trying to piece his words together. Her hands dropped.

Punch-bag jerked her arms back to the mid-air position. 'I'm going back to see where he hid the notes.'

Her heart pounded. Balancing out in front of her, her hands shook. 'There were notes?'

'*Ja*, that made hunting him more interesting, but your brother was clever at hiding stuff. We never found his notes. Mm, should I use the perfect murder weapon again? The one I used to kill your brother.'

Kelby froze.

Punch-bag inhaled deeply and flexed his right bicep. Looking at it, he sniggered, 'But I may find another way to snuff you.'

132

A hot gush of hatred flooded into Kelby's blood, pumping vengeance to every part of her. Punch-bag's confession he'd killed Gary made her want to jump up and grab his throat and throttle him. The other half of her wished she had the strength to shake him and pound his head against the wall until it turned to pulp.

Instead, she decided to keep him talking until she could figure a way out of here. 'W-w-what did you do to him?' She didn't want to know, but maybe it would be useful later.

'You'd never believe … the perfect murder weapon is not really a weapon.'

Punch-bag pulled a lighter out of his pocket and flicked it on. He fanned the flame under her fingers and asked, 'You been burnt before?'

Too stunned to answer, Kelby watched him lean over the desk and lit the bunsen burner. Transfixed, she watched the burner ignite into a blue flame at the bottom, and ranging in colour from orange to purple.

'You know, most people don't know that third degree burns cause the most damage. That's because they burn through each layer of skin.' He spoke as though they were friends having a coffee.

Kelby fixated her gaze on the end of the flame, stretching up, trying to lick at her fingertips.

'The damage can even reach the bloodstream, fry the nerves and sizzle the bones. Makes an interesting death. Don't you think?'

In Kelby's mind's eye, Stacie's severed ear, blistered, leathered and charred, dangled in the breeze. She squeezed her eyes shut to get the horrific picture out of her mind.

Punch-bag slapped her hands into the flame. '*Luisteren!* Listen to me when I talk. Move your fingers away and I'll burn them.'

As her eyes flew open, Kelby yelped at the flame biting into her skin.

'You wouldn't want the dragon spitting flames before he's ready for you.'

Her stomach tightened as she glanced from Punch-bag to the hypnotic blue-purple flame.

Unperturbed, Punch-bag turned a few pages in the journal. His stubby finger tapped a page. 'See here. Cerbera odollam. That's how Gary died.'

With simmering hatred, Kelby kept her eyes on the bunsen burner.

'When you went to Spain did you see that pretty bush many people have growing in their gardens, the oleander?'

In silence Kelby watched him reading from the journal.

'Oleander's seeds contain a toxin called cerberin, a potent compound capable of disrupting calcium ion channels in human heart muscles.' His eyes checked on the position of her hands so she held them still. He continued reading, 'This can lead to an irregular heartbeat. It's fatal if the toxin is ingested in high enough quantities.'

The heat in Kelby's scorched fingers made her arms rise higher above the flame. Punch-bag jolted his fist on them. The flames licked at Kelby's fingers again, this time searing through the blistered tips and singeing the rest of her left hand.

As she bit down on the pain, Punch-bag continued reading from the journal. 'Five hundred cases of fatal cerbera poisoning have been found between 1989 and 1999 in the south-west Indian state of Kerala alone.' He glanced at her hands, 'Mostly young wives who don't wake up.'

A deep furrow ridged her brow.

'You know, they don't wake up and fit in with Indian culture.'

His eyes glanced at her hands again. The muscles in her upper arms strained to keep them still. 'Don't you think plants are amazing? All I had to do was cook a spicy meal for your brother to ingest enough cerberin. I even made him write his own suicide note. Pretty clever, hey?'

After a moment of watching him gloat, she forced out a whisper, 'Where's Stacie?'

'Ahh. Think back to the time your mother forced castor oil down your throat.'

Kelby grimaced. How did he know? Maybe he forced it out of Gary before he died. Or maybe he assumed most parents did that.

'Disgusting stuff! I bet you'd never have guessed it came from one of the most poisonous plants in the world.'

'Castor oil?'

He nodded. 'Willow showed me this toxin called ricin.'

For a moment, Kelby focused on one word: Willow. Gary had introduced her to the homeopathic doctor to help her conceive. And later she had entrusted Annie into his care. Roy was right. Willow must be involved. Her heart skipped a beat. *Where was Roy?*

Punch-bag smashed his fist onto the top of her hands again. 'Listen!'

The searing pain of the flame forced her to look at him. 'I'm listening.' Her mind throbbed as much as her burning hands.

She had to find a way to escape.

133

María choked on the smell of burning flesh. A sour odour filled her nostrils. She had only ever smelt that dreadful odour once before when her mother had started roasting a piglet and had to rush off to deliver a baby. She had been a child at the time, and didn't know how to cook, so she ended up burning the family roast. The sickening stench of her own rotting flesh reminded her of the smell when Padre tanned leather over a flame.

Thinking she was in the middle of a terrible nightmare, María squeezed her eyes tight. When she opened them again the horror remained: her hands and feet were tied to the chair with Madre beaten, bruised and bleeding nearby.

Her mother clawed her way to her. 'María! María!' Madre's voice broke through the haze of pain.

María shook her head and tried to focus. The soldiers' threat came back. The young soldier would not be gone long, and the others could be back at any time. She would have no chance against all four of them. María clenched her jaw against the searing pain in her arms. Beside her, Madre tore at the knotted rope. Straining to glance over her shoulder, María once again choked on the stink.

The ropes were burnt and tattered. Long streaks of raw flesh swelled and bubbled up her arms. Under the blackened ropes, her wrists were raw with large blisters. Her hands had swollen to double their size. It was the worst pain she had ever felt. This was much worse than the time she had burnt her palms when lifting a heated pot.

With precise fingers, Madre picked at the ropes as though plucking the last few fine feathers out of a slaughtered chicken.

'What are you doing, Mama?'

'The rope is nearly off, María, then you must … go.' Her mother's voice lifted and dropped in a breathless attempt to save her daughter. 'Take the journal … hide it in the grotto … get Padre's *piedra* and run as far away as you can. These soldiers will do terrible things to you.'

'I will not leave you, Mama. I will take you with me.'

'But I cannot walk.'

'I will help you.'

'I pray you!' Madre's gaze pointed to the back of her legs. 'Look.'

Only now did María see several deep slashes in her mother's calves. The soldier's dagger had inflicted these wounds.

'They severed my muscles so I would not walk again.'

134

Kelby glared at Punch-bag, nodding to show him she was listening, despite the searing agony of the bunsen burner flame biting into her palm.

'*Goed.* Keep listening. The dragon gets angry when he's not taken seriously. As I was saying, the ricin is concentrated in the beans which castor oil is made from. One raw seed is enough to kill a human in two days.'

Kelby winced as he shook the jar of seeds that looked like ticks. Punch-bag looked smug as he added, 'Undetectable in autopsies, but it gives a long, agonising and unstoppable death.'

Kelby wanted to block her ears.

'Within a few hours Stacie's mouth and throat started burning. Then her guts would have ached. Bloody diarrhoea and vomiting made it entertaining. After she took the seeds, the rest was unstoppable.' He shrugged, 'So ... I didn't do anything.'

'But her ear —'

'Just a bit of fun. She died of dehydration.' Punch-bag leaned over Kelby, stared into her eyes and muttered, 'Hmm, I haven't decided if I should burn you, poison you or strangle you while the dragon takes his pleasure.'

Shivering from fear and the heat in her fingertips, Kelby held his steady gaze.

'Which would *you* prefer?'

She remained silent.

'Answer me!' He slammed his fist onto her balancing hands. Again, the flames ate at her flesh. Too afraid to move, Kelby bit down on the grunt of pain.

Trying to stop her left hand trembling in agony, she gagged at the smell of charred flesh. It smelt like the fried beef pet mince she had sometimes cooked for Fat Cat.

She fixed her eyes on Punch-bag and whispered, 'Do whatever you like to me, but don't hurt my niece.'

Kelby glanced around the desk, noticing a jar had a label: *Strychnine and brucine.*

She tried to remember what the journal had said about strychnine poisoning. Something about a heart toxin. Now, she wished she had listened to those lessons in her biology and science classes.

'Maybe I'll try all three. Because you're the third Wade.' He ambled along the shelf, glancing at the row of bottled dead animals.

Kelby tried to zone out and think of other things, but she kept seeing horror images of her dead family.

Distracted by the hum of the fridge in the corner, Punch-bag opened the door and leaned in. 'I have her other ear in here.'

Kelby took her chance. She ducked under the operating table and hurtled towards the door on the other side of the room.

In two long strides Punch-bag was behind her. His arm swung out and slammed into the back of her head. She reeled from the force of his bones crunching against her skull. Her head buzzed in agony.

A large sweaty hand caught her by the jaw. Gripping her, he yanked her backwards. The dragon arm snaked around her neck like a python. For a moment, it squeezed. A long, slow, deliberate constriction. Crushing her windpipe.

Choking, Kelby's frantic gaze darted around the room. Nothing within her reach to stop him. She wished she had Zelda's long red talons to dig into his arms. Instead, she sunk her teeth into the red dragon. Tasting his salty sweat in her mouth, she grimaced, but bit harder.

Punch-bag yelped and slapped his other hand across her cheek.

Kelby reeled from the blow.

As she jolted backwards, his hand darted out and yanked the blood-stained lab coat off the peg. Punch-bag tossed the coat over her head, gagging her. The stench of blood and decaying meat made her nauseous. Leaning backwards, he tugged it tighter and tighter.

Through the suffocating cotton, Kelby heard him mutter, 'Right devil, time to face the dragon.'

135

Kelby coughed and spluttered, struggling to breathe. Instinctively, she shoved her elbows backwards, jabbing into his chest with all the strength she could muster.

His vice grip slackened. She hurtled forward, but his grip tightened again. The stinking coat slipped off her face. Still in his clutches, she twisted around. Facing him, she rammed her knee into his groin. Punch-bag's grunt sounded like a thundering explosion in her ears. Caught off guard, he dropped his hands to clutch himself.

Kelby scrambled up onto the operating table. From her elevated position, she leapt over the cabinet, hoping she wouldn't hit the glass jars. Both feet crash landed on the mad scientist's desk, right beside the bunsen burner's flames.

A bottle rattled, pens scuttled across the top and rolled off onto the floor and the lamp toppled over. The test tubes crashed to the floor, scattering splintered glass.

Punch-bag advanced towards her, one hand still clutching his groin. She lifted a powder bottle that read: *Strychnine and brucine*. 'Get out!' She lifted the glass jar and aimed it at him.

He continued to move towards her.

Kelby hurled the glass jar at him, but Punch-bag ducked. The bottle sailed through the air, struck the light bulb above him and shattered.

Punch-bag looked up and gasped. '*Kijk uit!* Look out!'

A fine spray of dusty powder drifted over him. He spat out a mouthful. 'Urrgghh! *Bliksem.* That's vile!'

Ignoring the pain in her burnt hand, she lifted two more jars, arming herself with one in each hand. Punch-bag sneezed.

Kelby noticed that one had no lid. It had been labelled: *Na+C=N*. She bellowed at him, 'Get out! Or I'll drop this deadly powder over you.'

He sniggered. 'You don't know what deadly is.'

Kelby threw the bottle at him, striking him on the side of his head and scattering more toxins over him. He leaned back as some of it drifted towards him, using his hand to wave the dust away. She reached to grab the last glass jar. It felt powdery in her clammy palm.

Punch-bag used the moment to lunge at her. He grabbed her ankles, yanking her off the desk and into his open arms. 'Ah, now we can get friendly.'

Without looking down, Kelby stomped her heel on his instep. He grunted and momentarily lightened his grip. Kelby bent her leg, pulled her knee towards her torso and kicked his shin.

Punch-bag staggered and loosened his grip, but fumbled to get her back into his clutches. '*Nee*, little devil, that's not nice.'

With a powerful arm, he shoved her into the wall of dead animal jars. His sweating hands held her shoulders as he stared at her. 'I didn't think you'd fight back, but I have to admit … I like it.'

Desperate to claw her nails across his face, but without any nails, Kelby's gaze darted to the door. A few feet too far.

'Wait till you see what I mean by friendly.' The dragon arm crossed her chest, pinning her to the shelf of bottled monsters. His other hand crept around her trousers.

Kelby winced and tried to distract him. 'What did you do to Stacie?'

'The same as I'm going to do to you.' He spluttered as though short of breath.

She jumped as his fingers clenched her buttocks. One stubby finger jabbed into her arse.

'In my old job, women used to crawl all over me for a back-ender.'

Kelby cringed.

'I miss them, so I take every opportunity I get.'

From the corner of her eyes, she spotted the cat's tongue rammed inside a glass jar. Beside it, the rabbit's teeth mocked her. With her back lined against dead things, she knew she would be joining them soon.

He noticed her eyes darting sideways and said, 'Nice touch, don't you think.'

Kelby followed his gaze to the cat's head. Her mouth went dry.

'Although you wouldn't recognise him now.'

She inhaled sharply. Was it really Fat Cat? Tears threatened, but she refused to let him see her anguish. A sudden, bone-aching tiredness overwhelmed her.

Kelby sagged against the shelf.

136

María suppressed a deep sob along with the desire to lie in her mother's arms and weep. Despite the terrible dagger cuts on her mother's legs, she couldn't give up now; she had to survive. To save them.

After sniffing, she inhaled deeply to clear the weakness rising in her chest. 'You will walk. We have the rizado to heal those wounds. I will read the journal to find your remedy and we will get you walking again.'

Madre's hand shot out and cupped María's cheek. 'Sweet little *mi querida*, always the strong one with so much faith.'

'I learnt that from you, Mama.' She glanced over her shoulder again. The tangle of burnt rope was almost off her wrists. 'Hurry, Mama, hurry.'

Her mother picked for a few more minutes and the last strand broke, freeing María's singed arms. She stared at the scarred mess for a moment. It would be an annoyance to do many things with crippled hands. Worse than all, she wouldn't be able to write. Once again, that feeble maiden's weakness threatened to consume her. María swallowed hard.

The deep lust for life, gained on her journeys with Padre, filled her with renewed determination. Never would she live in bounds. Never would she assign limits to the desires she had always strived after. No, she would write, even if every word filled her with pain.

María joined her mother, picking the ropes at her ankles. She ignored her raw fingertips and crunched on the inflamed agony. Every movement shot flashes of torment up her arms. After a few minutes they finally got her legs free.

'Wait here, Mama. Let me check outside.' María jumped up and raced to the door. Cautiously, she pulled it ajar with her fingertips and peered out. The young soldier was nowhere to be seen.

Just then the sun burst over the hills in an orange fireball, lighting the garden. María stepped out and raced around the house. Everything outside was as it should be. In the early dawn, the birds chirped and flapped in the nearby trees, while the animals brayed their impatience to be let out of their pens.

Today she could not attend their calls.

María ran back inside. With careful, precise movements to avoid knocking her wounded hands, María reached into her stone hole and retrieved a wad of notes. The completed herbal *manuscrito* lay hidden in the underground cellar inside one of Madre's clay pots, but this was other rizado notes.

Flinching in pain, she stuffed the notes into her breeches. Everything she touched scraped her raw skin, magnifying the torment. It had to be ignored.

María knelt beside her mother. 'Come, Mama, let us be out of here with much haste.'

'María, take the journal and hide it at the grotto. Then come back for me.'

'No, Mama, I am not leaving you here alone. The young soldier will be back in minutes to inflict more suffering.'

'But María —'

'Mama! Never will we surrender. Better we die trying to escape than die by giving up.'

137

Still pinning the devil to the experimental shelf, Olaf flexed his neck. Ever since she had tossed one of Willow's experimental poisons over him, his face had started itching like hell.

Now his neck started stiffening. He wondered what had been thrown over him. His mouth still tasted disgusting. Strangely, he could taste something that reminded him of almonds, but this tang was too bitter.

While Willow had been trying to piece together compounds that could fit the rizado formula, he'd spent a lot of time experimenting with natural poisons. Most of the dead things lining the walls had experienced horrific deaths.

As Olaf shoved his elbow into the devil's neck, he noticed his dragon had turned a bright cherry-red, with goose bumps bristling his favourite body art. His armpits started sweating. He felt beads of perspiration lining his forehead as well. The bright light gave him a throbbing headache and flashed and popped like paparazzi camera bulbs.

A sudden dizziness overwhelmed him. Excitement at the thought of teaching the devil the lesson she deserved made his heart beat faster. His breathing accelerated and he panted in time with his heart.

Then he frowned; he didn't usually react this way. Sure, he got excited when the *animaal* stirred and needed to break free. But this bizarre behaviour confused him. Half of him wanted to lie on the floor and sleep. Mad, totally mad.

So far he'd enjoyed fighting the devil, but he couldn't understand his sudden weakness. Olaf's vision blurred. He shook himself, trying desperately to maintain control.

'Stacie's head is too big, but I'm sure I can get other parts to fit into a bottle.'

138

A bitter burst of bile shot into Kelby's mouth. Fear squeezed into her chest and closed its iron fist around her heart. The bastard had killed Stacie! And he was about to do the same to her.

Gary had sent her here. Not to give up, but to take these journal notes to the authorities. 'You've destroyed my family.'

'Not everyone. I can't wait to introduce the *meisje* to the dragon. Little girls dream of dragons.'

The abrupt realisation that Punch-bag had not harmed Annie revived Kelby. 'Where is she?'

His eyes rolled up. As he blinked, his eyeballs protruded and his pupils dilated. His eyelids flickered a few more times.

Kelby followed his gaze. 'She's here?' A hot wave of excitement surged through her veins.

'Under lock and key.' His eyes glanced in the direction of the underground tunnel.

'What do you want with a little girl? She can't harm you.'

'For now, she's an insurance policy.'

'I'll give you anything you want — everything I own. Please just let her go.'

His hand closed over her mouth. *'Je praat te veel!* You talk too much.'

139

Once again, María knelt beside her mother, and placed her hands under her back in an attempt to lift her. A searing bolt of pain shot through her body, tipping her forward. She stumbled and righted herself. Breathing deeply, she tried again.

Although she was far from the fire, it felt as if the flames still licked at her arms. Under the skin they played with her flesh making it feel as if her arms were still deep in the heat. María grunted and gritted her teeth to stop herself flinching. She didn't want her mother to witness her agony.

'It's no use.' Madre tried to sit up, but instead leaned to the side, like a tree falling in a storm. 'María, we must heal your hands before you can help me.'

María tried again to lift her mother, but yelped in pain as a blistered layer of skin came off one of her arms. The smell of her burnt flesh was still so thick and rich she could taste it.

'Stop! Ana-María de Carbonela! Listen to me.'

Startled by her mother's tone, María stared at her.

'You are wasting time. Take the journal and get a huge bunch of rizado, we will heal your hands and then you can help me.'

'But if they come back, they will kill you and hunt me down.' María stood her ground. 'I will not leave you, Mama.'

'¡Por dios! You are as stubborn as your father! If you refuse to listen, go fetch his tool bag.'

'By my faith!' María exclaimed as an evil thought struck her. Had Mama the same thoughts as she? No, Madre did not have a bad bone in her body.

Gently laying her mother back on the floor, she mumbled, 'As stubborn as my father, you say?'

Madre frowned at her. 'Pray tell. I see the look of mischief in your eyes.'

María dropped a light kiss on her mother's turbaned head. 'Yes, Mama. My *imaginacion* may save us after all.'

Knowing the young soldier would not be far from the house, María peered out and leapt across the cobbles. When she reached Padre's workshop, she stopped and glanced down the track, half expecting to see the young soldier. He would be back any time now. Every minute counted.

Thankfully, Madre had refused to clear out Padre's workshop. Padre had used a wide variety of tools to shape stone blocks and slabs into homes for the local poor villagers and the rich land owners. María knew his tools for shaping stone, such as his range of mallets and chisels of all shapes and sizes. He also had hammers, some to use with a chisel to split rock. Others were used to produce rubble.

María ran to the back of the workshop. With throbbing fingertips, she picked a long chisel with the thinnest, most pointed shaft, and Padre's stonemason's hammer. It had one flat surface with a long chisel-shaped blade. Many a time she had watched Padre use it to chip off small pieces of stone, without needing a separate chisel.

Armed with Padre's tools in her aching hands, she raced back to the kitchen. Madre still lay on the floor, but strained to move.

'Don't, Madre. Lie where you are.'

'Did you get the *Piedra*?'

'What stone?' María frowned, Madre must be in so much pain she now talked in riddles. 'When the soldier returns we will pretend all is as he left.'

'Why? You must escape before he —'

'There is no time, Mama. Please do as I say.' María slumped into her chair and coiled a piece of the shredded rope back around her ankles. At that moment, they heard heavy steps thumping onto the cobbles.

'Mama, turn your head and do not look this way. I do not wish for you to see what I am about to do.'

For once, Madre obeyed.

140

Olaf cupped the devil's mouth to shut her up. He had no idea why he needed a desperate pee. Anxiety never did that to him. Maybe the throbbing in his groin was a hard on? More than likely.

Oh, he'd make sure the devil got a hard jousting. He needed to relieve his frustration somehow. What it was, he couldn't focus on right now. He needed to slip back into the forest. 'This fighting is getting us nowhere.' He jiggled his jaw from side to side. All it wanted to do was lock up.

The devil stared at him. For a few seconds her eyes roamed around her forehead, juggling above and below each other. Then a third eye appeared. Olaf shook his head and focused his vision. Only two eyes again. In the right place this time. He drew his strength into his biceps. 'See this.' He indicated the dragon. 'You ever been fucked by a dragon before?'

The devil's eyes widened.

'I have.' His voice dropped to a whisper, 'It'll turn you into an *animaal.*'

Olaf felt his strength returning. His mind flashed to the forest and the carnal pleasures he had despised for so many years. Eventually, he had embraced them, and used them for his own tainted desires. Many a time he needed to be the forest *animaal*. The more he thought about it, the more his body energised.

'When the dragon gets horny, there's no stopping him.'

Suddenly, the devil fought against him. With all three of her eyes watching him.

141

María held her hands behind her back; one armed with the chisel and the other with the hammer. She tried to calm her breathing. Whatever happened, she must not alert the young soldier. She hung her head to stop her racing heart.

The young soldier kicked the door open and marched to her side. He reeked of sweat while his clod-laden boots sent a damp, earthy smell up María's nose.

'Where is the well?' He bellowed in her face, spitting his foul breath onto her cheeks. 'You are a lying witch! *¡Diablo!*'

María waited. Her head hung low over her pounding chest.

The soldier leaned over and yanked her hair. María launched herself into the air, both arms thrusting up. She lunged the chisel into the soldier's chest and slammed the hammer over his head.

He fell against her, gripping his chest and groaning in anguish. '*¡Diablo!* You witch!'

As the sunlight burst into the window, blinding her, a fuse kindled inside María. Without thinking, she shoved the soldier off her and clubbed him again with the hammer. Hundreds of tiny sparks of pain shot through her hands. But María ignored them; she had only their escape to worry about.

One last feeble groan spilled from the soldier's lips as he slumped on the floor beside Madre. María bent over him. A pool of dark blood oozed out of his head. She knew that sign. Although she loved animals, she had had to kill them for food. The same colour blood as of a slaughtered animal now seeped from under the soldier's lifeless body.

María spun around to Madre. 'Mama! We must go. Now!'

Madre nodded and lifted her arms. She didn't look at the soldier.

María helped her mother use every ounce of her strength to haul herself to her knees. 'Here, grab hold of me. Hold me around my shoulders. Lean on my back so I can keep my hands free.'

Madre nodded and lifted her arms. María and Madre spent the next few minutes grumping and groaning as they tried to get into a comfortable position to walk away from their home. Keeping her hands free, María used her elbows and hips to shunt her mother into position. She insisted her mother lean on her so she could drag her.

'María, wait, you must get Padre's precious stone.'

María ignored her mother's remark. 'Please, Mama, we must go.'

Before they had taken one step, María realised it would take hours, maybe days to get to the grotto. It was usually a short walk, but with her burnt hands and Madre's tattered legs they would be lucky to get to safety before the men returned.

'Here, Mama, hang on me. I will drag you, like a mule dragging a plough.'

'Except I am a useless plough!'

'We will mend your plough, Mama. That is what you have always done. You have put our community of people back in order when their bodies have come apart. You have taken care of any ailment you have met as an adversary. Now we will do the same for you.'

Madre smiled and took one last look around their kitchen. In a rasping whisper, she asked, 'Do you have any writing hidden there?'

María followed her mother's gaze to her hiding place in the stone alcove beside the fire. 'No, it is in the cellar with the journal.'

Determined to get out of there, María stepped forward with her mother hanging from her shoulders like a ragged drape. '*¡Vamos!* Let's go.'

326

142

Kelby grimaced at the sweat pouring off Punch-bag's brow. More ran down his arms and hands gripping her face and into her mouth.

'Yuck!' She shook her head vigorously trying to stop the flow, but her words were muffled behind his hand.

'Once the dragon ... infects you, then you'll ... know what deadly ... *duidelik* means.' His voice faltered.

A sudden kick from him made Kelby glance down. She frowned at his leg kicking out in every direction.

'If you hated Stacie that much ... you ...' He shook his head violently. 'You would've enjoyed ... watching her ... get infected.'

Oh my God! Kelby stifled a scream. What terrible things had he done to Stacie? She clenched her fists at her sides, suddenly realising she still clutched a bottle.

'But the dragon ...' Punch-bag muttered, his words fading.

Kelby gripped the bottle's lid and slammed it backwards, against the wooden shelf. The glass bottle splintered in her hand, breaking in half. Ignoring the sudden biting pain of broken glass stabbing into her palm, she plunged the jagged edge of the bottle into his thigh. Punch-bag crashed down beside her, gripping his leg with both hands and groaned.

Kelby grimaced at the sight of the bottle's neck sticking out of his leg. She wiped her bloodied hand against the wooden shelving. A sharp splinter of wood stabbed into her thumb's pad. She yanked her hand away and sucked the wound.

As Punch-bag leaned over in an attempt to pull the bottle out of his thigh, she sidled sideways. Noticing movement, he reached to grab her, but his hand stopped in mid-air. His muscles twitched. With bulging eyes, he leaned against her, as though trying to keep himself up. '*Sle-eett.*' He slurred, 'What did you throoo ... at meee.'

Now, Kelby remembered the label: *Strychnine and brucine.*

He must be reacting to the poison. Thank God, none had touched her. If she could shove him off and run away, he'd be much slower at catching her. His fingers shuddered and his arms began to spasm. His body leaned into her, and she felt the sheer weight of him pressing her into the shelf. Behind her, bottles rattled. On the end, one crashed to the floor, splashing its vile contents across his feet.

She watched in horror as his face slowly distorted into a monstrous grimace. 'Blik-semmm.' He frothed at the mouth.

To Kelby, it looked like an alien had suddenly possessed his body. Thrashing about, he rasped for each breath. His arms flapped. Kelby tried to shove him off her, but his weight kept her pinned between him and the shelf.

'I ... *animaal.*' He clutched his throat, struggling to breathe.

As he fell sideways, Punch-bag's body convulsed. He hit the floor and his body contorted into a stiff arch.

Then it lay still.

143

Madre took a step and cried out in pain. She stumbled and sank to her knees, dragging María to the floor with her.

'God protect us! We will not make it.'

'We will, Mama. We will go slowly, one step at a time.'

'Why will *you* not listen to your mother? I think it is better if you fetch rizado to heal you and then we leave.'

'And *I* think we should persevere. *And* make haste. They could return at any moment, Mama.'

'*Dios!* It's like having your father back with us.'

María chuckled. 'Then it is good fortune you can talk with him again.' Stretching her back, María raised her mother into a standing position. 'There. Now, seek out the place under your feet that gives you the least pain when you stand.'

For a few moments, Madre tried placing her weight on different parts of her feet. For each area, she grunted and lifted her foot.

'Can we go?'

Madre flinched, but nodded.

María took a step and dragged her mother behind her.

It took nearly an hour to get out of the door. She'd rather die than leave her mother here to the mercy of those soldiers.

Dragging her mother over the croft proved to be the worst part of the journey. They tripped over each cobble. A few times Madre's arms came loose. Each time it happened, María knelt on the cobbles, and shuffled her body under her mother's. At a woeful sluggard's pace, they hobbled closer to the underground cellar. María had to use her foot to kick open the stable door before they made their way to the cellar at the back.

The pain in her hands frustrated María. Madre had little strength left. If only she could use her hands to lift her mother. She wouldn't be able to carry her mother, she was too heavy, but at least she was able to drag her along. With toiling, she might even be able to pierce one of the chemises between two strong branches, and drag her mother along behind her, as she had seen traders lugging bags of vegetables to the market. But her hands were useless.

Suddenly the sound of hooves startled María. The soldiers! They were back.

144

For a long moment Kelby stared at the body on the floor at her feet. She couldn't work out if he was dead or unconscious. Not daring to go near him, in case he suddenly grabbed her ankle, she had to get away from here fast. And find Annie.

Punch-bag had hinted she was upstairs, but this place was abandoned. Maybe he had taken her to the clinic next door. She remembered his eyes indicating the direction of the tunnel. Kelby pulled herself together and darted out of the room. At the door, she remembered the journal. Leaping over Punch-bag's stiff body, she grabbed the journal from the desk.

Kelby tried Roy's number, but her phone didn't respond. She squinted at the bars on her phone. No signal. She'd have to get out of here and try again. She dumped the phone back into her sling bag.

Glancing left and right, she spotted a tunnel winding its way to the basement of the sprawling mansion. Dim globes strung along the roof showed raw bricks arching into the dark. Compared to the rest of the mansion's once splendid décor, the tunnel looked bare.

Kelby shivered with cold and unease, yet she turned into the tunnel. Despite the sensation of stepping into a horror film, she descended into the gloomy passageway. The overpowering odour of damp and mould almost forced her back. The rancid smell made her feel as though she were entering her own grave. But this wasn't nearly as putrid as the stench of those dead things floating in chemicals.

Wishing Roy were with her, she stepped into the bricked tunnel. Fighting against her instincts to escape, Kelby crept along, using her right hand on the rough chipped bricks to guide her. The dirt encrusted stones underfoot hadn't seen the light of day in centuries. A cobweb, dangling from the brick ceiling, floated over her cheek. Kelby squealed and bolted forward.

Her hand chafed along the rough walls. A few bumps and jutting bricks caught her knuckles, scratching the skin off them. Heat still emanated from her burns. She had to ignore the pain. She couldn't focus on anything except finding Annie.

Following the yellowed, flickering globes, Kelby bit down on the fear welling inside her. Refusing to think of Punch-bag and what he had revealed, she resisted looking at her blistered fingers and raw palm. Although tears threatened, she denied them. Her whole body trembled, but she stumbled along blindly.

She had one focus. Get out of here before anyone else found her. After no more than five minutes that seemed like hours, she came to the end of the tunnel.

A heavy oak door barred her way.

145

María and Madre stood frozen in their tracks. They listened to the hooves in the distance, expecting them to come closer. After a few minutes the sound disappeared and they remained still, holding their breath.

'*¡Dios santo!* We must hurry, Mama.'

'The soldiers are everywhere, María. You must leave me. You can get to the village and get help. There will be time before they kill me.'

'*¡Cállese!* Be quiet, Mama, I am not going to let them have you.'

'Wait, María, I have an idea. Leave me in the cellar. They will never find me there locked under the ground. You go ... get rizado to heal your hands ... and hide the journal. Then, come back for me.'

María tried to interrupt, but Madre poked her back.

'When you see ... they are not here, open the cellar. We can smear ... rizado over me.' Madre took a deep breath and continued, There is food enough for ... many days down there. We can hide until ... we are strong enough to escape.'

'But Mama —'

'*¡Por dios!* By God, this is the ... only way. Can you not see your ... stubbornness will only get us ... killed? Like ... your father. When the wall was falling ... he refused to give up and he got trapped. Don't let me ... lose you too!'

Her mother's desperate weeping made María squirm. It was a good suggestion, she had to admit. If she could get her hands even a little better she would be of more use to them both.

'As you will, Mama. I will hurry back.'

María used her remaining strength to drag Madre to the cellar. After she lifted the hidden wooden lid, she gritted her teeth against the agony of helping her mother down the steps.

A sense of victory spurred her on, even though the smell of her burning flesh would never leave her.

146

Kelby flung herself against the solid door and heaved. It didn't budge. She tried again and a slow creak groaned at her. Shoving her weight against the door, Kelby huffed. It moved a little, but not enough.

Placing one foot far behind the other, Kelby anchored her front toe against a crack in the floor and leaned her weight onto it. She heaved against the door, and it creaked open a little more — enough for her to squeeze through.

Something dangled onto Kelby's hair. She jumped back, thrashing her arms in the air. The thought of spiders and other creepy crawlies made her twitch.

An old-fashioned light switch, dangling on a long cord, swung back and forth in front of her face. She yanked on it and the room lit up.

Homerton's basement.

In front of her, an old-fashioned set of iron stairs led upstairs. Along the far side, an empty hospital trolley bed leaned against the wall. Beside it, another exit showed a sloping ramp that didn't look Victorian. Maybe it had been built when the clinic was renovated.

Kelby thought of medical trial patients being taken to the mad scientist's lab. She shuddered, but raced up the wrought iron stairs. At the top, she entered another cellar. Under the bright lights, this one didn't look dirty or feel scary. She thundered up the wooden stairway, clomping her way to the top and into the clinic's reception.

Kelby came face-to-face with Jon Thompson.

147

María glanced around the stone cellar. Its wooden shelves were rickety with the weight of the meat supplies and without Padre's constant attention.

Long ago, she had transcribed another copy of *Herbal de Carbonela*, and concealed the grotto map between the double layers of calf skin. Then, she had hidden the leather book inside one of Madre's clay pots for safe keeping.

Now, she lay her mother in the far corner and ran back to the house. Using her elbows, she gathered an armful of bedding and clothing to place under her mother. A second journey brought over her mother's medicina basket. 'Here, Mama, you can smear the last of your rizado on your wounds.'

Madre gave a weak smile, and María could see she wouldn't have the strength to do it. Her breasts were in a terrible state. María returned to the house and collected a few of mother's chemises. After smearing the remaining rizado paste from Madre's medicina basket over her mother's breasts and the cuts on her calves, María wrapped three chemises around Madre's body.

'This will protect your wounds until I bring more rizado back from the grotto.'

A third trip to the house allowed her to give her mother cooked food and a pail of water. She lifted Madre's shorn head to help her sip. 'You need food and water to build up your strength so we can escape.'

After Madre had a drink, she clutched María's hand. 'You are a good girl, strong like Padre. You will never let anyone or anything beat you.'

'You are strong too, Mama. You will survive this.'

'María, you must find Padre's stone, it will protect you and bring you back to me.'

María saw Madre grimace in pain. In that moment a flood of determination filled the space inside where hatred boiled. 'Mama, these soldiers and their queen will not win.'

Madre nodded. 'I am proud of you, María.' A smile filled her eyes and removed the agony from her face.

Although she left supplies right beside her mother, poor Madre was too exhausted and in too much pain to feed herself. 'Mama, I am going now. I will be back soon.'

Her mother didn't answer. María leaned closer to see her mother was asleep. The slow, shallow rise and fall of her chest assured her that her mother was still alive. She must hurry to get the rizado to heal her hands, and return to attend to her mother's wounds. With one last glance at her mother, María exited the cellar. She placed a few twigs and a layer of green branches over the wooden lid. Covered in animal feed it looked part of the stable floor.

The animals brayed to get free of their pens. Her heart skipped a beat. Getting help for Madre came first.

She glanced at her blistered raw palms. Even if her hands were able to free the animals, the returning soldiers would know she was strong enough to escape. They would ransack the farm in their search and they might find the cellar.

María had to get to the grotto fast.

The grotto's secret held their only hope.

148

Kelby's heart beat in time with her panting breath. 'Jon, thank God, you're here!'

He immediately spotted her burnt hand, 'My God, Kelby, what happened?'

Two of her fingertips looked like roasted prawns. For a moment, she wanted to shrug it off as nothing. Perhaps seeing someone familiar or the desperate need to share her horrific experience below brought the pent up fear tumbling out, 'There's this huge thug downstairs. He's in the other part of the building. And —'

'Wait, calm down. What other building?'

'There's another place next door where they're doing terrible tests on animals and maybe even humans. It's disgusting. There's body parts in bottles and it stinks.'

'Your hand, Kelby, how did you get burnt?'

'I told you, the thug.'

'You're not making sense.'

'He followed me. He's been stalking me on Twitter for ages. And he killed Fat Cat and put him in a bottle.'

Jon gaped at her.

Kelby suppressed a sob. 'I know, isn't it terrible? Who would want to harm a cat? He trapped me in the lab and burnt my hand while he told me how he killed Stacie and Gary.'

'God, Kelby, I am so sorry.'

Tears leaked from the corners of her eyes. 'I need to find Annie!'

Jon placed an arm around her shoulders, leading her towards a door. 'Come on, we can talk in private in the office. Then we'll find Annie.'

149

María entered the thick copse of trees that surrounded the grotto. She waded across a shallow pond where the rizado grew on the rocks.

Before collecting the slimy herb, she had one more task to carry out so she must make haste. María glanced up. High above, a dark black hole scarring the rocky outcrop hid a secret *cueva*.

Normally scaling up, she only reached here and there for support. Today though, she reached out every few steps. The horror of the past day made her weak and helpless. And the pain in her hands sapped the last threads of vigour she had left.

At the *cueva* entrance, María had to rest for a moment to catch her breath. Whenever she came to collect rizado and explore the grotto, she passed the sharp rocks along the walls and ceiling. Yet now, the tunnel leading into the hidden cave looked as though it bared its jagged teeth, forbidding anyone to enter. Normally, the damp sour smell of earth didn't trouble her, but today it made her retch.

From inside the cave, with a ceiling three times the height of her cottage, she could look out at the rizado pond below. Beyond, the wooded copse kept the grotto hidden. Inside, at one end of the grotto, water plunged into a huge pool. Here, María could dive into water that shone as blue as the sky.

In the middle, the cave's roof opened up, like clouds parting to let the sun through. On the far side, the pool descended into another lower cave in the depths of the earth.

Climbing deeper into the back of the cave, María searched for her hiding place. On some rocks, skinny figures brandishing spears, chased a group of umber buck across the rocky wall. The yellow ochre buck leapt into the air, escaping from a shower of arrows. María spotted her beloved painting on the rock and went straight to it.

Her usual hiding place for her secrets.

150

Kelby explained everything that had happened to her and Roy. It took only minutes to get the bare facts out. She finished with a plea. 'Please help me to find Annie.'

'Of course. Look, there's no signal in here so I'll go and call the police. Wait here. I'll be back in a minute.' He shut the door on his way out.

Adrenaline raced through Kelby like electricity. She had an odd feeling she'd been trapped on the wrong side of the door. She stood in the office, trying to decide if she should bolt around the clinic to find Annie or wait for Jon to return.

Kelby spotted a tray with a bottle of water and realised how dry her mouth was. Her shoes clomped on the tiled floor as she loped across. She grabbed the bottle and squeezed the lid. It remained clenched shut. She stuck the bottle cap in her mouth and tried to turn it with her back teeth. It still wouldn't budge. Looking around for something sharp to stick under the plastic lid, she spotted a letter opener inside the briefcase lid.

She lifted a decorative emblem of an angel out of the sheath. In its centre a ruby gleamed. Kelby spotted a magnifying glass beside it with the same angelic decoration. Strangely, the magnifying glass bore the same sharp end as the letter opener. Using the blade on the other end to prize off the lid, Kelby grimaced as the blade sliced right through the plastic.

'Phew, that's sharp.' Kelby gulped the water, and replaced the blade, being careful not to cut her finger.

Agitated, Kelby paced the room. She couldn't wait around for Jon to call the cops. She needed to find Annie. Fast and before Punch-bag's conspirators found her.

Suddenly her phone beeped a few times. Signal at last. She watched as a rush of messages came flooding in. The last one was from someone called Gabrielle Abelli. The preview read:

I am Teresina Piccoli's solicitor

Kelby opened the email and scanned it:

I spoke to her before her accident. As her solicitor,
I wouldn't do what I am about to do, but I was also
her friend. In the last hours of her life Teresina was
afraid. She asked me to send this unsent letter to you
if anything happened to her. I am bound by law not to
divulge my client's confidentiality, but maybe you can
help me find out what happened to her. Someone killed
her. I can stake my life on that! And I think it could be
the man in this letter.

Kelby tapped on the attachment and read the letter. It was addressed to Jon Barker Thompson. Kelby flicked on the desk lamp to read the tiny writing on her phone. The fluorescent tube lit the windowless room, casting shadows into the corners.

My name is Gabrielle Abelli. I am Teresina Piccoli's
solicitor. You are named as the father on Majella's birth
certificate.

'What?!' Kelby gasped, 'Majella is Jon's daughter!' She tried to recall if Jon had ever mentioned being that close to Teresina. Did Jon know about this?

She thought of Teresina's call only hours before she died. For the hundredth time, a pang of guilt shot through her, and she regretted not accepting the call. Maybe that could have saved Teresina's life.

Could Jon have killed Teresina? But why? Kelby swallowed the lump in her throat and read the email again.

Someone killed her. I can stake my life on that! And I
think it could be the man in this letter.

Then, another thought struck her like a lightning bolt striking a tree: Jon killed his own daughter. In killing Teresina he had taken his own child's life. He had known Majella was in the car with Teresina that day. If he could kill his own daughter, he'd kill Annie without flinching.

The door handle turned and Kelby's eyes flicked up. The man who had killed Teresina was about to enter.

151

The first time she had seen the painting of the huge charging bull, his head down and horns ready to attack, María had stared at it for hours, dreaming up scenarios for her stories. When she had run her fingers along his powerful chest, coloured in a lively burnt brown, and around his twisted horns of white chalk, she had discovered a hollow alcove.

Since then, she had used it as a hiding place for keeping secrets even Madre did not know. 'Take care of my notes, el Toro.' she whispered.

With careful movements María squeezed the rizado notes, still curled in the calf skin, into the hole. For now, rizado would be safe beside her Spanish bull. When Queen Isabella had forgotten about her, and the soldiers no longer hunted for Ana-María de Carbonela, she would return to find her notes. Right now, it held too many dangers for her to carry it with her. Turning back, she glanced at the rock wall. The bull stood proud, his head turned slightly as if he watched her every move.

Back beside the grotto's pond, María slumped and used her burnt fingertips to pluck rizado off the rocks. The only way to crush the curly, mossy herb was between her singed palms. Glancing around, she found a thick twig and lifted it, placing it between her teeth.

With clumps of sticky rizado resting on her palms, she ground the mossy herb between her hands. The rubbing made them bleed again. Biting hard on the twig, María kept crushing the herb into her wounds. Spasms of agony clawed up her arms. Within seconds, her whole body trembled. Her breathing leapt around in her chest like a frog chasing an insect.

When she could take no more, María fell back against the damp grass and shrieked in pain. '*Dios*, why, why, why?'

María had always been a good Catholic girl, believing God would do the right thing. God, would never — should never — want to hurt her innocent mother. Something had gone wrong, but now she had no time to question her faith. It had perished along with the use of her hands.

Her hands needed healing so María could rescue Madre before the soldiers returned.

152

Barker had been obsessed with two women for so long. Like Teresina, Kelby was a devil when she was angry or upset. Her constant rejection only made him want her more. Almost the same as when he'd first met the Italian she-devil.

Having Kelby think he was one of the good guys, he loved. Having his plans go awry, he hated.

He couldn't let anyone know he was linked to rizado; yet he had to warn Willow. If Kelby found the flaky bastard, he would probably panic and reveal all. Not only that, Willow would have to lock down Homerton Hall. If she reported what had happened in Willow's lab, hell would break loose. MG couldn't afford to have the cops snooping around. Neither could he.

His throat dried from his rushed breathing. He had to calm down. He had come too far to let a snag get in his way. The evidence could easily disappear and no-one would find out the truth. If matters took a turn for the worst, MG would take a hit, not him. Although, it would take years to pin anything on them; Gordo had covered his tracks better than a bushman hunter. Besides, Kelby thought Olaf was the stalker. Best he leave it that way, especially if the thug was dead.

Barker decided to let Willow sort out the body in the basement. It wasn't his problem. Gordo would hire another hit man to clean the mess so nobody would be found. Maybe they'd run a smear campaign to make Kelby look like she'd lost it after her brother and his wife had died.

Either way, he'd get Willow and find out everything he could about MG's project. He wasn't going to let this setback stop him. Now or in the future.

Adrenaline rushed through his body giving him renewed motivation. He'd find a way to be the global God he dreamed about. The rizado would be his. No matter what happened.

Kelby was in the right place. At the right time.

153

Jon entered Willow's office and kept his back to the door so Kelby couldn't bolt. He had never got over the effect her eyes had on him. Every time she looked at him, the impact of those incredibly blue pools caught his breath.

Now, Kelby fired an accusation at him. 'Did you have an affair with Teresina?'

He flinched. 'What are you talking about?'

'I've had an email to prove it.'

Without meaning to, Jon muttered, 'An affair? That sounds sordid. No, we didn't have an affair. Teresina was my first love.'

Kelby gasped.

Jon realised he'd slipped up. He remembered his and Teresina's wild love making, their wanton desire to try new things. Both of them had treated their relationship in the same way as their daily lives. The continual thirst for expensive toys, such as cars and unobtainable art and exotic properties, brought on a hunger for new sexual experiences. Each new tryst was boring unless they took their erotic adventures to another level.

The female trio didn't bother her too much, but their fire and passion burnt out with the male threesome.

Normally, he wasn't into that, but his need to see her sexually fulfilled had led him to agree. Seeing her satisfied by another man had given him intense spikes of jealousy, but he'd cleverly used the situation to dominate the other man and try things he had never dreamed of doing.

Their competitive streaks had created an envy fest, with each of them goading each other into going beyond their level of experience and comfort, gorging on the unsuspecting male until they were sexually satiated.

Yet it had destroyed their union. Teresina believed he wanted the triad more than she had, conveniently forgetting it had been her idea.

'Teresina plied me with erotic wonders and started blackmailing me.' He blinked several times as he remembered that night ten years ago. That part of his life would always remain secret, and the pain of his first love lost still haunted him. However, Teresina had threatened to tell the world how the eligible bachelor lived his life so he had waited a long time to get the she-devil back.

Now, he stared at Kelby. Being confronted like this, he hated. Having a plan of attack of his own, he loved.

'Life is about secrets, Kel.'

Through her blackmail letters, Teresina had promised their secret would die with her. And so it did.

But he wasn't about to let Kelby's secrets go to the grave. Her rizado secrets were about to be unlocked.

154

Kelby stared at Jon in disbelief.

Jon frowned at her. 'Me and Teresina ... it was a long time ago. Besides, I didn't see her again until I invited her to join the show.'

Kelby's voice dropped to a hoarse whisper. 'What happened?'

'When I found out the tyre tread monitor was faulty I thought it would come in handy. A few sharp turns in high speed and it blew the tyre.'

Kelby bridled, as if a sudden bad smell had caught in her nose. 'Why?'

'The bitch wanted money for keeping the ins and outs of our relationship quiet.' He peered at her through narrow eyes. 'Lots of money. Like the time she threw a party for Majella's tenth birthday.'

Kelby inched sideways.

'It was a medieval costume ball in Florence, in the Corsini Palace. Majella did a school play on Shakespeare. So Teresina conjured up the party of any young Italian girls dreams. Cost me a hundred grand. Can you *believe* that?'

Shock waves vibrated through Kelby. 'I trusted you. I even confided in you about the threats.' As the pieces started falling into place, she shook her head in disgust. 'You even arranged my surveillance and set up my security.'

'So I was able to get the codes. Poor Hawk had no idea it was me. Too trusting, like you. And, come to think of it, your brother was the same.'

Kelby shoved her face into his, hissing, 'You're despicable! Why did you have Gary killed?'

'Now, wait a minute, Kel, I had nothing to do with Gary's death. He came back from Spain with this amazing stuff that healed a wound on his arm and —'

'The rizado?'

'Yes.' He stared at her shocked expression. 'Didn't you know?'

She grabbed her pendant. 'Was it anything to do with this?'

Jon's jaw dropped. He stepped towards her, still staring at the symbol. 'Where did you get that?'

'Gary had it made for me. I thought it was a kind of Spanish emblem. But it appears to be a symbol off the rizado herbal book.'

'So, *that's* where Robson got the symbol. Well, if you think the foolish doctor is your white knight, he can't play that role anymore.'

'What have you done with him?'

'He's out of bounds so to speak, rotting away downstairs in a dungeon. Anyway, let's not bother with him now, I need to know *your* secrets, Kel.'

Jon closed the gap between them. 'Tell me where to find the rizado.'

155

Biting on the twig once more, María ground another batch of sticky rizado. In slow motion, she smeared the slimy green paste across her hands and up her arms.

The odour of Madre's scalded hair, blended with her own burnt flesh, still clung to her nose. María dropped her face into the water and shook her nose around to rid herself of the horrible smell, lest it sicken her even more.

As María sat beside the pond, she remembered the day it started, the day she had rescued the wounded goat.

Now, for the first time, she noticed how the water was thicker with slime at the edges beside the rocks, where the rizado grew. She trailed her palms across the surface. The cool water licked at the sticky paste, giving her instant relief. The heat inside her skin cooled, so she spent a few more minutes stroking the water. As she did so, she wondered if the water increased the healing powers of rizado. It certainly felt that way.

The grotto's peaceful tranquillity relaxed María. The heat of the mid-day sun gave everything around her a chance to rest. She lay back on the grassy bank with her hands hanging in the water, her mind drifting and her eyes closing.

Hours later, María woke with a start. She sat up and peered around her. The sun headed towards the horizon.

'*Dios!* I must get back to Mama!'

She leapt to her feet, vexed she'd slept through the afternoon's warmth.

For a moment, she glanced up at the blue sky. Another lovely day had passed her by.

Suddenly something else caught her eye.

Billows of smoke rose into the sky from the direction of Fuente Prado!

156

With unwavering poise, Kelby raised her head to meet Jon's towering torso. She pressed her index finger into his chest and hissed, 'First, tell me where's Annie?'

'Annie's fine, although a bit drowsy. She's locked away upstairs, but you can see her when I have the rizado.'

Kelby's, anger flared. Pouncing on him, she slapped his face and ran to the door. She yanked on it, but it wouldn't budge. A sharp pain filled her head as Jon gripped a handful of her hair and dragged her backwards.

'Willow told me about you being barren. You always wanted a kid of your own. Now you've got one. You should be grateful.'

Kelby elbowed him. Caught him in the ribs, sending him sprawling. She raced for the door, but Jon righted himself. He grabbed her by the shoulders and whirled her around to face him. As Kelby stumbled backwards, Jon pinned her against the desk.

With him towering over her, she scoffed, 'I saw the letter from Teresina's solicitor.' Behind her, her right hand scrambled around on the desk and into the briefcase, her fingers searching for something heavy to hit him with.

'What letter?' Jon's palm slammed Kelby's cheek. The force flung her sideways and her arm swept a pile of things off the desk. As Kelby hit the floor, the letter opener clattered beside her on the tiles. With Jon towering above her, Kelby saw the fire in his eyes. She scuttled backwards like a cockroach, but her back struck the desk's edge. She was trapped.

From the corner of her eyes, Kelby spotted the angel letter opener. Its ruby gleamed in the lamp's fluorescence as though the angel held a hand over a bleeding heart.

Above her, Jon patted her head. 'Poor little Kelby. You're a tough cookie, but nothing can match an angry man's strength.' In an abrupt motion, he buried his hand in her hair and yanked a handful upright, pulling her to her knees.

Kelby screamed.

Jon leaned down and glared at her. 'Tell me about the letter, Kelby.'

Face-to-face with Jon, she watched hatred burning his eyes. 'It was from Italy, saying you're Majella's father'

Jon's head shot up, his eyes glazed over. 'What?'

From the look of devastation on his face, Kelby realised he didn't know about Majella. 'She's my —'

'It said Teresina listed you as the father on the birth certificate. It said you were trying to kill her.'

Jon let out a whoosh. 'My daughter ...'

'Yes, you killed your own daughter.' Adrenaline rushed through her, leaving her edgy and twitchy. She didn't think about the consequences of her words, nor did she care. Kelby's fingers touched something cold. She flinched, as the shaft's end pricked her finger.

The angelic letter opener.

157

Kelby plunged the blade into Jon's stomach.

Jon groaned in pain, 'You fucking devil!'

Kelby could only see the angel sticking out of him. The rest was embedded in his bloodstained shirt. His knees crashed to the floor as he ripped the blade out of his flesh. Kelby scampered along the tiles on all fours, like a caged animal let loose. But Jon grabbed her ankles, and hauled her back towards him.

As she tried to crawl away, her hand gripped onto the desk's leg, dragging herself towards it. His strength overpowered her. In a split second, he wrenched her into his lap in a contorted position. Jon's arms wrapped around her, and he stroked her hair in a caressing motion. His hands, matted with blood, stuck to her head, and plucked the fine hairs around her ears.

With her back to his chest, Kelby could feel his heart beating as fast as hers, and she could hear his ragged breath rattling in and out of his throat like hers.

Kelby wriggled in his arms, struggling to break free, but Jon tightened his grip on her.

'You won't escape. Don't even try. I am ten times stronger than you.' Jon rose, stuffed his hands under her armpits and pulled her up. As he twisted her around to face him, she glanced down, and spotted the angel at Jon's feet. Its ruby centre glinted while its blood smeared shaft shimmered like a butcher's knife.

Using one hand, Jon clutched the bloody wound on his side. 'Having my extravagant plan for your death foiled, I hate. But coming up with a new death strategy, I love.'

A sudden worm of dark blood escaped from the corner of his lips. Without realising it, as Jon shuffled forward, he kicked the bloodied angel closer to Kelby's foot. She bent her knee and drove it into Jon's groin. He keeled over, both hands groping his loins and Kelby lunged for the angel.

Jon's long arm reached it first. 'Why don't you listen? I said, don't try.' He shoved his knee between her legs, forcing them apart. His height gave him advantage with his knee pinning her hips to the desk. Kelby watched him through slitted eyes.

Jon stroked the long shaft, smearing his blood onto his fingertips. With an abrupt motion, he licked the blade. Still pinned between him and the desk, Kelby glanced down to see his feet entwined with hers. He had her trapped as though they were locked in loving embrace.

Leaning closer, he flicked a piece of her hair out of her eyes, with the tip of the angel's blade. 'A good hair cut will make you look years younger, Kel. Maybe a few highlights to stop your face looking so overworked. I'd do it here and now, only,' his nose shrivelled, 'we're out of time. I have to find Willow, he has interesting toxins downstairs. I think you found his lab with his experiments floating in jars. I'll be sure to ask him to preserve those lovely eyes of yours. Otherwise I'll miss gazing into them.'

Jon took a deep breath as though he needed to re-energise himself. Then, he reached out to steady himself. 'On second thoughts, maybe I'll get Willow to attach your eyes to stalks.' He sneered at her. 'Maybe we can add Stacie's and Annie's as well. A kebab of Wade eyes.'

Kelby grabbed his wrist and shoved the blade away from her face. Using both hands, she twisted the blade back towards him. Jon struggled against her sudden burst of strength. As they twisted and turned the angel, the blade sliced Jon's arm, slashing flesh from the inside of his elbow to his wrist. Staring at the blood streaming from his arm, Jon's fingers weakened and the angel fell from his hand.

Kelby caught the handle. Wincing in pain as her scorched hand closed over it, she felt his blood coating her burns, its stickiness soothing the fire under her skin. She swapped hands and held it to his face. 'Take me to Annie, or you'll get this.'

Jon snorted but Kelby stood her ground. The dark blood pooling in the creek of his lips escaped, and snaked down his chin, as though his teeth had disturbed a nest of tiny black snakes. 'You won't use that Kel, you're too soft.'

His good arm came up out of nowhere and he punched Kelby under her chin. 'Jesus, that should have flattened you. You're lucky I'm indisposed at the moment.'

Reeling, she clung onto the angel, and pointed it back into his face. 'Don't try any more tricks. I *will* use this!'

Jon's good arm rammed out in attack mode, but this time, Kelby was ready for it. She swung away from him. Still embedded in her fist, the angel's rapier slashed across the front of his neck.

Jon grabbed her hand, but Kelby lunged forward.

The blade shunted over his cheek and the tip pierced his left eyeball.

Kelby screamed and let go of the angel's hilt. Jon's neck spurted blood for a few seconds, spraying Kelby's face.

She wiped her cheeks with the back of her hand. Each beat of his heart, propelled blood out of the breached flesh, forming an arcing pattern of blood stains across their shirts. Jon choked and gurgled and his legs caved in under him. As he slumped to the floor, the angel's emblem knocked on the side of the desk and spun away, taking Jon's embedded eyeball with it. Blood pooled around his body.

Kelby's hands closed over her mouth, muffling a scream. One lifeless eye stared at her while the other gaped like a bottomless gory pit. For a long horrific moment, Kelby stared back, paralysed with fear.

She had killed Jon Thompson.

158

María raced to the Finca and gaped at the destruction. Fire consumed their cottage and dead animals lay scattered near their pens. Madre's pots and pans littered the cobbles around the house. The soldiers had returned and searched the house.

María called out. 'Mama!'

Only then, did she discover the worst. In their anger the soldiers had set the donkey stable alight. The blaze had twisted the stone pillars from their foundations, crushing the stable roof on top of the cellar.

María dropped to her knees and tried to lift the smouldering thatched roof. The weight of it and the stone walling was too much for her. Even if her hands weren't recovering from the burns, she would never be able to get into the cellar.

'Madre! Madre!' María yelled. She ran around the shed and tried to crawl in between the rubble. No space was large enough for her to creep into. How could she get into the cellar to rescue Madre? She couldn't even see the cellar's wooden door under the pile of burnt wood and blackened stones.

'Mama, can you hear me?' María lay flat against the ground and hollowed into the earth. Madre may be sleeping. The destroyed stable wouldn't have harmed her mother hidden under the ground. María glanced over her shoulder, grimacing at her home burning to the ground. Spotting a metal bucket amongst the broken stone, she raced to grab it and ran to the water barrel. She sunk the bucket inside and threw water over the flames at the back of the house. It wouldn't save their home, but she tried anyway. She spent the next hour dousing the flames until the final drop of water had been used.

Then, hoping Madre would hear her this time, María ran to the rubble on top of the cellar and called out, 'Mama! Mama!'

Still no answer.

159

Kelby took one last look at Jon and tiptoed along the hallway. She peered back down the steps. Remembering Jon's words about Roy rotting away downstairs, she stood where she had bumped into Jon. This was probably a basement level in the former mansion and not used much in the clinic.

She had two choices. Barge upstairs, demanding to see Willow and accuse him of kidnapping Annie. The staff would probably gang up on her and lock her up. Or she could sneak into the tunnels looking for something that resembled a dungeon to find Roy. With him it would be easier to find Annie and a better chance of getting Annie out of there alive.

Even though Kelby didn't want to go near the place ever again, she opted for the second choice. Creeping back into the tunnel, she bit her lip, hoping Punch-bag didn't suddenly appear. Or Willow. Or anyone else involved in the rizado conspiracy.

A haze of suspended pain hung over her. Her burnt hand still screamed with agony and heat. The other trembled. She couldn't get the feeling of shunting the blade into Jon out of her mind.

Her footsteps echoed on the wooden stairway going back into the clinic's bowels. As she slipped down the dark tunnel, her eyes strained against the gloom and her nose twitched against the tunnel's dank smell. Somewhere in the dark, gurgling water choked through pipes, then it exited above her with a plink-plink-plink.

Kelby shivered with cold and unease. As she descended deeper into the gloomy passageway, she had the sensation of stepping into a horror film. The acidic odour of urine and musk made her nauseous.

Although Kelby was heading back towards the horrific lab, Jon's words about Roy rotting away in a dungeon kept her going. A cobweb, dangling from the arched brick ceiling, floated over her cheek. Kelby squealed and bolted forward.

The tunnel suddenly split into two.

160

Kelby peered into each split in the tunnel in confusion. When she had charged through here a while ago to get away from the lab, she hadn't noticed another passageway.

A thought struck her. Kelby delved into her pocket for her phone and checked. One battery bar left. She rang Roy's number.

A phone rang at the far end of the right corridor. She immediately cut the call and hit redial. Again a phone echoed in the distance. Cutting the call, she raced down the darkened hallway.

Her trembling hand scraped along the rough walls, scratching bits of skin off them. The tunnel suddenly stopped with only a steep set of iron stairs spiralling downwards. Kelby gingerly stepped onto the first step and listened. Only the empty sound of silence.

Using her good hand on the cracked and cold stone wall, Kelby guided herself down the spiral steps. She had to take each rusting stair at a time, planting her foot onto the inner, wider part before taking the next spiral. At the bottom, a door hung off its hinges. The door's lock had long ago perished. It creaked and swung out at her when she prised the door open. As she crept inside, she accidentally kicked a paving stone that had derailed out of the floor pattern.

Kelby held her phone high above her head to light the room. Another old-fashioned light switch dangling on a long cord swung back and forth, in front of her face. Kelby yanked on it and the room lit up. A sad and decayed dentist chair stood abandoned in the flaked and paint-chipped corner. Kelby's gaze fell on something familiar.

A body.

161

Overhead a crack of thunder erupted. Within seconds the darkening clouds opened, mourning with María. Huge raindrops deadened the last of the flames eating away at her home. As the thunder rolled across the sky, it revealed the truth María couldn't face. Madre had died of her wounds. Probably soon after María left for the grotto.

Allowing the rain to wash away her grief, María lay beside the cellar. Overcome with guilt and despair, she wanted to close her eyes and never open them again. Her stories, and determination to show off that a woman could be a writer had killed Madre.

How could she be so foolish?

The lump in her throat ballooned, making it hard to swallow. *Oh Mama, I am so sorry!*

María still lay beside the stable ruin. Finally, bitterness and disappointment forced her to her feet. She paced around the farmyard, a penned panther looking for escape. After staring at her shattered and ruined home, María stopped to tug on the dead little goat's beard. Then she stroked the slaughtered goose's bloody feathers. 'Thank you for those quills.'

Padre's workshop had been saved, but had been ransacked. She stepped over the broken door and perched on the tree stump where Madre had often sat to talk to Padre.

'Padre, what do I do? I have to leave, but where do I go?'

Tears welled in her eyes again. She was alone in the world. Maybe she could find Tío. His *mishpacha* would give her refuge. Maybe they would find a place for her on the sea voyage they were backing for Cristoforo Colombo.

María finally allowed her tears to flow freely. She sat on the wooden stump with her eyes closed. When she opened them, the tears had dried up. She dared not wipe her face while her hands were still healing and so she left the sticky tears on her skin.

For a long time María had longed to wear her father's loose clothes. Now, she spotted a pile of them hanging where Madre had stored them when she had been unable to part with anything of his. Without thinking, she changed into Padre's tunic, doublet and woollen breeches.

Glancing around, she spotted a rusting knife amongst her father's tools. She grabbed a chunk of her hair and with a sawing motion cropped it to her neck.

Outside the burst of rain finally stopped. The sky too had shed its tears. Dried eyed, she started preparing to leave. The soldiers would be back.

162

Roy lay unconscious in the middle of the room on an old-fashioned rusting trolley bed with corroded wheels. An arm and foot hung off the bed. His chin sagged onto his chest while his face was a bloodied pulp.

Kelby ran to him. Under her feet grit and dirt crunched into her heels. She shook him. 'Roy!'

He didn't answer. She lifted his chin and grimaced at the blood caking his face. Some had dripped onto his shirt. He muttered through swollen lips, 'Hey, fancy meeting you here.' He smiled at her through bloodied teeth.

Kelby threw her arms around him.

'Watch out!'

Kelby pulled back.

He reached out and stroked the side of her cheek. 'I'll take a rain check on the hugs when the ribs stitch back together. Okay?'

She nodded and wiped the blood off his face with her sleeve. 'God, you look awful.'

'I was hoping for something like — you're a sight for sore eyes or better still... God, what a handsome devil you are, even with a bent nose and blood-stained teeth.'

She grinned, feeling a little of the terror leak out of her. 'Are you okay?'

'How did you find me? I thought I was a goner.'

As Kelby spotted his eyebrows jiggling up and down, she chuckled.

'What's so funny?'

Using her index fingers, she held his eyebrows still.

'What're you doing?'

'Those eyebrows need taming. I'm trying to get them under control. I can't think when they're dancing around.'

He grinned sheepishly. 'A bit of a nervous reaction I have.'

'You? Nervous?'

He chuckled. 'Despite my worldly, confident manner, I get nervy around devils.'

Kelby smiled. 'Listen Rob Roy, I've got to get you out of here. Come on.' She lifted his arms and pulled him up. An intense desire to put her head on his chest overcame her. As if he felt the same he threw his arms around her and hugged her tight. 'Forget the bruised ribs. You're a sight for swollen eyes.'

For the briefest moment, her fear seeped away as his warmth crept into her, reviving her battle-torn spirit. Kelby wanted to bury her face in his chest and stay there, but time wasn't on her side. She had to find Annie.

Kelby stepped back and helped him swing his legs over the trolley. 'We've got to go. Come on.' She took his arm and led him to the door.

'I don't need anyone to chaperone me. I'm perfectly capable —'

Kelby turned to see him smiling and noted he had mimicked her words in the hospital, 'If you stop chattering and listen for a moment, I'll explain.'

He grinned at her. 'Go ahead, my knight with no armour.'

'Annie is somewhere here, I don't know where, but I think she's been drugged.'

'That's what I suspected. The meds she was taking shouldn't have made her so sleepy. Where's her mum?'

Kelby grimaced. 'Stacie's dead. And Hawk.'

'Oh my God! Kelby, I'm so sorry. What happened?'

'It's a terrible story and a long one. I'll tell you everything later.' She helped him to hobble along beside her. 'How did you get here? I can't imagine someone as tall and strong as you could be dragged down here.'

'Another long story. With your long story and mine, we'll need to get together and chat for a long, long time.'

'Agreed.'

They reached the top of the spiral staircase and hobbled to the split in the tunnel. In the basement, Roy stretched tentatively to test the severity of his wounds. He raised his arms and wiggled them as though trying to touch the ceiling. Then, he bent over and touched his toes.

Kelby frowned at him. 'What *are* you doing?'

'Stretching the bones. And warming up for a fight.'

His body sprang back into shape. 'Where to?'

Kelby pointed up.

163

Every part of María wanted to bury her animals. But the soldiers knew who she was and had orders from the queen to find her. They would not return to the Monarch in dishonour. If they saw animal graves, and her home cleaned they would know she was alive.

The soldiers would be back.

They would hunt her down. Maybe they would ransack the local village thinking someone was harbouring her. They might search the area and find the grotto.

She wished the sun would appear and lift her spirits. Instead, a peaceful, yet plaintive call wafted towards her. Woo-oo-oo. A strange tranquillity descended and drew her outside. She glanced at Madre's bakehouse and ambled towards it. Its door had also been broken down. The soldiers had found nothing inside, but baking tools. When Padre had received wild game as payment, Madre had used the bakehouse to hang the flesh to contain the smoke for drying or salting. Testing the use of her fingertips, María lifted a pan and dusted it off.

'Your favourite pan, Mama.' She had no idea why she spoke aloud, but hearing the words comforted her, as though Madre was there, listening to her. Placing it in the back of the stone oven, she said, 'I loved the bread you used to make with the herbs inside.'

María potted around, clearing the bakehouse and wishing she could fix the door. Stepping outside, she shook her head at Madre's trampled herb garden. She hoped Madre's herbal secrets were safe in the cellar. She felt a bitter twinge of irony that her mother's precious herbal *manuscrito* would die with her.

'Never mind, Mama. I will write another journal about your herbs. You said I had a good memory.'

Talking to Madre eased the emptiness in her heart. At last, she understood why Madre had done that every day, since Padre's passing. María went back to his workshop intent on cleaning it too, but she had to leave it. Her mother had insisted she escape so she could live. She would do that and make her mother proud of her from the grave.

As she crossed the croft, María glanced at the cottage, the rain soaked beams still hissing and the thatch smouldering with acrid smoke. With the smell of death and destruction wafting around the farm, María's knew what she would do.

Tío had given her many history lessons. They had fuelled her imagination. His lessons had given her mind many stories to write.

María turned back to the bake house, sat on the doorstep and told Madre her plan. 'I never told you this, Mama ... my biggest dream has been to journey to more places. I used to love to go with Padre to new towns. When Tío taught me about a sailor who was chancing everything to journey to far off lands, it filled me with excitement and dreams.'

Dreams a girl dared not dream.

164

Roy and Kelby leapt up the last step and stood staring at the normality of a bustling ward. A radiant light spilled out of a circular stained glass window in the middle of the reception.

Kelby was instantly reminded of Punch-bag throwing Hawk's body down the Hall's rotting staircase, and him landing in the shadows at the bottom. Her lasting image of Hawk would not be with horrible weapons poking out of him; it would be how he ended his life suffused with colour.

Retreating back to the stairwell, Roy pulled out his phone and dialled a number. 'Joyce. It's me. Sorry, I'll explain it later. Get the police to Homerton Clinic. There's a murderer on the loose.'

He ended the call, turned to Kelby and took a deep breath. 'You ready?'

'Yes.'

'No, you're not.'

She frowned at him.

'You need this first.' He threw his arms around her again and held her tight. Kelby almost caved in at the knees. The fresh tang of an orange shower gel lingered on his body, mingled with the coppery smell of blood on his clothes and the sweaty confines of his prison. As he pulled away, she spotted him flinching. He touched his ribcage.

Kelby stood a moment, still in a daze and enjoying his closeness. 'Thank you, I needed that.'

He jiggled his eyebrows and said, 'Let's go.'

'How do you know where we're going?'

'Instinct. I've been around enough hospitals to imagine a rough layout of this place.'

'Let's hope your instinct will find Annie.'

Still towering over Kelby, Roy marched to the desk. 'Hello. We're here to see Annie Wade.'

The receptionist had just bit into a sandwich and blushed. 'Oh, um.' She gulped, trying to swallow her mouthful.

'Her ward and room number please.'

The receptionist chewed frantically and swallowed what was left. With her hand in front of her mouth, she mumbled, '2B.'

Roy marched off, pulling Kelby behind him.

'Wait!' the receptionist called out, 'Is Doctor Willow expecting you?'

'Yes.' Roy called over his shoulder, 'Tell him Doctor Robson is back for our meeting.'

Kelby noticed the blush on the receptionist's cheeks pale as she immediately picked up the phone.

Roy led the way down the ward. At the door to 2B, he stopped and faced her. 'Brace yourself, Kel. I'm not sure what we'll find.'

She nodded and peered over his shoulder, eager to see Annie's face. At that moment she heard a shuffle behind her and turned to see Doctor Willow marching along the ward's corridor towards them.

165

As Kelby stiffened, Roy swivelled to see Willow and whispered to her. 'Let me handle this.' He stepped past her, gently shoving her behind him.

Willow stuttered, 'Wh-where did you get to. I-I lost you in the —'

'Forget it, Willow. There's no toxicology lab. You were —'

'There is!' Kelby dug in her sling bag and pulled out the journal. 'I have the proof.'

Willow's long fingers reached out to grab it, but Kelby pulled back. 'I can show you more horrible proof downstairs!'

'Okay.' Roy shoved Willow aside, 'In that case, Willow, we don't need you anymore. Kelby Wade is now Annie's legal guardian so we're taking her home.'

Doctor Willow halted in mid-step and glanced around him as though looking for an escape. Roy rushed into the room with Kelby following close on his heels. Leaning over a sleeping Annie, she whispered, 'Is she okay?'

Doctor Willow edged closer to the door. Kelby spun around and glared at him. 'What have you done to her?'

'Nothing. I mean, I've changed her medication and —'

'You've drugged her!'

Roy did a quick assessment. Thankfully the tubes in her nose had been removed and Annie's cheeks were brighter.

Roy patted Kelby's arm. 'It's okay, Kel, she looks better than last time.' He turned to Doctor Willow. 'Seen any improvements?'

Doctor Willow scratched his scalp. 'Before she left St Adelaide someone ordered an ABG.'

Kelby bent and kissed Annie's cheek. 'Hey, pumpkin, Aunt Kel is taking you home.'

Annie's eyes fluttered open and Kelby's heart almost burst at the look of elation in her niece's eyes. 'Aunt Kel,' Annie's voice was faint and breathy, like the flapping of butterfly wings, 'You came back.' She threw her arms around Kelby's neck. 'I thought you had lefted me too. Like Daddy. When can I see Mummy?'

Kelby knelt beside the bed and stroked Annie's head. 'Pumpkin, Mummy has gone to heaven to look for Daddy.'

'When will she be back?' A sob choked Annie.

'Let's talk to Daddy when we get home and see what he says.'

'Will you go there too or will you stay with me?'

'I'm with *you*, all the way.' She gave Annie a tight squeeze. 'You and me … we're going to live where we can swim in the hot sun every day.'

'Yippee!' Annie's voice got stronger by the minute. 'May-ree promised we'll swim in her special pool. She told me she has cream for my hands.'

Roy and Kelby looked at each other.

Kelby whispered, 'It's her. She's communicating with Annie.'

Roy nodded, his expression thoughtful, 'We can talk about it later.'

Willow hovered, unsure what they were discussing, but pretending to make himself useful. 'Sunlight can help eczema, but you must be careful of sunburn.'

Kelby ignored him as though he weren't in the room. She leaned over Annie and said, 'Listen, pumpkin. Doctor Rob Roy is going to pick you up now and he'll carry you, okay?'

Annie smiled at Roy and took Kelby's hand. 'I'm ready, Aunt Kel. Mummy has been gone for so long and my ants need feeding.'

Elation roared through Kelby. Annie was her old self.

At the door, Doctor Willow fiddled with the buttons on his suit. He stared at Roy. 'What will you do now?'

'Well, Annie will recover fully without the wrong drugs fed into her little body.' Roy lifted Annie into his arms and held her against his chest.

'No, I mean —'

'I know what you mean, Willow. You know what's coming to you. I don't need to explain.'

'But I *can* explain. It wasn't me.' Doctor Willow backed to the door. With the awkwardness of a crane preparing for flight, he turned and rushed down the ward corridor, flapping his hands about in a fluster.

'He won't get far.'

Kelby followed Roy into the lift. 'By the way, I need to pop around the corner and fetch an army boot.'

'A *boot?*'

Kelby rolled her eyes. 'Yes. That's another story.'

166

María spotted a metal ladle lying near the doorway and leaned over to touch it. She ran her peeling fingertips over the baking instrument. Her scarred hands looked like a man's and would profess to a life of manual labour.

A sudden thought gripped her. She darted back to the burnt kitchen and hopped through the smouldering embers. Spotting the soldier's dagger still lying in the back of the hearth, she used the ladle to haul it out. The dagger's hot metal scorched her hands, but she threw it into the dry sand outside to cool off. It would be essential on the journey ahead of her.

María picked her way over the burnt timber of the shed to Madre's burial cellar and knelt down. 'Mama, you know how I would dress in Padre's clothes?' She glanced behind her at the crushed herbal garden. 'Well, now I will dress as a man. The sailor I told you about is called Cristóbal. The Italians call him Cristoforo Colombo. I will labour aboard this sailor's boat. I will take Padre's name.'

Her intelligence and writing skills could persuade the great sailor to chart his journey into the unknown.

'I'll go with him to find the new world. You'll be proud of me. I'll be the first woman to sail across unknown waters.' María felt a lump in her throat. 'My promise to you Mama, is to continue your work. I will honour you and find a way to keep your *medicina* healing the people of this land you love.'

She stood and went over to the bake house and patted the walls.

A few minutes later, María gathered together a few things to help her on her passage. Now she would be on the run from the queen's soldiers, and trying to find Colombo, it was best to hide her writing secrets in a sturdy leather cloth that would withstand the long journey ahead.

Many years ago Padre had made a leather satchel from sheep skin to carry his tools. María knew where he used to keep it and quickly found the satchel.

After throwing out most of the tools, María added a few of Madre's *medicina* potions. Then, she wrapped two quills and a few sheets of hidden parchment into a piece of calfskin, tied it in a thin leather strip to make a watertight pouch. If, by chance, her satchel was stolen by vagabonds, she could at least dangle the leather pouch from her belt. The last book she had made lay hidden near Madre, in one of her clay pots.

With the bundle slung over her back, María took one last look over her shoulder.

Suddenly her eye caught something. Hung up on the back wall was Padre's boots. She glanced at her feet and knew her shoes wouldn't make the long journey ahead. She stepped back over the discarded tools on the floor and grabbed Padre's boots. Unlike her shoes, made from softened leather, Padre's were simple yet heavy ankle boots laced up at the front. He had made a thick leather sole to endure his many journeys.

In Padre's boots her feet would not suffer the hardened mountain tracks she would surely have to pass through to journey to the sea. Determined to keep them for the worst part of her passage, María tucked them into the satchel.

A chunk of black shiny rock fell out of one boot. As it hit the ground a shaft of sunlight streamed in through the door and fell upon the stone.

Bursts of fiery orange shone up out of the stone.

167

After Roy positioned Annie on the back seat, she curled up. He dropped a kiss on Kelby's forehead and headed to the driver's side. Kelby leaned in and tucked the clinic blanket around Annie's thin body.

Kelby hugged her again. Sometimes she wanted to squash her with love. She straightened and closed the back door. The spot on Kelby's forehead where Roy had kissed her radiated heat like a sonar beacon.

Suddenly Annie jumped up and yelled through the window. 'Hey, Aunt Kel, I nearly forgot!' Annie grabbed her mouth in mock horror.

'What did you forget?'

'Daddy said his lost foot has been itching to tell you something.' Annie started giggling. 'How can his foot tell you something? Daddy is *sooo* funny sometimes.' She flopped backwards and snuggled into the blanket.

Kelby stood still for a moment. A drum beat in her ears. She raised her eyes to the sky with her jaw hanging ajar.

Roy's eyebrows knitted together in a deep frown. 'Care to share what's on your mind?'

'That boot I told you about. Let's go get it. *Now!*'

'Okay!' Roy jumped in and said, 'I'm calling Joyce first or the police will wonder what happened to us.'

Kelby reached into her bag and handed the police officer's card to Roy. 'Can she get this officer to come see us at my house?'

Roy made the call. 'Joyce, one more thing, we have to get Annie home. *And* Kelby is exhausted, but she has lots to tell the police. Please contact PC Pike and tell him to meet us at Kelby's home.' He gave Joyce PC Pike's shoulder number and personal contact phone number.

When Roy had hung up, he drove off with Kelby directing him around the back of the clinic to the lab. As before, the spooky mansion loomed up ahead of them. Kelby mumbled, 'Pull up behind Hawk's car.'

As Roy parked, she hopped out. In one fluid movement Kelby retrieved Gary's boot from the back seat. She slammed the door and jumped back in beside Roy. He had a finger on his lips to shush her and threw a glance over his shoulder.

Kelby followed his eyes and saw Annie had fallen asleep, so she whispered to Roy. 'I found this boot hanging on Gary's wall, surrounded by his precious mementos. I had no idea at the time why I took it.' She shrugged, 'Sentimental, I guess. But after Annie's last comment, I think we may be on to something.'

'Why?' he whispered back.

'This is Gary's lost foot. If he's communicating with Annie, he may want me to take a closer look at his boot.'

'What for?' Roy's voice rose to a shout.

'Shh! I don't know. Let's see what happens.' She pointed to the symbol.

Roy gasped. His eyes glued to the now familiar symbol etched into the army leather.

'I wanted to show you this, but we can discuss that later.' Kelby dug her hand deep into the boot and shuffled around. Her fingers came out empty. Next, she turned the boot over and scrutinised the heel. 'Nothing there.' She flipped it back and tucked her fingers in between the laces.

A hoarse whisper rose from Roy, 'Wait!' He grabbed the boot and spun it back onto its heel. 'If Gary's foot is itching to tell you something, it's most likely the heel.' He yanked at the thick army sole. Then, he held out a flat palm to Kelby and said, 'Scalpel.'

'What?'

'You know.' His eyebrows wiggled.

'Ah! My scalpel. Of course. I forgot I even had it with me.' She dug in her bag and retrieved Gary's Swiss army knife. She handed it to Roy and watched as he slid the knife's point between the sole and the heel. For a moment he fiddled and tugged.

Without warning, the heel suddenly popped off like a champagne cork and hit Roy in the eye. Kelby grabbed the heel as it sailed back into his lap. She flipped it over and exclaimed. 'Oh my God!'

Together they gaped at the heel. Tucked inside, in a neatly cut cubbyhole, sat a bright green USB stick. Written across the tiny computer memory drive, in thick black ink, were two numbers and a letter.

42A.

168

María knelt and lifted the glowing stone that had fallen out of Padre's boot. No sooner than it touched her aching palms, the stone radiated a soothing warmth into her burnt skin.

Something in the back of her mind stirred. She remembered that Padre had received a sacred stone from the nuns when he re-built a crumbling wall at Abadía de Torcal. María bit her lip and leaned closer.

Was this the precious *piedra* Mama kept asking her to find?

The stirring in her mind, burst into a real live memory. Only now did she remember Madre checking if Padre had his *piedra sagrada* in his satchel when he journeyed long distances for work.

Madre had always insisted his sacred stone would protect him. In their gratitude to Padre for not taking money for his labour, the nuns had bestowed their promise. Padre would often jest, but carried the stone to quieten Madre.

María leaned closer to examine it. Inside, a web of glass-like crystalline glowed. The particles of amber formed a shape which looked like back-to-back twisted Cs.

María gasped. It was the same sign Madre had carved onto the leather cover of her *Herbal de Carbonela*. At the time she had thought Madre's twisted Cs were in honour of her own name.

Another shaft of sunlight slanted through the stone's golden honeycomb. Gaping in amazement María lifted the stone into the late afternoon's rays. When the sun shone through the crystals the Cs seemed to expand and flare into fiery colour, whirling into an X.

Suddenly a chill ran through María.

Padre must have left the sacred stone behind on the day the wall crushed him!

Although she had been vaguely aware of the stone, she had never seen it. Up close, it was the most beautiful object she had ever seen. How could this smooth lump of rock, with its strange inner crystalline shape, save Padre? Was there indeed something strange going on at the abbey? She'd never know.

With haste, María rushed back to the trapped cellar door and knelt one last more time. 'Mama, I have Padre's *piedra sagrada*. I will keep his sacred stone with me. That is my promise to you and Papa.'

Although yearning to avow to Madre for bringing this upon them, María couldn't spill her terrible secret. It would remain in the bottom of her heart. Always there to be mindful of her promise to never give up.

A bird cried out in the sky above. María's head shot up, and she rose to her feet, staring at a pair of turtle doves flapping with whistling wings between the bake house and workshop. Silver-grey in colour, with dark blue spots on their tail feathers, they watched her with their beady eyes. One of them let out another cry. Woo-oo-oo.

María's heart lifted. Madre and Padre were with her. Up there.

Before any more tears could well up, María leapt up. She took one last look of longing around the Finca and down the beautiful rolling valley.

One day she would return to claim this land as hers.

María grabbed her journey satchel and ran into the woods. She refused to give in to tears.

Far off lands awaited.

169

A sob escaped Kelby. She lifted her gaze from the USB memory stick to Roy and whispered, 'His foot *was* itching. He left us evidence.'

'How do you know?'

Kelby screwed up her nose. 'It's a horrific place, but 42A is under that building.' She pointed to the derelict mansion. 'Let's get out of here, quick. We'll check at home, but I can almost guarantee this stick will have evidence of the rizado murders. Or whatever Gary found out about MG.'

A little hand slipped over Kelby's shoulder. 'Is that Daddy's lost foot?'

Startled, Kelby swivelled around to see Annie's face close to hers. 'Yes, pumpkin. Daddy was right, his foot is itching. When you speak to him again, you tell him Aunt Kel will scratch his foot for him, okay?'

Annie burst into giggles. 'Oh, Aunt Kel, you and Daddy crack me up.' She sagged onto the back seat like a graceful ballerina completing her performance.

'Hey, I didn't get to see much of Spain. How about you and I have our swimming lessons there?'

Annie perched up and punched the air. 'Double yippee!'

'Is that okay, Rob Roy? Can Annie travel?'

'Sure, she'd love it. I know a good swimming teacher.'

'Who's this teacher? Let's set it up.'

He grinned at her. 'Right away.'

Roy opened the front door for Kelby and leaned close to her. 'What about the TV stuff? That's a full-time job, but so is looking after Annie.'

'I don't care. I'm giving up public life.'

He grinned. 'That deserves another hug. But not in front of the children.'

'Why? Annie won't mind.'

'Because each time I hug you, I want to stay there.' Roy dropped a light kiss on her forehead and pushed her into the passenger seat. 'I'm taking you two girls home.'

Kelby called Jimmy, and he answered with a screech, 'Be-jaysus, it's yourself.'

'I'm sorry about the silence.'

'You're not gonna believe this? The producers called, they want you to head up a new series.'

'Forget it!'

'Sure, I told them already. I said Miss Wade is going to —'

She interrupted him, 'Stop and smell the flowers.'

'Roses. You stop to smell roses, not flowers.'

'Well, that's where we're going.'

'We?'

'Didn't you say you should run the office?'

'Of course! But where are *we* going?'

'Torcal.' Kelby kept her eyes on Roy. Even with his eyes staring at the road ahead, a smile creased his face.

'What?' yelled Jimmy down the phone, 'Where on God's good earth is that?'

'It's in Spain where I can —' She stopped in mid-sentence and started again, 'Where we can chill out for a few months until things settle down.'

'Why am I going with you to Spain, when you need me to run things here?'

'You're going to set up a home office for me. You can have a place of your own close by — maybe Malaga — and commute for meetings with me in Spain.'

For once in his life, Jimmy was speechless.

'I'll be spending most of my time with Annie, so you need to get things set up how you want them.'

He yelled again, 'You're not the Kelby Wade I used to know. But I like this one better!'

She glanced at Roy. Smiling, she said, 'One more thing, Jim, please set up a trust fund for Hawk's wife and child. He died saving me and I want to care for them the same way he would've.'

'That's grand. Well done, Kel.'

'I'll see you tomorrow to tie up the details.'

'Sure. Oh, wait, I nearly forgot to tell you. Zelda has pulled off a coup. She has the charities lined up to auction your dresses. And she's helping them to invite a pile of celebs and high profilers to get involved. The charities are hopping with excitement at the money they'll make.'

'Oh, wow! That's brilliant. You'll have to give her a bonus.'

Smiling, Kelby ended the call and turned to check on Annie, still curled up on the back seat.

'You okay, pumpkin?'

Annie nodded.

She turned back and glanced at Roy, only to find him staring at her.

'You're going to try it, then?'

'Yes.'

His squared jaw dropped. 'Really?'

'If rizado helps Annie, I'll fund the research myself.'

'Marina will be thrilled you believe in it that much.' He leaned over and squeezed her hand. 'But forget the funding. Get Annie back on her feet.'

'Yes, and we have to sort out these pharma monsters. I have other evidence, so they won't get away with this. I nicked Willow's journal with lots of notes on toxins. His lab is full of body parts.'

'Ooh,' Roy pulled a face, 'but the journal sounds intriguing.'

'Don't get too excited, it's your homework.' Kelby relaxed back in her seat. 'Will you help me get settled?'

'Of course! But you know I can't join you. I have my practice here and …' his voice sounded wistful.

'Marina told me you visit your family often. If I'm near them, you can visit me too.'

'Nothing will keep me away.' His hand reached over and squeezed hers.

'By the way, when are you going to tell me about all that stuff you kept telling Marina *not* to tell me? You know, all about secret societies and an abbey in Torcal.'

'That was only because you were pushed for time. Jimmy warned us that your diary was stacked.'

'Funny thing, my diary seems to have come apart at the seams. Looks like I'm about to have plenty time on my hands.'

Roy said, 'Let's chat about it over a glass of Rioja.'

At that moment, they pulled up outside Kelby's gates, a security guard jumped up demanding to know who they were. As Roy hopped out of the car and explained, Kelby glanced up the drive at a hive of activity.

An army of people scuttled in and out of two police cars and three security vans. She spotted someone attaching a surveillance camera to one side of the house. Another set of cameras were being fitted to the opposite side. A man on the roof ran wires along the gutters.

An alarm suddenly shrieked and everyone stopped dead in their tracks.

A voice bellowed, 'Okay everyone, that's the last test.' Then the owner of the voice appeared in the doorway and shouted at the men with the cameras. 'Alarm done. How you guys doing?'

The man running cables near the gutter shouted back, 'Every point between the boundary and the house is covered. No blind spots.'

Roy slipped back into the car. He leaned over and whispered to Kelby, 'You're finally verified and able to go inside your own home.'

Kelby stared at Roy and shook her head. 'Hawk.' She choked up and muttered, 'He did this.'

'Good man. He came through.'

After squeezing the car between the security vehicles, Roy jumped out and lifted Annie out of the car. She pushed his hands away gently. 'I'm fine, Rob Roy, I want to walk. Daddy taught me to never give up.'

As Kelby's breath caught in her throat, she exchanged a look with Roy.

Annie stood between them and took each of their hands in her own. 'I promised him he could share my two feet.'

A pair of silver-grey doves flew over them. Annie pointed up as one of them let out a woo-oo-oo cry. 'See, Aunt Kel, Daddy and Mummy are with us. Up there.'

Kelby watched the birds hide themselves in amongst the pine needles. A quiver ran through her. Was it the same dove she'd seen outside Gary's shed?

She shook her head. Now *she* was imagining things. Yet the sensation Gary was watching over them still lingered. Talking to him, as she had done with her mother, helped to heal the gaping hole he'd left in her life. She chuckled to herself, maybe she'd be talking to him through Annie in future.

They ambled to the front door and Annie tugged on Kelby's hand. 'No big work handbag, Aunt Kel?'

'Don't need one.' As Annie smiled at her, Kelby thought her heart would burst. 'It's just us three, Pumpkin.'

'And our ants.'

The End of
The Grotto's Secret

If you enjoyed reading *The Grotto's Secret*, please take a moment to share your thoughts with a review on Amazon, Goodreads or Kobo. It doesn't have to be glowing, only genuine and fair. All you need to do is click the review link on this book's page. Thank you for your support!

Coming soon...

The
Sacred Symbol

Join my mailing list to find out when you can read a sneak preview of *The Sacred Symbol*: http://paulawynne.com/vip-news

Bonus Material

Go behind the scenes of *The Grotto's Secret* at
http://paulawynne.com/the-grottos-secret

Bonus material is available at
http://eepurl.com/bEidgH

  * A map of the grotto's location
  * Behind the scenes information
  * Q&A with Paula about her inspiration behind
    the story creation
  * Things you don't know about some characters

You can download reading group questions at
http://bit.ly/21wEEMQ

Join Paula's mailing list to receive the latest news about
upcoming releases and specials and for the opportunity to get a
free review copy of her next book:
http://eepurl.com/byjPVT

Follow Paula on Twitter:
http://twitter.com/paulawynne

Author's Notes

Writing a historical novel creates challenges for an author. Especially when it comes to what is and isn't true.

The facts about the Spanish Inquisition have been carefully researched and are true. The witch hunts and torture methods are true. Many horrific devices were used to force people into being heretics or witches. I was fascinated with the idea that many 'witches' burnt at the stake may have been innocent mothers, like Madre.

I was inspired by Nicholas Culpeper (1616-1654) who wrote his own complete herbal. He was prosecuted for witchcraft by the Society of Apothecaries, but acquitted by a jury. *Culpeper's Complete Herbal* is still in print today.

Most of the facts I have used about plankton are true. However, rizado is completely fabricated.

The poisonous plants I have used to kill fictional characters can really kill humans and dogs. Some cause agonising deaths. The popular oleander bush, prolific in Spain, almost killed my puppy. You can read his story on my website at
http://paulawynne.com/the-grottos-secret.

You can also read about toxic plants on my Pinterest board:
https://uk.pinterest.com/paulagracewynne/writing-the-grottos-secret/

You can also check out my notes and timelines for the story at
http://paulawynne.com/infographics

Acknowledgments

Firstly, I want to thank my readers who trusted me enough to buy this book. Thank you for your faith in me.

I would like to express my gratitude to the many people who saw me through this book; to all those who provided support, talked things over, read, wrote, offered comments, allowed me to quote their remarks and assisted in the editing, proofreading and design.

Above all, I want to thank my husband, Ken, my son Kent, my mad puppy Dexter, and the rest of my family, who supported and encouraged me in spite of all the time it took me away from them.

Expert help

As I have researched and written *The Grotto's Secret* some extremely kind, generous and knowledgeable people have provided me with information. Their expertise and help has been rich in detail, brimming with constructive feedback. A thousand thanks to them all.

The following people are experts in their field and I am hugely grateful for their advice and feedback which has helped to improve the book. In no particular order I would like to thank:

Bob Bedford, Executive Director at the Foundation for the Advancement of Sephardic Studies and Culture. Bob enriched the chapters and discussion between Tío and María. His advice and suggestions added colour and authenticity to the characters.

Paul Newman, author of *Daily Life In The Middle Ages* and *Growing Up in the Middle Ages* helped in verifying facts about daily life in medieval times.

Timothy Graham, Professor of History at The University of New Mexico also helped me in ensuring the historical details were correct. Tim teaches keen students about handling medieval documents and manuscripts. He has had the privilege to work with the finest collections of medieval manuscripts in Cambridge and Oxford in England, along with rare collections in France and the USA. As proof of his expertise, Tim was awarded the 2016 Award for Excellence in Teaching by the Medieval Academy of America Committee on Centers and Regional Associations (CARA).

Frank Morey from Virtus Risk Management whose information and advice on celebrities needing security when threatened by internet stalkers made those sections come alive.

Kevin Robinson a retired West Yorkshire police inspector, who has over thirty years of British and international policing experience. Since retiring Kevin supports writers in making their fictional police officers and procedures more realistic.

Doctor Mike Rossiter, Consultant in Sport, Exercise and Musculoskeletal Medicine who helped me to ensure the doctors and nurses in my book sounded like real medical staff.

Rob MacNevin for reading the crash chapters to be sure even the tiniest details are correct.

And finally, thank you to Kent Wynne and Ryan and Niall Sheridan for being supportive sons.

My awesome beta readers

Beta readers are avid book-lovers who read final drafts of novels to advise the author of any major hiccups before the book goes into the editing process. These wonderful, caring friends read the book and gave their feedback and constructive advice on how to improve some sections of the book.

I am deeply thankful for the help given by Ros Brookman, Graham Bird, Angela Crouch, Helen Johnson, Mary Murphy and Amanda Connery.

And a huge thank you to my husband, Ken Sheridan, who picked out things that didn't make sense and suggested many ways of improving the book.

Last and not least: I ask forgiveness of anyone whose name I have failed to mention.

About The Author

Moving to Spain allowed Paula to fulfil her lifelong dream to write novels. During the hunt for their new home in rural Andalusia, Paula and her husband found a beautiful home with stunning views down the Valle del Guadalhorce to Malaga and Marbella.

Apart from a white-washed village in the far distance, the valley is lush with green wheat fields and rolling hills, shadowed by layer after layer of mountains.

Paula's first sight of the Guadalhorce Valley took her breath away and gave birth to the fictional location of *The Grotto's Secret*.

Paula received an 'Honourable Mention' in the 75th Annual Writers Digest Writing Competition for two unpublished novels, which inspired her to continue writing.

Paula and her husband Ken starred in the BBC Show, *Escape to the Continent*, which showed their quest to live in Spain.

When Paula is not writing, she will be pottering in her garden, walking her Springer Spaniel along the country tracks around her home or exploring caves and ruins in Andalusia.

Made in the USA
Middletown, DE
01 December 2016